Hands of Honor

TERRON SIMS II

iUniverse, Inc.
Bloomington

Hands of Honor

iUniverse books may be ordered through booksellers or by contacting:

iUniverse
1663 Liberty Drive
Bloomington, IN 47403
www.iuniverse.com
1-800-Authors (1-800-288-4677)

ISBN: 978-1-4620-2455-1 (sc)
ISBN: 978-1-4620-2456-8 (ebook)
ISBN: 978-1-4620-2454-4 (hc)

Printed in the United States of America

iUniverse rev. date: 5/31/2011

Fort Monmouth is located on the Jersey shore, conveniently one hour south of New York City and one hour north of Atlantic City. The Jersey shore is a popular summer haven for young adults and families from New York, New Jersey, and the Philadelphia metropolitan area. Fort Monmouth is a very small, obscure post that most individuals, including many active duty Army personnel, do not know exists. For the past several years, the Army has been transitioning to civilianize the instillation. The two major units at Fort Monmouth are the US Communication and Electronic Command (CECOM) and the United States Military Academy Preparatory School (USMAPS).

The mission of the United States Military Academy Preparatory School is to provide academic, military, and physical instruction in a moral-ethical military environment to prepare and motivate candidates for success at West Point. Cadet Candidates, as the Prep School's students are referred to, are specifically chosen because they posses leadership potential, yet lack the full academic skills needed to achieve success with the Academy's rigorous academic schedule. The majority of the Cadet Candidates graduate in the top of their high school classes, possess outstanding physical abilities, demonstrate strong leadership potential, and have a strong desire to attend West Point. By attending USMAPS, The Military Academy provides the Cadet Candidates an opportunity that they would otherwise have not received.

The Prep school is comprised of a three-company battalion: Alpha, Bravo, and Charlie. It receives between one hundred fifty and two hundred Cadet Candidates every July. The Department of the Army mandates that the Prep school admit a minimum of a fifty one percent US Army soldier population that consists of regular Army, National Guard, and reserve soldiers. The other forty-nine or less percent of the incoming Prep school class come straight out of high school and college. The large majority of the high school students are athletic recruits. The others are "regular" high school kids who West Point feels have what it takes to achieve success at the Military Academy, yet need an additional year to sharpen their math and English skills. Though the majority of the incoming high school students are athletic recruits, they are still required to meet West Point's demanding application requirements.

15 April 2000, 2000 hrs: Cornwall, New York

DUE TO THE RECENT EVENTS THAT occurred at West Point this past winter, the Department of the Army (DA) had initially decided to not allow Major to serve as a graduate assistant (GA) basketball coach at USMAPS. With the Army's officers' corps numbers so dramatically reduced for the next four years, DA felt it unwise to waste a perfectly good new second lieutenant for six months coaching basketball. Needless to say, West Point has a way of getting what it wants, when it wants it.

This particular evening, Major is at Coach Patrick's house watching basketball and eating pizza. The Army men's basketball team lost in the first round to John Chaney's Temple University Owls in a tough defensive battle. Now home, the basketball team does like the rest of the nation: watches the NCAA tournament on TV.

Being the competitors that they are, the Army team was disappointed in the loss, but not terribly so because they had accomplished their goal of winning the Patriot League tournament; thus, reaching the NCAA Tournament for the first time in school history. Now, like their football brothers who played their hearts out in the Independence Bowl against Auburn during the '96 season, they too have rings.

While intensely watching Duke battle it out on the hardwood against Florida, Coach Patrick takes a moment to ask Major, "Do you want to GA at the Prep?"

The question shocks Major and ensues in him a feeling of extreme joy. Calming down from his excitement, Major asks, "Can I call my dad real quick?"

"Of course," Coach Patrick replies.

Major leaps to his feet and heads for Coach Patrick's telephone, which hangs on the kitchen wall. He lifts the receiver to call his dad, COL Sydney Johnson, USMC. After three rings, a male voice answers the telephone from the other end.

Recognizing the voice, Major says, "Dad, Coach just asked me to GA for him down at the Prep,"

"For how long?" COL Johnson asks.

"Six months."

"What about your basic course?"

"I'll report to OBC in January."

"Is that going to affect your promotion to First Lieutenant?"

"I already checked into that. It doesn't. All of the guys who've done it in the past were promoted on time."

"Do you really want to do this?"

"More than you know. I've wanted to be a GA since I went to the Prep."

"Well, I don't see why not."

"Thanks a lot, dad! I really appreciate it. I'll talk to you later."

"All right, Milton. You take care."

Major returns the telephone to the receiver and says to Coach Patrick, "I've got you, Coach. My dad says it's cool."

"That's great!" Coach Patrick exclaims. "I want you to see me everyday so we can run through drills and watch some film."

"Good deal. I can't wait! You know. I always wondered what goes on in that crazy mind of yours when you're breaking down film."

16 April 2000, 1430 hrs: West Point, New York

IT IS THE EARLY AFTERNOON AT the United States Military Academy. More significantly, it is the coldest month of the year in upstate New York. Being a Cadet during the winter is extremely unpleasant because the issued uniforms do not do much of a job of keeping one warm. The thickest coat that is issued to the Cadets is a wool overcoat. Most Cadets, when it is extremely cold out, wear either their gray jacket or, if they have one, their varsity sweater underneath.

Weather wise, it is an average day at West Point. The sky is gray to the point that one is unable to tell wether it is covered in an enormous blanket of gray clouds or if the sky itself has changed colors to adjust to the cold temperature. The air is so crisp that the lungs seem to feel every frozen molecule that enters the body.

There is hardly a soul walking in Cadet Area, not counting the numerous construction workers who are rebuilding the Mess Hall, Washington Hall, and Eisenhower and MacArthur Barracks. The majority of the Cadets are either in class or relaxing in their rooms. If it were warmer out, some of the Cadets would be outside playing basketball or soccer, or just lying out somwhere enjoying the nice weather. But, since the weather is not nice, it is more comfortable just staying in their rooms.

Major is one of the few Cadets who is currently out of his room. Being that he has to meet with Coach Patrick in about an hour, Major is taking care of some personal business that he can only handle during his precious time off after lunch. Major heads for Grant Barracks so he can get dressed for practice. Passing by Nininger Hall, Major just happens to run into his company tactical officer (TAC), MAJ Weiss.

"How's it going, Major?" MAJ Weiss asks as he stops to speak to his former commander.

"Not bad, sir. You?" Major asks.

"Everything is good. I'm glad I ran into you."

"Why's that sir?"

"I just returned from a meeting and saw that you're on the list to GA at the Prep school."

"Roger, sir."

"Why do you want to do that?"

"I've wanted to do that since I went to the Prep, sir."

"I don't know, Major. I think you're making a mistake."

"How's that sir?"

"How long do you GA for?"

"Six months, sir."

"That's what I thought. You're going to miss some precious lieutenant time: time that you can't get back.

"Sir, I spoke to my dad, and he doesn't have a problem with me GAing."

MAJ Weiss shakes his head, then says, "I think you're wasting your time, Major."

"No disrespect, sir, but I don't believe I am. The Army will be there when I'm done GAing. I'll have plenty of time to be a lieutenant."

Again, MAJ Weiss displays his dissapointment in Major's decision to coach basketball at the Prep school.

Knowing that he is unable to change Major's mind, MAJ Weiss dissapointingly says, "Well, I guess you're going to do what you're going to do."

"Roger that, sir. I have to."

"Oh well," MAJ Weiss replies as he walks away from Major.

Before MAJ Weiss can walk too far away, Major states, "Don't worry, sir. You'll see that I made the right decision."

Deciding that the needs of the Army supersede those of the Prep School, The Department of the Army decided that it was not necessary to fill the additional GA positions: women's basketball, lacrosse, and soccer. The Prep school traditionally uses the soccer GA as its head coach and first semester English instructor, but is now forced to hire from the civilian sector, at least for the next three years.

Despite the needs of the Army, Major is not the sole GA for the school year. His four friends, Ben Irons, James "JT" Midland, Greg Wilson, aka G Dubs, and Tony Carlson, aka TC, are also coaching at the Prep school as assistant football coaches. Their jobs were procured more on the basis of the necessity of the Prep School operating at a functional level. The permanent football coaching staff only consists of two assistants, who serve as the offensive and defensive coordinators, and a head coach.

The four young men are fortunate to coach the positions that they played at West Point. Ben is the linebacker coach, JT is the quarterback and offensive line coach, G Dubs serves as the wideouts coach, and TC serves as the defensive backs coach. Without the football GAs, the Prep school football team is unable to compete at a competitive level, as it does every year.

Other than coaching, the GAs serve as assistant company TACs during the summer training session known as Cadet Candidate Orientation. The GAs lead the Cadet Candidates in morning physical training and teach honor, leadership, and military tactics classes.

As GAs, the newly promoted second lieutenants serve as role models for the Cadet Candidates: constantly mentoring and assisting them on how to better prepare themselves for a successful life at West Point. Major and TC, being Prep school alums, are true beacons of hope for the young Cadet Candidates who are striving to achieve entrance to and success at the Military Academy.

During the academic year, besides their coaching responsibilities, the GAs are also physical education instructors. Because the football team is currently in season, the four football GAs serve as the weight-training instructors. Because they are in season, the weight-training class consists mainly of the football and basketball teams. Major is the assistant swimming instructor, working alongside his basketball head coach, Bruce Peak, and the football offensive coordinator, Steven Nailer.

Major has no idea why he was selected to teach swimming. He had to take the class twice at West Point and barely passed it the second time. When Major took swimming the first time, his class was in the category known as *The Rocks*. The title speaks for itself.

Major and his four classmates, including JT, were such bad swimmers that they were known throughout the Department of Physical Education as the Fab Five. They were so notorious for their lack of swimming ability that when they repeated the course their Yearling year Plebes would approach them and ask if they were in the Fab Five.

The Fab Five were such bad swimmers that, at the end of just their fourth day of class, their instructor, CPT Oliver Armstrong, said, "I'm going to be honest with you guys. None of you are going to pass."

The Fab Five's hearts sank at the ominous news. Their worst fear was coming true- having to repeat Plebe swimming.

CPT Armstrong continued, "It's better that I'm honest with you. What I'm going to do is focus on preparing you guys to pass the class next year."

Fortunately for the Fab Five, they all passed Plebe swimming on the second attempt...during the first quarter of their Yearling year. They did not all pass with flying colors, but they all passed, nonetheless. Major now considers himself an expert swimmer...at the sidestroke. Why the sidestroke? Because he can breathe while he moves through the water.

8 JULY 2000, 1800 HRS: BRADLEY BEACH, NEW JERSEY

MAJOR PULLS INTO THE DRIVEWAY OF his new home for the next six months: a three-story, five bedroom yellow house located just two blocks from the beach. The house is very ideal for young bachellors who plan on doing nothing with their free time but party. The house is rather old, as are all of the other homes in the community.

Because Bradley Beach is a popular summer vacation spot, the majority of the residents rent their homes during the summer. Once the summer ends, Bradley Beach becomes very quiet and desolate, which maks the older residents eccstatic.

G Dubs, TC, and JT have already made it to the house. Major parks behind G Dubs' car and immediately jumps out of his 4Runner, leaving his bags in the vehicle. He is unconcerned with them. The only thing on Major's mind is seeing his friends and checking out his new home.

Major trots down the sidewalk and leaps up over the steps and onto the front porch. He swings open the screen door and turns the knob. Seeing that the door is unloked, Major bursts into the house.

With his first step inside, Major shouts, "Fellas, I'm home!"

From a side room, Major hears a familiar voice shout, "Major!"

"Big Swoll!" Major jovialy replies as he rushes to the source of the voice.

From the side room, JT strides out and meets Major where the dining and living rooms meet. The two friends happily embrace and pick one another up.

Releasing their grip on each other, JT says, "Glad to see you made it. You get all your stuff?"

"Yeah," Major replies. "How were my directions? You didn't have any trouble getting up here, did you?"

"None at all. David and Jeff were wrong though."

"About what?"

"There wasn't any traffic when I left your house: None what so ever. I was able to drive without any problems.

"Good deal. So, I'm guessing G's directions to the house were good to go too, huh?"

"Yeah. He staked the place out a while back."

From upstatirs, Major and JT hear someone shout, "Major, is that you?"

"Who else would it be, brother?" Major loudly replies.

JT and Major hear the sound of scurrying coming from upstairs, followed by movement down the stairs.

TC steps into the living room and says to Major, "It's about time you got hear."

The two friends shake hands and quickly embrace.

Major then asks JT and TC, "Where the hell is G? I see his car parked outside."

"Oh. He's probably next door," JT answers.

Major gives JT and TC a funny look.

Noticing Major's quizical look, TC says to JT, "He hasn't met Jimmy and them yet?"

"No. He just got here," JT replies.

"Who's Jimmy?" Major asks.

"Jimmy's this Italian dude who lives next door to us," TC replies. "He and his friends live in Staten Island and rent the place out on the weekeds during the summer. Let me tell you! Them guys are wild, man! You need to meet them. They're our kind of people!" TC then looks at JT and asks, "You want to come?"

"No," JT answers. "I'm going to mess around with my computer."

"Whatever, man," TC replies. "Come on, Major."

TC turns around and heads for the front door, with Major following close behind. Outside, TC looks down the street to his right and notices that there are cars parked alongside the road.

"Good," TC states as he leads Major off of the porch and down the stairs, "They're still home."

At the bottom of the steps, TC and Major turn right and head next door. Major follows TC up the stairs of their weekend neighbors' house and immediately take a left. The two friends stand before the front door, which is open, with the screen door closed. TC gives the screen door several hard knocks, then takes a couple of steps back. Major is unsure as to why TC steps back until his question is immediatley answered by the savage barking of two extremely large black rawtwhilers.

"Wo!" Major states, as he leaps back away from the door.

"Don't worry about the dogs," TC says. "Jimmy'll handle them."

Not sooner than TC speaks do the two friends hear from within the house, "What're you boys barking at?"

Major and TC peer through the srceen door and spot a rather large man exiting the kitchen and walking through the living room, making his way to the front door.

Looking through the front door himself, the man, recognizing one of the persons standing at his front door, shouts, "TC! What's up, brother?"

"Not much, Jimmy," TC replies.

The dogs still barking, the individual loudly yells at them, "Stop all that noise! They're friends!"

The individual then places a hand on the back of the dogs' necks and forces them to stand still. After a brief moment, the dogs calm down. Their master releases his grip on them and proceeds to open the screen door.

"Come on in guys," man states.

Dutifully, the rawtwhilers move out of the way to allow TC and Major inside the house.

TC takes the screen door by the hand and steps inside, saying, "Jimmy, this is my friend, Major."

Major steps inside, directly behind TC.

Major throws his hand out and, before he can say a word, Jimmy boastfully states with a huge grin, "Welcome to the neighborhood, Major. You hungry?"

"Not really," Major replies, "but I wouldn't mind eating right now."

"Good," Jimmy states. "We're cooking up burgers and dogs on the grill out back. Come with me."

TC and Major follow Jimmy through the living room and into the kitchen where they find two guys who are about their age sitting at the kitchen table.

"Major, this is Mike and Vic," Jimmy introduces.

Mike and Vic rise to their feet and shake Major's hand.

"You living next door with Greg and TC?" Mike asks.

"Yeah," Major simply responds.

"That's cool," Vic comments. "You're going to have fun living next to us."

"That's the plan," Major agrees.

"Come on out back with me," Jimmy states as he heads for the back door.

"We'll catch you later," Mike states as Major and TC follow behind Jimmy.

"All right then. It was good meeting you," Major replies before stepping outside.

In the backyard, Major and TC find G Dubs lounging in a chair, sipping on a beer. Happily surprised to see Major, G Dubs leaps to his feet and rushes over to meet his friend.

"What's up, brother?" G Dubs exclaims.

The two friends shake hands, then quickly embrace. While Major and G Dubs get reacquainted, Jimmy and TC go to the grill to get some food and converse with the four young ladies and two men who G Dubs was sitting with.

Major responds to G Dubs' question, saying, "Not much, G: Just got in about ten minutes ago."

"Glad to see you made it all right. You didn't have any problems with my directions, did you?"

"Not at all. They were pretty good. It's funny, though. I've never been this far south before: Never really had a reason to. How far are we from Monmouth?"

"Ten to fifteen minutes."

"Shoot. That's not bad."

"Ben here yet?"

"Naw. He said he was going to be here around six or so. I left my aunt and uncle's house thinking that I'd get here the same time as him. That's what I get for going off of Ben's schedule."

G Dubs laughs and says, "Yeah, I hear you. Ben isn't always good about being on time. Oh well. He'll get here eventually."

"Yeah, he will. Hey. I forgot to ask him when I spoke to him last night: Is he still bringing Jessica with him?"

"As far as I know, yeah."

"That'll be interesting. A woman living with all us guys."

Major and G Dubs laugh at the thought. As the two friends swap stories about their summer, Jimmy walks over and hands them a beer.

"Thanks, Jimmy," Major says as he receives the Coors Light from his new friend and neighbor.

"It's no problem, Major. Eat and drink all you want. What's ours is yours," Jimmy exclaims.

"Thanks, Jimmy. I appreciate that, man."

"So when's your friend Ben supposed to get here?"

"He's supposed to be here already," G Dubs answers.

As soon as the last word falls off of G Dubs' lips, his cell phone rings in his pocket.

"That might be him," G Dubs says as he reaches his right hand into his pocket to retrieve his ringing cell phone. The phone in his hand and out of his pocket, G Dubs instinctively looks at the screen display. He presses the answer button, and recognizing the telephone number of the incoming call, answers, "What's up, Ben? Where you at?"

"I'm on that street that dead ends at the beach," Ben replies. "I know I have to take a right, but I forget which right I have to take after that."

"Don't worry, man. I'll guide you in. Did you turn right yet?"

"I am right now."

"Okay. You're going to see a small diner to your front right. You want to turn right on the street immediately before it. The diner's on that street."

"I got you. I'm looking for the diner."

G Dubs pulls his cell phone from his ear and says to Jimmy, TC, and Major, "Let's meet Ben out front."

"All right," TC responds.

G Dubs returns his cell phone to his ear, while he heads around the side of the house for the front yard. Jimmy, TC, and Major follow G Dubs, as well.

"All right," Ben says. "I see the diner. I'm now turning right onto the street."

"The diner's to your left now, right?"

"Yeah."

"Good. The street's going to end."

"It just did."

"Take a left, then the immediate right."

"Got you," Ben states as he follows G Dubs' directions to the letter.

As Ben drives, G Dubs says, "You'll see us out front. We'll be on the left."

"Got you. Thanks for the help, G."

"That's what brothers are for," G Dubs replies. He then ends the call and returns his cell phone to his pocket.

"Is he almost here?" Jimmy asks.

"Yeah," G Dubs replies. "He'll be here in a few seconds."

Looking down the street, G Dubs notices a gray Chevy Yukon make a right turn. The Yukon drives slowly down the narrow, car congested, street.

Seeing the male and female passengers in the Yukon, Jimmy states, "Man! I thought that was Ben. I guess he still hasn't found his way over here yet."

TC gives Jimmy a funny look and asks him, "What're you talking about?"

"Your friend, Ben, he's still not here," Jimmy explains.

"That's Ben and his girlfriend who just pulled in," G Dubs responds.

Embarrassed, Jimmy states, "Ah, man. I thought...you know- I figured Ben was Black."

G Dubs, Major, and TC give one another a funny look, then break out in laughter at Jimmy's hick-up.

"You thought," TC laughingly states, "that Ben was Black because we're Black."

"That's funny as hell, man!" Major chimes in.

"You guys aren't mad at me?" Jimmy carefully asks.

"Why should we be?" Major laughingly asks as he gives Jimmy a big bear hug. "I'd have thought the same thing in your position."

Relieved, Jimmy laughs along with his three new friends. The small group makes its way towards the Yukon as the driver parks in front of JT's Eclipse. The four young men stand on the side walk and patiently wait as the male and the female passengers step out of the Yukon.

"What's up, guys?" the driver of the Yukon states when he sees his friends standing on the side.

TC steps forward with his arms wide open and says, "Welcome home, Ben."

12 September 2000, USMAPS

LIKE MOST MORNINGS WHEN MAJOR IS not teaching a swimming class, he pulls into work a little after eight-thirty. Major would ride into work with his friends, but since he is the assistant basketball coach, and not football, their afternoon schedules are not always in synch. This morning, Major was the last one to leave the house; he does not miss an episode of the *Cosby Show* or *A Different World*, if he can help it.

With his speakers blaring and his windows down, Major pulls into the Prep School parking lot that sits between the athletic building and Shea Barracks. Major turns the music down some, then comes to a quick stop and parks. Several Cadet Candidates walk from Shea Barracks towards the academic building. Major says hello to the Cadet Candidates, as he jogs to the athletic building. Entering, he turns right and strolls down the hallway.

At the end of the hall lies the GAs' office. It is a large open room with eight desks positioned against the wall and a large, old, metal table seated in the center. Placed on each desk is a desktop computer.

Major enters the office whistling the last song he had heard on the radio. His four friends are already sitting behind their desks, surfing the internet and talking about last night's series of John Madden football games they had played.

"What's up fellas?" Major asks as he leisurely walks to his desk.

"Hey," the four football GAs reply in unison, each throwing a hand in the air.

Major rolls his chair out from under his desk and sits down to check his e-mail. Glancing through his inbox, Major notices an e-mail from New York City club and party promoter Cris A.C.

Scanning the e-mail, Major's eyes open wide in disbelief. He cannot believe what he is reading. Never before has Major read an e-mail that has made him speechless. The immense awe of the e-mail causes Major to check it several times over.

"Fellas!" Major shouts to his friends, as his eyes remain glued to the computer screen in disbelief. "You've got to check this out!"

Ben, TC, G Dubs, and JT gingerly get up from behind their desks and walk over to where Major sits.

"What is it?" Ben asks: his hands in his black Prep school athletic jacket.

"I don't know how legit this is," Major opens, "but I just got an e-mail inviting me to the MTV Video Music Awards after party."

"You're kidding, right?" JT asks in disbelief.

"I swear to GOD!" Major attests.

"How'd you get the e-mail?" Ben questions.

"Beats me. I've been getting e-mails from this guy since early Firstie year," Major answers.

"What's his name?" JT asks.

"Cris A.C.," Major responds. "He's a club and party promoter in the City. I never got a chance to see if he's legitimate, because of basketball and what not, but now we have no choice. We have to check this bad boy out! We'll never forgive ourselves if we don't, especially if the joint is legit.

Shoot! If we get to the party and find out that this guy's a fraud, we can still go somewhere and wild out. You know what I'm saying?"

"I agree," G Dubs states.

"You think this guy's legit?" Ben asks Major.

"I don't see why he isn't. Look at it like this- if he weren't legit, he'd probably be out of business by now. You know what I'm saying?"

"I guess you're right," Ben agrees.

"So, when is it?" JT asks.

"This Thursday. The joint says to be kind of early because they're expecting a big crowd."

"What's early?" Ben asks.

"I don't know," Major replies. "Say ten o'clock?"

"That sounds all right, I guess," Ben agrees.

TC disrupts the flow of the conversation, saying, "I'm not going to be able to go."

"Why not?" JT asks.

"Me and Sherry have plans already," TC answers.

"Fool, please!" JT protests. "Bring her with us. She can help me holler at the ladies."

TC laughs, stating, "Sorry, man. Maybe next time."

"Your loss, nupe," Major says to TC. He then says to Ben, JT, and G Dubs, "I'll e-mail this Cris A.C. guy and get our names on the list. JT, check the train schedule and find us a time around nine."

15 SEPTEMBER 2000, 2000 HRS

G Dubs, JT, Ben, and Major ride on the New Jersey Transit rail system, headed for New York's Penn Station. If there is no traffic on the Garden State Parkway and the New Jersey Turnpike, the drive to New York City is only an hour from where the four young men live in New Jersey. The ride to Penn station on the train is one and a half hours. The guys do not like the long ride, but they truly appreciate the train's convenience. Driving home was not an option for any of them since they all are going to drink at the party. Because they all want to take full advantage of the night's events, they all knew they would not be in the right physical and mental condition to drive home.

The New Jersey Transit train that travels along the Jersey shore does not run continuously for twenty-four hours. At one o'clock every morning, the train stops running for maintenance and does not resume operation until three hours later. The train's hours are not an issue for the young men. They plan on partying until the sun comes up.

"Now arriving: New York's Penn Station," the conductor announces over the loud speaker.

JT, Major, Ben, and G Dubs rise to their feet and, in anticipation of the train stopping, stand in front of the nearest exit to beat the soon to be approaching mob. As the train creeps through the bowels of Penn Station, the other passangers in the car stand and begin crowding around the exits.

Finally, the train comes to a complete stop. Major, Ben, JT, and G Dubs, whose bodies are nearly pressed up against the exit doors, step off of the train just as the doors open. The four friends scurry off of the train, the small mob following close behind, and head up the escalator to the main floor. They make their way through the immense crowd: forcefully moving forward, but not in a rude manner. The four friends stride through Penn Station's vast lobby, passing several newsstands, coffee shops, and fast food restaurants.

Seeing a newsstand, JT says, "Let's get some beers for the road."

"Yeah. Let's do that," G Dubs boisterously agrees.

JT leads his three friends into the newsstand where they each buy a twenty-four ounce can of Coors Light. The cashier places each can in its own brown paper bag. The guys all grab their bags and return on their path to the street.

As the four young men briskly walk through Penn Station, much to their dismay, they see many homeless people: some panhandling and others just lying on the floor, attempting to disappear into the background. Major spots one homeless man seated against a concrete pillar, wearing a POW/MIA shirt.

He reaches into his pocket and hands the man a dollar, saying, "I don't know what you'll do with this dollar, sir, but I'm giving it to you in the hope that you do something positive with it."

The man looks up at Major and says, "That's kind of you, sir."

The man stretches out his hand. Major reaches forward and gives him a firm shake. Major releases the man's hand and continues on his way. He has to jog forward to catch up with his friends who only briefly paused while Major was being a Good Samaritan.

Outside on 17th Ave, the four friends stand on the street's edge. Cars irately speed down the street in both directions. Unafraid of the oncoming traffic, the four young men step out into the street, in an attempt to hail a cab for the ride to the MTV Video Music Awards after party at Club NV.

No cabs stop, as the young men waive down every yellow car that moves towards them. They pace back-and-forth in front of Madison Square Garden trying to get a heads up on the other people who are also attempting to hail cabs. Standing there, they watch cabs pull up and pick up people who stepped out of Penn Station after them

After several minutes of frustration, Major blurts, "This friggin' sucks! Ben you get the bad boy. We'll stand over here and look like we're not with you."

Ben laughs as Major, JT, and G Dubs quickly get out of the street and stand on the sidewalk beside a lamppost, appearing as though they are not with him.

The four friends must play this charade because of the difficulty Black men have in catching a cab in New York City. Major, JT, and G Dubs, being young Black men, experience this frustration nearly every time they go to the City. The entire situation upsets them, but usually, they just laugh it off, not because the situation is funny, but because it is sad that they and an entire group of people are stigmatized and alienated for the negative acts of a very small few.

Standing alone for only a brief moment, Ben is able to hail down a cab. The yellow cab pulls beside Ben and comes to a quick halt. Continuing the charade, Ben opens the back door as though he is going to enter the cab alone. Instead, Major, JT, and G Dubs immediately rush out into the street and jump into the open back seat. His friends in the cab, Ben shuts the door behind them, then jumps into the front beside the driver. Acting as though nothing strange had just occurred, Ben simply gives the cab driver the address to Club NV.

The cab driver is confused beyond belief. He is unsure as to what has just occurred. As far as he was aware, he was picking up just one man. Now, he finds four in his cab. The three men seated in the back seat were not the ones whom he wanted to give a ride. The entire situation causes a perplexed and confused look to grow on the cab driver's face.

The cab driver thinks to himself, 'Oh well. A fare's a fare. They look all right, I guess.'

His thought complete, the cabby puts his car in drive and peels off down the street for the MTV Video Music Awards afterparty at Club NV.

Ten minutes of the ride having passed, the cab pulls alongside Club NV. Major, G Dubs, and JT exit the rear of the cab. Before stepping out, Ben pays the driver ten dollars, then follows behind his friends, where they wait for him in a relatively short line. Since it is not eleven o'clock yet, they quickly move to the front of the line.

At the front of Club NV's VIP line, holding a clipboard and pen, is a rather enormous Jamaican. He stands over six and a half feet and looks to weigh nearly three hundred pounds. The Jamaican is not one to be messed with. The four friends make the proper assumption that the Jamaican is the doorman. Led by Major, the four friends step in front of the Jamaican.

Slightly looking up, Major says to the overly large Jamaican, "We're on Cris A.C.'s list."

Without looking at the clipboard, the Jamaican smiles, nods in approval, then waives in the four young men. As Major, G Dubs, JT, and Ben pass the doorman, he hands them a red poker chip.

The four friends walk into Club NV and approach the cashier. Ben, who has now moved to the front of the small group, reaches for his wallet after having placed his red poker chip on the cashier's counter.

The cashier sits in a small room that is separated from the public by an iron cage. The young, cute, twenty-something blond who serves as the cashier sits at her post with very little enthusiasm. Her face is free of any positive emotions.

When the cashier notices the red poker chip on the counter, she says to Ben, "You're good."

Somewhat surprised with hearing that he does not have to pay to enter the club, Ben happily returns his wallet to his back pocket. Ben looks up and locks eyes with the cashier.

Smiling, Ben simply says, "Thanks."

Whether it is Ben's voice when he says 'Thanks' or the extremely kind look that he gives the cashier, from out of no where, a rare smile grows across her face. The cashier is not accustomed to politeness and

17

manners from those who pass her booth every evening. Ben's simple act of courtesy makes her entire evening.

Seeing that Ben did not have to pay to enter Club NV, G Dubs, Major, and JT follow Ben's lead by leaving their wallets in their pockets. As each young man walks past the cashier, they all hand the cashier their red poker chip and say, "Thank you," to her as they pass.

Inside Club NV, the four friends stand in amazement.

"We're actually in!" G Dubs quietly exclaims.

"Was there any doubt?" Major confidently asks.

Ben simply looks at Major with a cynical expression and shakes his head. He then says, "Let's get out of the way."

"There's the bar." JT announces, pointing and leading the way.

At the bar, JT immediately orders four rum and cokes and hands them to his friends as the drinks are placed on the bar.

After standing at the bar for a while, Ben says, "I'm going to go walk around some."

"I'll go with you," Major states.

"I'm going to stay here for a while," JT replies.

"Me, too," G Dubs chimes.

"All right then," says Ben. "We'll be back."

Ben and Major take their drinks and head for the main section of the club. The two friends walk slowly through the club: taking their time to see what possibilities may lie ahead.

Major finishes the drink that he has in his hand and places the empty glass on a nearby table. He then says to Ben, "You want another drink?"

"Yeah. I'll take one," Ben replies.

Major steps away from Ben and leaves him to his own devices- mainly attracting the ladies within his vicinity. As Major walks to the nearest bar, a big smile appears on his face because, out of the corner of his eye, he spies Ben working his magic on the ladies. Major steps to the bar and patiently waits for a bartender to approach him.

As he idly stands, Major feels an ominous presence over and behind him. Before he is able to react Major hears a voice coming from the presence say, "Your dad know you're here?"

The voice, a familiar one, causes Major to throw his head back and spin around. Standing in his face is a giant, overpowering, chest. Major throws his head up into the air and glares into a huge pair of dark brown eyes and is totally surprised as to whose eyes are staring back at him.

Major takes a small jump back until his back is up against the bar. "Mac?" he shockingly asks.

"Didn't think I'd ever see you again, kid," Mac replies. "How've you been?"

"Man! I can't believe this! What are you doing here?"

"Let's just say I'm in a new line of work. Actually, I'm kind of working right now."

"What do you do?"

"I guess you could say I'm a bodyguard. The guy I'm working for, though, is a friend of mine."

"Who?" Major inquisitively asks.

"X," Mac simply states.

"Get out of here! You mean The X."

"The only other X I know is Malcolm, and he's been dead for a while."

"Man! That's tight!" Suddenly, Major remembers that he had left Ben to get some drinks. He says to Mac, "My friend Ben's here, too."

"Who?"

"The guy who was with me in Bradley who got shot when we ran into you and Killer."

"Oh yeah," Mac replies: his memory returning to him of last winter's events. "Where is he?"

"He's over there hollering at the ladies."

"Well, bring him over."

"Bet!"

Major leaves the bar and rushes over to where he had left Ben. As Major had anticipated, Ben is surrounded by a small group of women, all of whom are smiling and laughing at his every word. Usually, Major would attempt to become a part of the festivities, but not at this particular moment.

Major excuses himself past the young ladies and says to Ben, "Cousin. Mac's here."

Totally thrown back, Ben asks with a puzzled look on his face, "What? Where is he?" Ben is just as shocked at the news as Major was.

"He's over at the bar," Major informs, motioning in the direction from whence he came.

"I'll see you ladies later," Ben says as he follows Major back to the bar.

Standing immensely over everyone around him, Mac stands out in the crowd like a sore thumb.

"How's that leg?" Mac asks Ben as he and Major approach the bar.

Mac throws his right hand out and firmly shakes Ben's hand.

"It's pretty good. The round went straight through, so it wasn't as bad as it could've been. I was only on crutches for a few weeks."

"That's good."

With the back of his hand, Major hits Ben in the chest a couple of times, saying, "Mac's here with X, man."

"Get out of here!" Ben exclaims.

Seeing Major and Ben's reaction to his being X's friend, Mac asks, "You guys want to meet him?"

"Hell yeah!" Ben and Major ecstatically reply in unison.

Grinning, Mac leads Ben and Major through the crowd and to the VIP section. As they enter, Major and Ben cannot believe their eyes. Surrounded by a throng of women is X, who some would consider one of the most prolific Hip Hop lyricists of our time.

Mac notices that Major and Ben are mesmerized.

With a smirk on his face, Mac says to them, "Don't just stand there with your mouths open. Go over there and meet the man."

Mac places a hand on both Ben and Major's backs and lightly pushes them forward. With momentum behind them, Major and Ben walk away from Mac and head for the small crowd of women that surrounds X. As they slowly walk forward, Mac motions to X that the two young men are approaching. Major and Ben stand behind the women, unsure of what to do or say. The women appear to be way out of their league. The last thing that the two friends want is to embarrass themselves in front of a group of beautiful women.

Noticing Major and Ben's presence, X barks, "What's up fellas? Get over here!"

Nodding with satisfaction, Ben and Major carefully make their way through the ladies to the middle of the circle where X stands alone.

"So, where're the rest of your boys?" X asks.

"How did you..." Major begins to ask, but in mid-sentence, he realizes that Mac, being who he is, had to have known that G Dubs and JT are with them, as well. Mac must have signaled X somehow.

"Don't worry about them," X states. "I've got one of my guys getting them right now. Everything's on me tonight. If you're a friend of Big Mac's then you've got to be good people."

"Thanks a lot, man," Ben replies.

"No problem, dawg," X says, who then motions for some of the ladies to gather closer around Major and Ben. X then asks, "You know how me and King Kong over there became boys?"

"No," Major and Ben chime in unison.

"We served in the Marine Corps together. We were in boot together over in Paris Island. That place fuckin' sucked more than you know! The mosquitoes were the size of baseballs! But anyway, we served our first assignments together at Pendleton. I got out after my three year commitment. That fool stayed in. Don't ask me for how long, though. All I know, between the three of us, I think my man's been doing some black ops, secret agent type shit for the past few years or so. You guys know what I'm saying?"

Major and Ben nod their heads in agreement with X's monologue about Mac. Ever since Major and Ben ran into Mac last year, the one thing that they have never been able to figure out is how he and Killer showed up at West Point in the first place. Major has never asked and he does not think that he ever will.

Major, Ben, JT, and G-Dubs are having the time of their young lives. Never have they ever partied in such style and fashion. The women who surround the young men treat them like they are superstars. The fact they are somewhat acquainted with X is reason enough for the ladies to bathe them in overindulgence, attention, and affection.

Major dances with a young woman on the dance floor. She has at least five years on him, but Major is not concerned. All Major cares about is the fact that the woman is drop dead gorgeous and knows how to move on the dance floor.

On the dance floor with Major are G-Dubs and JT. G-Dubs is dancing with two women: one in the front and the other behind him.

The smile that permeates across his face fills the entire room. Looking at G-Dubs, one can tell that he is in total bliss.

JT is on the dance floor, as well: dancing with a lovely young woman. To further his enjoyment, JT grips a bottle of Moet in his left hand and drinks freely from the bottle. From time to time, he passes the champagne bottle amongst his friends and the young ladies who they have befriended.

"I could get used to this!" Major shouts, elbowing G-Dubs in the side.

Acknowledging Major's statement, G-Dubs throws his right arm in the air and smiles brighter than he has in a long time.

JT takes a swig of the Moet, then says, "Major, you're the mother friggin' man! I should never have doubted you about this!"

Ben is the only one of the four who is not out on the dance floor. Instead, Ben sits in a booth with a small group of women, sharing with them his storied tales from the gridiron.

"You are such an incredible athlete," one young lady comments.

"Why didn't you go pro?" another young lady asks. She reaches forward and pats Ben's inner thigh and says, "You're so strong."

In his own humble way, Ben says, "Serving my country means more to me than playing professional football."

"Modesty will get you everywhere," one young lady says as she slides closer beside Ben and softly kisses him on the cheek.

Ben smiles and thinks to himself, 'Can life get any better than this?'

As everyone is partying and freely enjoying themselves, four o'clock sneaks up on them in no time. Four o'clock is significant because the young lieutenants' train departs from New York Penn station at six. Major, Ben, G-Dubs, and JT rally around one another to figure out what they should do.

"We've got to roll," Major states.

"I know, but I'm having a great time!" JT blurts.

"I here you, JT, but we have our meeting with coach at eight thirty," Ben explains.

"Yeah, I hate to say it, but you're right," G-Dubs reluctantly agrees.

"Well, I guess we better get going, then," Major states.

The four friends prepare to leave Club NV. Before they do so, they seek out X to pay their respects. They find X amongst a small group of his crew.

Major reaches out and squeezes X's shoulder, saying, "Hey, X, we're going to roll now."

"Yeah, man. Thanks for all this! We had a great time!" JT adds.

"It was my pleasure, fellas," X states. "You little brothers can roll with me whenever. Just holler at Big Mac to see where the hell I'm going to be. Shoot! I don't even know where I'll be half the time!"

"Thanks, X," Ben responds. "We appreciate that."

"We don't have Mac's number, though," Major comments.

"My bad. Here you go," X apologizes as he reaches in his pocket and hands Major a business card containing Mac's business number. He then says, "Wait a second. Where you guys headed to, anyway?"

"Penn Station," Major replies.

"You guys can ride with me. I've got room in the limo," X offers. "You down for some breakfast first?"

"Hell yeah!" G-Dubs blurts.

"All right, then," X says. "Let's bounce so ya'll don't miss your train."

X leads his crew out of Club NV, along with Major, Ben, JT, and G-Dubs. They leave Club NV from the upstairs back exit and walk out onto the street, which is scattered with several small groups of people hailing cabs and getting into cars, SUVs, and limousines to take them to their next destination.

When G-Dubs, JT, Ben, and Major step outside onto the street, they are once again flabbergasted by what they see. The entire evening has been full of great surprises. Now, is yet another moment of a happy surprise. Standing before them is an Escalade stretch limousine. They have all seen an Escalade stretch at one time or another, but they have never ridden in one and never imagined that they would ride in one this soon in their young lives.

The four friends follow X and his crew into the Escalade. The anticipation forces them to quickly pile in.

Having almost forgotten that Mac is in the back of the small group, Major turns and asks him, "Hey, Mac. You rollin'?"

"Naw," Mac replies. "I'm calling it a night. I have some stuff I've got to do in the morning. You guys have fun. I do want to give you something before you go, though. Let me see that business card X gave you."

"I didn't know you saw any of that," Major comments. "Man, you're good!"

Major pulls the business card out of his back pocket and hands it to Mac. At the same time, Mac pulls his pen out from his front pocket. With his business card in hand, Mac quickly jots a number on the back, and then returns the card to Major.

"I want you to have this," Mac says to Major as he hands him the business card. If you ever need me for anything, don't be afraid to call. Against my better judgment, I'm giving you my personal number. Whatever you do, do not give this to anyone. All right? I can count the number of people on one hand who have this number, one who I haven't spoken to in years. This number is only for emergencies. I have friends who may be able to help you if you find yourself in a situation that you can't get yourself out of. You know what I mean?"

Mac's words slap clarity onto Major's face. The tone which Mac uses to explain his personal telephone number raises more questions in Major's brain as to what Mac's background truly is.

Somewhat sobered up by the conversation, Major replies, "Yeah. I know what you're saying. I appreciate it, man?" Major pulls his wallet out from his back pocket and slips Mac's business card into it.

"Don't lose that," Mac stresses.

"I won't," Major assures Mac.

"If you're even half the man your father is, then I know I haven't made a mistake in giving you my number."

"How do you know my dad, anyway?"

"Did you tell him I said hey?"

"Yeah, I did."

"What'd he say?"

"He didn't say anything really. He just laughed."

Mac chuckles a bit, while saying, "Yeah. Your dad hasn't changed at all, man."

Abruptly interrupting Mac and Major's conversation, JT throws his head out of the side door of the Escalade and shouts, "Major! You coming or what, man?"

In response, Mac slaps Major hard on the back and says, "You better get going. You don't want to keep your boys waiting. I'll see you around, kid."

"Bet."

Major and Mac give each other a pound. Major then jogs over to the Escalade stretch and leaps in, while Mac walks alone down the street.

The region known as the Lebanon has been inhabited for over two hundred thousand years. The first traces of Phoenician settlements existed around 3000 to 2500 BC. The Phoenicians were traders and merchants who were involved in international trade between the Middle East and countries located around the Mediterranean Sea. They were also transmitters of culture, new inventions, an alphabet, and currency. The Phoenicians did not establish large kingdoms because they limited their states to city-states, which accepted compromises with stronger neighbors and paid for peace and freedom to maintain their ability to trade freely.

Arabic is Lebanon's dominant language. Armenians master their native language of Armenian. French is still predominantly spoken because of the French mandate during the post-World War I era. Today though, English is the foreign language of choice.

Lebanon has a Muslim dominance of about fifty-five percent, but Christians make up a significant minority of about forty percent. There are many religious groups in Lebanon, and the divisions between these groups are often big and problematic. While Lebanon is comprised of a handful of different ethnic groups, they mean little compared to one's religious preference.

Lebanon's constitution divides power amongst its three religious groups: the Shia'a, Sunnis, and the Maronite Christians, who are Catholic. The president is always a Maronite and the prime minister is a Sunni. The speaker of the National Assembly is a Shia'a, which places the Christians as the most powerful group politically, with the Shia'a as the least influential.

The National Assembly has one hundred twenty-eight seats, which are up for free elections every four years. The seats in the National Assembly are however, distributed in advance between the different religious groups: Maronite Catholics (34), Sunni Muslims (27), Shia'a Muslims (27), Greek Orthodox (14), Druze (8), Armenian Orthodox (5), Greek-Melkite Catholics (5), Alawites (2), Armenian Catholics (1), Protestants (1), and other groups (1).

Syria still controls much of Lebanon's politics. Lebanon has a political system, which divides important positions amongst the religious groups. Lebanon's dependency on foreign powers is quite a normal situation in the country's history, where its neighbor, Syria, now has the upper hand. Inside the country, Christians have relatively more power than their percentage of the Lebanese population would normally allow, but the Muslims are awakening politically and have increased their turnout in national elections after the civil war.

The Lebanese school system is stamped by a de facto division between Christians and Muslims. School is not mandatory, though it is provided for all. While nearly all Christian children attend school, the mass majority of Muslim children do not take advantage. Despite this fact, Lebanon has an eighty-six percent literacy rate. Higher education in Lebanon is considered among the best in the Arab world, with five of the country's seven universities in Beirut. The other two universities are in Jounieh and Tripoli.

Beirut, the capital of the Lebanese Republic, with one and a half million citizens, is considered, by virtue of its strategic location, the crossroads between Asia, Africa, and Europe, and the gateway to the East. Its inhabitants are a unique blend of the eastern and western cultures.

Named Beroth, which in Phoenician means the city of wells, Beirut is one of the most ancient settlements, as evidenced by relics from the prehistoric communities. In Phoenician times, however, Beroth was dwarfed by thriving Byblos, Sidon, and Tyre.

When occupied by the Romans under the command of Pompey in 64 B.C., Beroth entered the most glorious period of its ancient history. In 15 B.C. Beroth was named Colonia Julia Augusta Felix Berythus and acquired the rights of a Roman city-state. What most contributed to its fame, however, was its School of Law which, under Septimus Severus, excelled the Schools of Constantinople and Athens and rivaled that of Rome.

To date, Beirut is heavily destroyed from civil war, anti-Israeli terrorist attacks, and the Syrian occupation from 1975 to 1991. Beirut is currently under reconstruction, but not in haste and at discount rates; thus in many sections of Beirut, destroyed and modern, elegant, new buildings lie next to one another. Downtown Beirut is rebuilt according to the old city plans; thus returning the capital's old charm and elegance.

The Lebanese civil war is what put Beirut on the map. The conflict started in 1975 when all possible groups began fighting one another in an almost confused manner. The Shia'a and Palestinians were among those who instigated the fighting. Israel intervened in 1982 under the cover of helping the Christian minority who were allegedly threatened by the PLO, who had taken refuge in West Beirut.

Beirut is situated on the east side of the Mediterranean Sea, making it a very valuable sea port. The capital is a great cultural mecca with great impact on the Middle East. Its eight universities have graduated a large number of the region's most influential people. Beirut's newspapers and publications are read by thousands throughout the Middle East. It also remains the publishing center for the region.

Beirut is divided into three regions: the east for the Christians, west for the Sunnis, and the south for the Shia'a and Palestinians. The capital is an amalgam of western and Arabic architecture, but it is not organized very well. Residential and commercial areas are intermixed, at times, along with industrial activity.

Beirut serves as the commercial, banking, and financial center for the Middle East, with about eighty-five Lebanese and foreign banks, countless import/export companies, arbitrage and triangular trade operations, and a free exchange market. Beirut. Despite the civil war, surprisingly much of the economical life survived in Lebanon.

Today, Beirut is strongly returning to the international arena. The country enjoys much goodwill from countries in the west and in the Arab world. Lebanon is currently in a transitory process, with an extreme foreign trade deficit, high unemployment, and often modest control of investments and profits.

3 January 2001: Beirut, Lebanon

THE SUN HANGS HIGH OVER THE desert landscape. The haze in the sky causes the sun to appear more auburn and larger than it would appear in other locales. Men and women crowd the streets of Beirut: moving in all directions. The arid heat does not cease their regular activities. Though the people occasionally complain about the heat, they are so accustomed to it that it is not much of an issue, especially since it is cool, considering how hot it is during the months of July and August.

All throughout the square are a multitude of sounds and noises: people holding conversations, merchants selling their wares. The overall surrounding sound is at such a high level that one can barely hear oneself think, or even speak to another outside of a close proximity.

As the men pass one another, they shake hands and kiss each other on the cheek: two or more kisses if they are closely familiar with one another. Those women who are clad in black move through the streets like solid shadows: receiving hardly any attention from anyone as they move from one place to another. The cosmopolitan women move with much greater freedom. They have no social restrictions are not constrained like their ultra-conservative Islamic sisters. Like the men, the women greet one another as they pass, but not with the same overexuberance as the men do with one another.

The thick air is filled with the shrill sound of an imam calling for prayer from a local mosque tower. An imam is the Islamic equivalent of a priest or minister. Those unfamiliar with Islam would assume that the populace would either rush to the mosque as prayer is called or stop where they stand, drop to their knees and say their prayers to Allah. In reality, that is not the case. To the average citizen, the call to prayer is as natural to the ear as an airplane flying overhead; the sound is simply a part of the overall background noise.

When it is time for the imam to call for prayer, he goes to the top of his mosque's tower and recites a preprescribed prayer. He stands in the tower because, before the days of electricity, standing in a high place was the only way for the surrounding area to hear the call to prayer.

The call to prayer is not spoken; it is sung. Praying is the only form of religious singing in which Muslims are permitted to take part. Once the imam has completed his call to prayer, those who wish to pray go to the mosque or a private place, lay out their prayer rug, if they own one, and pray.

Within the immense crowd a small current forms, creating a moving gap in the middle of the street. Standing in the center of the gap is a group of five distinguished old men garbed in black. A stern and determined look is locked on their faces. These men are serious, and those they walk past are very aware of this fact. The men walk tall and proud through the crowd: untouched as they move forward: closer and closer to the mosque.

At the head of the group is a man ripe in his years. He too is dressed in all black, except that he wears a green shawl on his head. The elderly man has a deep gray beard that touches his chest whenever he puffs his chest out, which is whenever he is in the public eye or amongst his followers.

The Al-Omari Mosque stands on the street on which the five men walk. It is an ominous, yet glorious sight. The Al-Omari Mosque is one of Beirut's oldest intact buildings and one of two mosques that date back to the 13th century. It was constructed on the remains of a Byzantine church, the church of St John, originally built by the Crusaders. Before this, the site shows evidence of being a Roman temple, so it's a complete record of Beirut's multi-religious past.

After the Islamic Conquest was fought during the reign of the second Caliph, Omar Bin Khattab, the site was reconstructed by Beirut's Muslims into their own religion's place of worship where it has stood ever since. Sadly, the mosque did suffer damage during the civil war, but through Beirut's major restoration program of important buildings, it is now open to worshippers and respectful visitors alike. The imam for the Al-Omari Mosque is a highly respected elder amongst Islamic circles.

Approaching the Al-Omari Mosque, two of the men behind the elderly gentleman rush to the front and open the mosque doors on cue for the elderly gentleman to enter without missing or shuffling a step. He steps into the mosque, where the two men who were behind him then pass. In the front, they then open the double doors, allowing the elderly gentleman to enter the mosque's inner sanctuary. The four men fall in behind the elderly gentleman and continue forward.

Needing to cleanse themselves before they pray, the five men turn left down a small hallway and then take an immediate left. In the bathroom, the men remove their headgear and commence to washing their faces and hands. Against the wall is positioned a long wooden, cushioned, bench. The five men take a seat, then remove their sandals from their feet. Their feet bare, the men profusely wash their feet. Feeling clean, the men stand to their feet and put the headgear back onto their heads. They exit the bathroom and return to the main lobby.

In the main lobby, the elderly gentleman leads his group forward to the prayer room, which is located beneath the mosque's onion dome. The high ceilings give the prayer room the feeling of immense space. The sides of the prayer room are made of cedar. Etched in the cedar walls are verses from the Quran. The ceiling is layered in marble in one single pattern. Contained within the marble, but in a different pattern, the ceiling is covered with verses from the Quran. The form of Arabic script used on the walls and the ceiling is not solely for a spiritual purpose. It is against Islamic law to have images of people or animals hanging in a mosque. To substitute for the absence of artwork, the Arab Muslims converted verses from the Quran into an art style. From wall to wall, the room is covered with multiple Persian rugs and carpets of random colors. The carpet layer is thick to such a degree that one seems to bounce when walking on the soft surface.

The elderly gentleman approaches a large, red, Persian rug that lies in the center of the prayer room and slowly lowers himself down to the ground. He sits up on his knees for a few seconds, then leans forward and sprawls his torso forward down onto the ground. The four men, standing diligently behind the elderly gentleman, follow suit.

Daily prayers are an act that these men take very serious. Every call to prayer, the men report to a mosque and pray in their reserved locations. Today, to those unaware, is a normal day for the five men, but it truly is not. Today, the men are praying at the most holy mosque in Lebanon. Other than conducting their regular prayers, the elderly gentleman, the Ayatollah Ali Hussein Ishmael, must conduct some business, as well.

Rising and standing on cue and in unison, the men say their three prayers to Allah. While the five men pray, another elderly gentleman steps out from the front of the mosque and stands diligently waiting for the five men to finish their prayers. Ten minutes having past, the five men rise to their feet for the final time. They take a moment to adjust their clothes, then walk forward to meet the lone standing elderly gentleman.

As the five men approach, the waiting elderly gentleman bows his head and says, "Sayed, it is always an honor to have you in the mosque."

The two elderly men approach one another, shake hands, then kiss each other's cheeks three times.

Releasing their grip on one another, the Ayatollah, says, "It is always good to see you, my dear friend."

"As it is you, sayed," the elderly gentleman replies.

The Ayatollah and his old friend walk together through a side door of the mosque. Entering a wide hallway, they turn left. Walking in front of the four other men, the two old friends approach two black-garbed men guarding the third door on the right. In front of the door, the guard on the left swings the door open, then jumps back to the position of attention.

The six men enter a large room with a high, immense mahogany ceiling. Verses from the Holy Quran line the ceiling in gold. The floor is covered with Persian rugs of various sizes and colors. The rugs have been in place for so many years that no one is sure what the actual floor looks like.

The two elderly gentlemen sit beside one another in separate suede armchairs. The other four men sit along the wall on a long, brown leather couch. As they sit, a middle-aged man enters the room, carrying a tray of tea and baklava. Keeping his head bowed while in the room, the middle-aged man quickly serves the refreshments, then promptly leaves the room.

"I was very pleased when I received your message the other day saying that you wanted to meet with me after your noon prayers," the elderly gentleman says to the Ayatollah, beginning the conversation.

"Many thanks, Ibrahim," the Ayatollah responds to his old friend. "It is very important that we speak. I see a very dark period ahead for us in the near future."

Reacting to the Ayatollah's words, Ibrahim leans forward in his seat and asks, "What's the grim news?"

"The Christian is giving his speech to the National Assembly in three nights."

Ibrahim casually takes a sip of his tea, then says, "Yes. I know. What is grim in that? He speaks to the National Assembly every six months to report his progress and issue his agenda."

"This, I know. It's what he is going to say that is very detrimental to our people, our nation, and to Islam."

"How so?"

"From what one of my men informed me last night, the Christian is going to implement a series of changes that will surely lead us down the path of the infidels."

Ibrahim shoots up in his chair and says, "What do you mean, sayed?"

"The Christian wants to begin this change by following Egypt and Jordan's example of recognizing the Zionist invaders as a sovereign nation."

Enraged, Ibrahim leaps to his feet and shouts, "He cannot do that! Does he not know what the implications of such an action is?"

"Obviously he does not. Such an act would force every radical group to attack in some form or another. Lebanon could seriously erupt into civil war again. More importantly, though, Palestine is our land. It belongs to Islam."

"I see where you are coming from. What other issues are there?"

"The Christian is going to push for Lebanon to end its relationship with Syria and push for a more secular government. He wants to gain favor with the infidels…"

"America?"

"Yes: The infidels. He wants us to gain favor with them. He aims to make Lebanon's status with them higher than that of Jordan's."

"Isn't Lebanon secular enough as it is? My GOD! So many of the women, Christians and Muslims alike, walk the streets showing their skin for any man to see. Alcohol is served for anyone who wants to purchase it. Isn't Lebenon enough like America for him? The Christian's plan for Lebanon will mean the end," Ibrahim states, shaking his head slowly as he returns to his seated position.

"If the Christian is able to get the legislature to side with him, then yes, our society is doomed," the Ayatollah says after sipping his tea. "On the other hand, there is a way that we can quiet the oncoming storm."

"What do you plan, sayed?"

"I cannot say, at this time. Plus, I do not want to put anything into motion unnecessarily. Allah willing, the Christian will eat his words when he speaks before the legislature. If that is the case, as I pray, then he will ruin himself; there will be no need for me to act. The politicians will run the Christian out of town."

"But if he is successful?"

"If the Christian happens to fool the legislature into standing behind his new, dumbfounded cause, then I will have no choice but to use extreme measures to cease his plans."

"How extreme, sayed?"

"I cannot say, at this time. Let's just say that Allah is guiding me and all of the decisions that I make and will make in the very near future."

"All praises to Allah. With him, you will not fail."

Having said his piece to Ibrahim, the Ayatollah and his four associates exit the Al-Omari Mosque in the same fashion in which they entered: chests puffed with self-endued pride.

As they re-enter the crowd, the people again move to the side: being very careful not to touch the Ayatollah and his four followers. Each person that the Ayatollah passes bows his head in respect. His head held high, the Ayatollah slightly nods his head in recognition to some and slightly waving to others. The five men walk in such a manner that their robes give the appearance of them floating on the air.

Walking, one of the men accompanying the Ayatollah asks, "Sayed, do you believe that Sayed Ibrahim is going to back us as he said?"

"There is no question that Ibrahim will support our actions. He and I grew up together. We were with the Ayatollah Komeini when he returned to Iran on Allah's holy mission. I confided in him because I knew that he would support us. The people will follow his word because he is truly a man of GOD."

"What of the others, sayed?"

"If you are referring to the radicals, no I do not require their assistance. They will create nothing but a distraction. The Christian is our target, not the Christian people. If we allow those fools to assist us, we will do nothing but make life worse for ourselves and our children."

"As always, sayed, you are correct."

"Only through Allah's guidance and the words of the prophet am I able to walk the true path."

6 January 2001, 1945 hrs

The Lebanese National Assembly hall is filled to standing room capacity. For several weeks now, the word has spread throughout the country and the Arab world that the President, in his annual address to the National Assembly, has several key, ground breaking points to make to the Lebanese people, and to the world. Not in remembered history has the National Assembly anticipated such a momentous Presidential address. Usually, only those who hold a position in the three branches of government and the senior military officials attend the President's address. Tonight, amongst the regular attendees are also Lebanon's most prominent citizens: religious and community leaders, businessmen and women, and a handful of prominent educators, authors, scientists, entertainers, and athletes.

As the clock strikes eight, loud bongs are heard throughout the hall from the main clock. At the sound of the final bong, the main doors to the hall open wide, and out steps the President. He takes a quick look up and around, feeling the presence of everyone in the hall. It is fortunate that the President is not claustrophobic or he would probably break out into a panic attack. An extreme number of those in attendance stand shoulder to shoulder in order to catch a good glimpse of their president. Though the hall seats one thousand people, its high ceilings give the impression that it is much larger than it truly is.

Walking proud, and without hesitation, the President heads down the center aisle. Each step is sure and precise. The President understands how important image is to the people; therefore, he knows that the last thing he needs happen is for him to trip as he walks across the rough red carpet.

As the President passes through the immense crowd, those able to reach the aisle throw their hands out. The President grasps each hand as he slowly makes his way down the aisle. Each hand that the President shakes relaxes him ever so much. What level of anxiety the President had prior to his arrival has nearly dissipated by the time he reaches the dais.

Standing before the entire assembly, the President pauses for a short while to gather himself. He quickly, yet carefully, scans the room, looking at every set of eyes that stares back at him. As the President had anticipated, not every face in the crowd is a pleasing one. There are several amongst the crowd who are not, by no means, anticipating what he has to say.

Having looked into every observer's eyes, the President smiles. He opens his speech book, which lies before him on the dais. The President bows his head and closes his eyes, saying a quick, silent, prayer, 'Heavenly Father I ask that you bless my words and, I pray that the people receive my words with openness and fairness. In your holy son's name: Amen.'

Finished praying, the President raises his head and dives into his speech. "To the people of Lebanon, I greet you this fine evening. I stand before you all today, not as your President, but as a citizen of Lebanon. A man who, every waking hour, strives to make his country, our country, a better place for our children. A land where the rest of the world can look and say, "We want to be Lebanese." That, my friends, is the goal. We do not want the world to envy us, but at the same time, we want the world to look upon Lebanon as one of its shining examples: A country where Christians and Muslims live together in peace and harmony: A country that does not war or cause unneeded drama with its neighbors. It is time for Lebanon to grab hold of the Middle Eastern and Mediterranean reigns of leadership and lead the region, as we move forward into the twenty-first century. We have the capabilities, the talent, and the resources to do it, and do it well!"

"We the people are not far from reaching that goal. The goal is truly an attainable one. There are several things, though, that we as a nation must do first in order to reach our goal. We must denounce radicalism in all of its forms. All of Lebanon's citizens have the freedom of speech and assembly, but not the freedom to act on said speech. I love Lebanon and the Lebanon I love respects all religions and ethnicities. Whether you are Sunni, Shia'a, Christian, Druze, Arab, Turk, Assyrian, Armenian, or Palestinian, we all should live together in peace and tranquility. To those who disagree with my words and dare to act upon them, your days are numbered!"

The listening crowd jumps to their feet at the President's exclamation.

The President pauses and waits for the cheers to die down before continuing. "Lebanon is a proud nation with a rich and diverse history and culture. The civil war has been over for nearly twenty years. It is time for all of us to move on. I am not saying to forget the ills of the past. No!

We need to embrace that dark period of our history and learn from it. To assist us in moving on to a brighter future, I am enacting a mandate that will repair all of the civil war damage within the next three years."

"We are a very proud people. Lebanon's resources are aplenty and its people are stronger than any in the world. Pride, as we all know, is dangerous, at times. It forces one to, at times, make irrational decisions. Lebanon, we must put our pride to the side and reach our hand out to the west. We must allow the west to assist us in jump-starting our economy and strengthening our military forces. I am not a fool in assuming that Lebanon will become a world superpower, but at the same time, there is no reason why Lebanon should not be the military might and envy of the Middle East and the Arab world. We are an independent nation. No longer will we allow Syria to dictate our policies and regulate us as a second-class nation. We deserve better than that. By whatever means it takes, we will loose Syria's grip from our throats. This, I promise!"

Again, the crowd leaps to its feet, applauding the President's words. Many shout in agreement: elated that someone is finally bold enough to stand up to Syria's tyrannical rule.

"Today is the day that we tell Syria that enough is enough! As much as some of you may dislike the United States, we must look at our position in the world with a clear mind and understand that a friend of the United States' is a very strong and powerful nation. Befriending the United States does not mean that we allow our society to spoil as it has. Lebanon, we will take the best from the United States and use it to make Lebanon stronger and more beautiful than ever before."

"To gain a friendship with the United States, we must follow Egypt and Jordan's example. As much as many of you listening this evening may disagree, it is imperative for Lebanon's growth that we recognize Israel as a sovereign state. I know this pains many of you, but we must make hard decisions and sacrifices in order to ensure that Lebanon's future is a bright one, for the sake of our children."

Once again, the crowd cheers, this time, though, not as loud as the two previous times. There are a few snickers and hisses amongst the crowd: again, nothing that the President was not expecting.

"In closing, I pray that you all support my plan for the year, and I pray that you assist me in showing the world that Lebanon is the jewel that we all know it is. May GOD bless and keep you. Good night."

The President softly shuts his speech book. As he does so, nearly everyone in the National Assembly leaps to its feet, applauding. They cheer in excitement, positively anticipating the radical changes that are soon to come. The President entered the hall showing very little emotion. Now, he grins from ear to ear, knowing that he clearly made his point to the people. The President can feel their sincerity pouring over him. The adulation makes him feel good.

The Ayatollah is not at all pleased with the outcome of the President's speech. He had prayed that the National Assembly would rise up and run the Christian out of the hall. Unfortunately, the exact opposite is occurring. The people praise President Paulos in such a manner that they do everything short of carrying the President on their shoulders. The President continues his slow and triumphant walk down the center aisle, shaking every hand that is thrown before him.

The Ayatollah stands amongst the crowd with his four companions, waiting for the President and the elated crowd to walk past. Cheering and clapping is not an action in which the Ayatollah participates. The Ayatollah has just witnessed his worst fear; the National Assembly believes and supports the Christian's proposition. He now must take matters into his own hands.

"Let us leave this den of infidels," the Ayatollah coolly says to his entourage.

Loyally, the four men follow the Ayatollah out of the hall, through a side door. They enter the lobby, which is about fifty meters away from the large, elated crowd. Seeing the crowd, the Ayatollah, surprisingly to his men, decides to head in its direction. The Ayatollah could easily take a side exit, but he wishes to make a statement to those in attendance.

Reaching the crowd, as the Ayatollah is accustomed, the people step to the side. They make every concession not to touch him. Each person whom the Ayatollah passes bows his head, ever so slightly, out of respect. Dutifully, the Ayatollah's four companions walk with him: two behind and two to each side. Further into the crowd the Ayatollah leads.

Nearing the center, the Ayatollah approaches the President. Someone motions to the President that the Ayatollah is walking in his direction. Hearing the message, the President quickly turns around:

locking eyes with the Ayatollah as he passes by. The Ayatollah glares into the President's eyes with a controllable rage.

The President, not sensing the Ayatollah's anger, waives his hand in a friendly gesture and says, "Good evening, sayed."

The Ayatollah ignores the President's words: his anger too intense to hide his distaste with a fake act of courtesy. Acting as though no one has spoken a word to him, the Ayatollah and his four-man entourage walk on through the crowd and out the main entrance of the legislative building.

When the five men step out onto the street, a black Mercedes is there waiting alongside the road, idling. The Ayatollah flashes the driver a signal. The driver, seeing the signal, gets out of the Mercedes and speeds over to where the Ayatollah stands. The driver dutifully opens the rear passenger's side door for the Ayatollah to enter. As the Ayatollah situates himself in the Mercedes, one of his men takes the place of the driver. Once the Ayatollah is seated in the Mercedes, the remainder of his entourage enters the car, as well: leaving the original driver standing on the side of the road.

With all five men in the Mercedes, the Ayatollah says to the new driver, "It is time to enact the plan. Take me to the Mountain."

The Assassins were established by Al Hasan Ibn Al Sabbah, a Persian from the southern Arabian Himyarite kings. As a young man, Al Hassan received instruction in the Batinite system. After training for a year and a half in Egypt, Al Hasan returned to his native land as a Fatimid missionary. In 1090, Al Hasan gained possession of the strong mountain fortress Alamut, which was strategically situated on an extension of the Alburz mountain chain and on the shortest, yet most treacherous, road between the Caspian Sea and the Persian highlands. Al Hasan had acquired a central stronghold of strategic, primary importance.

Using Alamut as his staging area, the Assassin grand master and his disciples executed surprise raids in various directions, in order to obtain other fortresses. The Assassins' primary weapon was the dagger. Their mastery of the dagger elevated assassination to an art.

The secret organization, which is based upon Ismaelite antecedents, developed an agnosticism which aims to emancipate the initiate from the trammels of Islamic doctrine, enlighten him to the superfluity of the prophets, and encourage him to believe nothing and dare all.

Elegant pavilions and palaces surrounded the garden of Alamut. Only the Assassins were permitted to enter the garden. There was a fortress at the garden's entrance that was strong enough to hold off any attack. No other entrance existed.

In his court, the grand master kept several youth from the surrounding country, ranging from twelve to twenty years of age. The grand master initiated the youth by allowing them into his garden, making them first drink a potion, which cast them into a deep sleep. Asleep, the youth would be lifted and carried into the garden. When the youth awoke, they found themselves in the garden, surrounded by beautiful dancing and flirtatious women. The experience was so overwhelming that the youth thought that they were in Paradise.

The Assassination of the illustrious vizir of the Seljuk sultanate, Nizam Al Mulk, was the first of a series of mysterious murders that plunged the Muslim world into sheer terror. The same year, the Seljuk Sultan, Malik Shah, sent a disciplinary force against Alamut. The Assassins easily repelled the besieging army. Other attempts by caliphs and sultans proved equally futile, until finally, the Mongolian Hulagu, who had destroyed the caliphate, seized Alamut in 1256, along with its subsidiary castles in Persia. The attack equated to the destruction of all of the Assassins books and records.

As early as the last years of the eleventh century, the Assassins had succeeded in firmly establishing themselves in Syria and winning as a convert the Seljuk prince of Aleppo, Ridwan Ibn Tutush. By 1140, the Assassins had captured the hill fortress of Masyad and many others in northern Syria.

One of the most famous Assassin masters was Rashid Aldn Sinan. He resided at Masyad and bore the title Shakkh Al Jabal, which the chroniclers of the Crusades translate to "the Old Man of the Mountain." It was Rashid's Assassins who struck awe and terror into the hearts of the Crusaders: Thus beginning the mysterious legend of the Assassins and the Man of the Mountain.

After the Mongolians captured Masyad in 1260, the Mamluk Sultan Baybars dealt the Assassins their final blow in 1272. The attack sparsely scattered the Assassins throughout northern Syria, Persia, Oman,

Zanzibar, and especially India, where they number about 150,000, and go by the name of Thojas and Mowlas. They all acknowledge as titular head the Aga (Great) Khan of Bombay, who claims descent through the last grand master of Alamut from Isma'il.

The world, for all intents and purposes, considers the order of Assassins long extinct. The world is very much mistaken. Having augmented its practices and means of execution, the Assassins operate under extreme forms of covertion and knowledge from the outside world. Only a select few are aware of the Assassins' existence and operations.

The Khan who leads the Assassins, shares the same bloodline with the Aga Khan. The Aga Khan is aware of the Assassins' existence and whereabouts, but due to his public status, is not permitted to associate directly with the order. The Khan who leads the Assassins is the true Assassin figurehead. He sets the standards and states which missions are executed. He does not report to the Aga Khan. The Aga Khan reports to him.

The Syrian night is quite tranquil. Across the entire sky, there is not a single cloud in sight. The star filled sky is like that of a black silk sheet with an uncountable number of bright, multi colored pinholes. Small herds of camels seem to wander aimlessly and unguided through the barren desert. Other than the occasional Bedouin herdsman, the landscape is vacant of human life. Following behind the camels, the Bedouins travel-guiding their herds towards an unknown, far off destination.

In the backdrop of the desert landscape lays a large mountain. The mountain stands alone, as though GOD thought to himself one day to place a monstrous amount of rocks and dirt on one specific location. There is not a mountain range within eyes view. Not too many people approach the lone mountain: no mountain climbers, bikers, or campers. Several legends exist concerning the mountain. The legends keep the people away: Not out of fear, but out of respect.

The Ayatollah and his men approach the base of the mountain, and come to a slow stop: approximately one hundred meters away. All of the men exit the black Mercedes and walk closer to the mountain. Nearly touching the side of the mountain with his body, the Ayatollah scans the stonewall that stands before him. In all directions, the Ayatollah's hands inspect the side of the mountain. After only a couple of minutes of feeling and prodding, the Ayatollah touches a spot on the mountain that is just above and to the right of his head. Suddenly, yet gradually, the stone portion that the Ayatollah has touched roughly slides into the mountain. Instantaneously, a secret door opens in front of the five men. Before the door can open entirely, the five men quickly scurry into the mountain. Upon entry, the door quickly shuts behind them: concealing them in complete darkness.

One of the Ayatollah's men swings his robe open and retrieves a large flashlight, which he hands to the Ayatollah. The Ayatollah turns the flashlight on so that he and his associates are able to see in the dark cavernous room. Aiming the beam of light down a dark passageway, the Ayatollah leads his men through the dark mountain passage.

The passageway is just over shoulder width high and three feet wide. In order to move forward, the men must hunch themselves over. The Ayatollah and his men uncomfortably walk for what seems like hours. The rocky journey is up hill in its entirety. After every few minutes, or so, the group encounters several turns and cut offs. The Ayatollah confidently takes each turn without hesitation. His men do not worry whether or not their leader knows where he is going. They have faith in their leader. Around and around the path winds: slowly taking the men further and further to the top.

The Ayatollah and his men are determined. Though they are tired and their bodies ache from their physical position, they continue on their path. Their motivation comes from above. Because the Ayatollah and his men believe that Allah blesses their journey, they know that they must continue on: that their strength comes from Allah.

Unbeknownst to them, because their heads have been down for the majority of the journey, the Ayatollah and his men approach the end of the path, which opens up into a large cavernous room.

His spirit nearly broken, one of the Ayatollah's men pants, "Sayed, what do we do now? There is no where for us to go."

Out of breath, yet still calm and full of strength, the Ayatollah replies, "Just because we cannot see the remainder of the path does not mean that the path does not exist. Trust in Allah, Assam, and he will trust in you."

"Yes, sayed," Assam replies, bowing his head in shame. "I apologize for my lack of faith."

The Ayatollah waives his hand, dismissing Assam's words. The Ayatollah understands that one is always growing in Allah's ways. Perfection is a goal to strive for, yet never attain.

While the Ayatollah motivates Assam, a rope ladder decends from above. The Ayatollah smiles at the sight of the rope, silently thanking Allah as he leads his four men forward and up into the seemingly endless black cavern.

Not very athletic by any stretch of the imagination, the five men clumsily struggle up the gangly ladder. Their rate of ascent is very slow. There are moments when the Ayatollah and his men come to a complete stop: holding onto the rope ladder for dear life as they regain a few ounces of their strength and energy.

As the old men climb higher and higher, the rope ladder swings in all directions. Their non-fluid body motions that are not rhythmic in nature causes the rope ladder to swing. It takes all of their effort and will power to not fall to their deaths.

Further and further up the ladder the Ayatollah and his men climb. The men feel as though they are climbing the Biblical Jacob's ladder. Reaching an unknown height, the Ayatollah looks up and spots a dim glimmer of light. Hope, though never diminished, is strengthened at the sight of the light- symbolizing that their journey is nearing an end.

The Ayatollah's men notice the light a brief moment after their leader. Their hearts fill with joy and their bodies fill with a new inner-strength that they have not felt since their journey had begun. The light sub-consciencesly causes the five men to increase their rate of speed up the rope ladder. They move so fast that their hands and feet barely touch the ropes as they ascend.

Finally reaching the end of the rope ladder, the men pull themselves up onto the cliff's edge, which is roughly twenty feet in diameter. On both sides, there are more cliffs that jut further up into the mountain. The ledge and the jutting cliffs create an image of a series rocky porches. To the front of the edge and cut into the cliffs is another pathway that is much larger than the one that the Ayatollah and his men had begun their journey.

Exhausted, the Ayatollah and his men stand hunched over with their hands resting on their knees. Profusely heaving, the men suck in as much air into their lungs as they are able. Some of them sit on the ground in an effort to relax their underused muscles.

Unaware of their surroundings, a man steps out of the shadows and, in a deep bass voice, says to the Ayatollah and his men, "Come with me."

The sound of the voice startles the men, causing them to stand erect. The Ayatollah and his men face the direction from whence the voice came and stare into the shadows. Peering, the five men eye a man standing a head above them. His skin is a light brown; his face is covered with a thick, black beard. The man wears a deep purple robe with a white shawl covering his head. On his right side is a long, broad sword that glimmers from the small amount of light that reflects off of its shimmering surface.

The Ayatollah and his men dust themselves off, then walk towards the man from the shadows. Nearing him, the man from the shadows turns and heads down a path. This pathway is the exact opposite of the path that the Ayatollah and his men first encountered. The walkway that the men currently tread is several meters high and wide. Every two meters, lit torches line the pathway. From the fire's glow, the Ayatollah and his men read Arabic script enscribed on the wall. Some of the writing is from the Quran. Others, the Ayatollah is unsure of their origin.

The man from the shadows reaches a heavy wooden door. He bangs a series of knocks, then takes a couple of steps back. The door swings open towards the group. The man from the shadows leads the beleaguered group through the doorway and out of the cavern. Through another long hallway, the men walk. The hallway is much like the one within the cavern, only better lit. On the right side of the hallway are written in gold, quotes from the prophet Mohammed and on the left, the words of Ali, Mohammed's grandson.

The Ayatollah looks in amazement as he follows along. Though he knows that Allah is guiding his path, he still cannot believe that he is actually going to have an audience with the legendary Man of the Mountain.

The man from the shadows stops and swings a large wooden door open. "Come in here," he states.

The Ayatollah and his men obey and step into the doorway. Inside, the door quickly shuts behind them, leaving the five men alone in a seemingly empty room, in the dark. Suddenly, an overly illuminating light shines upon them. The light is so overpowering that the Ayatollah and his men are unable to see outside of their circle of light. They know that they are surrounded by darkness, but they have no idea what awaits them in the dark.

Unsure of what to do, the Ayatollah decides to boldly walk forward, yet just before the Ayatollah is able to take his first step forward, a voice from the darkness states, "Step forward, Ali."

Obeying the voice's commane, the Ayatollah and his men walk forward, but their movement is interrupted yet again- the voice in the dark stating, "I said you, Ali. Not your men. They will wait where they stand."

The Ayatollah's men look at their leader for guidance. He nods his head, acknowledging his men to remain where they stand. The Ayatollah then continues forward, unsure of what or whom he is going to encounter.

When the Ayatollah steps out of the light and into the darkness, the sudden change in brightness momentarily blinds him. While the Ayatollah cannot see, he does not move. Eventually, the Ayatollah's eyes adjust to the darkness, as his sight returns to him.

Opening his eyes wide in an effort to focus, the Ayatollah spots an enormous wooden chair positioned against the far wall. In the chair sits a lone man. The man wears a long green robe that buttons up at the neck. Around his waist is tied a black sash. On his feet, the man wears a pair of black moccasin like shoes. His face has a short, thick, black beard and mustache. Leaning against the wall, to his right is a curved sword in a seemingly golden sheath. The man's hair is black and curly and is just short of touching his shoulders. The man is not very old in age: not as old as the Ayatollah would have expected. The man appears to be in his mid-forties.

The man seated in the wooden chair says to the waiting Ayatollah, "You may come into the light, Ali."

The Ayatollah continues walking forward: stopping when he stands directly in front of the man.

"So," the man opens, "I see you actually made it. I had my doubts as to whether you would make it up here. At your age, I was not sure you could survive the journey. Some have died in their quest to hold an audience with my predecsors and me. As you would assume, there is a much easier way to get here. Of course, there are not too many who are privy to that information. I guess you truly do believe in your holy cause."

"Great Khan," the Ayatollah humbly replies, bowing his head low, "I am honored that you allow me to stand before you. Allah be praised for his glory."

The Khan callously waives his hand at the sound of the Ayatollah's words.

The Khan then states, "Before you begin, Ali, understand that if it were not for my father's connection with your family, you would not be standing before me."

The Ayatollah nods his head in recognition and the truth behind the Great Khan's words, which take the Ayatollah's mind back to when he was a young child.

"Come, Ali it's time for bed," the future Ayatollah's father states.

The young Ali runs down the hallway and sprints past his father who stands against the wall. Entering his room, Ali leaps into bed, where his two younger brothers lay waiting. In the bed beside the three little boys are their two sisters.

"Daddy, daddy! Tell us a story!" the children shout.

Their father walks down the hall and enters his children's room. He pulls a chair up from against the wall and positions it between the two beds.

"Let's see," their father states. "What story should I tell tonight?"

"Tell the one about the guy who saves the girls from the bandits," Ali's older sister requests.

"No, no, no!" Ali's youngest brother shouts. "I want to hear the one about the man who kills twenty men by himself with a sword."

The children's father laughs. His most precious time of the day is the evening when he sits with his children and tells them stories.

"You know," Ali's father begins, "I like Layla's suggestion. I'm going to tell the one about the hero who saves the young ladies from the bandits."

During his youth, the Ayatollah's father began every bedtime with a story of great adventure. The Ayatollah's father passed away when he was only ten. The only solid memories the Ayatollah has of his father are of those nights when he would tell his siblings and him their regular bedtime story. The Ayatollah always assumed that his father was simply a great storyteller who had a great gift of connecting and reciting words in such a manner as to entertain and retain the attention of young children.

The Ayatollah's father's stories always reminded him of the tales of the Arabian Knights. The stories were always filled with constant danger and death defying feats: stories that featured men of great honor who never failed in a task which they were presented: men who never faced an enemy they could not defeat. The Great Khan's words force the Ayatollah to question whether there was more reality than fiction to his father's stories.

While the Ayatollah's mind lingers on childhood memories, the Khan states, "I know why you are here, so there is no need for you to verbalize your request. As you are aware, I have people everywhere. I will grant your request, as long as you are still willing to accept the terms."

Complying with the Great Khan's agreement, the Ayatollah nods his head. The terms for accepting an Assassins' contract is for the one placing the contract to turn over a five-year-old male family member, who will train in the ways of the Assassins. The setback to the agreement is that the young man is unable to re-enter society until he has reached the age of consent, which varies from person to person. The age of consent ranges between eighteen and twenty-two. By the time the young man is able to leave the fabled mountain, he has very little recognition of his past family. The only family he knows is the men and women who are affiliated with the Assassins. The Ayatollah has sacrificed the youngest son of his eldest son to the Great Khan.

The second set of terms is that if the Assassin who the Khan sends to execute the contract is killed while fulfilling the contract, then he who requests the contract must financially compensate the Assassins for its loss. The price tag for a fallen Assassin is twenty-five million dollars: paid in full one year after the Assassin's death. If the price is not met, then the Assassins will take the life of he who requested the contract.

The two terms that one must meet to open a contract with the Assassins are why so few seek out the Assassins for its assistance. Since its inception, the Assassins' terms have always been too high for most to meet. Over time, the Assassins were not sought out, except for rare and exceptional cases. Because the public lost visibility of the Assassins, they simply became a part of myth and legend.

"Since you agree to the terms, then I want something to be very clear before you leave here. Know that I do not care about this self-righteous jihad that you are undertaking."

The Khan's words cut through the Ayatollah's heart. His eyes suddenly widen in disbelief. The Ayatollah cannot believe the words that are coming from the Khan's mouth. The last person the Ayatollah expected to be against Allah's plan was the Great Khan: Surely he is mistaken.

Noticing the Ayatollah's reaction, the Great Khan continues, saying, "Surprised, aren't you, Ali? I knew you would be. We of the mountain worship Allah in an entirely different manner than you and your followers. We worship Allah in Islam's purest form: the way that Allah and the Prophet had intended. We practice a gospel of acceptance and inclusion. Not exclusion and alienation, as you do. You and your followers would be quite surprised on how we live here in the Mountain." The Great Khan takes a moment to pause, then says, "I will have the Lebanese President killed for you, but understand that I do not do it in the name of Allah. Murder is not Allah's work. Allah's path is that of love and peace. But, I am wasting my breath saying all of this to you, Ali. You will never understand."

Disappointed in what the Great Khan has stated, the Ayatollah hangs his head low, not understanding how or why the Khan does not believe in the plan that Allah has placed before him.

"Hold your head up, Ali. Your shame and disbelief is not yours alone to bear. Know though, that your grandson will be well taken care of. His mother will see him again. Now, take your men and go. If I need to contact you, I will find you. Do attempt to contact me."

The Ayatollah, again, nods his head in acknowledgement. Internally, he is highly upset at the Great Khan's words.

'How can the Khan not agree with my cause?' the Ayatollah thinks. 'It has to be obvious that Allah is on my side. Obviously, the Khan is misguided and confused. Unfortunately, any word I say could mean my life, so I will stay silent and strong for my people.'

"Oh, I almost forgot," The Great Khan says while the Ayatollah is in mid-stride. "Do not worry about using that passage way after you have left, if you are thinking of returning for some unknown reason. My people will seal it off as soon as you and your entourage leave. Now, go, and may Allah be with you."

10 JANUARY 2001: BEIRUT, LEBANON

P RESIDENT PAULOS SITS IN HIS OFFICE, going over some last minute paperwork with his staff, prior to leaving for home. Tonight is Tuesday, and every Tuesday night, during the late fall, President Paulos makes it a point to attend his youngest son's futbal games. His position as the President of Lebanon does not allow him to be as active in his children's lives as he would like, so President Paulos makes it a point to stress one aspect of each of their lives as regularly as he can. Since the president is a futbal fanatic, it is not a difficult decision for him to leave work early on Tuesdays to see his son, Arminak, play.

When President Paulos was growing up, he spent every waking moment playing futbal: so much so that when the young president disobeyed or disappointed his parents in any way, they would disallow him from playing futbal for an extended period of time. Fortunately for the president, he was a relatively good child and earned good marks in high school. When it was time for President Paulos to attend college, he applied and was accepted to Oxford University, in London, England. There, he tried out for and made the futbal team where he played as a midfielder for the varsity team his junior and senior years.

President Paulos sits impatiently behind his desk, while frequently looking at his watch. Three of his staff members, who sit directly in front of him, continuously hand President Paulos documents and speak to him as they do so. President Paulos is half aware of what they are saying. It is not that he is ignoring his staff or that he does not care about his work. It is just that he really wishes to leave.

Out of frustration, President Paulos points to his watch and coolly asks, "Are we almost done yet?"

"Yes, sir," one of the staffers replies. "You just need to sign this." The staff member places a packet before the president.

"What is it that I am signing?"

"Sir, this is the legislature's bill on creating a college scholarship program for women."

The president slowly nods his head in acknowledgement, as he reads through the bill. Assured that the bill has the proper substance, President Paulos takes his ballpoint pen and signs it.

The bill signed, President Paulos drops his pen down on his desk, leaps to his feet, and says, "Can I leave now?"

"Yes, sir," his staff laughingly replies.

"Good!" President Paulos slams his hands down on his desk with a large grin on his face. He moves from behind his desk and grabs his blue suit jacket that hangs in the back right corner of his office. Standing at the doorway, one of the staff members patiently waits with the president's briefcase in hand.

Exiting his office, President Paulos takes his briefcase from his staff member and says "See you in the morning."

Unlike the President of the United States, the Lebanese President does not live and work in the same building. The President of Lebanon works in an executive building, which he shares with the Sunni Prime Minister. Though security is relatively strict in the executive building, the public is still able to enter the building without much difficulty.

Every workday during the mid-afternoon, the executive building hallways are extremely congested with all of the people leaving for home. Just over a thousand personnel work in the executive building. There are only four ways out of the building for general use, so at the end of the workday, people are shoving their way out of the doors. No one acts in an impolite manner, but bodies are quite close, and at times, are forcefully moved through the halls like a log in a stream current, out the doors. The movement out is so immense that the security guards do not allow anyone to enter the executive building between the hours of four and five in the afternoon.

President Paulos steps out into the hallway and joins the flowing traffic that is heading out of the executive building. His security detail is always frustrated with their president during moments such as these because he does not protect himself from the people. President Paulos loves his job and the people so much that he is unwilling to leave through one of the secured back doors. He loves to spend as much time amongst the people as he can, even if it is shoulder-to-shoulder. The president feels very positive and confident when he walks amongst those whom he serves."

When President Paulos first took office, he told his chief of security that the only way he would allow his security detail to act as they please is the day his life is placed in jeopardy. It has been three years since the president made that statement, and so far, his life has not been in any form of danger.

President Paulos does not usually leave his office at the same time as the general staffers. Typically, he is in his office way after dark: not getting home until eight or nine o'clock in the evening, and at times, even as late as ten o'clock. Tuesdays in the autumn are President Paulos' opportunity to interact indirectly with the people. He loves throwing people off by striking up a conversation with them before they realize that they are speaking to their president. That always gives him a good laugh.

President Paulos walks to the right and a step behind a young twenty-something year old male. He carries a black briefcase and swings it frantically as he moves down the hall.

"How's it going?" President Paulos asks the unsuspecting young man.

"Pretty good. You?" the young man replies, without looking back.

"Not too bad. I'm getting ready to go to my son's futbal game."

"Very nice. What position does he play?"

"Midfielder, like his old man. Who do you work for?" "Minister Ziad."

"That's great. He's a good man and a great person to work with."

"You've worked with him in the past?"

"You could say we kind of work together now."

"Really, I..." the young man begins to say. In mid-sentence, the young man turns his head and is shell-shocked by who he is staring at. Stammering, he then says, "Sir, I apologize. If I would have known it were you..."

President Paulos cuts the young man off in mid-sentence, saying, "What? You wouldn't have spoken to me? It's okay. There's nothing wrong with good conversation between two people. Now is there?"

"No, sir. There isn't."

President Paulos extends his hand, asking, "What's your name, son?"

"Haneen, sir: Haneen Rahib Al Yakdan," the young man replies, shaking President Paulos' hand.

"Well, Haneen, it was a pleasure speaking with you. I'll tell Minister Ziad you said hello."

President Paulos extends his stride and passes young Haneen. Leisurely strolling down the hall, President Paulos quickly moves, with two of his personal security detail walking close behind. The people in the hall, recognizing who he is, step out of their president's way. Not too many people are able to walk unscathed in the hallway during rush hour. President Paulos is one such person who can. As President Paulos walks through the gauntlet of people, he cordially waives to the crowd. The president does not stop to speak to anyone else though, because he is too focused on leaving the executive building and attending his son's futbal game.

Facing the left wall near the executive building's main exit is a janitor wearing a light blue jumpsuit and black shoes. The janitor stands a mere five foot three inches tall. He has a scruffy beard that appears as though he has not groomed it in days. The zipper to his jump suit is unzipped down to the upper part of his chest. He wears his uniform in such a manner in order to allow the air to keep his body cool as he works. The janitor appears unaware of the monstrous crowd that swarms around him. He pays no attention to the people. The janitor simply cleans the wall as the people pass.

President Paulos continues on his way towards the exit. Twenty feet from the door, his security detail darts in front of him in order to open the doors for their leader. The detail, having to move in front of President Paulos, begrudgingly forces them to turn their backs to him. The president's security detail does not like doing so and have complained to their higher on numerous occasions, but to no avail. Striding alone, President Paulos heads directly for the exit. To his right, he passes one of the numerous janitors who spends the entire day keeping the executive building clean.

Touching the janitor on the shoulder, President Paulos says, "Have a good evening, sir."

Acknowledging the president's kind gesture, the janitor turns his head and cordially nods and smiles. President Paulos smiles at the janitor in return, as he continues along his way. The security detail reaches the doors and quickly opens them for the president to have an easy exit. As President Paulos' security detail turns around, they witnesses their biggest fear has just now become a reality.

President Paulos passes the janitor with nothing but futbal glory on his mind. Unaware of what is occurring behind him, President Paulos feels a sharp, intense pain shoot up his back. From the center of his gut, President Paulos lets out a monstrous roar. His natural reflexes force him to turn around in the direction from the source of the attack.

Much to President Paulos' disbelief, his eyes are set on the janitor he had just passed. The smile that was previously on the janitor's face is now replaced by a sinister cowl. The janitor stands before President Paulos, tightly gripping a bloody dagger in his left hand. With President Paulos' chest now in his face, the janitor strikes at his heart. The president lunges to the right, causing the janitor to stab him in the shoulder. With barely any strength remaining, President Paulos throws his body forward, pushing the janitor up against the wall. The janitor hits the wall with a great force, but is still able to stab President Paulos in the gut. The president groans in agony and bends over from excruciating pain. Using the reactionary forward motion to his advantage, President Paulos head butts the janitor, ramming the top of his head in a fierce collision with the janitor's nose, causing it to break and bleed profusely.

The counterattack causes the back of the janitor's head to crash up against the wall. The sheer force of the janitor's head hitting the wall causes the dagger to fall from his hand. Weaponless, the janitor shoves President Paulos out of the way. The janitor then bends down in an attempt to retrieve his dagger. The janitor, having let his guard down for just a brief moment, gives Presdident Paulos another opportunity to defend himself. President Paulos, now on one knee, springs forward and tackles the janitor as he is scampering on the floor for his dagger.

A very weak and battered President Paulos now lies sprawled on top of the janitor. Weaponless, the janitor realizes that he is unable to kill the now blood covered president; thus, he scurries from underneath him in an attempt to escape. Lying on the floor near death, President Paulos struggles to pick his body up from off of the ground. He gets to one knee and uses the wall to help himself up. Standing on his two feet, President Paulos' knees begin to wobble and he instantly collapses to the floor.

On his feet and unhindered, the janitor bashes through the crowd, as he attempts to escape. President Paulos' security detail, their pistols now drawn, race after the blood stained janitor. The security detail shoves everyone out of their way as they pursue their president's attacker, who no one in the crowd attempts to apprehend. Fear controls their minds and bodies, causing them to act passive. The people simply stand and watch the horrific scene as though they were watching a scary movie in their living rooms.

One of the men in President Paulos' security detail stops and fires a warning shot into the air, shouting, "Everyone, down!"

Reacting to the gunshot, the people crowding the hallway scream in distress and quickly drop to the floor. The janitor remains the only person standing on his feet, causing him to silhouette himself in the immense hallway.

The janitor continues his escape, running over the lying people and even stepping on a few of them, yet his efforts to evade the president's security detail are to no avail. With no one obscuring the janitor's route of escape, the security detail easily has him in their sights. Each man pauses and takes four shots at the janitor: hitting his head and upper back. The force of the rounds throws the janitor's lifeless body forward a few feet in the air, before it hits the marble floor with a soft thud.

With President Paulos' attacker now neutralized, the security detail races to his near lifeless body to check on his condition. They quickly reach where President Paulos lies, and kneel beside him. Roughly two meters around President Paulos, the once white and light gray marble floor is now stained crimson red with his blood. President Paulos now lies near death in a small pool of blood.

One of the men on the security detail says, "He doesn't look good!"

"Where the hell are the paramedics?" the other says as he swings his head from left to right, looking for the help that should already be at the scene.

"They better hurry the hell up or he isn't going to make it!"

53

1800 HRS

"**T**HIS IS NOT GOOD. NOT GOOD at all," the Ayatollah nervously says as he paces back and forth in his living room.

The Ayatollah now carries a very heavy burden on his shoulders. An hour ago, one of his men came to his home reporting, "Sayed! Sayed!"

"Jabar, Has Allah's plan been fulfilled?"

Jabar takes a moment to answer the Ayatollah. He knows that his leader is not going to take his report very well.

Realizing, though, that keeping the truth from the Ayatollah is not going to make the situation any better, Jabar calmly replies, "No, sayed. Things did not go as planned."

Mortified by Jabar's news, the Ayatollah's eyes grow extremely wide, as though they are going to fall out of his head. The Ayatollah takes several steps back and waivers some, to the point where two of his men leap to their feet and rush to his side. Grabbing him, they place the Ayatollah in an armchair, where his body then slumps over in grief.

After a few minutes of solitary melancholy, the Ayatollah forces himself to relax. He straightens himself out then sits up properly in his seat.

Calm, the Ayatollah says to Jabar, "Tell me everything you know."

Jabar kneels beside the Ayatollah and reports, "Sayed, the assassin was in the guise of a janitor. Our people in the executive building said that the assassin attempted to kill the Christian while he was leaving his office for home. The Christian was stabbed in the back, in the shoulder, and his abdomen."

"Our people were very surprised when the Christian began fighting for his life. He was actually able to knock the assassin's knife out of his hand. The assassin tried to pick the knife up from off of the ground, but the Christian found some hidden strength and tackled him to the ground before he could pick the knife up. The janitor got off of the floor and tried to escape. I guess he didn't think he could kill the Christian."

"The Christian's security detail was able to get the people to lie on the floor. With the area clear, the Christian's security had a clear shot. As the assassin ran, they shot him several times in the head and the back. The assassin was dead before he hit the ground."

The report causes the Ayatollah to throw his head into his hands.

From out of no where, the Ayatollah shouts, "Allah, why?"

Shocking his associates even more, the Ayatollah begins to sob. The Ayatollah's men look at one another in bewilderment. They are totally confused. They have never seen their leader lose control of his emotions in such a manner.

The Ayatollah is not an emotional man, but the unthinkable news that he has just received causes him to react in such a manner that is unbecoming of his personality. The Ayatollah sobs profusely. His men hand him a handkerchief to wipe his face.

Breaking the noise of the Ayatollah's sobbing, the telephone rings. Everyone stares at the telephone for a brief moment before one of the Ayatollah's men decides to answer it.

"Hello?" is all that Kareem is able to muster.

"Listen closely and do not say a word," the voice on the other end of the line coldly states. "Tell Ali that as soon as I hang up, he needs to go to the Hussenia Mosque in the Altwani sector. Someone will be there to speak with him."

The voice ceases and the phone goes dead. Kareem replaces the receiver onto the telephone, then slowly walks behind his leader.

Kareem bends over and whispers into the Ayatollah's ear; "Sayed, you are to meet someone at the Hussenia Mosque now."

"I don't understand, Kareem," the Ayatollah says as though he did not hear Kareem's words. "Where did we go wrong? I have never doubted Allah's power or went against the Prophet's teachings. I was sure that Allah required me to end the Christian's life. Wasn't it evident? It was so clear."

The Ayatollah slowly stands to his feet. Assam grabs the Ayatollah's black shawl and places it across his hunched shoulders. The Ayatollah usually stands perfectly erect with his back straight, full of pride and self-confidence. Today's events have changed his composure in every way imaginable.

Now, the Ayatollah stands with his back bent over. His chest is not puffed out in pride; his beard, instead of touching his chest, now hangs low in the air. The Ayatollah does not hold his head up high. Now, the Ayatollah's head is bowed: his eyes glued to the floor, as though he is forcing himself to watch where he carefully places each step as he walks forward.

"Let us go," the Ayatollah says to his four companions. "I must speak with the Khan."

Out of character, the Ayatollah walks forward and opens the door for himself- slowly opening it just enough for him to pass. Ahmed, who stands behind the Ayatollah, catches the door on its edge and opens it wider so that he and his compariots are able to exit the house.

1900 HRS

THE MARKET AREA IS QUITE CROWDED. The setting sun marks the period of the day when everyone leaves their homes and enters the streets to socialize with one another. People walk in all directions: going from stand to stand buying kabobs to eat and tea and coffee to drink. Because the neighborhood is quite poor, there are no cafés or restaurants where the people can sit and relax. Instead, they lay old blankets and rugs out on the sidewalk and sit and lie on them, pouring their friends coffee and tea as they stop for a visit.

The streets are covered with sewage and trash. Due to the lack of infrastructure and the noticeable remnants of the civil war, the sewage from the homes has nowhere to go but out onto the streets. The adults do what they can to avoid stepping in the sewage, but the children pay it little mind: splashing and playing in the sewage as though the water is clean.

The Ayatollah and his men walk through the filthy neighborhood as they head for the Hussenia Mosque. Because the Ayatollah cannot stand the stench that the sewage produces, he covers his mouth and nose with his shawl. The Ayatollah's men carefully navigate through the streets, bypassing all of the sewage that they encounter. The last thing that they want is for their leader to get his feet dirty.

As he is accustomed, the Ayatollah moves through the street unscathed. Even though he rarely visits the Altwani sector, the people still know who he is and show him the proper respect. The Ayatollah does not expect any less from the people. His title of Grand Ayatollah carries much weight in most of the Shia'a world. Tonight though, all of the Ayatollah's clout and prestige is as useless as a pair of reading glasses on a blind man.

The Ayatollah and his entourage reach the Hussenia Mosque. It is not nearly as elegant as the mosques he is accustomed to frequenting.

There is neither a giant, onion shaped dome nor a sky sprawling tower for the imam to call for daily prayers.

Before the Ayatollah stands a run-down, two story building. Nearly all of the mosque's windows are broken and the paint on the walls is extremely faded. Instead of an elegant tower, the Hussenia Mosque has a tall grouping of metal poles with a megaphone attached at the top.

The iron gate that separates the mosque from the street is spackled with faded turquoise paint and rust. Lying in front of the Hussenia Mosque are two seemingly homeless men. They lie beside the wall on cardboard mats. The men and their clothes are dirty to the point that the whole of them appear gray. The Ayatollah looks down at the unconscious men and scoffs.

He thinks to himself, 'These filthy men! Sleeping on the ground in front of Allah's house! The nerve of them! Obviously these people are not following the words of the Prophet.'

Before the Ayatollah enters the gate, he stands before the Hussenia Mosque and places his hands on his hips, saying to his four men, "Look at this! It is a sin to treat Allah's house in such a manner. It does not matter that this mosque is in a filthy neighborhood. Whichever imam runs this mosque should keep it up as he was trained. Shameful!"

The Ayatollah, finished with his pompous tirade, swings the gate open and leads his men into the mosque's courtyard. The Hussenia mosque's appearance and the presence of the two homeless men seemingly wipe the Ayatollah's mind of his ill mood. Nearly forgetting that he is in a disastrous situation, the Ayatollah marches forward down the walkway to the mosque's main entrance.

Reaching for the door handle, the Ayatollah turns it and throws the door wide open. He pauses, takes a deep breath, and steps inside. Closely behind their leader, the Ayatollah's men follow. When the first of the Ayatollah's men steps into the mosque, without warning, he is suddenly met with a severe thrust to the chest. The immense force drives him back, causing him to fall into the man behind him; thus triggering a chain reaction that causes all four men to fall back outside of the mosque.

Not a moment after the four men hit the ground outside of the mosque, the door slams shut and a large bolt is heard locking on the other side. The Ayatollah's men leap to their feet and rush to the door. They fiercely attempt to open the door, but to no avail. Realizing that they cannot force the door open, they bang on it with all of their might, but no one answers their call: in the mosque or out on the street. Out of frustration, the four men stop banging on the door and take a minute to look at the environment in which they stand.

"Is it not odd that no one's reacting to our actions?" Jabar rhetorically asks his companions.

"Yes it is," Assam replies. "You would think someone from out on the street would have come to assist us."

"Or at least come to the gate out of curiosity," Kareem interjects.

"Well, we can't just stand here," Ahmed states. "We must check around the mosque for another way in. The Ayatollah's life may be in danger."

The door slams behind the Ayatollah. The sudden crash of the door slamming behind him immediately causes the Ayatollah to spin around. Much to his dismay, Jabar is not behind him, as he was when he had entered the Hussenia Mosque. The Ayatollah turns back around, knowing now that things are about to become very serious.

The Ayatollah hears a voice from somewhere to his back right say, "Continue walking forward, Ali."

The Ayatollah obeys the voice and begins walking forward again, down a short hallway. Fear begins to churn within his stomach. In a light whisper, the Ayatollah recites passages from the Quran to calm his nerves.

'If I am to die tonight,' the Ayatollah says to himself, 'I will die with dignity and honor. I will not allow the Khan to see the fear in my eyes. Allah has protected me thus far. I know he will continue protecting me now, in my darkest hour.'

At the end of the hallway, the Ayatollah approaches a small, open room, which appears to be the prayer room, yet is much smaller than the Ayatollah is accustomed. The prayer room is pitch black. Not a single particle of light penetrates the room's darkness. It is as though there is a solid barrier separating the light from the dark.

The Ayatollah stops just shy of entering the room.

He hears the same voice state, "Go into the room, Ali."

The Ayatollah obeys the mysterious voice's command and steps into the dark prayer room. Suddenly, a thick tarp drops from the ceiling, creating a border between the prayer room and the hallway. As soon as the bottom of the tarp touches the floor, the lights cut on. Because the Ayatollah has been in the dark for such an extended period of time, the unexpected brightness causes him to go blind, for a brief moment.

Quickly, though, the Ayatollah's vision returns to him. As his vision clears, the Ayatollah looks to his front to see if anyone is in the room with him. Wide eyed, the Ayatollah is shocked to find a strange old man sitting before him.

"Where is the Khan?" the Ayatollah is quick to ask.

Taking his time to rise to his feet, the old man calmly states, "It would be wise of you, Ali, to hold your tongue. It is not in your best interest to upset the Great Khan any further."

"How can I upset him if he isn't here?"

"Do you not think that I will not report every word that is sayed here tonight?"

"Where is the Khan?"

"The Great Khan does not leave the Mountain for petty issues. Your situation, Ali, does not warrant his leaving the Mountain."

The Ayatollah is shocked at the old man's words. He has always thought himself a great and powerful man. The Ayatollah has held council with every major Islamic leader and head of state. People bow their heads and make way for him where ever he walks. All Shia'a Muslims pray to Allah for his steady health and well-being. Now, the Ayatollah stands before an old man who he has never met who has just informed him that he is not important enough to warrant an audience with someone.

The old man, seeing that the Ayatollah has calmed down, slowly returns to his seat.

Seated, the old man states, "Here is what the Great Khan says. Because the Assassin was able to act upon his assignment, the Assassins are not going to make another attempt on the Christian's life. Because the Assassin was killed while fulfilling his assignment, you owe the Assassins the agreed upon twenty-five million dollars."

"I don't have that kind of money!" the Ayatollah exclaims.

"The Great Khan does not care, Ali. That is for you to figure out. You have one year, beginning the day you agreed to the contract, to fulfill your end of the contract. After the one-year has passed, at twelve midnight, you will bring the money here, to Sheik Hassan Jalal. If you are unable to fulfill your end of the contract, the Assassins will take your life. May Allah have mercy on you."

As the word 'you' leaves the old man's lips, the room suddenly goes dark again. Unexpectedly, the Ayatollah is lifted from off of his feet and is thrown over someone's massive shoulder. The Ayatollah cannot see who is carrying him, and truthfully, does wish to know.

The Ayatollah has discovered a new refined faith. Allah has presented him with a new opportunity. More importantly, though, the Great Khan has extended his life another year. The Ayatollah must now take actions to ensure that his life is extended further and not snuffed out by the Khan and his Order of Assassins.

The large figure carrying the Ayatollah storms out of the room. Unimpeded by the now lifted tarp, he moves quickly down the hallway. The Ayatollah hears the large bolt to the front door unlock. He then feels a gust of wind rush through the hallway and brush across his face, signaling that the door is now open. Suddenly, the Ayatollah is thrust off of the large figure's shoulder and is thrown high into the air. The Ayatollah hits the ground with a large thud. He is tossed with such a force that he does not have enough time to scream. Hitting the ground, the Ayatollah rolls to his left and looks up at the mosque. Much to the Ayatollah's dismay, the door closes shut before he is able to get a look at the man who threw him out of the mosque.

Hearing the door slam, Jabar, Kareem, Assam, and Ahmed rush to the front of the mosque. Much to their delight, they find their leader pushing himself up from off of the ground. They sprint to the Ayatollah's side and assist him onto his feet.

"Sayed, are you all right?" Assam asks.

"Physically," the Ayatollah answers, "yes, I am."

"What happened in the mosque, sayed?" Jabar asks.

"Allah is testing us," the Ayatollah mysteriously answers. "We have just under a year to come up with twenty-five million dollars."

"Sayed! Why so much money?" Kareem asks.

"I first thought that Allah wanted us to punish the Christian through his death. I was mistaken. It is not for man to always know what Allah truly has planned for him. I believe Allah has made that path much clearer now. All praise to Allah and his blessed prophet Mohammed."

MG Philip H. Sheridan staked out the site, now known as Fort Sill, on January 8, 1869. His mission was to lead a campaign into the Indian territories to stop hostile tribes from raiding border settlements in Texas and Kansas. MG Sheridan constructed Fort Sill as the staging area for his campaign.

In its infancy, Fort Sill was entitled Camp Wichita and referred to by the Indians as the Soldier House at Medicine Bluffs. MG Sheridan later named Camp Wichita in honor of his West Point classmate and friend, BG Joshua W. Sill, who was killed during the Civil War. The first post commander was Brevet MG Benjamin Grierson and the first Indian agent was Colonel Albert Gallatin Boone: the grandson of Daniel Boone.

MG Sheridan mobilized six cavalry regiments for his early winter campaign, those of which included the 7th Cavalry regiment, the 10th Cavalry regiment, the 19th Kansas Volunteers, and a distinguished outfit of *Buffalo Soldiers*. Several historical figures accompanied MG Sheridan on the campaign, including frontier scouts *Buffalo Bill* Cody, *Wild Bill* Hickok, Ben Clark and Jack Stilwell.

Several months after Fort Sill's establishment, President Grant approved a peace policy that placed responsibility of the Southwest tribes under Quaker Indian agents. Fort Sill soldiers were restricted from taking punitive action against these Indians, who in turn interpreted the restriction as a sign of weakness. The Indians reacted to the restriction by resuming their raids in the Texas frontier, using Fort Sill as a sanctuary.

In 1871, General of the Army William Tecumseh Sherman arrived at Fort Sill. During his visits, GEN Sherman discovered several Kiowa chiefs boasting about a recent wagon train massacre, which they had participated. When GEN Sherman ordered the arrest of the Kiowa chiefs during a meeting on Brevet MG Grierson's porch, two Kiowas attempted to assassinate him. In memory of the failed assassination attempt, the Commanding General's quarters was christened, *Sherman House*.

In June 1874, the Comanches, Kiowas, and Southern Cheyennes went on the warpath. The south Plains once again shook with the hoof beats of Indian raiders. The resulting Red River Campaign, which lasted an entire year, was a war of attrition: involving relentless pursuit by converging US military columns.

Without a chance to graze their livestock and faced with a disappearance of the great buffalo herds, the hostile tribes eventually surrendered. Quanah Parker and his Quohada Comanches were the last to abandon the struggle. The Comanches' arrival at Fort Sill in June 1875 marked the end of Indian warfare on the south Plains.

Until the Oklahoma Territory opened for settlement, Fort Sill's mission was one of law enforcement. The soldiers' main mission was to protect the Indians from outlaws, squatters, and cattle rustlers.

In 1894, Geronimo and three hundred forty-one other Apache prisoners of war were brought to Fort Sill where they lived in villages on the range. Geronimo was granted permission to travel for a while with Pawnee Bill's Wild West Show. He had the opportunity to visit with President Theodore Roosevelt before his death of pneumonia at Fort Sill, in 1909. The remainder of the Apache tribe remained on Fort Sill until 1913. LT Hugh L. Scott taught the Apaches how to build houses, raise crops, and herd cattle.

LT Scott commanded L Troop of the 7th Cavalry regiment, which was a unit comprised entirely of Indians and considered one of the best in the west. Famous Indian scout I-See-O and other members of the troop are credited with helping tribes on the south Plains to avert the Bloody Ghost Dance uprising of the 1890s, in which many died in the northern Plains.

The Last Indian lands in Oklahoma opened for settlement in 1901. Twenty-nine thousand homesteaders registered at Fort Sill in July for the land lottery. On 6 August, the town of Lawton, located directly beside Fort Sill, was founded and quickly grew to become the third largest city in Oklahoma.

With the disappearance of the frontier, the mission of Fort Sill gradually transformed from cavalry to field artillery. The first artillery battery arrived at Fort Sill in 1902 and the last cavalry regiment departed in May 1907.

The school of fire for the Field Artillery was founded at Fort Sill in 1911 and continues to operate today as the world-renowned U.S. Army Field Artillery School. During its many phases, Fort Sill has also served as home to the Infantry school of Musketry, the School for

Aerial Observers, the Air Service Flying School, and the Army Aviation School.

Today, as the U.S. Army Field Artillery Center, Fort Sill remains the only active Army installation of all the forts on the south Plains that was built during the Indian wars. Fort Sill serves as a national historic landmark and home of the Field Artillery.

One of Fort Sill's most important missions is that of instructing new second lieutenants in the field artillery through the Field Artillery Officer's Basic Course (FAOBC). FAOBC is a five-month crash course in the technical and tactical aspects of field artillery. The second lieutenants are instructed in such a manner that, upon graduation, they will have a well-rounded understanding of all of the tasks and jobs that their soldiers and NCOs know, once they arrive to their units.

15 February 2001, 1015 hrs: Fort Sill, OK

MAJOR STANDS JUST OUTSIDE OF THE Gunnery School's academic building, resting against a handle rail. He and his classmates have finished the first hour of yet another grueling gunnery class. Major never realized that when he signed up to become an artilleryman that computing mathematical equations was a serious part of the job: talk about false advertisement.

As Major allows his brain to relax, he begins to rhythmcly tap his ring hand on the guard rail. The sound of his West Point ring striking the rail makes a very crisp and distinctive sound. When calm, Major tends to "make beats" whenever his mind clears itself of thoughts, which he tends to do quite often: a habit that some of his friends find a bit annoying.

Still striking the rail with his ring, Ben steps outside to join Major during their class break. Accompanying Ben is Marcos Paulos Bakoos, a young lieutenant in the Lebenese Army. The Department of Defense has a program that admits US allies to send a number of its officers to US military training and doctrine schools. The field artillery officer's basic course is one such school.

"Major, do you really have to do that?" Ben asks upon hearing the noise that Major is making with his ring and the rail.

"My bad. I'm not kicking beats- just practicing the morse code we learned in signal class yesterday. I figure if I know the numbers and the letters, then I'm good. You know what I'm saying?" Major explains.

"I guess so," Ben simply replies. He then turns the conversation to Marcos' direction and asks, "How're you liking the States so far, Marcos?"

"I like America, Ben. Thank you for asking. I actually have family in Detroit who I have visited before," Marcos replies.

"Oh, so this is nothing new for you then," Major comments.

"Well, Oklahoma is new. Detroit is not," Marcos explains

"Oklahoma's new for all of us," Ben jests.

The three young men laugh at Ben's half joke mainly because Fort Sill is in the middle of the praire and they are all used to the big city and the suburbs.

"Yeah it is," Major replies with a slight chuckle. After a brief pause, Major changes the topic of the conversation. "Hey, Marcos, how were you able to come here for OBC anyway?"

"Your country holds a few slots for my country every year. I wanted to serve in the Army for a few years and, though I do not like to admit it, my dad's influence helped me get this slot," Marcos explains.

"Your dad?" Ben asks. "How was he able to help? Is he an ambassador or something?"

"Close," Marcos states. "My father's the president of Lebanon."

"Get the hell out of here!" Major exclaims.

"I am serious," Marcos replies.

"We believe you, Marcos," Ben chimes in, just as shocked as Major. "It's just that it's not everyday that someone tells you that their dad is the president of a country."

"I can understand how that would seem out of the ordinary," says Marcos.

"So, what're you getting into for the four day, Marcos?" Major asks.

"I am flying to Detroit as soon as we finish class today. There is no point in staying here if I do not have to," Marcos replies.

"I hear you on that," Major agrees.

"Hey, I was just thinking," Marcos blurts. "You and Ben should come to Lebanon for a visit this summer."

"Lebanon?" Ben and Major say in unison.

"Yes. Come to my home and meet my friends and family. You wll have a great time. The women in my country are beyond beautiful."

"Let's do it," Major says to Ben.

"You seem to forget, Major. We have this little thing called Ranger School that we have to go to right after OBC," Ben states.

"Oh, yeah," Major replies.

"I did not know you were going to Ranger School. I am glad that you are my friends," Marcos jokes. He then suggests, "Since you cannot come this summer, how about New Years? My father holds a party that will impress even you two."

Major says, "I never really have anything to do for New Years, so why not? Yeah, I'm down. Lebanon for New Years…man!"

"We may as well make the most out of our lives while we're still young and take advantage of opportunites that present themselves, so yeah, I'll go too. Thanks for the invite, Marcos. I appreciate it," Ben says.

"The pleasure is all mine, Ben," Marcos replies. "We are going to have a memorable and exciting time!"

15 JUNE 2001

MAJOR'S ALARM SOUNDS, ALERTING HIM THAT it is time to get out of bed and start yet another day. He rolls over and reads his digital clock. In a bright red light, the clock flashes four-thirty. "Uh," Major groans as he sits up out of bed. "GOD I hate this!" he murmurs as he stands to his feet.

Every weekday, Monday to Friday, Major wakes up long before sunrise. Unfortunately, his painful routine is necessary. Major has to do what is referred to as Ranger PT. Ranger PT is the special PT session that only select FAOBC students take in order to prepare them for the physical rigors of Ranger school. Today, though, is not a Ranger PT day. Today is the final OBC Army physical fitness test (APFT).

The APFT consists of three tested events: push-ups, sit-ups, and two-mile run. Major usually dreads APFTs, not because he finds them difficult, but for the simple reason that he just does not like to take them. On the other hand, Major does quite well on APFTs. Today's APFT is different than most. Major is vying for the highest APFT score in his FAOBC class. He knows that it is an attainable goal and one that he must earn for pride's sake.

The maximum score for the APFT is three hundred. The Army, though, has an extended scale. The extended scale is the one that matters to Major, and many of his friends, as well. For every additional push-up and sit-up that Major does over the seventy-two and eighty max, respectively, is an additional point to his score. Every six seconds that Major runs faster than the thirteen-minute two-mile max is an additional point to his run score.

Major grabs his black PT shorts from off of the ground and quickly slips them on. Half naked, Major walks into his TV room, in search of his running shoes. Major has a tendency to place his belongings in the same place, most of the time. As soon Major enters the TV room, he locates his shoes sitting beside his LAZ-Boy, where he had left them last night after a good night of watching WCW wrestling. Instead of sitting in the LAZ-Boy, Major sits on his coffee table, grabs his running shoes, and quickly slips them on.

His shoes on his feet, Major stands erect. He then goes to his computer desk and snatches his keys, which sit on the right side of his monitor. Major turns around, then walks past his couch and grabs his Army PT shirt that lies on the far end. With his PT shirt in hand, Major heads for the door and exits his apartment. As he trots down the stairs, Major slips on his PT shirt.

Outside, Major turns right and cuts across the grass, heading for Ben's apartment stack. Major leaps up the three steps and enters the stack. Inside, Major turns, faces the door on the right, and pounds on it a few times. After a couple of seconds, a sleepy eyed Ben answers the door. Too tired to speak, Ben simply waives Major in. Major walks into Ben's apartment and takes a seat on his couch.

Ben disappears in the back. Major does not sit for long before Ben walks back out from his bedroom. Seeing Ben enter the TV room, Major jumps to his feet and heads for the door. Major swings the door open and exits the apartment- Ben following close behind. The two friends exit the apartment stack and walk to Major's 4Runner.

Major drives he and Ben to Honor Field, which is where all Fort Sill personnel conduct their APFTs. Being that their entire class is taking the APFT, parking is hard to come by. After a short time of searching, Major finds an empty spot on a side road and parks. Ben and Major slowly get out of the 4Runner and walk the short distance to Honor Field.

Honor Field is swarming with officers. Second lieutenants stand, waiting to take the APFT. Most of them are quite nervous and dread the fact that they have to take it. A few, Major being one, cannot wait to get the APFT started.

As Major steps off of the road and onto Honor Field, he shouts, "Let the game's begin!"

Ben shakes his head at his friend's loud, boisterous outburst.

Major and Ben walk to the large group of second lieutenants and find their friends from school, JT, G Dubs, TC, as well as those who were graduate assistants at West Point, Alan Gamble, Nick Lake, and Simon Terror. As with the Prep school, West Point only allotted for the four football graduate assistant positions, due to the Mess Hall incident from the previous winter. The fourth graduate assistant, Daniel Clayton, is currently at Fort Benning, Georgia. Daniel has recently completed the Infantry Officer's Basic Course and is now waiting for the next Ranger school course to begin. Simon, Ben, and Major will join him in a month's time.

"You ready for this, Major?" JT asks, getting hype himself. JT slams his giant hands on Major's shoulders and firmly squeezes.

"Hell, yeah!" Major boasts. "I've got this!"

"You're crazy," Simon sternly remarks in reference to Major.

"You've got to be a little crazy to stay sane in this world," Major retorts.

"I guess so," Simon states. He and Ben then share a cynical look.

The close friends continue conversing, mostly about what they are going to do later in the evening. After a few minutes of talking, the NCO who is administering the APFT moves to the middle of Honor Field and has the second lieutenants gather around him for the APFT brief.

"Gentlemen, and ladies," SFC Carmen states, "today I will be administering the APFT. This APFT is for record. If you don't pass this APFT, you won't graduate from OBC."

Briefing the second lieutenants, SFC Carmen runs through the minimum and maximum requirements and proper method in performing each of the tested events. As he briefs, a young captain demonstrates the proper form for executing each of the tested events.

The brief complete, SFC Carmen states, "Behind you, there are ten lines. Go to one and make sure that they're even."

The second lieutenants move to the ten lines. Major walks to the line that is to the far left, where he immediately moves to the front. JT goes to the line immediately next to Major's.

As Major stands and waits for the APFT to begin, he mentally prepares himself. Major begins to bounce, thinking, 'You've got this, Major. It ain't no thang. You can break one-o-six. It's all in the mind, son. It's all in the mind.'

While Major gets himself hype, his grader approaches him and asks, "What's your name LT?"

"Milton Johnson, sir," Major answers.

The grader, a CPT Thomas, writes Major's name down on a scorecard, then says, "Here. Fill in your social, then pass it on to the rest of the guys."

"Roger, sir."

Major writes his social security number down in the appropriate space, then passes the card on to the second lieutenant standing behind him.

With all of the scorecards properly filled out, SFC Carmen, with a mega phone to his mouth, commands, "Testers, take your positions."

The group of lieutenants in the front of their respective line goes down to their knees. Major takes his time moving to the ground. He knows that SFC Carmen cannot begin the test until everyone is in position. As Major feels, there is no need to rush the inevitable.

Seeing that the ten second lieutenants before him are on their hands and knees, SFC Carmen then states, "Testers, ready."

The second lieutenants move to the push-up position. Major does not. Instead, he slowly rocks back and forth, as though he is timing the start. Major knows that SFC Carmen is not going to wait for him to move into the proper position, which is exactly what he anticipates.

Immediately after ready, SFC Carmen states, "Begin."

The second lieutenants commence to pushing. Major, timing the ready perfectly, moves to the push-up position and begins executing his push-ups, as well. Major's reasoning behind waiting for the command of "Begin" to move into to the push-up position is due to his theory on the conservation of energy. As Major sees it, there is no need to needlessly waist energy and tire oneself, if it is not necessary.

Major's speed and intensity is unbelievable. He pushes at a rate that few others can even imagine to maintain. Major does not think as he pushes. He simply pushes. Major treats the push-up event like a sprint, as though he is running the four hundred meter dash. He does not worry about pacing himself, which he deems as pointless.

Major hears CPT Thomas count his repetitions. CPT Thomas is barely able to keep up with Major's speed. The count softly echoes in Major's head, as his repetitions steadily increase.

At repetition number eighty, Major pauses for a brief moment to rest his arms. As he locks his arms out in the up position, Major lets out a mighty roar; "Ahhhhhhhh!"

Everyone on Honor Field, hearing the loud shout, turn their attention to Major's direction. Even some of the second lieutenants who are testing briefly cease their movement to look at Major.

Unaware and uncaring of the sudden attention, Major continues with his repetitions, as though he had not stopped. Having done so many push-ups, though, Major's arms begin to tire, but he does not allow that to faze him.

Pushing and pushing, Major finally reaches his goal of one hundred six. Again, Major loudly shouts. This time, though, he does pause to do so. Having reached his goal, Major seems to suddenly hit a brick wall. Slowly, Major continues to push. One-o-nine. One-ten. Every time Major pushes up, he lets out a grunt. Major attempts repetition number one hundred eleven, struggling to do so. Repetition one hundred twelve is even more of a struggle. With all of his will, Major forces himself up, completing his one hundred twelfth push-up. Quickly, Major lowers down to execute number one hundred thirteen. Again, Major fights with all of his might, in an attempt to execute the repetition. Fighting and fighting, Major grunts and exhales, using all of his remaining energy to push up. As valiant as his effort is, though, Major is unable to execute repetition number one hundred thirteen.

With no strength remaining in his arms, Major collapses to the ground. Not sooner than he hits the ground, Major leaps to his feet and barks like no one has heard him, let alone anyone else, for that matter, bark before. Major is beside himself because he did seven push-ups over his personal best. Major runs in the rear of the test lines, barking and throwing up the Omega Psi Phi sign over his head.

Though Major has only completed one of three APFT events, as far as he is concerned, the test is complete. He does not really care about the remainder of the APFT. His attitude towards the two-mile run and the sit-ups does not reflect his efforts or his execution. In fact, Major regularly maxes both events to the same level as he does the push-ups. The difference with push-ups is that to Major, the push-up event is a spiritual experience. Something burns inside of him whenever he does the push-up portion of the APFT. The same feeling is not felt during the two-mile run and sit-ups and also is not felt when doing random push-ups. The feeling only surges through Major's soul when he is testing; Major is a gamer.

Calming down some, Major returns to his line. The second lieutenants in the line congratulate Major as he returns.

JT, who had executed the push-ups in the same iteration as Major, joins the jovial group and asks his friend, "How many'd you do?"

"One twelve, dawg!" Major boasts.

"That's what I'm talking about!" JT shouts. Overjoyed by Major's performance, JT bangs Major in the chest with his fists.

While the group celebrates Major's accomplishment, CPT Thomas walks over and joins them as they wait for the two minutes to end.

Laughing, CPT Thomas jokingly remarks, "Man! LT Johnson did enough push-ups for a third world country!"

The APFT complete, Major and Ben slowly walk back to the 4Runner. They would walk fast, if not jog to the truck, because they are more than ready to return home, but they do not over exhort themselves due to the fact that their bodies are extremely worn out. Though the APFT consists of only three events, for whatever reason, it never fails to drain one's body to the point where the person wants to do nothing but pass out.

"Good job on the push-ups, Major," Ben congratulates.

"Thanks, cuz," Major replies.

"Hey, man. You worked hard for that. You earned it."

"Yeah I did. I should have the highest score in the class now."

"There may be some guys who're close to you, but I think you got it."

"Yeah. Me too. I'm not too worried about it."

The two friends reach the 4Runner and immediately head for home.

"You driving?" Major asks Ben as they pull out of the parking spot, referring to their nine o'clock class.

"Yeah. I'll drive," Ben answers.

"Cool. I'll meet you at your place, then."

"That'll work." After a slight pause, Ben continues, saying, "I can't wait for tomorrow."

"What're you talking about? You're excited about the field?"

"Of course not, but it's the last three days. Tomorrow is the first day of the last days, brother."

What Ben is referring to is the three-day field problem that the FAOBC students execute prior to graduation. Though the field problem is a graduation requirement, no one ever fails any of the taskings. Each of the three days is divided into three separate stations: fire direction (FDC), fire support, and basic gunnery. Each of the three platoons circulates through each station. The Marine platoon is separated by squad and sent to the individual stations

During the FDC phase of the field problem, each squad functions as a fire direction center. The FDC is in control of processing the fire missions down to the howitzers. When the FDC moves into position, it receives the observer's location and their location from the advance party. Based upon that data and the azimuth of fire, once the FDC receives target data, it is able to process a mission and send it to the howitzers.

Many variables are involved when the FDC processes a fire mission: wind speed and direction, the temperature, whether or not it is raining, the time of day, the height of the target, howitzers, and observer, and how many times the howitzer has fired, to name a few. FDC functions truly prove that modern artillery is not about raising the gun tubes and firing. Accurate computations and calculations are involved before the howitzers are given the green light to fire.

While in the FDC portion of the field exercise, each squad member performs the job all of the FDC positions: fire direction officer (FDO), fire direction NCO (FDNCO), computer operator, horizontal chart operator (HCO), vertical chart operator (VCO), ammo tracker, and radio operator (RTO). The purpose of the second lieutenants performing each of the FDC functions is to ensure that they have learned all of the required tasks and, most importantly, understand what they are to expect from their soldiers and NCOs in the very near future.

At the fire support phase of the field problem, the second lieutenants are required to locate, then call the targets down to the FDCs. The FDCs that the second lieutenants call their fire missions to are those of their classmates at the FDC station. Some of the second lieutenants serve as forward observers and others run the mechanized infantry lane.

The forward observers are the soldiers who locate the targets and send the fire missions to the FDCs. Forward observers come in many forms: either as a single individual or a fire support team. The observers send the FDC their location by an eight-digit grid coordinate. When they report the target location, they can either send another eight-digit grid coordinate or the direction and distance to the target.

When the second lieutenants run the mechanized infantry lane, they ride in Bradley Fighting Vehicles and FISTVs. The second lieutenant playing the role of the company commander has all of the responsibility while on the lane. As he crosses each phase line, the acting commander radios in to his tactical operating center (TOC). When the commander crosses a particular phase lane, which is the trigger for the FDC to fire the mission that the observer had called in earlier.

The third station that the second lieutenants undertake is gunnery. Gunnery, for the field exercise, consists solely of firing the howitzer. Each squad serves as a gun section on either a M198 Howitzer or a M119 Howitzer. Both artillery pieces are towed: the M198 by a 5-ton and the M119 by a HMMWV. Fort Sill does not have a Paladin unit and the MLRS is too expensive to fire for a regular field exercise. For this reason, those second lieutenants reporting to light units fire the M119 and those reporting to mechanized and cavalry units fire the M198.

Gunnery consists of more than firing the howitzer, but due to safety requirements, the second lieutenants are not permitted to lay and safe the howitzers prior to firing. They focus solely on the functions of a howitzer section. As with the FDC, the second lieutenants perform the role of each of the howitzer section's positions, except for the driver: chief, gunner, ammo chief, assistant gunner, canoneer number one, RTO, canoneer number two, and canoneer number three.

The chief is the NCO in charge of the howitzer. His gun does not fire without his command. The gunner's function is to lay on the target using the gunner's sight and an aiming point, generally two aiming poles and a calometer. He sets the howitzer's deflection. The ammo chief is responsible for preparing the rounds for firing. The assistant gunner sets the howitzer's quadrant. The RTO receives the missions from the FDC, annotates the received information, and reports it to the chief. The canoneers perform the physical function of loading and firing the howitzer.

When it comes to firing the howitzer, the M198 is much more difficult than the M119. The M198 weighs over two tons, where as the M119 weighs about a third of that. In addition, the M198 HE (high explosive) round, which is the primary round that is fired, weighs just over eighty-five pounds, but the M119 HE round weighs just over forty pounds. The round is so heavy that it requires a minimum of three men to ram the round into the tube; thus the numerous canoneer positions.

The howitzer sections fire several types of fire missions throughout the day, including high angle, out of traverse, and illumination. The sections spend all day and night firing, mainly because they have to wait until twilight to fire the illumination missions.

Firing the howitzer is probably the most fun of the three stations. When the fire mission comes down from the FDC, the second lieutenants move with intense speed: hustling to fire the round before their peers. Though they move at a high rate of speed, safety is always a factor. The second lieutenants do not sacrifice safety for speed.

As Major drives past the high rises, he says to Ben, "I'm dreading the FDC, man. I suck at all that."

"I hear you," Ben agrees.

Major and Ben pull into their apartment complex and park. The two friends step out of the 4Runner and head for their respective buildings.

"I'll see you bro," Major states as he walks away from his truck.

"Yeah. I'll see you," Ben retorts, stepping onto the sidewalk.

Major jogs to his apartment complex, with his Army PT shirt in hand, to prepare for his last day of class.

Because it is the last day of class, the session ends just after the regularly scheduled lunch break time of eleven thirty hours. The second lieutenants are ecstatic because they are one more step closer to achieving freedom, or so they foolishly assume.

The second lieutenants do not hesitate to leave class. As soon as their instructor, CPT Scott, dismisses them, the second lieutenants rush out of the classroom like a herd of stampeding buffalo. Not in much of a hurry themselves, Ben and Major walk out of the classroom together, as they normally do, and head for the parking lot, which is located just under a quarter of a mile down the street.

As the two friends walk, Major asks Ben, "You get your passport yet?"

"No, I haven't," Ben replies.

"You got your stuff for it?"

"Yeah. My mom mailed me my birth certificate last week."

"Cool. You want to go get our passports before we lift?"

"Works for me."

"You going to do Ab Attack?"

"No. I didn't get any results from it. My sit-ups actually went down on the last PT test."

"Fudge, man. That sucks. Mine improved some. Oh well. I'm going to do Ab Attack, so we should drive our own trucks so you don't have to wait for me."

"Sounds like a plan. Do you know where to get the passports?"

"At the courthouse."

"That's over by the mall, right?"

"Yeah. Oh, okay. I know how to get there, but I'll follow you, anyway. What time do you want to leave?"

"Not sure yet. I'm going to give JT a call to see if he can lift early."

"All right, then. It's no big deal. Just come get me when you're ready."

"Cool deal, I'm going to need a little time, though, so I can pop my pills."

"I will too, so you want to say about two o'clock or so."

"Yeah. That'll work."

Ben and Major reach Major's 4Runner and promptly get in. Major backs out of his parking space and heads for their apartment complex so they can change and get ready to lift and get their passports. Less than five minutes later and the two friends arrive at their apartment complex. They step out of the 4Runner, Major going his way and Ben his own.

Inside his apartment, Major picks-up his telephone and dials JT's phone number. Major waits as the telephone rings five times, which is generally his hang up limit, but being that weight lifting is very important to Major, he allows the telephone to ring five more times.

'Maybe he's on the toilet or something,' Major thinks to himself as he listens to the phone annoyingly ring in his ear.

After the tenth ring, Major frustratingly hangs up the telephone, quietly saying, "Where could that fool be?"

Major takes his cell phone and scrolls through his phone book. Finding JT's number, Major presses the call button and again, waits as the telephone rings. Much to Major's relief, his second attempt is successful.

"Major! What's up brother?" JT boisterously shouts as he answers the phone.

"JT!" Major happily replies.

"So, what's up, brother?"

"I've got to run an errand at two out in town. You want to meet me at Gold's for three?"

"Yeah. That works for me. I was going to go running, anyway."

"Cool deal. I'll see you at three, then."

"See you then."

1400 HRS

MAJOR HAS TAKEN SOME OF HIS Advocare supplements, as he religiously does prior to his working out. The other supplements that Major needs to take later, he ensures that he has onhis person prior to stepping out of his apartment. It is important to take the supplements as directed. In Major's case, he is very strict with the suggested time limit restraints that Advocare asserts will give one optimal performance and results. For this reason, there is a pill that Major must take an hour and a half prior to his work out, two others an hour before his workout, and another five minutes before his workout.

Major walks into the kitchen that he and TC share and shouts, "TC, I'm out!"

"We still going out tonight?" TC shouts in response with the theme music from a Playstation 2 game blares from within his apartment.

"Most definitely!"

"All right then. I'll see you when you get back."

"Yep."

Major grabs a jug of his energy and rehydration concoction from out of the refrigerator and quickly heads out of his apartment. He glides down the stairs and dashes outside, sprinting the short distance to Ben's apartment complex. Approaching the steps, Major leaps over them and, as his foot touches the cement, he reaches for the door handle. Major turns the handle and smoothly opens the door. Inside, Major knocks on Ben's door.

"Yeah!" Ben shouts, hearing Major's knocks on the door.

Major enters Ben's apartment with Ben stating, "Let me get my shirt."

Major quietly stands by the door as Ben makes his way to his room. Ben immediately returns wearing a white cotton t-shirt. He then goes to the kitchen and fills a bottle with water.

"I'm ready," Ben proclaims as heads in Major's direction.

"Let's roll," Major replies as he turns and leads the way out of Ben's apartment.

In the parking lot, Major jumps into his 4Runner and Ben his gray Yukon. Though Ben has a relatively good idea of where the courthouse is, he nonetheless follows Major, just in case.

When Major drives, he is all about one thing: time. Wherever Major goes, whether he is walking, running, or driving, his number one priority is to arrive at his destination as fast as he possibly can. That does not mean that he drives in a reckless fashion. What it means is that Major takes the most expedient routes.

In the case of driving to the courthouse, Major does not drive through Lawton. There are too many stoplights. Since Fort Sill is located alongside US Interstate 735, Major takes it in order to by pass as much traffic as possible. The drive south on the interstate is quick and effortless. When Major approaches the third exit, he pulls off of the interstate and veers right, heading down a main street. Major drives a few blocks and approaches a Ford dealership, which is to his front left. He veers to the left and when the traffic is clear, takes a left turn.

Turning left has placed Major and Ben in old downtown Lawton. Many of the stores that they slowly pass are permanently closed. The street ends, bringing them to the mall, which is located to the front left.

Major turns right at the stop sign and drives down the road only a few hundred feet. He and Ben parallel park their SUVs alongside the curb to their right, in line with a row of shops. Before Major steps out of his 4Runner, he takes two of his weight lifting pills, anticipating the fact that he will begin his workout in an hour.

Immediately across the street is the county courthouse. Together, with their folders in hand, Ben and Major walk across the street and head for the main entrance. Inside, instead of aimlessly roaming through the courthouse, the two friends find the directory and search for the office that issues passports. Reading the directory, Major and Ben discover that the office in which they seek is on the main floor, just around the corner.

Ben and Major step away from the directory and head directly for the passport office. They walk around the first corner, turning left, then walk to the end of the hall, where the passport office is located.

The passport office is constructed in such a manner that unauthorized personnel are unable to enter. The office is nothing more than a large rectangular open room with several desks positioned in various locations. Four walls cover the perimeter of the office. On the front wall, there is a large rectangular space that has a four foot high counter strung across it. Today, there are four women in the office: three sitting behind a desk and one leaning on the counter. The women are all in their mid to late forties.

Major approaches the counter first, saying, "Good afternoon, ma'am. How're you doing today?"

"I am fine, dear. Thank you for asking. And how are you?" the woman behind the counter states.

"I'm doing great, ma'am. Thank you."

"How may I help you, today?"

"I need to get a passport, ma'am."

"Okay. That shouldn't be a problem. Let me get the paperwork for you real quick." She walks away from the counter and asks one of her colleagues, "Barbara, where do you put the passport forms?"

"They're in the file cabinet, Diane" Barbara informs.

Diane gingerly walks over to the row of file cabinets and searches through a few of the drawers before she finds the one that she is looking for. She opens the drawer and pulls out a small stack of passport forms and pushes the drawer shut.

Returning to the counter, Diane says, "We just finished remodeling. There's stuff everywhere." She then hands a passport form to Major and says, "I'm going to need you to fill out lines one, two, three, four, five, and six."

Major takes the sheet and spins it around so he can read it. At the same time, Ben walks up to the counter and stands beside Major.

"Are you getting a passport, too honey?" Diane asks Ben.

"Yes, ma'am," Ben politely responds.

Diane hands Ben a passport form, saying, "Fill out lines one, two, three, four, five, and six for me, please."

Ben pulls a pen out of his pocket and fills the passport form out as instructed.

While Major and Ben fill out their passport forms, Diane asks them, "Do you gentlemen have your birth certificates and a head shot?"

"Yes, ma'am," Major replies.

Major and Ben promptly open their folders and remove their birth certificates and head shots that they had taken the end of their Firstie year at West Point.

As Ben and Major continue writing, Diane asks them, "So where are you young men planning on going?"

Without looking up, Ben replies, "Beirut, ma'am."

"Beirut? Oh my Lord!" Diane exclaims. "What would ever make you want to go there?"

"We have a friend who lives there, ma'am," Major explains.

"Beirut's not as bad as it was in the eighties," Ben adds.

"I don't know," Diane states: "Sounds kind of dangerous to me."

Major and Ben simply smile at Diane's pessimism.

When Major finishes filling out his form, he slides it to Diane, along with his birth certificate and head shot. Diane takes the small stack and places it to the side. Ben completes his form and hands all of the proper materials to Diane, as well.

With both Ben and Major's forms, Diane says to them, "Your passports are going to cost you fifty dollars."

"Do you accept a check, ma'am?" Major asks.

"Yes we do. You can write a check or money order. No cash, though," Diane explains.

"Man," Ben remarks. "Hey, Major, can you spot me? I brought cash."

"I got you," Major states.

"Can I write one check for a hundred?" Major asks Diane.

"I'm afraid not, dear. You'll have to write two," Diane explains.

"Thanks, ma'am," Major replies.

Ben hands Major fifty dollars, which he then folds into thirds and places in his right front pocket. Major then writes two checks: one for himself and the other for Ben.

"Who do I make the checks out to, ma'am?" Major asks.

"Here you go," Diane says as she places a cardboard sheet in front of Major, which has on it the State Department address.

Major looks at the cardboard sheet and annotates the proper information onto the checks, then hands them to Diane. Now that she has all of the necessary documents and items from Major and Ben, Diane places them into separate manila envelopes.

"All right gentlemen. You're all set," Diane says as she tosses their envelopes into the mail drop. She then says, "You boys have a good time on your trip and please, take care of yourselves."

"Yes, ma'am. We will," Ben replies as he steps away from the counter.

"Thanks for your help, ma'am," Major states as he follows Ben.

Major and Ben stride out of the county courthouse and return to their SUVs. Situated, they pull away from the curb and head for Gold's Gym.

The majority of Major and Ben's friends from West Point who are currently going through FAOBC and who are stationed at Fort Sill are members of the Lawton Gold's Gym. Lifting for them is like business, but it is also like a mini-reunion whenever they meet.

Ben and Major drive from one end of Lawton, to the other to get to Gold's Gym. Unlike going to the courthouse, they do not have the luxury of taking the interstate to expedite their trip. Driving through Lawton during the early afternoon is rather smooth. The roads are not too crowded. Four o'clock is when rush hour begins in Lawton.

After driving just over ten minutes across Lawton, Ben and Major finally arrive at Gold's Gym. As Major had anticipated, JT is waiting in the parking lot for him in his car. Major pulls up alongside JT's car and Ben parks a few parking spots away from Major. Seeing Major, JT leaps out of his car and stands, waiting for him.

Major gets out of his 4Runner, saying to JT, "You ready?"

"You know it, big dawg!" JT blurts.

Major and JT give each other a pound, then head into Gold's Gym, while Ben follows close behind.

"You going to do Ab Attack?" Major asks JT as they enter.

"Wouldn't miss it," JT replies.

JT and Major head for the water fountain so JT can take his supplements. Major, in the mean time, takes his supplements and washes them down with his energy drink.

"Let's do this!" JT says as he sticks his head up from the water fountain.

JT leads the way as he and Major enter the weight lifting area.

Major lifts with JT for three reasons: one, because they are very good friends, two because JT knows what he is doing, and three because JT is one of the most muscular guys that he knows.

Today, JT and Major lift their backs and chest: four chest exercises and four back. For their chest workout, JT and Major do dumbbell bench press, decline press, dumbbell flies, and incline press. Their back exercises consist of isolated front rows, kneeling rows, seated rows, and dead lifts. JT and Major perform two sets of eight to ten repetitions of each exercise: alternating each muscle group as they move through their workout.

The end of every workout, Major and JT perform four-way manual resistance neck and weighted dips. To perform four-way manual resistance neck, one lies on a bench on his chest, back, and both sides and executes twelve repetitions for each of the four positions. They perform this exercise last because it saps the body of its last bit of energy.

Major and JT stand beside the dip machine, preparing to execute the exercise, as they usually do. When the two friends do their dips, they set the weight to the maximum allowable pounds: two hundred ten. They run through their first set and now prepare to finish their last.

Before JT takes a seat, he scans the room and physically analyzes everyone in the gym. One of the things that JT and Major hate are people who go to Gold's Gym to socialize. As far as they are concerned, the weight room is a place of business. One can socialize later. Major and JT truly hate the women in the gym wearing fresh make-up and hair does. It is obvious that they are looking for a man.

Having scanned the room, JT looks at Major and says, "You know, we're two of the strongest guys in here."

"Really?" Major asks, not truly believing JT's words.

"Look at these guys. They're not putting up the kind of weight we are. We're easily two of the strongest guys in here, if not the strongest," JT adamantly proclaims.

Major scans the room, as well, to confirm JT's findings. A brief moment of investigation leads Major to come to the same conclusion as JT.

"I guess you're, right, dawg," Major states as he prepares to spot JT. "I never really paid attention."

JT finishes his set of dips, then Major. The two friends then do their four-way manual resistance neck exercise to complete yet another enjoyable day of weight lifting. Finished lifting, JT and Major gingerly head for the aerobics room for Ab Attack, which is a half hour abdominal workout that is led by a certified aerobics instructor.

Before Major enters the aerobics room, he finds Ben and says to him, "Me and TC're going out tonight. You want to roll?"

"Yeah," Ben replies as he places a set of dumbbells down on the floor. "Who's driving?"

"TC."

"All right. That works for me."

"Cool then. Come by the house around eight or so."

"All right," Ben says as he bends back over and picks up the dumbbells that he had just placed at his feet.

Major walks away from a focused Ben and chases down JT, who is getting ready to walk into the aerobics room with some other of their friends.

"You ready for this?" JT asks Major as he joins the small group.

"You know she's going to break us off today," Major laughingly states.

"Yeah she is," JT replies as he too laughs.

JT and Major, along with some of their friends, enter the aerobics room together laughing and joking amongst the dispersed group of women who prepare for Ab Attack.

20 JUNE 2001, 1000 HRS

GRADUATION FROM FAOBC IS NOT A very exciting or memorable moment. The second lieutenants are merely happy to have successfully completed the five-month course so they can get on with their lives. Major, as he had wished and anticipated, received a certificate for achieving the highest APFT score in his class: 347. With the graduation complete, all the second lieutenants care about is clearing housing and leaving Fort Sill for their much-earned thirty days leave.

Major and Ben meet at the top of the aisle of the auditorium, waiting for one of their friends. Spread throughout the perimeter of the auditorium are several men dressed in black suits with small earpieces in their left ear. Standing beside Major and Ben are two of the black suited men.

"I guess Marcos wasn't kidding about his dad, huh?" Major asks.

"There's no reason why he would've been," Ben states.

"True," Major agrees. He pauses, then says, "I was kind of in a rush to get down to Polk, but since his dad's taking us to lunch, I'll just crash at Tweeter's place tonight."

"Yeah," Ben retorts. "I guess I'll stay there as well. As much as I wanted to get home, it isn't every day you get to hang out with a president of a country."

"Well, unless you're you and me," Major jokes.

Major and Ben laugh and elbow each other in the ribs because they had spent time with the President of the United States on Christmas Eve of 1999 when Major received his Medal of Honor. Though that President is no longer in office, Major and Ben still maintain contact with him to this day.

Peering down the aisle, Ben and Major watch Marcos and his father converse with a couple of generals and a small gaggle of colonels. Though Major is impatient and hates waiting for anyone or anything, he does not have much of a choice but to wait for Marcos and his father. Ben and Major bide their time by talking about whatever random subjects come to mind. As they wait, several of their friends approach them on their way out of the auditorium.

Major and Ben's friend and classmate, 2LT Nick Lake, better known as Tweeter, strolls up the right side aisle and stands with them.

"You guys still coming over tonight?" Tweeter asks as he approaches his two friends.

"Yeah, Tweeter," Major answers. "I'm not sure what time, though."

"No problem," Tweeter replies. "I'll be home all day."

"We'll give you a call when we're on our way," Ben informs Tweeter.

"That'll work," Tweeter states.

"We still rollin' tonight, right?" Major asks.

"Yeah. You want to go to Cowboys?" Tweeter asks.

"May as well," Major answers. "It'll be our last hurrah in Lawton."

"You want to go, Ben?" Tweeter asks.

"I don't see why not," Ben replies. "I'm going to keep it low key though. I want to get on the road at eight."

"Sweet!" Tweeter exclaims. "You can DD, then."

While Ben, Tweeter, and Major continue their conversation, Marcos and his father slowly make their way up the center aisle towards the three second lieutenants. The closer Marcos and his father reach Major, Ben, and Tweeter, the closer the secret service looking gentlemen step behind them. By the time Marcos and his father are standing before the three second lieutenants, they are practically surrounded on all sides.

Marcos extends his hand and states, "Nick, Ben, Major, this is my father, President Paulos Bakoos Sargon."

The three second lieutenants firmly shake President Paulos' hand.

Shaking hands, President Paulos says, "It is a pleasure to meet you gentlemen. I have heard so much about you. I greatly appreciate you befriending my son as you have."

"It's no problem, sir," Ben replies. "Marcos is a good dude."

"Good dude?" President Paulos inquisitively asks.

Major jumps into the conversation saying, "Sir, good dude is a term that we use at West Point that legitimizes someone's credibility with a group of people. When we say that someone is a good dude, we're saying you can trust him. Good dude is the best compliment that you can give someone."

"Well," President Paulos retorts, "I'm glad to hear that Marcos here is a good dude."

Everyone laughs at President Paulos' comment.

As the laughter subsides, President Paulos continues, asking, "So, where are we going to lunch?"

"Hey Marcos, how about that Mexican joint we took you to a while back?" Major suggests.

Marcos nods his head several times in agreement. He then says, "You'll like the restaurant, father."

"Well then," President Paulos states, "the Mexican restaurant it is."

"You are more than welcome to join us, Nick," Marcos notifies.

"Thanks, Marcos," Tweeter replies. "I really appreciate it."

The small group, closely led by President Paulos' bodyguards, exits the auditorium and head for the limousine, which has been idling since the FAOBC graduation began.

As they walk outside, President Paulos asks, "So, Major, Ben, are you still coming to pay us a visit over New Year's?"

"Most definitely, sir," Major exclaims.

"Yes, sir," Ben adds. "We're really looking forward to visiting Lebanon."

"Well, I'm glad to hear it," President Paulos states. "My family is very excited that you are coming to spend the New Year with us." President Paulos then turns his attention to Tweeter, asking, "Are you coming as well, Nick?"

"Thank you for asking, sir, but no. I'm not going to be able to go. I have some family obligations I have to attend to during that time," Nick explains.

President Paulos places his hand on Tweeter's shoulder and says, "I respect that. Family should always come first."

Marcos breaks his father's conversation, saying, "I'm going to meet Ben and Major in Baltimore so we can fly together."

"I thought you were going to your uncle's in Detroit?" President Paulos asks his son.

"I still am. My flight home from Detroit connects in Baltimore. Ben and Major are going to meet me in the terminal and fly with me from there."

"Oh. I see. Did you make all of the necessary arrangements?"

"Yes, sir. Everything's all taken care of."

"Good." President Paulos, who now stands beside the idling limousine, places himself between Major and Ben. Placing his hands on their back, President Paulos states, "Gentlemen I am so honored that you are coming to visit us. You will love Lebanon. Maybe we'll find you a wife, but for now, let us go to lunch."

20 July 2001, 1200 hrs: Fort Benning, GA

HENRY LEWIS BENNING, FOR WHOM FORT Benning was named, was a soldier, attorney, politician, and a Justice on the Georgia Supreme Court. A Georgia native, Benning's career began in Columbus in 1835 when he set up residence and began practicing law. At the age of 39, two years after an unsuccessful campaign for Congress, he was elected associate justice on the Georgia Supreme Court, making him the youngest man to hold that office.

Benning was a staunch advocate of States Rights and took a prominent part in the conventions concerning secession prior to the Civil War.

When the Civil War commenced, Benning recruited men to form the 17th Regiment of Georgia Volunteers. During the first year and a half of the war, he fought with General Robert E. Lee and attained the rank of brigadier general. Because of his coolness in battle, Benning's troops began referring to him as "Old Rock."

After the war, Benning returned to his law practice in Columbus, GA. He died in 1875 at the age of 61.

Fort Benning is known as the "Home of the Infantry." It is here that the famed United States Army Infantry School was established, and through the years, gradually emerged as the most influential Infantry Center in the modern world. Fort Benning and the Infantry School are so intertwined that it is virtually impossible to trace the history of Fort Benning without recording the evolution of the school.

From 1918 until the present, the development of Fort Benning has been directly proportional to the progress of the school. Throughout the years, the mission of Fort Benning and the Infantry School has remained fundamentally the same: "To produce the world's finest Combat Infantrymen.

The trend of instruction at the Infantry School became increasingly combined-arms oriented. In 1963, the 11th Air Assault Division was formed at Fort Benning to test the air assault concePT that led to the airmobile concept of the First Cavalry Division.

As Fort Benning proved its significance locally, it also began to make its mark nationally in the quality of the leaders it produced. The Infantry School has either trained in its officer courses or honed in its command structure some of the nation's most prominent military figures. Leaders like five-star generals Omar Bradley, Dwight Eisenhower, and George Marshall and others, such as George Patton and Colin Powell, learned their craft at Fort Benning.

With the Infantry, the Queen of Battle, as the nucleus, Fort Benning has added other very significant missions as the years progressed. Among them, Airborne School, where soldiers learn to engage in battle from the sky; Ranger School, where soldiers learn advanced tactics and skills warfare; the 29th Infantry Regiment teaches soldiers how to operate and maneuver the Bradley Fighting Vehicle in combat. Fort Benning's 36th Engineer Group has been at the forefront of the Army's post-Cold War mission of providing aid; and Fort Benning is on the cutting edge of future technology, with BattleLabs shaping the way the military of the 21st Century will fight its wars.

Generals and privates alike have shared the experience of learning the art of soldiering at the Home of the Infantry. They also share the heritage that has evolved over the years to make our troops and our post second to none.

Ranger training at Fort Benning, Georgia, began in September of 1950 with the formation and training of 17 Airborne Ranger companies during the Korean War by the Ranger Training Command. In October 1951, the Commandant of the United States Army Infantry School established the Ranger Department and extended Ranger training to all combat units in the Army. The first Ranger class for individual candidates graduated on 1 March, 1952. On 1 November, 1987, the Ranger Department reorganized into the Ranger Training Brigade, establishing four Ranger Training Battalions.

The Ranger Training Brigade's mission is to conduct the Ranger and Long Range Surveillance Leader courses to develop the leadership skills, confidence, and competence of students by requiring them to perform effectively as small unit leaders in tactically realistic environments.

The Ranger course is designed to further develop leaders who are physically and mentally tough and self-disciplined and challenges them to think, act, and react effectively in stress approaching the level found in combat. The course is over nine weeks in duration and divided into three phases: Benning phase, Fort Benning, Georgia; Mountain phase, Dahlonega, Georgia; and Swamp phase, Eglin Air Force Base, Florida. The Long Range Surveillance Leader course is designed to train long range surveillance leaders to better prepare them for the training and tactical leadership of their units/teams.

The Benning Phase of Ranger training is designed to assess and develop the military skills, physical and mental endurance, stamina, and confidence a soldier must have to successfully accomplish combat missions. It is also designed to teach the Ranger student to properly sustain himself, his subordinates, and maintain his equipment under difficult field conditions during the subsequent phases of Ranger training. If a student is not in top physical condition when he reports to the Ranger course, he will have extreme difficulty keeping up with the fast pace of Ranger training, especially the initial phase.

The Benning Phase is executed in two parts. The first part conducted at Camp Rogers in the Harmony Church area of Fort Benning. This phase consists of an APFT consisting of 49 Push-ups, 59 Sit-ups, and two mile run in running shoes in 15:12 minutes or less. In addition, applicant must execute six chin-ups and perform the Combat water survival test, 5-mile run, 3-mile runs with an obstacle course, a 16-mile foot march, night and day land navigation tests, medical considerations class, rifle bayonet, pugil stick and combatives. Advanced physical training assures physical and mental endurance and the stamina required for enhancing basic Ranger characteristics, commitment, confidence, and toughness. Additionally, the student completes the water confidence test at Hurley Hill, terrain association, demolitions, patrol base/ ORP and an airborne refresher jump at Fryar Drop Zone.

The second part of the Benning Phase is conducted at nearby Camp William O. Darby. The emphasis at Camp Darby is on the instruction and execution of squad combat patrol operations. The Ranger student receives instruction on boxing, field craft training, executes the Darby Queen Obstacle Course, the fundamentals of patrolling, the warning order/operations order format, and communications. The fundamentals of combat patrol operations include battle drills, ambush and reconnaissance patrols, entering clearing rooms, airborne operations, and air assault operations. This phase uses the crawl technique during the field training exercise (FTX), which allows the student to practice the principles and techniques that enables the patrol to successfully conduct reconnaissance and ambush patrol missions. The Ranger student must then demonstrate his expertise through a series of cadre and student led tactical patrol operations. As a result, the Ranger student gains tactical and technical proficiency, confidence in himself, and prepares to move to the next phase of the course--the Mountain Phase. Following the Benning Phase students are transported to Camp Frank D. Merrill, Dahlonega, GA.

During the Mountain Phase, students receive instruction on military mountaineering tasks, as well as techniques for employing a squad and platoon for continuous combat patrol operations in a mountainous environment. They further develop their ability to command and control a platoon size patrol through planning, preparing, and executing a variety of combat patrol missions. The Ranger student continues to learn how to sustain himself and his subordinates in the adverse mountain conditions. The rugged terrain, severe weather, hunger, mental and physical fatigue, and the emotional stress that the student encounters afford him the opportunity to gauge his own capabilities and limitations as well as that of his "Ranger Buddies". In addition to combat patrol operations, the Ranger student receives five days of training on military mountaineering. During the first three days of mountaineering (Lower), he learns about knots, belays, anchor points, rope management, and the basic fundamentals of climbing and rappelling. His mountaineering training culminates with a two day exercise (Upper) at Yonah Mountain, where he applies the skills he learned during Lower Mountaineering. During the two FTXs, Ranger students also perform patrol missions, which require the use of their mountaineering skills.

Combat patrol missions are directed against a conventionally equipped threat force in a low intensity conflict scenario. These patrol missions are conducted both day and night over a four day squad field training exercise (FTX) and a platoon five day FTX that includes moving cross country over mountains, conducting vehicle ambushes, raiding communications/mortar sites, and conducting a river crossing or scaling a steep sloped mountain. The Ranger student reaches his objective in several ways: Cross-country movement, air assaults into small landing zones on the sides of mountains, or an eight to ten mile foot march over the Tennessee Valley Divide (TVD). The stamina and commitment of the Ranger student is stressed to the maximum. At any time, he may be selected to lead tired, hungry, physically expended students to accomplish yet another combat patrol mission.

At the conclusion of the Mountain Phase, the students move by bus or parachute assault into the Third and final (Florida) Phase of Ranger training, conducted at Camp Rudder, near Eglin Air Force Base, Florida.

The third, or capstone, phase of Ranger School is conducted at Camp James E. Rudder, Eglin AFB, Florida. Emphasis during this phase is to continue the development of the Ranger student's combat arms functional skills. He must be capable of operating effectively under conditions of extreme mental and physical stress. This is accomplished through practical exercises in extended platoon level patrol operations in a Jungle/Swamp environment. Training further develops the students' ability to plan for and lead small units on independent and coordinated airborne, air assault, small boat, ship to shore, and dismounted combat patrol operations in a low intensity combat environment against a well trained, sophisticated enemy.

The Florida Phase continues the progressive, realistic OPFOR scenario. As the scenario develops, the students receive "In Country" technique training that assists them in accomplishing the tactical missions in the phase. Technique training includes: small boat operations, ship to shore operations, expedient stream crossing techniques, and skills needed to survive and operate in a jungle/swamp environment.

The Ranger students are updated on the scenario that eventually commits the unit to combat during techniques training. The 10-day FTX is a fast paced, highly stressful, challenging exercise in which the students are evaluated on their ability to apply small unit tactics/techniques. They apply the tactics/techniques of raids and ambushes to accomplish their missions.

High standards are required and maintained despite the stressful environment in Ranger training. The Ranger course produces a mentally hardened soldier, who possesses an enhanced capability to perform combat arms related associated functional skills and is more confident in his ability to overcome obstacles, withstand the stresses of combat and accomplish his mission under extremely adverse conditions.

During the Ranger course, the Ranger proves he can overcome seemingly insurmountable mental and physical challenges. He has demonstrated, while under simulated combat conditions, that he has acquired the professional skills and techniques necessary to plan, organize, coordinate, and conduct small unit operations. He has demonstrated that he has mastered basic skills needed to plan and execute dismounted small unit day and night operations, low altitude mountaineering, and infiltration as well as exfiltration techniques via land, air, and sea. As a result of proving that he can successfully accomplish these tasks during the Ranger course, he is authorized to wear the Ranger Tab.

Major, Ben, and Simon stand outside of the reception area, waiting to step onto a bus that will take them to the Ranger School training area. The three friends are surrounded by swarms of young men who are all within their age group. A few of their classmates from FAOBC stand with them. It is good to see familiar faces at such a stressful time.

"I'm not going to lie to you guys," Major says to Ben and Simon. "I'm friggin' scared."

"I feel you," Ben simply replies. "I could do without the butterflies right now."

"I don't think I should have eaten all of those eggs this morning," Simon jokingly comments as he pats his stomach

The three friends laugh at their remarks. Anything they can do to get their mind off of their stress is a much-needed release.

After having waited for about half an hour, a white school bus pulls up alongside the reception center. Major, Simon, and Ben pick their duffle bags up from off of the ground and slowly make their way to the bus. They do not rush to get on. What is the point? Everyone who is boarding is going to the same place anyway.

Boarding the bus last, the three friends sit with each other in the two front row aisle seats: Simon and Major in one seat and Ben across from Simon. They place their duffle bags between their legs and attempt to enjoy the last quiet, stress free, moment they will have for a long time.

As Simon, Major, and Ben attempt to get comfortable, the bus driver, an old burly man in his late fifties, turns to them and sarcastically asks, "You boys ready for some fun?"

The three friends laugh softly at the joke.

Simon answers, "If this tops two-a-days and lifting with Satan, then I've come to the right place."

Major shakes his head and smiles. He then leans his head forward and rests it on top of his duffle bag, as the bus pulls out onto the road.

His eyes closed, Major silently prays; 'GOD! I hope I know what I've gotten myself into. This is going to suck. No real food or sleep for nine weeks. I must be crazy. I love food and sleep too much to be doing this. Oh well. I'm here now. I've got no choice but to go through with it. I pray I don't lose too much weight or start talking to rocks and trees like I've heard other people do. Yeah. That's all I need: a stimulating conversation with a tree.'

Major turns his head to the left and looks over at Ben, whose eyes are wide open and staring straight ahead. Major can tell that Ben is concentrating: psyching himself up for what's to come. He then looks at Simon and sees that he too is mentally psyching himself up. Major smartly decides to leave his two focused friends alone to their thoughts. They would be pissed as hell if he were to break their concentration.

The bus leaves the Fort Benning main post area and heads into the woods. It turns onto a compact dirt trail and continues on its course. There is nothing around but pine trees: no buildings, people, or animals.

After driving through what seems like an endless forest, the bus approaches a small opening. To the rear of the opening are groupings of small white buildings. Approaching the buildings, the bus begins to slow down.

Major, feeling the change in the bus' speed, opens his eyes and raises his head. He peers out the window to see where he is. To his front right, Major notices a long line of black t-shirt clad men wearing camouflaged pants, tight black t-shirts, and donning black baseball caps. The sight causes Major to slightly shake his head up and down twice.

The bus creeps to a halt. The bus driver looks up through his rearview mirror, and with a huge smile on his face says, "Welcome home, boys. I hope you enjoy your stay!"

The bus driver swings the door open and immediately, a sergeant first class rushes onto the bus. The NCO stands roughly five feet, six inches, but what he lacks in height he makes up for in muscle. His black t-shirt is skin tight, as though it were painted onto his torso. His hat sits on his head just enough to stay on, but looks as though it would fall off with the slightest gust of wind.

Seeing the NCO, Major says to himself with a small, confident smile on his face, 'Let the games begin.'

"Get on your feet and get off my bus!" the NCO shouts.

The Ranger School students leap to their feet and scamper to retrieve their bags from off of the floor. They hurriedly rush off of the bus to begin the most physically and mentally grueling nine weeks of their lives.

25 September 2001, 1030 hrs: Dumfries, VA

MAJOR WAKES UP FROM A LONG slumber. His first night home from Ranger School graduation was a rough one. Major and his best friend, David Smoke, and a couple other high school friends celebrated Major's return by partying all night in DC. Sitting up in his bed, Major softly rubs his head. He barely remembers much of the night. It is mostly a blur to him. Ninety days of Ranger school caused Major to lose all of his alcohol tolerance, so much so, that after four long island iced teas, he was feeling light on his feet. Being the responsible person that he is, though, Major knew his limit and did not drink himself into a stupor.

Major rolls out of bed and goes to the computer that is positioned against the wall. It is not much of a struggle for Major to get to the computer, much to his satisfaction. The room is so small that the computer desk chair always sits up against the bed.

The room that Major sleeps in is not the one he had when he was in high school. When Major reported to the Prep school back in June of 1995, the first thing his parents did was give his little sister his old bedroom. Whenever Major comes home on leave, he sleeps in the computer room, which is nearly half the size of his old room. The computer room is so small that with the full sized bed, the dresser, the nightstand, and the computer, there is hardly any room to walk, especially when Major goes home and simply throws his bags on the floor.

Major sits in front of the computer to check his e-mails, which have accumulated due to his being away the entire summer. After quickly deleting the junk e-mail and reading the ones from his friends, Major finally gets to writing Marcos an e-mail, as he had promised he would do.

'sup marcos,

how's it going man? i just got back from ranger school. that joker was hard as hell. i swear to GOD the rocks were talking to me after the third week. you know how i like to eat? well, let me say that food was one of those things that i had little access to. we could only eat when the RIs said so, and don't let them catch you eating while on the trail. let's just say i got up close and personal w/a tree after my RI caught me eating a cracker while on patrol. life hadn't sucked that bad since my days at the prep w/ssg auburn. it's all good, though. ben and i graduated on time. thank GOD! i don't know what i would've done if i had to recycle through a phase.

so you know, we're still coming to see you, so let me know what we need to do and what not, prior to us meeting up. we already got our passports, so everything's good from that end. i guess all we need is your itinerary.

well brother, you take care. tell your dad that i said hello. until next time...

Finished typing his e-mail to Marcos, Major checks the plethora of e-mails that had accumulated while he was away at Ranger school. Major first highlights all of the junk e-mails and deletes them. With the nonsense out of the way, Major begins reading the e-mails from his friends.

Having read all of his e-mails, Major exists the internet and shuts the computer down. Major gets up from behind the computer and bends over, grabbing a pair of black Army football shorts and his D-1 t-shirt. He quickly slips on his clothes, then sits on the bed and puts on his running shoes. Dressed, Major grabs his ring from off of the dresser and leaves the room.

In the bathroom, Major turns the radio on. Since his family first moved into the house during the summer of 1991, Major has always kept a radio in the bathroom. There is nothing Major loves more than good music, especially Hip-Hop. Even though Major has not lived at home since he graduated from high school in 1995, the radio has remained locked to WPGC, 95.5, the number one radio station in the Washington, DC metropolitan area.

The reason the radio has remained unchanged for such an extended time is because Major's younger brother and sister, Will and Jasmine, listen to WPGC, as well. Every young, Black person in the Washington, DC metropolitan area does. Moving to the rhythm of the music, Major quickly brushes his teeth and washes his face and hands. When Major finishes with his hygiene, he exits the bathroom, while at the same time, leaving the radio on.

Major trots down the stairs and goes to the kitchen, where he immediately retrieves his keys, wallet, and cell phone from off of the counter. Major then walks to the pantry in search of something to eat. Even though he is getting ready to lift, Major loves eating too much not to. Eating is like a hobby to Major. Searching through the pantry, moving and shifting several food items and packages around, Major finally finds what will satisfy his craving. He pulls his hand out of the pantry, holding onto a plastic package containing six blueberry bagels.

"This'll work," Major says aloud as he opens the package and retrieves a bagel.

With the bagel in his mouth, Major walks out of the house and heads for his 4Runner, which he had left with his parents while he was at Ranger school.

Major starts his 4Runner up and immediately speeds out of the long driveway. Driving down the road, Major picks up his cell phone and scrolls through his phone book. Finding the number he needs, Major places the earpiece in he ear, then hits the talk button. After a few rings, a groggy voice answers.

"Major," the groggy voice slowly says.

" Cousin!" Major shouts. "I see you had a good time last night, too."

"Don't yell. My head hurts"

"My bad, bro. I e-mailed Marcos just a little while ago to let him know we're still on for New Years."

"Good. We're still doing everything as we planned, right?"

"Yep. We're going to link-up with Marcos at BWI, then fly on to Lebanon from there. You still coming down here for a few days before we leave?"

"Yeah. I'm going to stay with my uncle in DC. Can you pick me up from his place the day before we fly out?"

"Come on now! What kind of question is that? Of course I can get you. That's not a problem. Family looks out for each other. You know what I'm saying?"

"I hear you. Hey, I'll give you a call back later. I need to sleep some more."

"I've got you. I'm getting ready to go lift now, anyway."

"All right then. I'll talk to you later."

"Peace."

Major hits the red button on his cell phone to disconnect his call with Ben, then scrolls through his phonebook again. Finding the next number, Major hits the talk button. The phone rings a few times before someone answers.

"Hey honey. How are you?"

"You know me. I'm always well."

"Yeah, I know. It's just good to hear your voice."

"Well, thank you, babe, but more importantly, how're you doing?"

"I'm at work right now, but otherwise, I'm okay."

"That's good."

"What do you have planned for today?"

"I'm driving to the gym right now. Other than that, who knows? See some of my people: check out a flick with David: Nothing much really. I got tore the hell up last night, though. GOD! We hit up DC. It seems like forever since I've done that."

"Well, I'm glad you had fun last night. Making up for lost time, huh?"

"You better believe it! Now begins the painful payback."

"What are you talking about?"

"I'm friggin' small now! I lost like twenty pounds at Ranger school."

"Why don't you take some time off and let your body rest?"

"Wish I could, but I can't let my soldiers see me like this. I'm the MAN. I have a reputation to uphold."

95

"Sorry," Terry sarcastically states. "I forgot I was talking to the MAN."

"That's right," Major jokes. "So, when are you getting up here?"

"In about three weeks or so. I'll e-mail you my itinerary when I get off the phone with you."

"Cool. I can't wait for you to get up here."

"I must be crazy wanting to drive to Louisiana with you."

"I knew there was a reason why I love you."

"Ha ha. Are you and Ben still going to Beirut for New Year's?"

"Yep."

Terry sighs, then states, "I thought you would have changed your mind about that."

"Come on now, babe. I thought you knew me better than that. How can I turn down an opportunity like this? When will I ever get another chance to go to Lebanon?"

"I guess you're right, but I still don't like it."

"I'll be okay. It's not like anything's going to happen to me. My friend's the son of the President for GOD's sake. There'll be security up the yin yang wherever we go."

"Do me one favor then."

"It depends. What is it?"

"Get an international plan for your cell."

"Huh?"

"An international cell phone plan."

"What for?"

"So I can call you dummy."

"Do you really think that's necessary?"

"No, but I'll feel a lot better knowing I can get a hold of you if I need to."

"Do you know how expensive that is?"

"It's only for your trip. So you have to pay it for a month. I think you can handle that."

"I'll look into it. All right?"

"Please do, Major." Someone walks into Terry's office, causing her to say, "I'm sorry baby, but I've got to get going."

"No problem, babe. Make that money! Give me a call later, if you can."

"I have a late night tonight, but I'll give you a call before I go to bed."

"That'll work. I'll holler at you later, then."

"Bye, honey. Love you."

"Love you, too."

FORT POLK, LOUISIANA

FORT POLK WAS ESTABLISHED IN 1941 and was named in honor of the Right Reverend Leonidas Polk, the first Episcopal Bishop of the Diocese of Louisiana and a Confederate general. Since its inception, Fort Polk has adapted to service during every U.S. military crisis.

Thousands of soldiers learned the basics of combat at Fort Polk during the World War II Louisiana Maneuvers. Afterwards, the post was opened and closed for the Korean War and for large-scale exercises Sage Brush and King Cole.

The Berlin Crisis prompted the post's reactivation in 1961, and Fort Polk became an infantry training center in 1962. Three years later, it was selected to conduct Vietnam- oriented advanced training, and in 1973 became the sole training center qualifying basic infantry soldiers. More than a million men graduated from basic and advanced individual training before the training center colors were retired in 1976.

The Fifth Infantry Division (Mechanized) became Fort Polk's major tenant in 1974. Hundreds of millions of dollars in construction made Fort Polk one of the most modern installations in the Army. In 1993, Fifth Infantry Division was re-designated as the Second Armored Division and moved to Fort Hood, Texas, as a result of changing defense requirements.

With the reduction of U.S. forces spurred by the end of the Cold War, Fort Polk, again, adapted to a challenging transition. On 12 March 1993, Fort Polk officially became the home of the Joint Readiness Training Center, which was relocated from Little Rock Air Force Base and Fort Chaffee, Arkansas.

Fort Polk is also home to other units with varied military missions. The Second Armored Cavalry Regiment is affiliated with the XVIII Airborne Corps and has a quick deployment mission. The Warrior Brigade contains several units with early deploying wartime missions.

Medical, dental, and military police commands are also assigned to the post.

In recent history, soldiers of Fort Polk have been called to serve around the world. They were in Panama to seize Manuel Noriega's headquarters during Operation Just Cause. They served in Operation Desert Storm, and they were in Somalia for Operation Restore Hope. Fort Polk units have also served in Honduras, Cuba, and Suriname during Operation Safe Haven and the United Nations Mission in Haiti for Operation Uphold Democracy. Fort Polk soldiers have also deployed in support of peacekeeping operations in Bosnia.

14 OCTOBER 2001, 2000 HRS: LEESVILLE, LA

AFTER A TWO-DAY JOURNEY HALF WAY across the United States, Major and Terry finally arrive in Leesville, Louisiana. To ease the journey some, Major and Terry stopped in Atlanta for a couple of days and stayed at David's. The drive from Dumfries, Virginia to Atlanta, Georgia is about eight hours. From Atlanta, Georgia to Leesville, Louisiana is roughly a nine hour drive.

As Major and Terry reach the Leesville city line, Major is taken aback by what he sees, or in this case, what he does not see.

"There's got to be more to this town than this," Major says to Terry as he eyes the directions to his house.

Every February at the United States Military Academy, the First Class Cadets participate in what is referred to as Post Night. During Post Night, the Firsties assemble with those cadets of their respective branch at 1830 hours. The night's event determines which installation the future second lieutenants will serve their first tours.

Due to the West Point incident of December 1999, there were not as many post selection options because of the drastic decrease in the size of the four cadet classes. Fortunately for the Army, not as many cadets lost their lives as could have that fateful day. To offset the loss, the Department of the Army increased the number of post options to ROTC (Reserve Officer Training Corps) cadets.

All of the Firsties who have branched field artillery assemble in the auditorium on the third floor of Bartlett Hall. A large number of the cadets who file into the auditorium are members of the football and basketball teams. At West Point, the field artillery branch is fondly known as Football Alumni because it seems that nearly every football player branches field artillery every year.

Field artillery was not Major's first choice: armor was. West Point has a regulation requiring that eighty-five percent of the male population must branch combat arms. The Class of 2001 did not make that initial goal, so combat arms was forced upon those who did not have the foresight to select the proper branch. Major fell victim to the overhaul; thus his receiving his second choice of field artillery.

Major chose the field artillery as his second choice, not because he finds the branch interesting, but because it is what most of his friends branched. In all honesty, Major wanted to cross branch to the United States Marine Corps, and would have been selected if he were to have applied, but being that his long term plans in the Army are uncertain, he decided that it was best to be around his friends as much as possible. Unfortunately for Major, the Marine Corps cannot facilitate that desire.

From front to back, the future second lieutenants sit in class rank order: the highest ranking in the front and the lowest in the rear. Major takes a seat in the second to last row. It is simple to say that Major is not a stellar cadet when it comes to academics, but he is graduating on time with all of his friends, and for him, that is all that truly matters.

With everyone seated and assembled, the captains and majors commence with the post selection process. The highest-ranking field artillery Firstie, CDT Solomon Hutchinson, steps forward to the counter. Before him on the counter lie several sheets of paper. Each sheet contains a series of columns with empty slots for each of the Army's active duty posts. Once all of the slots are filled it means that the post is filled.

CDT Hutchinson stands at the counter and writes his name in the first Fort Hood slot, which means he will be assigned to either the First Cavalry Division or the Fourth Infantry (Mechanized) Division. Several of the Firsties are shocked when they discover that CDT Hutchinson has selected Fort Hood. Traditionally, the highest ranking cadet selects Vachinsa, Italy as his first duty station. CDT Solomon is from Houston, Texas and desires to be near home, so as far as he is concerned, someone else can go to Italy.

Following CDT Solomon, all of the other Firsties, maintaining their rank order, approach the counter and select their post. Major anxiously sits and waits his turn. After about half an hour, it is finally Major's turn to select his post. The posts remaining for him to select from are Fort Bragg, Fort Drum, Fort Sill, and Fort Polk.

Major does not want to go to Fort Bragg because the thought of jumping out of a perfectly good airplane does not excite him in the least. Fort Drum is an easy one for Major to cross off of his list of choices because he loathes the cold. Major can take the cold, but he has no desire to train in the field in extreme cold weather, if he can help it. In terms of Fort Sill, COL Wood warned him of the ills of choosing a TRADOC post. Major does not want to take the chance of being assigned to a basic training or AIT (Advanced Individual Training) unit. The only post remaining for Major to choose is Fort Polk.

Fortunately for Major, there are several reasons why he would select Fort Polk. Fort Polk has a cavalry unit, the 2d Armored Cavalry Regiment (ACR), which means he would be permitted to wear a Stetson and spurs, once he earns them. Major knows he would look good in a Stetson. Also, he would not be far from Lake Charles, Louisiana, which he considers one of his second homes. Living near Lake Charles would give Major a chance to spend time with his grandmother, Muh, and reconnect with relatives whom he has not seen in nearly ten years.

Major walks down the auditorium stairs, passing all of his seated friends and classmates who have already selected their posts. At the counter, Major picks up a lying pen and scans the sheets for the Fort Polk column.

"Well, that's that," Major says as he returns the pen to the counter top.

Major steps away from the counter and returns to his seat. He spends a few minutes joking around with his friends, as they wait for the official portion of Post Night to end.

Almost complete, it is time for one of Major's close friends to select his post. CDT Andre Cosby slowly stands to his feet. Everyone turns their heads to look at CDT Cosby, mostly because he is the third to last Firstie to select his post. CDT Cosby stands six feet, five inches tall, and weighs two hundred fifty pounds. He was a starting offensive lineman and weighed just shy of three hundred pounds, while in season. Andre is one of the biggest guys that Major knows, or knew, because he is not nearly as big as he once was.

CDT Cosby lazily side steps out from the last row and turns left to head down the aisle. On his third gentle step down, Andre shocks everyone. Those who were not paying attention now are.

Andre throws his arms in the air and cries, "Fuck! This isn't fair!"

Tears pour from out of Andre's eyes and down his cheeks. His face turns red and his eyes become extremely puffy. It is quite evident to those in the auditorium that CDT Cosby is not too happy with his remaining post choices.

'Man!' Major thinks to himself. 'I didn't think he was going to take it so hard!'

Still sulking, CDT Cosby stomps down the aisle as he quickly makes his way to the front. When he approaches the counter and scribbles his name under the Fort Sill column.

"Fuck it! I don't care!" he shouts as he tosses the pen back onto the counter.

Upset beyond anyone's belief, Andre stomps back to the back row and plops down into his seat.

Major turns around and asks Andre, "Giant, brother, you going to be all right?"

Resting his head on his right hand, Andre looks at Major and replies, "Yeah, Major, I'll be all right. There just weren't any choices left!"

"I feel you, bro," Major sympathizes. "Mine sucked, too"

"Yeah, Fort Polk. I heard that place sucks."

"I don't know about all that, but I do know that I get to get myself a cowboy hat when I get to that bad boy. You know the MAN looks good in a cowboy hat."

Cheering up some, Andre sarcastically says, "What ever man."

Andre leans forward and punches Major in the shoulder. The two friends laugh as Andre slowly becomes less upset about his future.

All of the cadets have selected their posts, thus ending the official portion of Post Night. Now begins the unofficial portion: when the Firsties head down to the Firstie Club to celebrate with their friends. The field artillery Firsties rush out of the auditorium and hurriedly exit Bartlett Hall. With much haste, they make their way to the Firstie Club.

Along the way, the field artillery Firsties run into several other of their classmates who are headed in the same direction.

The large and rowdy, camouflaged clad mob finally makes it to the Firstie Club. The guard on duty, so overwhelmed with Firsties does not take the time to check identification, as he would typically do. At the same time, though, the Firsties probably would not have given him the opportunity to do his job, being that so many of them desire to enter without hesitation.

Near the front of the pack, Major enters the Firstie Club, along with Ed and JT to enjoy one more milestone in their careers as cadets at the Untied States Military Academy.

When Major selected the Second Armored Cavalry Regiment as his unit, he discovered that two of his friends, Charles Jefferson and Winston Smith, were going there, as well. Major and Charles have been friends since day one. They were in the same platoon during Beast Barracks and maintained their friendship throughout the years. Major and Winston, though, did not meet until the end of their Cow year when they, along with Charles, met regularly to prepare for their staff positions for Mounted Maneuver Training (MMT) at Fort Knox, Kentucky.

When the three friends discovered they were all going to Fort Polk, they decided to rent a house together. Because Major was a GA and went to Ranger school, and the fact that FAOBC is longer than any other officers' basic courses, he is the last one to arrive.

Charles was the first to arrive at Fort Polk. After graduating from the Armor officers' basic course (AOBC), Charles opted not to attend Ranger school. Winston, on the other hand, did. He and Charles graduated from AOBC together, leaving Charles responsible for ensuring that they all had a place to live when they arrived at Fort Polk.

Charles, being somewhat financially suave, lived on post for three months. He did not see the point in wasting money on rent when he was going to be the only one living in the house. He spent the time alone, saving his money and shopping for a house. As soon as Winston graduated from Ranger School, Charles cleared housing. Having found a nice, three-bedroom house not far from the local Wal-Mart, Charles moved off post and got everything together for his two friends.

The year that Major was separated from Charles and Winston, he maintained contact with them to ensure that everything would be ready for his arrival. When Major called Charles prior to he and Terry's drive, he was quite relieved to discover that Charles had the house all situated. Major was not worried. He knew that Charles would not fail, but, nonetheless, it felt good to hear that the house was ready for him to move into.

Just within the Leesville city limits, Terry takes the directions out from the cup holder and reads them to Major. The couple drives through Leesville, amazed at the size of the town, or better put, the lack there of.

"There has to be more to this town than this," Major says as he takes a right turn.

"I don't think there is, hon, but you never know," Terry retorts.

Major continues driving, overly amazed at the small size and rustic environment that is Leesville, Louisiana.

Somewhat disappointed, Major says to Terry, "You know, when I researched this place, I was under the impression that there was a reasonable population here."

"Really?" Terry asks with a snide look.

"Yeah. I mean, shoot! The sign even says welcome to the city of Leesville. Someone needs to change the criteria for what makes a place a friggin' city 'cause GOD knows that this place ain't it."

Terry just laughs at Major's little tirade.

The couple drives through a modest neighborhood. Being that they are not in the suburbs, no house looks alike, which is a positive for Major, since he thrives on originality.

"There's the house," Terry says pointing to a brown, wooden framed house.

"Good deal," Major says as he pulls into the driveway.

Parking, the front door opens and Charles comes walking out.

Excited, Major jumps out of the 4Runner and shouts, "What's up boy?"

Charles, with a huge grin on his face, strides towards Major. Meeting in the yard, the two friends firmly embrace, then push each other back. An arms distance away, Major and Charles playfully hit each other in the chest a few times.

Somewhat calm, Charles states, "It's about time you got here you dork."

"I'd have gotten here a lot faster if I wouldn't have had to ask a cow for friggin' directions to this place."

Laughing, Charles simply says, "You haven't seen anything yet."

"Huh?" Major inquisitively asks.

"You'll see. I'll take you guys out tomorrow."

"GOD help me."

As the two friends catch up on old times, Terry gets out of the 4Runner and walks to where Major and Charles stand in the yard. Because Major has not acknowledged her presence, Terry punches him on his right shoulder to get his attention.

Hit, Major looks at Terry and chuckles. "My bad, babe. Charles, this is my girlfriend, Terry. Terry: Charles."

Charles and Terry shake hands. Charles then says, "You must be amazing for dating this bone head."

Terry laughs, replying, "Yeah. I consider this guy my community service project."

"Yeah. Ya'll are funny," Major retorts, hitting Charles in the chest, then giving Terry a slight squeeze. He then says, "Hey, bro. Give me a hand with the bags."

"Got you," Charles answers, following Major to the rear of the 4Runner.

As Major begins pulling the bags out of the 4Runner, a thought suddenly pops in his head. "Where's Guns?"

"He doesn't live here anymore," Charles replies.

"What? When'd that happen?"

"A week after he moved in."

"I'm confused. That fool was supposed to be here. That was the plan."

"I know, but he all of a sudden wanted to live by himself."

"He's living on post?"

"Yeah."

"That's cool, I guess. We have another roommate, then?"

"Yeah. JD."

"Oh. That's cool. We've been tight since Beast."

Major and JD met during Beast Barracks the first day of ability group runs for PT. Major was in Echo Company and JD was in Foxtrot Company. The ability group runs were split up amongst the companies: i.e. there was an ability group for each company, except for the green and black groups because they are the two fastest, thus had the fewest people.

Green group, the fastest group, was very small in size. On the first day of ability group runs, the green group began with nearly one hundred people. By the end of Beast Barracks, the green group was down to a platoon size element: just under fifty people.

JD, or what is written on his birth certificate, James Peter Davis, attended AOBC with Charles and Guns. JD ran cross-country and the 800 meters on the track team. He escaped death that fateful day at West Point because he was participating in an indoor track meet.

As Charles, Major, and Terry take the bags inside, Major asks Charles, "Where the hell is JD, anyway?"

"He and Guns're in the field," Charles answers as he leads Terry and Major to their room.

"Man! That sucks. When're they getting back?"

"Next Tuesday, I think."

"Good deal. They'll at least get to meet Terry before she leaves."

Dropping his bags on the floor, Major asks, "What's for dinner?"

"I ate a sandwich," Charles blurts.

"Well, let's go get some real food. I'm hungry as hell."

"Why not? There's a Chinese buffet that's not too bad."

"Cool. Let's hit that up." Major turns to Terry and asks, "Is that cool with you, babe?"

"That'll work," Terry answers.

The three friends leave the room. Major and Terry head out of the house, while Charles goes to his room to retrieve his keys and wallet.

Outside, Charles says to Terry and Major, "I'll drive."

"Works for me," Major replies. "I'm tired as hell, anyway."

The three friends converge into Charles' gold, 1993 Nissan Pathfinder. Charles jumps into the driver's seat.

Major opens the front seat for Terry, but she stops his action, saying, "Sit with your friend, big head."

"Cool deal," Major jests as Terry turns and opens the back passenger side door for herself.

Major promptly jumps into the front seat as Charles starts the engine. They pull out of the driveway and head for the Chinese buffet.

As they turn onto US HWY 171, Charles asks Terry, "How long are you staying?"

"I leave on the twenty-ninth," Terry answers. She scoots to the middle of the seat and leans forward to better participate in the conversation.

"That's cool. I'll be able to show you guys around before you go, not that there's much to show you."

"What is there to do here?" Terry asks.

"Tomorrow night, I'll take you guys to Las Margaritas. They call it a sports bar, but it really isn't. I'm going to be honest with you. The place sucks, but it's the best we've got, so we make due. You know?"

"Well, it's good to know that you're making the most of it."

"Yeah. We do our best. There's also a movie theater. The place sucks, but it's the closest theater within an hours drive from here."

Major interrupts saying, "You're kidding me, right?"

"Nope. Other than the one in Leesville, the nearest movie theater is in Alex, which is about forty-five minutes away. After that, it's Lake Charles."

"What about a mall?" Terry asks.

"The same thing," Charles answers. "Leesville doesn't have a mall. There's one in Alex and Lake Charles, but they're both small as hell."

"Is there another main road that runs through this town, or is this it?" Major asks

Charles laughs, replying, "This is it, man."

"You've got to be friggin' kidding me!" Major exclaims. "GOD help me!"

"If you hate small towns, you're going to hate Leesville. The best thing this place has going for it is Wal-Mart."

"I hate Wal-Mart!" Major takes a couple of seconds to calm down, then asks Charles, "How far are we from Lake Charles?"

"Just over an hour. Why?"

"My grandmother lives in Lake Charles. At least it won't take me long to visit her."

"I didn't know your grandmother lived in Lake Charles."

"Yeah. My dad grew up there. Shoot! My dad's mom's side of the family is all from southern Louisiana."

"Really?"

"Yep. I'm Creole."

"Man! Then welcome home."

30 October 2001, 0745 hrs

MAJOR HAS SIGNED ONTO POST AT the In-and-Out Processing Center at Ft Polk. It took him a few days to process through several different offices: housing, finance, the provost marshal, and legal. Though there are not many offices to sign-in, it takes several days to complete in-processing, due to the 0900 to 1600 hrs workday. Because he has completed in-processing, Major could have signed into his unit a day early, but his orders state that he report no later than 30 October 2001. As far as Major is concerned, the Army is going to get everything out of him that it can. He may as well, rest and enjoy himself as much as he can now.

Major wakes up to the soft beeping sound of his alarm clock. Major likes to wake up to music. It helps him in the transition from sleeping to waking up; unfortunately Major has no such comfort. There is no regular Hip-Hop and R&B radio station in the Leesville area, so instead of waking up to country music, Major opts for the beep.

Rolling over slowly, Major gets out of his bed in order to turn off the alarm. He stands fully erect and stretches his arms high into the air to knock the cobwebs out of his system. Now fully awake, Major bends over and hits play on his stereo. Hearing the latest DJ Green Lantern mix-tape CD puts a smile on Major's face.

With the loud Hip-Hop sounds blaring in his room, Major walks to his closet and removes a set of summer BDUs (battle dress uniform) from off of a hanger. Major then grabs a pair of highly polished black boots, a pair of socks, and a brown t-shirt. He steps out of the closet, then tosses his clothes onto the bed, except for the boots, which he drops to the floor. Still standing, Major puts his BDU pants on then sits down on the bed. He then puts his socks on and slips his boots onto his feet. Major carefully tucks his pants legs into his boots: pulling the bottom of each pants leg tight and then to the side. His boots tied and laced, Major takes his brown t-shirt and slips it on. Nearly dressed, Major rises, picking up his BDU top, simultaneously.

Major does not put on his BDU top. Instead, he walks out of his room and heads for the bathroom. In the bathroom, Major places his BDU top on the toilet seat to free up his hands. Major takes care of his personal hygiene: brushing his teeth, shaving, and washing his face. Major does not have to worry about combing or brushing his hair because he does not have any. He has been in the habit of shaving his head since the mid-point of FAOBC. A bald head is low maintenance.

Finished with his personal hygiene, Major retrieves his BDU top and heads for the door. As he steps out of the bathroom, Major bumps into JD, who is wearing nothing but a purple towel around his waist and a pair of slippers on his feet.

"What's up, brother?" Major happily says to JD.

"Not much, man. Just got back from PT," JD replies. "You finally going to work today, huh?"

"Yeah. Why not?"

JD laughs at Major's remark, then says, "I'm in Apache troop. Make sure you come over and see me."

"Most def."

"Cool then. I'm going to take my shower now."

Major and JD give each other a pound. JD steps into the bathroom and Major heads for the kitchen.

In the kitchen, Major makes himself a breakfast sandwich: three eggs and three sausage patties stacked between two slices of cheese toast. It only takes him about ten minutes to fix his food. With his plate in one hand and a large glass of Kool-Aid in the other, Major heads for the den to watch a little television while he eats.

As Major sits down in front of the television, Charles comes walking down the hallway, heading for the kitchen.

Seeing Major partially dressed in his BDUs, Charles states, "It's about time you decided to go to work, you lazy bum!"

Major does not return with a verbal reply. Instead, he turns and faces Charles, while at the same time holding his cup of Kool-Aid high into the air with a huge grin on his face.

Major returns to his original position and picks up the remote control from off of the coffee table. He scrolls through several television channels until he finds the one that he is looking for. As he had expected and much to his delight, Major is able to find his favorite TV show: *The Cosby Show.* Happy, Major leans forward with his sandwich in hand, and enjoys his breakfast.

23 May 1836, President Andrew Jackson commissioned the 2d Regiment of Dragoons. The Regiment has had the distinction of being the oldest continuously active regiment in the United States Army.

After serving with distinction in the Seminole Wars, Congress called for the elimination of the Regiment. Compromise was reached and the Second Dragoons were re-designated as a rifle regiment, though they spent a year as infantrymen before they were remounted as Dragoons.

During the Mexican War, the Regiment served with distinction. At the Battle of Resaca de la Palma, the Dragoons, led by Captain Charles May, charged a battery of Mexican artillery guarding the Matamoras road. The Dragoons overran the battery and May's order of the day became the Regimental motto: *Remember your Regiment and Follow your Officers.*

In 1861, the Regiment was recalled to the east and renamed the Second US Cavalry Regiment. They fought with distinction in the First Cavalry Division of the Army of the Potomac. Throughout the course of the Civil War, the Regiment participated in the battles of Fredericksburg, Antietam, Chancellorsville, Gettysburg, The Wilderness, Manassas, Spotsylvania, and Cold Harbor. For its gallantry, the Regiment received fourteen battle streamers. Five of its troopers are Medal of Honor recipients.

After the Civil War, the Regiment was stationed on the frontier and fought in the Indian Campaigns. The Regiment saw action against several tribes, including the Sioux, Cheyenne, and Nez Perce.

During the Spanish-American War, the Second Cavalry was deployed for action and was the only regular mounted cavalry unit to fight in the war. The Regiment participated in the battles of El Caney, San Juan Hill, Aquadores, and Santiago. Three years after the American victory, the Regiment remained in Cuba as part of the pacification force.

After Cuba, the Regiment also saw action on the other side of the globe during the Philippine Insurrection. They then returned stateside to fight alongside General John J. Pershing's expedition into Mexico against Poncho Villa.

With the outbreak of World War I, the Second Regiment found itself again under General Pershing as part of the American Expeditionary Force. The Regiment has the singular distinction of being the only American unit used as horse cavalry during the war. The Regiment participated in the Aisne-Marne offensive and the reduction of the St. Mihiel Salient, as well as the last Allied offensive, the Meuse-Argonne.

With WWII underway, the Regiment was reorganized in 1942 as the Second Armored Regiment, and in 1943 as the Second Cavalry Group, Mechanized. They fought in France as part of Patton's Third Army and distinguished themselves in the Ardennes-Alsace, the Rhineland, and Central Europe campaigns. The Regiment was awarded a Presidential Unit Citation and a Belgian Croix de Guerre for its part in the Battle of the Bulge. Elements of the Regiment fought in the Pacific theater and were awarded battle streamers for Leyte and Ryukus, and a Philippine Presidential Citation.

In 1948 the Regiment was re-designated the Second Armored Cavalry Regiment and played a vital role guarding the Iron Curtain until the end of the Cold War in 1990.

Operation Desert Storm found the Second Armored Cavalry Regiment as a cavalry screen for VII Corps. When the Ground War commenced, the Regiment played a vital role in advancing quickly upon Republican Guard positions, while additional divisions were committed through or around the Regiment to destroy the heavier divisions of Republican Guards. After the fighting ended, the Regiment moved into Iraq as a peacekeeping force.

The Second Armored Cavalry Regiment served in Bosnia-Herzegovina for an eight-month deployment. They were there to support the ongoing peacekeeping mission by performing the traditional cavalry duty of reconnaissance and area security, as well as to assist in regional elections.

0900 HRS: FT POLK, LA

MAJOR STANDS BESIDE THE S-1'S DESK. His orders have him reporting to 1st Squadron, 2d Armored Cavalry Regiment: War Eagles. The first step in reporting in to the unit is having a counseling session with the squadron commander, which is why Major patiently waits beside the S-1's desk.

Not one who likes waiting very long, Major, to kill time, slowly paces in the S-1's office area: looking at the historic pictures that hang on the wall of the Regiment's storied past. Having looked at each picture and read all of the captions and plaques that go along with them, Major returns to his original waiting position.

After a minute or so of waiting again, a rather large man walks down the hall. Major watches the man walk down the hall. Noticing the black oak leaf on his right collar, Major knows that he is a Lieutenant Colonel, thus making the assumption that the man is his squadron commander.

With a smile on his face the Lieutenant Colonel stops in front of Major and thrusts his hand out towards him. "Good morning, LT Johnson. Welcome to War Eagle."

Now that the Lieutenant Colonel stands in front of Major, he is able to read his nametag: Jasper.

"Morning, sir," Major replies, firmly shaking LTC Jasper's hand.

"Let's go to my office."

"Roger, sir."

Major follows LTC Jasper to his office where he then motions for Major to take a seat. As Major sits in an armchair that is positioned to the right of the door, LTC Jasper shuts the door and takes a seat on a small couch that sits along the wall that runs perpendicular to the door.

Situated, LTC Jasper opens the counseling session. "Well, LT Johnson it is definitely an honor having you in the squadron. I guess I'll be saluting you, huh?"

Major smiles at his squadron commander's comment because his words are true. Because Major is a Medal of Honor recipient, everyone must salute him, even those who out rank him, such as his squadron commander, LTC Jasper.

"Do you know what the oldest active combat unit in the Army is?" LTC Jasper asks Major.

Unresponsive, Major thinks to himself, 'I think it's First of the First, but...'

LTC Jasper breaks Major's thought, saying, "The Second Regiment of Dragoons. As a fellow grad, you know that First of the First Infantry, which was formed during the Revolutionary War, is the oldest active unit, but they're West Point's garrison now. The regiment is the oldest active combat unit."

"That's cool, sir."

"Yes, it is," LTC Jasper replies with a huge grin on his face. He then asks Major, "With the way that the regiment is configured, do you know where we may deploy to next?"

"Not a clue, sir. The Philippines?"

"No, but that's a good guess, though. Columbia."

"Columbia, sir?"

"That's correct. Think about it. We are, in nature, a light cavalry unit. Our basic mode of transportation is the HMMWV, which is perfect for the countless number of trails that criss-cross throughout the jungle. Light infantry can't do it because they can't maintain their supply lines. Mechanized can't because they're too big. The Regiment is ideal. We're small and we are capable of sustaining ourselves for an extended period of time."

"Man, sir. I never thought about that, but you're right. Columbia wouldn't be a bad deployment, but GOD knows there'd be a lot of fighting."

"We are in the business of war fighting, LT Johnson. Always remember that we as officers are managers of death."

Major cocks his head back, replying, "Manager's of death, sir?"

"That is correct. It is our job, as officers, to properly position our men on the battlefield. We determine where fires go, what direction, and their duration: all of which is METT-T (Mission, Enemy, Troops, Task, and Time) dependent. We as leaders determine how much death we inflict on the enemy."

"I never thought of it that way, sir." Major immediately thinks to himself, 'Managers of death- I like that.'

"Now, for your job. My howitzer battery needs another FDO, so I'm going to place you there," LTC Jasper informs Major.

The news causes Major to grimace slightly.

Noticing Major's obvious disappointment, LTC Jasper asks, "You wanted to be an FSO, huh?"

"Roger, sir. I'm into tactics and maneuver. Artillery's too stationary for me. There's no real tactics involved."

LTC Jasper nods his head in agreement, then says, "Don't worry, Major. Our howitzer battery's the best in the regiment. I know you'll fit in just fine and pick-up on your job with no problem."

"Roger, sir."

"Your commander is CPT John Amsterdam. This is his second command. He commanded at Bragg, prior to joining the regiment. You should learn a lot from him." LTC Jasper looks down at his watch and says, "Well, I don't want to hold you up any longer."

"Roger, sir"

Major and LTC Jasper rise to their feet and then firmly shake hands. Major then exits LTC Jasper's office and returns to the S-1's desk.

"Sir," Major asks the S-1, CPT William Edwards, "how do I get to the Battery from here?"

"Did you walk or drive?" CPT Edwards asks.

"I drove, sir."

"Okay. This is easy. When you pull out of the parking lot, turn right when you get to the street. The road's going to split. Stay to your right. That will take you up a hill. At the intersection, take a right. The HOW BAT'll be to your right. You can't miss it. You'll see a large Cobra sign on the S&A."

"So I take a right onto the road, go up the hill, making sure that I stay to the right. At the intersection, I take a right, and I'll see the battery to my right: and a Cobra sign."

"You got it."

"Thanks for the help, sir."

"No problem, lieutenant."

Major exits the S-1's area and makes his way out of the squadron headquarters. Before exiting, though, Major takes a look at the wall, which has the pictures of the commanders and First Sergeants in the War Eagle squadron. Major's eyes slowly glance over each individual picture: taking a mental note and memorizing each face. Upon reaching the HOW BAT section, Major's eyes open wide. Quickly, he peers at CPT Amsterdam's picture so close that his nose is practically touching the frame.

'I don't believe this!' Major happily says to himself. 'I never thought I'd get a Black commander! I can count on one hand the number of

Black teachers or instructors I've had since kindergarten. This is friggin' incredible! It can't get any better than this!'

Major stands outside of CPT Amsterdam's office. Because the door is open wide, Major does not have to knock on the door hard. He knocks three times, catching CPT Amsterdam's attention.

CPT Amsterdam raises his head and waves Major in, saying, "Come on in LT."

Major properly enters the room, walking directly for CPT Amsterdam's desk.

Major stops three feet from the desk and salutes, stating, "Sir, LT Johnson reporting as ordered."

CPT Amsterdam returns Major's salute then says, "Take a seat."

Major sits on the edge of the couch that is to his left.

"Welcome to the Cobra Battery, LT Johnson. I never thought I would meet a real life hero." CPT Amsterdam scans Major's uniform with his eyes saying, "You're a Ranger, but you're not Airborne?"

"No, sir," Major answers. "I turned my Airborne slot down. I decided to go Air Assault instead. I have this thing about jumping out of a perfectly good plane."

"Well, I assume the old man told you that I commanded at Bragg before taking over here," CPT Amsterdam remarks. He leans back in his chair and with his thumb, points to his old battery colors that proudly hang in a frame behind him, stating, "Back in Bragg, we used to do that damn thing. There's no better division in the Army. If you want to be about something, you'll go to Bragg."

"Roger, sir," Major simply remarks.

"You'll be proud to know that you're in the best damn battery in the Army. No one on this post can beat us in anything. You name it: slanging bullets down range, sports. You name it, we're it. We're the current three time commander's cup champions for athletics. We just won our third straight Dragoon Thunder. No one can touch us. Joining the Cobra Battery is the best thing that could've happened to you. I'm going to make you the FDO for second platoon. Lieutenant King's the platoon leader and Smoke Barley's the platoon sergeant. Do you know your way around post?"

"Not really, sir. I know how to get to the gym and home and now here. That's about it."

From out of nowhere, CPT Amsterdam shouts, "LT Castillo! Come in here!"

Obediently, LT Castillo quickly stands outside of CPT Amsterdam's office.

Before LT Castillo can knock on the door, CPT Amsterdam coolly says, "Come on in, guy."

As LT Castillo enters his commander's office, he notices LT Johnson standing in front of the desk. The two lieutenants nod in recognition of one another.

With both lieutenants in his office, CPT Amsterdam says, "LT Castillo, I want you to show LT Johnson here around the post and take him to all of the places he's going to need to survive around here."

"Yes, sir," LT Castillo states.

A moment of silence passes, causing CPT Amsterdam to say, "You guys can get out of here now."

"Roger, sir," Major replies.

LT Castillo leads Major out of CPT Amsterdam's office, and into the lieutenants' office.

"Have you been to the training room yet?" LT Castillo asks Major as he makes his way to a desk.

"No, I haven't," Major replies.

"Okay. Before we go, I'll take you to SGT Miner. He'll square you away."

"Appreciate it man."

"You ready?"

"Yeah. Let's go."

LT Castillo leads Major out of the office and over to the training room.

Seeing LT Castillo enter the office, SGT Miner joyfully boasts, "What's up, sir? What can I do you for?"

"Hey SGT Miner," LT Castillo opens, "this is LT Johnson. He's second platoon's new FDO."

"Welcome to the battery, sir," SGT Miner states, extending his hand.

"Thanks, sergeant," Major replies, grasping SGT Miner's hand and shaking it.

SGT Miner then states, "It's good to see some more color up in here."

SGT Miner, the two lieutenants, and a specialist who also sits in the training room laugh at the comment.

Calmed down, LT Castillo says, "SGT Miner, LT Johnson needs to in-process into the battery."

"No problem, sir," SGT Miner states.

SGT Miner stands to his feet and opens a cabinet that is directly to his front. He selects several sheets from the cabinet, then shuts the door.

"You need to fill these out, sir," SGT Miner says to Major, handing him a small stack of forms. SGT Miner then states, "Let me see your folder."

SGT Miner rummages through Major's personnel folder and extracts various forms. He then hands them to his assistant, "Hey Thorpe, get me copies of these."

"Got you," SPC Thorpe replies.

SPC Thorpe leaps to his feet and snatches the forms from out of SGT Miner's hands, then quickly bolts out of the training room.

"I'll get those back to you later, sir," SGT Miner says to LT Johnson.

"Good deal, sergeant," Major replies. "I'll be back later."

"You ready to go?" LT Castillo asks.

"Yeah. Let's roll," Major answers.

"I'll see you, sergeant," LT Johnson says as he walks out of the training room.

"See you, sir," SGT Miner replies as Major leaves.

As LT Castillo leads Major out of the battery area, he says as he steps out of the door, "I forgot. I'm the FDO for first platoon. I just got here in May."

"I would've been here in July if I wouldn't have gone to Ranger school, but then again, if I wouldn't have coached ball at the Prep, I would've been here back in January."

With somewhat of a puzzled look on his face, LT Castillo asks Major, "Where'd you go to school?"

"West Point," Major replies.

"Oh. I didn't know West Point had a Prep school."

"Yeah. It's kind of like one of the Army's secrets. It's a one-year program. All we take is math and English classes. All you have to do is graduate with a 'C' average and you're automatically accepted to West Point."

"That's not too bad."

"You're telling me. Hindsight twenty-twenty, I had a great friggin' time. Where'd you go to school?"

"I went to NMMI (New Mexico Military Institute) for two years, then transferred to San Diego State."

"Nice! I know some people who went to NMMI."

"Yeah? I knew some guys who ended up going to West Point. Who do you know?"

"Lindbergh and Spears were in my Beast platoon."

"Man, I know them."

"Who else?"

"Did you know Krueger? He was my military training NCO when I was his commander. That dude gave up his commition to go to West Point. Now that's dedication for you!"

"Yeah, I know him. I remember him doing that. Man this is wild!"

"What about Brand?"

"Guy or girl?"

"Girl."

"No. I don't think so. Maybe if I saw a picture of her or something. Did you know Cooper?"

"Tim or Hank?"

"Tim."

"I knew him, but we weren't boys or anything."

"That's cool. Where're you from?"

"Well, my dad's a Marine, but I claim northern Virginia: DC metro area."

"My dad's a retired Marine sergeant major."

"That's tight, man!"

"Were you ever at Pendleton?"

"Yeah, but that was way back when I was three. We were there from '79 to '82."

"My dad retired at El Toro."

"Man! There's nothing but sand and palm trees out there, or at least that's what my dad's told me. I've never been there before."

"You haven't missed much. Trust me. It's like you said; there's nothing but sand and palm trees there."

The two lieutenants reach LT Castillo's green GMC pick-up truck. Major trots over to the passenger side, while LT Castillo gets in on his side.

In the truck, Major says to LT Castillo, "Dude, between you and me, I don't do last names. My name's Milton. No one calls me that, though, except for my mother, I think. My people refer to me as Major."

"Well, Major, I'm Ryan. Welcome to the Cobra Battery."

24 December 2001, 1200 hrs: Woodbridge, Virginia

CHRISTMAS EVE IS THE DAY WHEN most people spend their time preparing Christmas dinners and ensuring that hidden gifts are still in their proper hiding places: unscathed. Major and Will, on the other hand, are not most people. The brothers have a personal tradition where they do their Christmas shopping on Christmas Eve. Why? There is no real reason, really. Shopping is something neither brother likes to do, so as far as they are concerned, Christmas Eve is just as good a shopping day as any other. A bonus to doing their Christmas shopping on Christmas Eve is that the malls are engulfed with sales. Major, being the frugal individual that he is, loves taking advantage of a good sale, especially if he has no choice in having to go shopping.

Major hates shopping because when he and Will were young, too young to stay at home alone and watch themselves, their mother would take them to the mall with her cousins nearly every Saturday. Now, going to the mall as a child is not a bad thing, but what Major was never able to understand was that no matter how many times and how nice he asked, his mother would never take him and Will to the toy or electronic stores. What stores did they go to? The ones that are geared solely to women. There were times when Major and Will were so bored during their shopping experience with their mom and cousins that they would fall asleep on the floor. Usually, they would choose the fur coat section, for obvious comfort reasons.

Major hates shopping to such a degree that he will not even make a quick grocery run with his mother when he is home on leave. His mother does not understand why, even after he tells her his story. As far as Major is concerned, he is scarred for life, but not in a bad way. Major looks at shopping as a means of acquiring things that he needs: In and out. Get what you need, then leave. It is as simple as that. Shopping is not a sport. It is a necessary activity one must perform to acquire things.

Major and Will do all of their Christmas shopping at Potomac Mills Mall: the number one tourist attraction in the state of Virginia. Major hates Potomac Mills, but he does not want to take the fifteen minute drive north to Springfield Mall. Potomac Mills, on the other hand, is only five minutes from the house, give or take the traffic, lights, and other uncontrollable factors. Though he likes Springfield Mall better, it is as what was stated earlier; Major hates shopping so he will rarely go the extra mile to buy something, unless he really wants/needs it. Potomac Mills serves all of Major and Will's shopping needs: books, clothes, paintings, music, perfume, etc.

The brothers stroll through the immensely packed mall at a pace that most people are unable to maintain. The people run frantic throughout Potomac Mills doing their last minute shopping. The fact that it is Christmas Eve and three o'clock in the afternoon cause Major and Will to smile because they know that everyone is stressing over buying all of their Christmas gifts before the stores close. Will and Major, on the other hand, have bought gifts for everyone except for themselves and their dad.

Major and Will always buy each other what the other wants. They do not believe in the whole surprise factor in gift giving. Past history has shown that Christmas is much more enjoyable when one receives what he wants, not what someone else wants them to have or thinks they would like.

Dodging and making their way through the crowd, Major sees a book store to his front right.

"Let's check it out," Major states as he heads into the bookstore: Will following close behind.

"You know what you're going to get?" Will asks as the brothers work their way through the bookstore.

"Let's see now. We're going into a bookstore, so maybe I'll buy him a t-shirt," Major cynically answers. "What do you think, dummy?"

"My bad, son. Just asking," Will replies.

Major, who has already walked through the entire bookstore, returns to the front where the New York Times Bestsellers are kept on display.

'There's got to be something up here that dude'll like,' Major thinks to himself as he scans each of the books.

Scanning, Major's eyes lock onto a book cover that displays a portrait of President Theodore "Teddy" Roosevelt, who happens to be Major's favorite US president.

Major reaches for the book, saying to Will, "I'm a get him this."

Will nods approvingly, though he really does not care what Major buys their dad for Christmas.

As Major and Will walk to the cash register, he asks Will, "What're you going to get dad?"

"I don't know," Will responds. "I'll probably go back to that tie store and get him that joint I was looking at earlier."

"That'll work. He'll like that."

The book bought, Major and Will head out of the bookstore and return to the shopping mob streaming through the mall. Will leads the way through the crowd this time, as the two brothers head for the tie store.

At the tie store, Major does not go inside. Instead, he hangs out near the entrance, while Will walks directly to the display where the tie he wants to buy their dad hangs. Will snatches the tie off of the rack and heads straight for the cash register.

Having bought his father's Christmas gift, Will walks to where his brother patiently stands.

"Good to go?" Major asks Will as his brother approaches him.

"Yeah," Will blurts.

Nearly complete with their shopping, the brothers continue their trek through Potomac Mills. They move like two speeding dolphins through a fast moving current.

After walking for only a couple of minutes, Major says to Will, "I'm friggin' tired, man. What about you?"

"Yeah, man," Will agrees. "Let's finish this up some other time."

"Bet. We'll get our gifts on the twenty-sixth before I get Ben at his uncle's."

"That works for me, man. I feel like I'm going to pass out."

Tired and fed up with the frustrations that surround the mall, the two brothers cut their Christmas shopping short and head home.

Major was tired from shopping, but as soon as he and Will returned home, he seemed to not be tired anymore. With several bags in hand, Major heads for his room. He throws the bags on his bed, then takes a seat in front of the computer.

'Let me check my e-mail real quick,' Major thinks to himself as he turns on the computer.

After a couple of minutes the computer kicks on and is ready for Major's use. Major double clicks on the Internet Explorer icon. When the screen appears, Major types in the Hotmail address. Clicking on the 'send' button, much to Major's delight, the Hotmail webpage immediately appears. There is nothing Major hates more than slow.

With the Hotmail page up, Major enters his e-mail address and password, then hits send. Major waits a few moments before his inbox appears on the screen.

"Good deal!" Major joyously states softly. "Marcos shot me an e-mail."

Major clicks on Marcos' name and waits for the message to appear. Marcos' message opens, reading:

My Dearest friend Major,

I wish you and your family a very merry Christmas. I hope that you and Ben are ready for your visit. We are going to have a great time. I am in Detroit now with some of my family. Maybe I will call you before we depart. I see that your cell phone number is below. If I do not call, I will see you in a few days

Your friend,
Marcos

'It's on, boy!' Major silently shouts in his head. 'This trip's going to be money! Best thing I could've done!'

Major hits the reply button to return Marcos' message, in the hopes that Marcos will read within the next day or so. When the reply screen appears, Major types:

homeboy,

it's good to hear from you! yeah, man. me and ben are looking forward to the trip. i can't wait. if you don't get a chance to call, it's all good. i'll holler at you at the airport. peace!

25 DECEMBER 2001; 0800 HRS

COL JOHNSON WALKS INTO THE ROOM where his eldest son sleeps and says, "Time to get up for church."

Major barely reacts to his dad's voice. He rolls his head and looks at his dad.

Groggy, Major asks, "What time is it?"

"It's eight."

"What time are we leaving?"

"I'm pulling out of the garage at eight forty-five."

"Man! I've still got another half hour."

Major turns his head away from his dad and throws the covers back over it.

"Don't be late," COL Johnson simply replies as he shuts the door to the room.

Half an hour later, Major leaps out of bed, which he does so in order to wake up quickly. Major only does this when he truly does not want to get out of bed, but must.

Whenever Major goes home on leave, he never unpacks. His mother hates it, but there is nothing she can do about it but complain, which she often does. Major never unpacks because he is lazy. He gives his mother other reasons, such as he is never home long enough, but the truth of the matter, which he and his mother both know, is that as soon as his bag hits the ground, that is where it is staying, along with all of its contents.

Major walks to his black West Point basketball team dress bag and bends over to retrieve an outfit. He pulls out a white, long sleeve, dress shirt from the middle of a pile. Looking at the shirt and realizing that it is wrinkled, Major selects a dark blue sweater to cover the wrinkles. Major does not see the point in ironing a shirt if he has the ability to cover it up and conceal the wrinkles from prying eyes.

Major tosses the shirt and sweater onto the bed. He then takes a pair of wrinkle free black pants from off a hanger and quickly slips them on. Next, Major retrieves his black Stacey Adams from a large pocket in his dress bag. Inside each shoe is a black and blue designer dress sock, which he slips onto his feet. Major takes the dress shirt and slips it on, then quickly throws on his dark blue sweater. Finally, Major puts his shoes on and kneeling, quickly ties the laces. Before exiting his room, Major grabs his billfold, watch, glasses, and class ring.

Major enters the bathroom to take care of his hygiene. He enters the bathroom, then turns left to enter the bathtub and toilet area, but his progress is hindered due to the fact that the door is locked shut.

Major pounds on the door and barks, "Who's in there?"

"It's me!" a girl's voice replies.

"I need to brush my teeth, brat," Major says to his little sister, Jasmine, through the door.

"Hold on," Jasmine replies.

A moment later, the bathroom door cracks open. A small hand grasping a toothbrush comes through the door.

"I need my wash cloth, too," Major states.

The door shuts, and again, Jasmine's hand reaches out through the cracked door gripping Major's wash cloth.

"Are you good?" Jasmine asks Major.

"Yeah," Major replies.

"Good," Jasmine states as the door shuts.

"Turn the radio on," Major orders his sister as he puts toothpaste on his toothbrush.

A moment later, the radio turns on and, instantaneously; Major bobs his head up and down to the music.

It only takes Major a few minutes to brush his teeth and wash his face. Though he started after Jasmine, Major finishes before her. Instead of bothering Jasmine with his toothbrush and washcloth, Major simply folds the washcloth into thirds and hangs it over the sink's edge and places his toothbrush into an empty space in the extra toothbrush holder. Major steps out of the bathroom and bumps into Will as he approaches the stairs.

123

"'Sup fool?" Will says in a deep voice.

"Chillin'," Major replies, tapping Will on the shoulder with his right fist.

Major heads down the stairs to grab some breakfast from the kitchen, where he finds his dad eating at the table.

Seeing his dad eating, Major asks, "Got any for me?"

"Nope," COL Johnson replies. "I'm leaving in five minutes."

"Don't worry, dad. I'll be ready."

Major grabs the instant oatmeal container from out of the pantry, then retrieves a Tupperware container from underneath the cupboard. He pours a handsome amount of oatmeal into the bowl, along with some sugar and butter. Major turns behind him and goes to the sink. From the faucet, he pours some water into the bowl. Using his right index finger, Major stirs the contents, then throws the container into the microwave for two minutes. As the oatmeal cooks, Major goes to the refrigerator and removes a pitcher of milk, placing it beside the stove. When the timer goes off, Major grabs the container from out of the microwave and immediately pours a generous amount of milk into it.

Finished with his breakfast, COL Johnson rises to his feet and says in a voice just short of shouting, "It's time to go."

"Coming!" Jasmine and Mrs. Johnson shout from upstairs.

Will, instead of yelling his readiness status, discreetly walks down the stairs.

As the rest of the family heads downstairs, Major picks up his oatmeal and quickly drinks it as though it were a giant milk shake. Because time is of the essence, Major does not feel the need to use a spoon like most civilized people. He is quite civilized, but he definitely has his peculiarities.

While Major drinks his oatmeal, COL Johnson, with his Bible in hand, walks out the door into the garage. Will, Jasmine, and Mrs. Johnson all follow COL Johnson out into the garage before the door has a chance to close. Finished with his breakfast, Major tosses the empty container into the sink.

Major grabs the car keys from off of the counter and follows his family out into the garage. Major jumps into the driver's seat of the Volvo as his parents back out onto the driveway in the Infiniti. Will and Jasmine sit in the Volvo waiting for their brother.

Situated in the Volvo, Major starts the engine, then backs up. Out of the garage and still driving backwards, Major zooms down the fifty meter driveway. Major considers himself the greatest backwards driver in the world. Well, actually, Major considers himself the greatest driver in the world, period, but because he is currently driving in reverse, his skill in that action is what is currently on his mind.

The drive to First Mt Zion Baptist church is a quick one. Major is very pleased because the only light that is between the church and the Johnson home is green when Major approaches it, making the trip only two minutes in duration. There is nothing Major loves more than expediency.

As Major turns right into the First Mount Zion parking lot, he drives past his parents who are already walking towards the church. Major finds a parking spot near where his parents have parked and quickly pulls in. The three siblings step out of the Volvo and head for the church.

Major is a very sociable person, and so naturally says hello and Merry Christmas to most of the people whom he encounters. The people happily return his salutations, waving and smiling. Major does not know most of these people, though because his parents joined First Mount Zion during his Yearling year at West Point. Major's home church, where he knows everyone and has been a member since the summer of 1987 is Ebenezer Baptist Church in Occoquan, Virginia, which is only ten minutes or so north from his parents' house.

Jasmine, Will, and Major enter the front lobby of First Mount Zion and head for the sanctuary, in search of their parents. As they step foot into the sanctuary, the three siblings stop at the doorway and do a quick scan of the room.

Jasmine discovers their parents first, saying in a soft voice and pointing, "There they are."

Jasmine takes off down the aisleway without waiting for her two brothers. Major and Will follow Jasmine down the aisle to where their parents sit and take a seat. Sitting behind and around their parents are several of the Johnson family friends: the few members of First Mount Zion who Major has known for several years. Seeing them for the first time since the past summer before going to Ranger school, Major makes it a point to quickly say hello to all of them before sitting, especially his good friend from high school and church, Al Meadow.

Al and Major have been friends since they were juniors in high school when the Meadows' joined Ebenezer Baptist Church prior to the Johnson's returning from Okinawa. Major and Al also were in several of the same classes and, nine times out of ten, were the only two Black males in any of their classes.

Al and Major, along with their friend Kenny York, applied to West Point together, with the assistance of Kenny's dad who is a member of the Class of 1974. Al and Kenny received direct appointments to the United States Military Academy, while Major spent his first year at the Prep school.

Major sits and listens to the church service. The Christmas service is not very long, much to Major's delight. Major believes that GOD is very punctual and does not waste or take time for granted. The Christmas service is one of those rare moments when Major feels GOD and man are in synch.

With the opening of the service, the congregation stands and the choir leads them in singing *Joy to the World*. The one thing Major loves about singing traditional church songs is that he tends to not need the hymnal to sing along. Having grown up in the church, Major knows most of the songs that are sung from the hymnals.

Finished singing *Joy to the World*, the congregation returns to its seats while the choir, without the initial assistance of the congregation, sings the Temptations' version of *Silent Night*. Full of joy and excitement, several members of the congregation leap to their feet and joyfully sing along with the choir. With the completion of *Silent Night* and the congregation settling back down and returning to their seats, the pastor, Dr. Tobias Washington, rises from his seat and approaches the pulpit.

Pastor Washington is not wearing one of his traditional pastoral robes. For the Christmas service, the First Mount Zion Baptist Church family does not dress up as it would for a regular Sumday service. Most of the congregation is dressed rather casually. A few wear suits and dresses, while others wear sweat suit type outfits. The majority of the congregation though, is dressed wearing a nice pair of jeans or slacks and a casual shirt. Pastor Washingotn is wearing a pair of blue jeans and a purple Polo short sleeve shirt.

Pastor Washington, as he opens his large, worn, red Bible, smiles at the congregation and happily says, "Good morning, church! Merry Christmas!"

"Merry Christmas!" the First Mount Zion congregation joyfully responds.

"Turn with me to the Book of John, chapter one, verses one through four," Pastor Washinton says as he smooths the pages out in his Bible.

Everyone in the congregation immediately stands to its feet and turns their Bibles to the book of John, chapter one, verses one through four. Those who do not have Bibles look on with the person standing beside them.

Seeing that everyone has turned to the scripture, Pastor Washington begins to recite. The congregation reads aloud with him, saying, *"In the beginning was the Word, and the Word was with GOD, and the Word was GOD. The same was in the beginning with GOD. All things were made by him; and without him was not any thing made that was made. In him was life; and the life was the light of men."*

With the recitation complete, the congretion close their Bibles and returns to its seats.

Seeing that everyone is situated, Pastor Washington says, "Let us pray."

Automatically, the congregation bows its heads and closes its eyes.

Pastor Washington bows his head, as well, and prays, "Dear Lord. Thank you for this day. Thank you for what you've given us. Lord, forgive us of our sins and bless those who are less fortunate than we are because we know that we've been blessed. Lord, I ask that you bless my words this morning. Grant me the ability to properly interpret your word. I pray that I say something that will bless someone this day and bring them to you. Allow my words to glorify you and your son Jesus' name. All this I ask in your holy name, father. Amen."

"Amen," the congregation responds as they and Pastor Washington raise their heads and re-open their eyes.

Pastor Washington opens the Christmas sermon saying, "When the general population thinks of Christ during the Christmas holiday, they always picture him as an infant and refer to him as the 'Baby Jesus' or the 'Christ Child.' Now, when one thinks of an infant, certain adjectives come to mind, such as innocent and helpless. We tend to think of babies as being defenseless and in need of protection. I know you parents made sure that you bundled up your young ones in big winter coats, scarves, gloves, and hats so they wouldn't feel the effects of the frigid weather on the way to church this glorious morning. We as parents do everything in our power to protect our children, whether it's from the cold or the many evils of the world."

"It's very easy for people to fall into the trap of thinking of Christ as a normal child. One could say that Christ's entrance into the world in physical form is an oxymoron."

"How so, you ask? Well, look at it like this. The most powerful comes to us in the most defenseless, harmless forms imaginable. I can honestly picture GOD laughing when he came up with the concept. Can you imagine GOD telling Jesus he's going to earth?"

"Hey, Jesus. I'm sending you to earth to redeem man's soul."

"Great! Am I going with fire and brimstone?"

"Sorry, son. That comes later. I'm sending you as a newborn. Fire and brimstone come later."

Everyone in the church laughs. Even the children understand Pastor Washington's suttle joke.

As the congregation settles back down, Pastor Washington continues with the sermon. "Though Christ came to us in physical form as an infant, he never was a baby or a child in the conceptual sense. Yes, Christ was once in infant form and had to grow to adulthood like you and I, but growing physically is not the same as growing spiritually or mentally. Christ had to come in the form of an infant because that was the only way he could genuinely be human and fulfill prophesy."

"Being that GOD is all-powerful, Christ could have come down from heaven and taken a human form, but then he would not have fulfilled the prophecies. Isaiah chapter seven verses thirteen and fourteen reads, *And he said, Hear ye now, O house of David; Is it a small thing for you to weary men, but will ye weary my GOD also? Therefore the Lord himself will give you a sign; Behold, a virgin shall conceive, and bear a son, and shall call him Immanuel.*"

"If you turn to Isaiah chapter nine verses six and seven you will see that it says, *For unto us a child is born, unto us a son is given: and the government shall be upon his shoulder: and his name shall be called Wonderful, Counselor, The mighty GOD, The everlasting Father, The Prince of Peace. Of the increase of his government and peace there shall be no end, upon the throne of David and upon his kingdom, to order it, and to establish it with judgment and with justice from henceforth even for ever. The zeal of the Lord of hosts will perform this."*

"Isaiah eleven, verses one through five states *And there shall come forth a rod out of the stem of Jesse, and a Branch shall grow out of his roots: And the spirit of the Lord shall rest upon him, the spirit of wisdom and understanding, the spirit of counsel and might, the spirit of knowledge and of the fear of the Lord; And shall make him of quick understanding in the fear of the Lord: and he shall not judge after the sight of his eyes, neither reprove after the hearing of his ears: But with righteousness shall he judge the poor, and reprove with equity for the meek of the earth: and he shall smite the earth with the rod of his mouth, and with the breath of his lips shall he slay the wicked. And righteousness shall be the girdle of his loins, and faithfulness the girdle of his reins."*

"Reading those three prophesies of Christ's coming, one gets a clearer picture of GOD's role for Christ here on earth and the fact that Christ will come from David's bloodline. As most are aware, one of the principle animals that the Jews sacrificed in the temple to cleanse their sins was a lamb, thus Christ being referred to as the lamb of GOD. It is evident that GOD planed for Christ to come in the form of an infant. It was necessary for GOD's plan to achieve success that his son come in a pure form. If Mary would have already had known Joseph prior to Christ's birth, then there would have been doubt and controversy of Christ's legitimacy as the true son of GOD."

"If Christ had not come from David's bloodline and just appeared as he did during the resurrection, the temptations that he encountered throughout his life would have meant nothing. In all actuality, they probably wouldn't even have occurred. Don't be fooled, the devil isn't dumb. He would've been wasting his time tempting Christ into turning the stones into bread to satisfy his hunger, for what does GOD have need for food? But if GOD is in human form, then obviously, he can become hungry, thus the temptation to turn stones into bread, when prodded by the devil, is plausible. The devil knew that he could not tempt the deity, but he could definitely tempt the flesh. I guess it was a valiant effort on Satan's part, but definitely a waste of time.

The congregation laughs again at Pastor Washington's biblical joke. Some of the children laugh, as well, but too many of them. The joke was somewhat over their heads.

Pastor Washington waits a few seconds for the congregation to calm down some, then continues the sermon, saying, "The world uses the Christmas holiday to celebrate the birth of Christ, and that is a great thing, but as with most things, the world does not have it completely right. The world tends to believe that Christ did not come into the Biblical picture until the latter days of Octavius Caesar when his parents had to report to Bethlehem for the census, thus forcing Mary to bear him in a cave on the outskirts of town. People treat Christ as though he is solely a major player in the New Testament."

"If you turn to Genesis Chapter one, verse twenty-six, you'll see that it states, *And GOD said, Let us make man in our image, after our likeness: and let them have dominion over the fish of the sea, and over the fowl of the air, and over the cattle, and over all the earth, and over every creeping thing that creepeth upon the earth.*"

"Genesis makes it clear that GOD is speaking to someone who is of him. He isn't speaking to the angels because, as most of us are aware, GOD out ranks the angels in the spiritual hierarchy. Angels are flawed creatures, to begin with. At the time of creation, Satan and the third of the angels had already attempted to rebel against GOD and were tossed out of heaven. Now you tell me. Why would GOD create man in the image of something that had already turned against him once before? I think not. It is safe to assume that GOD is not having this conversation in Genisis with the angels, but instead is speaking to Christ, and you can probably throw the Holy Spirit in there, as well.

Again, Christ's presence is inferred when the Babylonian emperor, Nebuchadnezzar, threw Shadrach, Meshach, and Abednego into the fiery furnace for not worshiping the image of gold. Daniel, chapter three, verses twenty-four and twenty-five reads, *Then Nebuchadnezzar the king was astonished, and rose up in haste, and spake, and said unto his counselors, Did not we cast three men bound into the midst of the fire? They answered and said unto the king, True, O king. He answered and said, Lo, I see four men loose, walking in the midst of the fire, and they have no hurt; and the form of the fourth is like the Son of GOD.*"

"Much to Nebuchadnezzar's surprise, he witnessed the son of GOD standing with the three Hebrew friends and protecting them from near death. It's no wonder that Nebuchadnezzar was quick to get Shadrach, Meshach, and Abednego out of the fiery furnace. No need to upset the Son of GOD anymore than you have to."

Again, the First mount Zion congregation laughs at Pastor Washington's subtle biblical joke.

Pastor Washington waits a few seconds for the laughter to die down, and then continues with the sermon saying, "Even after our Lord's resurrection into Heaven, he makes two more appearances in the New Testament. First in Acts chapter nine, verses three through seven, which reads, *And as he journeyed, he came near Damascus: and suddenly there shined round about him a light from heaven: and he fell to the earth, and heard a voice saying unto him, Saul, Saul, why persecutest though me? And he said, Who art though, Lord? And the Lord said, I am Jesus whom thou persecutest: it is hard for thee to kick against the pricks, And he trembling and astonished said, Lord, what wilt thou have me to do? And the Lord said unto him, Arise, and go into the city, and it shall be told thee what thou must do.*"

"Christ's second set of appearances in the New Testament is throughout the book of Revelations when he gives the Apostle John the signs of his return. Christ is rather blunt in defining his infiniteness when he says to John in Revelations one, eight; *I am the Alpha and Omega, the beginning and the ending, saith the Lord, which is, was, and which is to come, the Almighty.*"

"Can Christ be any more direct in telling us that he was here in the beginning and will be with us in the end? Man, I could have opened and ended the sermon with that scripture," Pastor Washington says with a slight chuckle and a smirk on his face.

The congregation shares in its pastor's laughter, realizing that he is technically correct with his self-assessment of his sermon.

Calm, Pastor Washington continues. "The point I make by mentioning these two appearances is to illustrate the fact that Christ is yesterday, today, and forevermore. He is not a character who pops up once a year as a baby with a bright sun star over his head. Christ was with us in the beginning, He was with us when we needed him to redeem our souls, and He will be with us in the end."

"If we are to celebrate anything, it is Christ beginning his journey to save the world from eternal damnation because we have all sinned and fallen short of the glory of GOD. Through his grace alone are we saved. I want you all to go home thinking of Christmas as the day when GOD decided to enact his plan to save man from himself."

The sermon complete, the organist softly plays. In unison, Pastor Washington raises his hands and says, "If there is anyone who wants to accept Christ into their life, please come forward. Christ has always been here for us. He was with us in the beginning, He is with us now, and he will be with us in the end. Come. We don't know when our day on earth is done. We don't know when he will come again. Please, come and accept Christ into your life, while you are still able."

No one amongst the congregation steps forward. As the organist plays, those who know the song, mainly the deacons and deaconesses, softly sing along as they wait for someone to approach the alter.

Seeing that no one is going to approach the alter to accept Christ into their life, Pastor Washigton says, "If you are looking for a church home; If you are looking for a church that preaches the forward, that puts Christ first, then come and join the First Mount Zion family."

Again, no one steps forward, mostly due in part that those in attendance this early morning are all First Mount Zion members or family of members. During the 'welcome visitors' portion of the service, the only people to stand were the relatives of First Mount Zion members. There were no regular church vistors this mornong. First Mount Zion rarely receives new members during its Christmas morning services.

Smiling, knowing that no one is going to step forward to join First Mount Zion Baptist Church, Pastor Washington says, "Rise and let us sing the benediction."

The congregation quickly rises to its feet in anticipation of leaving. The organist begins to play and cues the congregation as they all sing the benediction.

"Glory be to the Father, and to the Son, and to the Holy Ghost. As it was in the beginning, is now and ever shall be: World without end. Amen. Amen."

The singing of the benediction complete, Pastor Washington steps off of the pulpit and strides down the center aisle. At the main entrance, he stops and turns around. He then raises his arms to head level and says to the congregation, "Go in peace and have a merry and blessed Christmas."

Upon hearing Pastor Washington's words, the congregation relaxes because the service is now complete. Before departing from church, of course, everyone takes time to say hello to one another and wish them a merry Christmas.

Major turns around in his pew and says, "What's up Face?"

"'Sup man?" Al replies.

"Chillin', son. You know how I do."

"You comin' by the house today?"

"It wouldn't be Christmas if I didn't show up at your house right when ya'll're ready to eat."

"Christmas? You mean every meal."

"True. True."

Al and Major laugh at their verbal exchange.

Major thinks to himself, 'Where's Kenny? He ought to be here.'

Al and Major step out from their pews and into the aisle. Their families are already at the entrance of the sanctuary, speaking with Pastor Washington. The two friends walk up the aisle, slowly pursuing their parents.

As they walk, Al spots Kenny standing with his family and says to Major, "There's Ken."

Major follows Al to where Kenny idly stands.

Seeing his two friends walk towards him, Kenny throws his left hand in the air in acknowledgement.

"What's up fellas?" Kenny says to Major and Al as they approach.

"Same old nonsense," Al answers

"When'd you get home?" Major asks Kenny.

"Couple days ago. You?" Kenny asks Major.

"I got home on the twenty-third," Major replies.

"That's cool. My mom told me you're going to Beirut in a few days," Kenny states.

"Yeah. My mom told me the same thing," Al chimes in. "Are you crazy?"

"Come on fellas. Ya'll know me," Major replies.

"Yeah, we do," Al states. "That's why we know you're crazy."

"It's like I always say, not that I don't say a lot of things, but in this case, like I always say, you've got to be a little crazy to stay sane in this world."

"I guess so," Kenny hesitantly agrees. He then asks, "Why Beirut, though? I asked my mom, but she didn't know."

"I got a boy whose pops is the president of Lebanon. His dad invited me and Ben over for New Year's," Major answers

"That's cool and all," Kenny states, "but it's still Beirut. People die over there."

"Man, people die in DC," Major defends.

"That's true and all, but there's a big difference between DC and Beirut, Major," Al explains.

"Potatoes potatoes," Major sarcastically replies.

"Potatoes potatoes, my butt," Kenny interjects. "There's a huge difference between DC and Beirut."

"If you say so."

"Whatever, man," Al states, shaking his head. "All I know is that you better watch yourself out there and not get into any more trouble like you did last year."

"Come on now. I don't know what trouble is," Major boasts.

"You don't know what trouble is?" Al jests.

"Man!" Kenny agrees. "We leave you on your own for six months and the Mess Hall gets blown the hell up."

"True, but if I wouldn't have been around, GOD only knows what would've happened to the place," Major says in self-defense.

Al and Kenny nod their heads in agreement, followed by the three friends all laughing together.

1830 HRS

MAJOR HAS JUST LEFT FROM AL's house, where he stopped in for Christmas dinner, after having first eaten at his own home. In all actuality, Major paid the Meadows' a visit for the simple fact of saying hello, but he just happened to arrive when they were preparing to serve dinner.

Whenever Major goes to the Meadows' home on an early weekday evening, he has an uncanny knack of arriving at their home as they are preparing to sit down and eat dinner. Mr. and Mrs. Meadows love how Major seems to have an uncanny sense of when they are going to eat. Major is like a third son to the Meadows, so his walking in for an unexpected free meal is not seen as an intrusion, but as a welcomed invitation. This Christmas is no different.

Major now drives to David's parents' house for his regular Christmas visit. Major's relationship with the Meadows, in terms of him walking in on a meal, also applies to David's family, except that Major is only able to work his magic on Christmas and Thanksgiving.

While Major drives, he picks his cell phone up from the cup holder and scrolls trough the phone book. Finding the number he was looking for, Major presses the call button and waits for a voice to answer.

"Merry Christmas, baby!" Terry happily states.

"Merry Christmas to you too, babe," Major returns the salutation.

"You do anything special today?"

"I wouldn't say so. You?"

"No. Just your typical Christmas."

"Yeah. Me too, except for the fact that Dear wasn't here."

"Oh. How is Dear, anyway?"

"She's cool."

"Why didn't she visit you for Christmas this year?"

"Dear's coming down this summer. She does the one trip a year thing, unless my dad begs for her to come for both. He didn't beg this year. He asked, but he didn't beg."

Terry laughs at Major's comment about his dad.

She then asks, "What about, Muh?"

"Muh doesn't visit that often. Last year was an anomaly. You know what I'm saying?"

"Yeah, big head. I know."

"Muh loved it when I brought you over to the house last summer."

"I had a great time hanging out with her."

"Yeah, Muh's a cool old lady. She has a good arm, too. HA!"

"She had to having to raise nine kids all by herself. I don't know how she did it."

"Well, I always mess with Muh about going dancing all the time, 'cause she hasn't been in a few years, 'cause of her arthritis, and what not. Going to the zodeco with her when I took you down to Lake Charles friggin' made her world."

"Did it really?"

"Trust me on this. It was good seeing her out there on the dance floor doing her thing. I almost wanted to knock a couple old Grady looking dudes out though."

"You're a mess."

"I know I am. That's why you love me, though."

"Butt head."

"Anyway, the next time Muh comes up to VA for a visit won't be until the Brat graduates from high school in three years."

"How is my girl, anyway?"

"I don't call her the Brat for nothing."

"Ha ha. How is she?"

"Check out what this little girl did. She's handing out Christmas gifts, right. She gives my mom one, hands my dad one, then passes out all of the other gifts: then, she friggin' gets up and sits next to my mom."

"What's wrong with that?"

"What's wrong with that? The girl didn't get me and Will a Christmas gift!"

Terry laughs.

"Oh, you think that's funny, huh? You want to know what the girl said when we asked her why the hell she didn't get us a gift?"

"What did she say?"

"She friggin' spent all her money buying gifts for her dumb little friends. Her friends! Can you believe that nonsense?"

"That is kind of sad."

"Yeah it is. Now don't get me wrong. It's not the fact that she didn't get us a gift, 'cause even if she would have, we probably wouldn't have liked it anyway. The issue is that she thought of her little punk friends before she thought of her brothers."

"I guess she did do you guys wrong."

"Yeah she did, but oh well."

"So what're you doing now?"

"Driving to David's for dinner. You?"

"I'm just relaxing now. We just finished eating dinner."

"Your brothers come over?"

"Brian did. Ron spent Christmas with his wife's family, though."

"That's cool. Tell them I said what's up."

"I will. My mom wants to know when you're coming here for Christmas."

"Who knows? Maybe next year. We'll see."

"I can't believe you're still going to Beirut on the twenty-seventh."

"I know! It's tight, isn't it?"

"No! It's not tight, but you're going to do what you're going to do."

"I wish everyone would stop worrying about me. Ken and Face friggin' hemmed me up in church today over my trip. Their moms're trippin', too."

"What about your mom?"

"She knows better. Let's just say that the umbilical chord was cut a long time ago. Any worrying she did to me would have no effect, and she knows that."

"Whatever. You just take care of yourself when you're out there."

"I will, babe."

"You call me before you get on the plane."

"Yes, ma'am."

"I'll let you go now. I love you."

"Love you, too."

26 December 2001, 1900 hrs

"You know," Major says to his mother, "if this were two years ago, you guys would've already have taken me to the airport, and I'd be back at school right now."

"Yeah, and now you're going to Beirut for New Years. Woop-dee-do," Mrs. Johnson cynically replies.

Mrs. Johnson knows that the only reason why her son is speaking to her is to get a rise out of her. He has succeeded.

"What time is your flight tomorrow?" Mrs. Johnson asks Major.

"Ten in the morning," Major answers.

"Ben's staying with us tonight, correct?"

"Yeah."

Mrs. Johnson's question causes Major to look down at his watch.

"Fudge!" Major exclaims, "I've got to give him a call."

Major jumps to his feet and leaps up the stairs. Entering his room, Major goes to the dresser and snatches his cell phone. He then scrolls through the phone book, finds Ben's number, then presses the call button.

After a couple of rings, Ben answers his phone, saying, "What's up Major?"

"'Sup, cousin?" Major asks

"Nothing really. Just waiting for your call."

"Bet. How do I get to your uncle's house?"

"Here, let me put him on so he can give you directions."

Ben's uncle replaces Ben on the phone and gives Major directions to his house in Washington, DC. Major writes the directions down on a note card, then repeats them back to Ben's uncle to ensure that he truly knows how to get to the house. The directions given, Major thanks Ben's uncle, who then returns the phone to his nephew.

"So, you good?"

"Yeah. I've been over near where your uncle lives. I'm going to pick up David, then swing by the house. I shouldn't be any more than a couple of hours."

"All right then. I'll see you when you get here."

"Peace." Major hangs up his cell phonep, then shouts, "Hey, punk! You ready to roll?"

From the other side of the hall, Will shouts, "Yeah, fool! I was waiting for you!"

The two brothers meet out in the hall and head down the stairs together.

As Major enters the kitchen he opens the refrigerator and grabs a jug of Kool-Aid, while saying to his mother, who is still in the den, "We're out."

"Okay. I'll see you in the morning."

Major throws up the deuces as he follows Will into the garage.

Lake Ridge is a large suburban community in Prince William County, Virginia. Major had lived there from the late spring of 1987 to the summer of 1991, when he was in the fifth to eighth grades. During that time period, Major attended three different schools: Lake Ridge Elementary, Fred M. Lynn Middle School, and Lake Ridge Middle School.

Lake Ridge Middle School holds a special place in Major's heart for many reasons. For one, Major created the school colors: blue, gray, and white. Also, he and three other friends, Dean Gourd, Jeff Hummel, and Manny Love hold the school record for the four by four hundred meter relay. During the district track meet, they came within two seconds of breaking the county record, which was set back in 1968. Jeff gave Major hell for running the slowest leg of the four.

In the summer of 1991, the Johnson family moved to Okinawa for two years. After a quick and exciting two years, MAJ Johnson received orders for the Pentagon, thus sending the family back to northern Virginia. Instead of returning to Lake Ridge, though, the Johnson's moved to Montclair. Instead of attending Woodbridge Senior High School, as he had hoped, Major entered CD Hylton Senior High School for his junior year in the fall of 1993.

During this entire period, one thing remained constant for Major: his friendship with his best friend David Smoke. Major and David stayed in contact with one another during the two years when Major was in Okinawa. It was Major's way of staying in touch with his past.

Major first met David during the mid-fall of 1990, when they were in the eighth grade. They were in band together. Major played the trombone and David, the saxophone. From there, other than the fact that they were two of the only six Black kids in the one hundred something class, Major and David are unsure, to this day, as to how they became so close. I guess some things were just meant to be.

Major and David may as well be brothers. As Major puts it, "They are brothers in spirit." David and Major do everything together. For some odd reason, unbeknownst to them, during the five years that they were away at school, Major at West Point and David at Morehouse, they were always home at the same time. At least whenever Major was in Virginia, so was David, and this was without any form of coordination. Now that the two best friends live in the real world, they have to coordinate to ensure that both are in Virginia when the other is.

David knows everything about Major and Major knows everything about David. Major is very big on confidentiality, so it is very important for him to have someone who he can fully trust and confide in without worrying about his business spreading throughout the street. Everyone should have a friend like that.

Major and Will pull into David's driveway. The two brothers jump out of the Volvo and head for the front door. At the door, Major does his special knock and doorbell ring so that David and his parents know that it is him and not some random person.

After a couple of seconds, David answers the door, allowing Major and Will to enter.

"You ready to roll?" Major asks David as he and Will enter the house.

"Yeah. Let me get my sweater," David replies as he heads up the stairs for his room.

"Mrs. Smoke!" Major bellows.

"Why are you yelling in my house?" Mrs. Smoke jokes with Major.

"I just want to say hello, ma'am."

"Hi, Milton." Mrs. Smoke then notices Will and says, "Will, is that you?"

Will answers by simply nodding his head in compliance.

Mrs. Smoke walks over to Will, who is still standing beside the front door, and says, "I haven't seen you in years. How old are you now?"

"Twenty."

"Oh my. I remember when you were this tall," Mrs. Smoke comments, gesturing with her hovering hand just above her stomach to indicate Will's height from the last time she saw him.

As Mrs. Smoke excites herself over how much Will has grown, Major makes his way to the kitchen where Mr. Smoke is sitting at the kitchen table eating a plate of left over turkey and dressing and reading the newspaper.

"How's it going, Milton?" Mr. Smoke asks Major as he takes a seat at the table.

"Pretty good, sir. You?" Major asks.

"I can't complain. So, you ready for your big trip?"

"Can't wait."

"Everyone's messing with you about it, aren't they?"

"If you only knew, sir. My boys, my girl, my mom: They're killing me."

Mr. Smoke laughs, then says, "Well, if you're not worried, then neither am I."

"Thank you, sir."

David comes running down the stairs saying, "You ready to go?"

"Yeah. Let's roll." Major rises to his feet.

Will is the first one out the door, mostly because he is becoming tired of Mrs. Smoke speaking to him as though he is still a little boy.

"I'll see you, sir," Major says to Mr. Smoke, shaking his hand.

"You take care of yourself, Milton," Mr. Smoke replies as Major steps out of the kitchen.

"Have a good trip, Milton," Mrs. Smoke says to Major as he walks by her.

Major and Mrs. Smoke hug, followed by Major saying, "You know I will, ma'am."

Major steps out of the house and follows Will and David to the Volvo. The three young men get into the car and pull out of the driveway, on their way to Washington, DC to pick up Ben.

Driving north, on interstate ninety-five, Major asks David, "So, Leslie and her girls are going to meet us at DC Live?"

"That's what she said when I called her right before you got to the house," David responds.

"She better be. That girl's been dodging me since I got home."

"Well, she'll be there tonight, so you can hem her up when you see her."

"Trust me. I'll do that."

Will interrupts the conversation, saying, "We're meeting up with Leslie tonight?"

"Yes, we are," Major answers. "You got a problem with that?"

"Yeah, I do. You know I don't like that girl."

"Well, get over it. No one's making you talk to the girl. There'll be other females for you to holler at."

"I was going to do that anyway."

"Well then. Sit back and chill the hell out. Aight?"

Major returns his attention to David, saying, "You know, it's funny. If Leslie would've had her act together, I'd have taken her years ago, but oh well. I've got Terry, now. I can't do too much better than that."

"What about Jasmine Guy?" David sarcastically asks Major, knowing that Jasmine Guy was Major's childhood celebrity love interest.

With a big smile on his face, Major replies, "I'll get back to you on that."

Major approaches interstate four ninety-five, which is the DC beltway. The way that interstate ninety-five was designed, one is unable to drive directly through Washington, D.C. To continue north, into Maryland, one must exit onto interstates four ninety-five and go around the nation's capital. If one's trip requires continuing north onto interstate ninety-five, one takes what is posted as interstate four ninety-five north. The opposite direction is posted as interstate four ninety-five west. West is the direction Major, Will, and David need to go.

Major turns right and drives down the off ramp and onto interstate four ninety-five west. Speeding down the highway, Major drives through Fairfax and Annandale. Five minutes into the drive, Major passes the exit for interstate sixty-six. Another five minutes, and the three young men cross the Potomac River, which lets them know that they have just entered the state of Maryland. The welcome sign at the far side of the bridge is another obvious signal. Crossing the Maryland state line is Major's signal to jump into the right lane.

At the first Maryland exit, Major turns off of the interstate and veers to the right. Yielding to oncoming traffic, Major pulls out onto the street at the first opportune moment.

Keeping his eyes on the road, Major reaches for the directions to Ben's uncle's house, which he had placed in the cup holder, and hands them to David. He then turns the volume down on the radio so he can concentrate while he drives.

"Hey bro, read these to me," Major says to David as he passes the index card to his best friend.

"I got you," David replies. He then states, "You need to turn left at the Amoco."

Three more blocks up the road and Major spots an Amoco gas station. At the intersection, he turns left.

"All right. Now you need to take a right at the fourth light. There should be a small shopping center and a Seven Eleven on the right and a Wendy's on the left. Across the street and to the right there should be a bank," David instructs as he reads the directions.

'One light,' Major says to himself when he crosses the first traffic light.

'Second light,' Major says to himself when he crosses the second traffic light.

'Light number three,' Major says to himself when he crosses the third traffic light.

"Here we go," Major softly states as he approaches the fourth traffic light.

Major decelerates and turns right at the intersection.

The three young men drive down a dimly lit street lined with black street lamps and brownstones. Major looks at his directions, then up at the brownstones. After a few moments, Major spots the house and pulls up along the curb beside it.

Parked, Major says to Will and David, "I'll be right back."

Major gets out of the Volvo, leaving David and Will waiting in the idling car. Approaching the front steps, Major leaps to the top. He then presses the doorbell and patiently waits for a response.

After a brief moment, the door opens. Standing before Major is Ben.

Ben opens the screen door and says, "Glad you made it all right, brother."

"Thanks, cousin. You ready to roll?" Major asks.

"Where's your brother and David?" Ben asks as Major enters the house.

"They're out waiting in the car."

"Let me get my stuff so we can get out of here then."

"Here. I'll give you a hand."

Major and Ben lift the luggage from off of the ground. As they do so, Ben's aunt and uncle step out into the foyer to see their nephew off.

"Hey, ma'am. How's it going, sir?" Major says to Ben's aunt and uncle.

"Glad to see you didn't get lost with those crazy directions I gave you," Ben's uncle jokingly replies.

"It was no problem, sir. I don't get lost," Major jests. "I was out this way before a few years ago over at Martha Washington College."

"Oh. That's just down the street a ways," Ben's aunt responds.

"That's what I thought," Major replies.

"You boys have fun and take care of one another," Ben's aunt states with a tear in her eye.

Ben places his luggage on the ground and walks over to his aunt, giving her a hug. He then side steps to his uncle and hugs him as well.

Major shakes hands with Ben's uncle and aunt as Ben heads for the door.

"Bye," Ben states as he steps out of the house.

As Ben and Major walk to the idling Volvo, Major says, "I got the hook up for you tonight."

"What's that?" Ben asks walking to the back of the Volvo.

"I've got seven of the baddest sisters you've ever seen meeting us tonight!"

"Really?"

"I know how you like the sisters. You're family. You know the MAN always looks out for family."

Ben laughs at Major's statement as they walk to the front of the Volvo.

"What's up fellas?" Ben states as he gets into the rear passenger's seat.

"What's up, Ben?" David replies as the two young men shake hands.

"'Sup?" Will simply states.

Ben and Will give one other a pound.

"Little brother hanging out with us tonight, huh?" Ben jokes.

"Someone's got to drive us home," Major answers.

"Real funny," Will replies.

As the four young men make their way into Georgetown, Major looks up through the rear view mirror and says to Ben, "Man! I forgot to tell you. All of the girls who we're meeting up with are up for grabs tonight. I'm just out to get my drink and my dance on and do a little flirting to make sure the MAN's still got it. You know what I'm saying?"

"I here you, brother," Ben laughingly replies.

"Shoot! We'll all give you mad props if you can get Leslie," Major remarks.

"I think he can," David states.

"Only if you're crazy," Will annoyingly comments.

"What's the deal with Leslie, anyway? You've mentioned her before, but you've never gone into any real detail. What's her story?"

Will and David start to laugh in anticipation for what Major may say.

"I remember the first time I met that girl," Major opens. "David had been friends with her since the end of our senior year in high school. This fool was always talking about how bad she was, but I never got a chance to meet her. Anyway, one weekend, when I was home during our Yuck year. I think it was Columbus Day weekend, but anyway, I was chillin' over at David's house when she called. David arranged for us to pick her up at her place and go to a movie. Let me tell you, I was friggin' excited. I was finally getting to meet Leslie. So anyway, to make a along story short, we showed up at her house a little late. That was my mom's fault, but that's another story."

"We pulled up in front of her house and there she was, standing in the yard impatiently waiting for us. You could tell she was pissed because she had her hands on her hips, and she was standing in that 'I'm pissed as hell at you pose.' Anyway, I stepped out of the car and walked into the yard where she was standing. When I got into the light and finally got to see her face, my mind went blank for a nanosecond. Dude! That's never happened to me before. I always have thoughts running through this bad boy. I couldn't believe how beautiful she was."

"She looks that good?" Ben unbelievingly asks.

"Yeah, man," David affirms.

Ben looks over at Will who nods his head in agreement with his brother and David.

Will then states, "As much as I don't like the girl, I can't take anything away from her. She is definitely a dime piece."

"So, what's the problem with her?" Ben inquisitively asks.

"She's got a lot of attitude," David states.

"Too much!" Will interrupts.

"Personally, I find the attitude sexy. The problem I have with her is her lack of focus," Major explains.

"What do you mean?" Ben asks.

"That's too complicated to explain, but I'll put it to you like this. As beautiful as she is, the girl is dumb, and I don't mean in an intellectual way, 'cause she's smart as hell. I mean the girl has all of this potential, but she won't tap into it. It's like she's afraid of the unknown or something. I don't know."

"Well, I'll see what there is to choose from," Ben comments.

"The pickings'll be good tonight," David blurts.

"Tonight's all about breaking hearts!" Will boasts.

David, Ben, and Major laugh at Will's flamboyant comment. Ben and David then turn and playfully punch Will in the shoulders and chest a few times. Will laughs as he tries to protect himself from the jovial onslaught that he receives from his "adopted" big brothers.

The four young men enter downtown Washington, D.C. Major drives through the streets in search of E street. DC Live is on F street. Major knows that he will not find a parking spot on E or F streets. His plan is to drive to the club, then search outward for the nearest parking spot. After driving around for about fifteen minutes, intermingled with a few drive by female interactions, Major finds a parking spot on a street that runs perpendicular to and just a few meters from an intersection with Pennsylvania Avenue, only four blocks away from DC Live.

Major, David, Ben, and Will slowly step out of the Volvo. Major and Will properly hide items in the Volvo that would possibly lead to a burglary or motivate someone who is just looking to do something stupid for the hell of it.

Ben takes a couple of drinks out of the back seat and hands one to David. The two young men drink unsparingly. When Major walks beside Ben and David, they both hand him their drinks, motioning to him to finish them off. Quickly, Major finishes the drinks then throws the containers in the nearest trashcan.

"All right. I'm ready," Major states as he locks the Volvo. He then tosses the keys to Will.

The four young men walk up the street two blocks then cross and turn left onto E street.

E street is alive with bright lights and thumping sounds. Young Black adults in their late teens and early twenties from all walks of life swarm the popular street every weekend. A large number of the population consists of college students who attend a wide variety of schools within the Washington, DC metropolitan area: Howard University, Morgan State, George Mason University, and Georgetown to name a few. The others are non-college educated persons who simply work for a living.

Young men slowly drive up and down E street, showing off their flashy re-modeled cars and trucks and displaying the massive amount of bass that booms from their sound systems. The young ladies dress provocatively to attract the attention of the young men. In response, the young men generally hang out of the windows as they pass by, hooting and hollering at the women to get some form of a reaction. The truly courageous men and those with a strong sense of bravado approach the young women in an attempt to make the weekend that much better.

As Will, Ben, Major, and David smoothly walk alongside the crowded street, they do not pay much mind to the craziness that is occuring around them. David, Ben, and Major definitely appreciate the event for what it is worth, but they are some of the oldest out on E street this evening, and thus are a bit more refined than the average male who is out tonight looking for a good time.

Will, on the other hand, is a different story. His cool comes from within. The last thing Will would ever do is get overly excited over seeing a beautiful woman, or in this case a large group of them. Respecting the obvious and being the men that they are, the four young men do coolly acknowledge when they happen notice a young lady who stands out from the crowd.

"Man! I wish I had my truck right now!" Major exclaims. "I'd blow these little boys out of the water!"

"Yeah you would," Will agrees.

The four young men reach the next corner and turn right. At the next corner, they take a left onto F street. A few meters up and to their left is DC Live. There is a long line to the front door, but it is moving pretty well.

Major is not used to waiting in lines at clubs. In New York City, through party promoter Cris A.C., Major rarely has to wait in line at a club, especially if he has a number of women with him. Washington, D.C., on the other hand, is a different story. Because he was at the Prep School and West Point for five years and David was down in Atlanta at Morehouse for school, they never had a chance to form any real connections in their home city. Atlanta and New York: no problem. Washington, D.C.: problem. It is not a real issue, though, being that Major and David go home only twice a year: Christmas and the 4th of July.

As the young men wait in line, David's cell phone rings.

David answers his phone, saying, "You here yet?"

"We're trying to find a parking spot right now," the voice on the other end answers.

"We're in line now. They're letting the girls in as they come, so you shouldn't have a problem getting in."

"Okay. I'll see you inside in fifteen minutes."

"All right. We'll be on the main floor. We'll see you when you get here." David hangs is cell phone up and returns it to his pocket, saying, "That was Leslie. They're looking for a park, right now. They should be here soon."

"Cool," Major simply replies.

Will rolls his eyes at the thought of having to be in the same room with Leslie.

The four young men finally make it to the front of the line. They show their IDs to the doorman as they pass through. They then stand to the side so security can pat them down. The procedure is necessary to ensure that no one brings any weapons into the club. Inside, they pay the ten dollar admittance fee, then enter the lobby, where they slowly strut up the nearest stairwell.

The top of the stairs opens to a short walkway, which then opens into a large, immense area. Major and David lead Will and Ben to DC Live's main floor. To Major's direct right, the wall is nothing more than an elongated mirror. The center of the room consists of the main dance floor. To Major's front left is the bar, which is in the shape of a square, allowing patrons to circulate around it.

"I told Leslie we'd meet her on the main floor," David informs Major.

"That's cool," Major replies. "We'll stay around here until she shows up."

The four young men occupy a table as they wait for Leslie and her crew to arrive. Major, David, and Ben pass the time nursing a beer as they, along with Will, converse about the last presidential election.

"You know Bush stole that election," David states.

"You're kidding me, right?" Major cynically asks.

"No, I'm not kidding. It's obvious his brother bought the election for him. He's the governor of Florida," David defends.

Major shakes his head saying, "Come on, D. You're smarter than that. No leader in this country has the power or ability to buy a friggin' election."

148

"I don't know, Major," Ben interjects. "Kennedy's dad and Frank Sinatra got the mob to help him win."

"That's true and all," Major explains, "but we're talking an elected official here: not the friggin mafia."

"Then what do you think then?" David asks Major.

"I don't know," Major honestly answers. "All I know is that the system worked."

"How can you say the system worked?" David replies. "The Supreme Court had to get involved."

"That's my point exactly. The Supreme Court decided that the electoral votes for Florida went to President Bush. Therefore he is unquestionably the President of the United States. The Supreme Court is unbiased. They have no vested interest in showing any."

"It shouldn't have to come to that, though, Major," Ben says.

"I agree," Major responds, "but it did, and it showed just how great our country is."

"How's that?" Ben asks.

Major takes a sip of his beer and answers, "Because most countries would've had some form of a civil war or a coup détente. We didn't. Al Gore, though he was pissed as hell, respected the Supreme Court's decision."

"That is true," David agrees. "I still don't agree with the decision, though."

"Oh well," Major remarks. "Not like you have much of a choice."

"All I know is that they need to revise the voting procedures and process in most states," Ben adds. "From what I've heard, Florida wasn't the only state that had some voting issues."

"I heard the same thing," Major chimes in.

While in the middle of the civil and multi-sided debate, Major feels two hands squeeze his waist and a sexy voice say, "Milty!"

Major spins around on his stool and raises his head some.

Looking up at the beautiful woman who has acknowledged his presence, Major replies, "What did I tell you about calling me that, Les?"

With her hands on her hips, Leslie replies, "I'll call you whatever I please, Milty."

Major simply rolls his eyes in playful frustration. He then turns to Leslie's girlfriends and says hello to them.

Ben, David, and Will stand to their feet out of respect for the ladies. Major does not. He simply sits on the stool and sips his beer.

"You're a fool. You know that, right?" Leslie scolds Major.

"That's why you love me," Major jokes.

"Ooh. I can't believe you're going to Beirut. You're crazy."

"That I am, but what are you going to do about it?" Major then turns his attention to Leslie's girlfriends and says, "I apologize for my rudeness. Ladies, this is my cousin, Ben. Ben, this is Michelle, Tracy, Mary, Ericka, Sarah, and Toya."

Major's introduction causes the young ladies to give him and Ben a funny look.

Major laughs to the point where he is unable to reply.

Michelle asks, "What's so funny?"

Ben picks-up where Major was supposed to begin, saying, "We're first cousins."

"No you're not."

"Yeah, we are. Major's dad and my mom are brother and sister. They have the same dad."

"Yeah," Major replies, gaining control of himself. "Grand dad was a rolling stone."

"You guys aren't cousins," Michelle interjects, shaking her head in disbelief.

"We are," Major responds.

"We didn't find out ourselves until the summer before our Yuck year at West Point," Ben defends with a straight face.

Michelle looks to her left and right, in an attempt to read everyone in the group on whether they are biting on Major and Ben's hellacious story.

"Seriously," Ben continues. "We got to talking one day about our families and where they're from. One thing led to another and we realized that it was possible. To confirm our suspicions, we called our parents and grandmothers."

"Trust me," Major continues, "No one was more shocked than we were." Major stands to his feet, then puts his arm around Ben's shoulders saying, "We're not just friends, we're family."

"Wow," Michelle shockingly replies. "You guys really are cousins."

Major, David, Ben, and Will look at one another for a brief moment, then burst out into a roar of laughter.

"You really think we're cousins, huh?" Major asks laughingly. He then snaps his face directly in front of Michelle's and says, "Gotcha!"

"Ah, you punk!" Michelle states, hitting Major in the arm. "I didn't believe you, anyway."

"Say what you want," Major replies. "You wouldn't believe how many girls used to fall for that. I just wanted to see if it still worked."

"Are you done playing now?" Leslie asks Major.

"My bad," Major replies. He then asks, "You ladies want a drink?"

Leslie's girlfriends all reply with some form of a yes. Major and Ben go to the bar, leaving Will and David to their own devices.

A brief moment later, Ben and Major return with the drinks, distributing one to everyone, except Will.

A cup in everyone's hand, Major raises his cup to eye level and states, "To me and Ben's last night in the US in 2001."

27 DECEMBER 2001, 0500 HRS

MAJOR HAD A VERY LONG NIGHT of partying with his friends: nothing overzealous, but very energy draining, nonetheless. In a way, Major is kind of happy that he is preparing to take a cross Atlantic flight. He can get some much needed sleep. Ben holds the same sentiment. He nearly fell asleep at DC Live. Major was somewhat surprised that he did not, but as he and Ben know, for some odd reason, Ben only falls asleep at Club NV. Thank GOD for good friends.

Though still a bit tired, Major gets out of bed full of exuberance. Today's trip has him fully energized. Major slips on a pair of athletic shorts and runs out into the hallway.

Major nearly bumps into his dad before COL Johnson says, "I was just coming to get you out of bed."

"I'm going to get Ben up," Major replies.

"All right. We're leaving at six. You're mom's going to fix us breakfast before we go."

"Get out of here! I've got to take a picture of this!" Major exclaims.

Rarely does Mrs. Johnson ever cook anymore. If it is not Christmas or Thanksgiving dinner, Mrs. Johnson does not cook, unless inspired. This morning must be a moment of inspiration.

COL Johnson returns to his room laughing at his son's sarcastic comment about his mother, as Major turns left and heads to the end of the hall.

Opening the guest room door, Major says, "Ben, you up?"

Ben moans.

"Hey, bro," Major continues, "it's just after five. My mom's fixing breakfast. We're going to leave the house at six, so we'll probably eat at around five forty-five or so, being that my mom isn't even out of bed yet."

Ben slowly sits up and says, "Thanks, man. I'll be up."

"Cool. There's a clean set of towels for you on the bathroom counter."

Major leaves Ben's room and heads for the bathroom to take a bubble bath. Being that he, Ben, and Will did not return home until about four in the morning, Major decided not to take a bath prior to going to bed. Major loves bubble baths more than most things. As far as Major is concerned, there is nothing like a nice hot bubble bath. When Major takes a bubble bath and time is on his side, he generally spends at least half an hour in the bathtub, but being that he is aware that Ben needs to bathe as well, Major knows that he cannot take long in the tub.

To maximize his time, Major first runs the bathwater. As the bathtub slowly fills, Major turns on the radio, and then retrieves his toothbrush and toothpaste and commences to brushing his teeth. His teeth clean, Major returns the items to the medicine cabinet, then takes his razor and shaving cream, in order to shave.

Major generally does not shave his facial hair when he is on leave: one because he hates shaving and two, because he takes every opportunity he can to see himself with a beard, which is rare. For this trip though, COL Johnson overly emphasized the fact of not looking too military during their travels- no point in drawing any unneeded attention.

Instead of shaving his face, Major simply shaves his head clean. Done shaving, which does not take too much time, Major returns the razor and shaving cream to the medicine cabinet. He then removes his shorts and gingerly steps into the hot water filled bathtub.

Stepping into the bathtub, Major slowly sinks his body in, allowing each part to adjust to the difference in temperature. Fully immersed in the tub, Major leans back, his knees high in the air, and lets out a slow sigh.

Unable to truly enjoy the heat that envelopes him, Major grabs the soap and washes his body. Clean, Major submerses his head to get the full effect of the hot water. After a few seconds, Major pulls his head out from under the water and pulls the drain plug; thus ending one of his most favorite experiences of the day. Major then steps out of the bathtub and quickly dries off. Major wraps the towel around his waist and leaves the bathroom, with the music still blaring as he walks out.

Before Major enters the room, Ben happens to pass him in the hall. The two friends raise their heads in recognition of one another before going their separate ways: Ben to take his shower and Major to get dressed.

When Major was young, Dear, his maternal grandmother, taught him and Will to always dress nice when they fly: as though they were going to church. Major has always lived by that rule. One would never catch Major wearing a pair of jeans, t-shirt, or athletic shoes on an airplane. Major does not go as far as to wear a suit, though. He goes with more of a comfortable leisure style. Since his coaching days, Major wears one of three Army Basketball polo shirts whenever he flies. He likes the shirts, not for their comfort, though they are comfortable, but because they are good conversation openers for other people.

Because Major is flying international, though, he is not wearing anything that would make others aware that he is in the Army or outwardly shows that he is a US citizen. He was going to wear his class ring, but Ben was adamant about not wearing them. COL Johnson suggested that they also place their military identification cards somewhere accessible, but out of view of the general public. He told them that they should keep their military IDs in their carry-on luggage in a discrete pocket, but ensuring that the bag is in arms reach of one of them at all times.

Fortunately for Ben and Major, when they had their passport photographs taken, their haircuts were pushing the Army regulation of no more than three inches long, an inch and a half deep, and not touching the ears. Major had a small afro when he took his passport photograph.

Ben's hair, though not three inches long, was hanging rather long as far as the officers at West Point were concerned.

For the flight, Major wears his black dress boots, dark blue sacks, and a white, blue and black striped sweater with a white dress shirt underneath. Major checks himself out in the mirror and likes what he sees. He carefully glances around the room, checking to make sure that he has not left anything important behind. Seeing that he has packed everything that he is going to take on the trip, Major throws his Nike team bag on one shoulder and his West Point Basketball dress bag onto the other, then grabs his brown leather briefcase from off of the ground. Fully loaded, Major heads downstairs.

"I'll be downstairs, Ben," Major states loud enough for Ben to hear.

"All right," Ben replies from his bedroom. "I won't be long."

"Cool," Major replies as he plops down the stairs.

When Major reaches the bottom, instead of stopping, he cuts hard right and walks through the dining room, and into the kitchen where his mother is cooking breakfast.

"Good morning, Milton," Mrs. Johnson greets her son.

"Hey," Major simply replies as he stops to briefly chat with his mother.

"I'm almost done with breakfast. Just got to wait for the biscuits."

"Cool. I'm going to go put my bags in the garage."

"Okay," Mrs. Johnson replies as Major walks out of the kitchen towards the garage.

Major enters the garage and places his bags on the ground behind the Volvo. He then returns inside and watches television as he waits for his mother to finish making breakfast.

A few moments later, Ben slowly enters the kitchen area.

"Let me help you with that," Major says as he walks over to assist his friend.

"Thanks, man," Ben replies, handing Major one of his bags.

As Ben and Major pass the kitchen, Mrs. Johnson says to them, "Breakfast is ready. You guys can eat when you come back in."

"Yes, ma'am," Ben replies as he and Major head for the garage.

Upon Major and Ben's return to the kitchen, they find COL Johnson seated at the table eating.

"You guys are slow," COL Johnson says to the two young men. "I've been waiting here with all of this bacon for forever."

"Okay," Major sarcastically replies as he and Ben take a seat at the table.

Spread unsparingly across the table are large bowls of grits, scrambled eggs, biscuits, and bacon. There is also a small crystal bowl full of grape jelly, but that's for COL Johnson. He has an affixation for grape jelly. He puts it on very type of bread one can think of and whenever he can. There is more than enough food for everyone to take as much as they want, which is exactly what Major and Ben do.

"This is really good, Mrs. Johnson," Ben politely comments.

"Thank you, Ben," Mrs. Johnson replies.

Everyone continues eating without flinching. Major and COL Johnson do raise their heads from their plates though, to tell an occasional joke.

COL Johnson, as is customary, is the first to finish eating. He rises from his seat and puts his plate in the sink, rinsing it off with hot water.

"Five minutes," COL Johnson states as he heads upstairs to get his car keys and wallet.

"Roger," Major replies as he too rises from the table to dispose of his breakfast plate.

Ben follows suit. He then attempts to clear the table off, but Mrs. Johnson disallows him from doing so.

"Don't worry about that, Ben. I've got it," Mrs. Johnson states.

"Yes, ma'am," Ben replies.

COL Johnson comes walking down the stairs. When he reaches the kitchen, he says, "Let's get to the airport."

Major and Ben dutifully follow COL Johnson into the garage. COL Johnson pops the trunk, allowing his son and Ben to place their luggage inside. As they do so, Mrs. Johnson opens the garage door.

"GOD, it's cold!" Major shouts as the cold wind from outside hits him.

"It won't be cold where you're going," COL Johnson informs.

Mrs. Johnson walks up to her son and gives him a hug. She gives Ben a hug too.

"You guys take care of yourselves. Have a safe flight." Mrs. Johnson states as she steps away from the car.

"We'll be fine mom. Plus, there's nothing we can do about the flight," Major jokes with his mother.

"You know you're not funny," Mrs. Johnson comments.

COL Johnson gets into the driver's seat. Major walks over to the front passenger's side and enters the car. Ben slides into the back seat. Situated in the Volvo, the three men pull out of the driveway as Mrs. Johnson stands to the side, waving.

'I've got a fool for a son, but he's all right,' Mrs. Johnson says to herself as the car disappears down the road.

0645 HRS: BALTIMORE – WASHINGTON INTERNATIONAL AIRPORT

BALTIMORE-WASHINGTON INTERNATIONAL (BWI) AIRPORT IS LOCATED fifteen miles south of Baltimore, Maryland and thirty minutes north of Washington, D.C. For Baltimore residents, BWI is very accessible. For the residents of the District of Columbia, Ronald Reagan National Airport is more accessible. Washington, D.C. residents, though, use BWI quite frequently because it is much cheaper to fly in and out of BWI than it is National. The price difference in the plane tickets is what causes Major and his dad to frequently travel the additional forty-five minutes to BWI: anything to save a buck.

Arriving at BWI, COL Johnson does not pull into the parking garage. Rarely does he ever park when he is dropping off or picking up someone. The last time Major remembers his dad ever parking at an airport was back when he was in the third grade and his dad picked up he and Will from the airport after having spent the summer with Dear and their grandfather, Papa. That was the last time Major and Will saw Papa before he passed away two years later.

COL Johnson drives the car beneath the Northwest airline sign, where he then puts it in park. Everyone steps out of the car. Ben is the first to the trunk, which he immediately opens. Major is directly behind Ben. With the trunk open, the two friends quickly, yet carefully, toss their luggage out onto the sidewalk. COL Johnson stands to the side as Ben and Major empty the trunk of their personal items.

"Got everything?" COL Johnson asks Ben and Major.

"Yeah," Major replies.

"Yes, sir," Ben simultaneously answers.

COL Johnson approaches the two young men. He first firmly shakes his son's hand, then Ben's, saying, "I know I don't need to say this, but I'm going to say it anyway. Watch out for each other. Be cautious, but still remember to have a good time. I'll see you guys when you get back."

"All right, dad," Major says as he shakes his dad's hand again.

"Thanks, COL Johnson," Ben states as he shakes COL Johnson's hand.

Having said their good byes, Ben and Major grab their luggage and head directly into the airport and head straight for the Northwest counter. Much to their delight, as they approach the Northwest counter, Major and Ben spot Marcos waiting for them, as he said he would.

Marcos notices his two friends walking towards him and so, walks towards Ben and Major, meeting them half way.

"Marcos!" Major shouts.

Marcos grins from ear to ear at the voice of his boisterous friend.

Standing before one another, Ben says, "It's good to see you, Marcos."

"You too, Ben," Marcos replies. "Here. Let me help you with those."

Marcos takes a bag from both Major and Ben.

"Thanks, Marcos," both Ben and Major say.

The three friends walk to the Northwest Airlines first class line, which really is not much of a line since there is no one standing in the queue. Ben is the first to approach the attendant, a tall brunette wearing a red Northwest Airline skirt uniform, whose hair is tied in a loose bun.

As Ben places his bag on the scale, the attendant asks, "What is your destination today, sir?"

"Beirut," Ben simply answers.

With a curious look on her face, the attendant remarks, "That's an interesting place to visit."

"You're telling me," Ben replies as he hands the attendant his plane ticket and identification. He then states, "Hold up. This may help."

Ben bends down and digs into his carry on bag. Finding his military ID card, Ben rises and hands it to the attendant.

Receiving Ben's military ID card, the attendant says, "I know I shouldn't say this, but seeing this makes me feel a lot better."

"I thought it would," Ben replies with a flirtatious smile on his face.

The attendant processes Ben's ticket then hands it to him, saying, "Your flight connects into Frankfurt, Germany with a sixty minute layover there. In Frankfurt you will switch planes and connect into Beirut, Lebanon. Your total flight time is eleven hours. I hope you have a good time and please take care."

Smiling, Ben takes his ticket and says, "Thank you. I will."

Ben steps to the side and makes way for Major.

Major jovialy says to the attendant, "I'm going to the same place he is."

The attendant shakes her head in disbelief.

Seeing the attendant's reaction, Major asks her, "What's wrong?"

"I can't imagine why you and your friend would ever want to go to Beirut," the attendant remarks.

Major leans on the counter and motions behind him, "You see that guy over there standing next to my friend?"

"Yeah."

"Well, that's my man Marcos. His dad's the President of Lebanon."

"Is he really?"

"That's right. You could say that Ben and I are official guests of the Republic of Lebanon."

Major's quick information dump immediately changes the attendant's demeanor. Major hands her his identification. While the attendant processes Major's ticket, he places his bag onto the scale.

"Here you go, sir," the now jovial attendant says to Major as she hands him his ticket and identification."

"Thank you," Major replies.

"I hope you and your friend have a great time."

"Oh trust me. We will."

Major, Ben, and Marcos sit at a bar, just a few yards from their terminal. As they relax and catch up on the past few months, with mostly Marcos prodding his friends about tales from Ranger School, an attendant announces the boarding of their flight over the public announcement system. Hearing their flight number called, the three friends drop a wad of cash on the counter and leave the bar for their terminal. Because they are flying first class, Marcos, Ben, and Major walk directly to the front of the line and hand the attendant their tickets.

In first class, Major and Ben sit beside one another: Major in the aisle and Ben at the window. Marcos has the seat across from Major, in the aisle. The three young men situate themselves for the long flight to Frankfurt, as the remainder of the passengers begin to board the plane.

After twenty minutes has passed, the senior flight attendant gives the safety brief over the intercom. Having flown all of his life, Major barely pays attention to what is said. The flight attendant finishes her brief, and a few moments later, the plane rolls down the runway, in preparation for take-off.

In the air, Major, Marcos, and Ben occupy the beginning of their flight with different activities. They first pick-up their conversation where they had left off at the bar. After an hour or so of talking, the three friends move on to singular activities. Major pulls out his notebook and writes, Ben reads a book on Chinese philosophy, and Marcos listens to music on his CD player.

Comfortable beyond his imagination, Major comments, "Mrs. Wood told me that once I fly first class, I'll never want to fly coach again. She wasn't kidding! This is the joint! I can get used to this."

"I hear you, brother," Ben agrees. "This is nice."

Ben leans his seat back as far as it will go. He then places a blanket over his head and immediately closes his eyes to sleep through the duration of the flight.

1500 HRS EST: FRANKFURT, GERMANY

B EN AWAKENS TO MAJOR NUDGING HIM and softly saying, "Hey, Ben, we just landed."

Ben slowly removes the blanket from over his head and places it between his back and the seat.

Sitting up, Ben asks, "How long was I out?"

"Four hours, friend," Marcos replies as he returns his CD player to his personal carry-on bag.

"Man, I needed that bad," Ben states as he squares himself away.

The airplane slowly taxis down the runway and does not stop until it reaches its terminal. Once the airplane comes to a complete stop, the seat belt sign shuts off, thus allowing the passengers to leave their seats and remove their bags from the overhead compartments.

Their carry-on bags in tow, Ben and Major follow Marcos out of the plane and into the Frankfurt terminal. Because they have to switch planes, the three friends head for the terminal of the connecting flight to Beirut, Lebanon. Their plane arrived in Frankfurt on time, so they are not forced to rush to their connecting flight, which is scheduled to depart at four o'clock in the afternoon: one hour from now.

When the three friends reach their connecting terminal, they do not sit down. Their bottoms are tired from seven straight hours of sitting. Instead, they huddle beside a pillar that is a few feet from the check-in counter.

"I forgot!" Marcos exclaims. "We'll barely have time to make it out to the night club."

"The night club?" Major jests.

"What is so funny?" Marcos asks.

Laughing, Major answers, "We don't say nightclub back home: just club. It just sounded funny when you said nightclub. That's all."

"Oh," Marcos responds. "Well, you will like the women in our clubs very much. They are very beautiful and very friendly. The fact that you guys are Americans makes it even better"

"Really?" Ben asks. "I didn't think that women in the Middle East could express themselves openly like that."

"Saudi Arabia is not all of the Middle East," Marcos explains. "Most of the major cities are great cosmopolitans and very modern. Most of the people love America. You would be surprised."

"I bet," Ben states. He then asks, "Is your dad still hosting his New Year's party?"

"Yes he is. I used to hate them when I was a child, but I have grown to appreciate them as a man."

"How so?" Ben asks.

"For many reasons," Marcos replies. "There are always important dignitaries present. This year, Turkey and Israel's Prime Ministers, as well as the President of Egypt and the King of Jordan will be there."

"Get out of here!" Major shockingly responds.

"I usually never get to talk to men of their position," Marcos explains. "I am introduced to them, but that's as far as the conversation goes. This year should be different, being that you guys are national heroes."

"Come on, man," Major says.

"Man, Marcos," Ben replies. "I'm really looking forward to that."

Marcos smiles and points his right index finger in the air, stating, "I said there were many reasons. The other is the simple fact that there'll be several beautiful women with a lot of influence and money who like to have a good time."

"I'm starting to like Lebanon more and more," Ben remarks.

The three friends continue to converse: excited about the anticipation of their trip. A few minutes later, one of the flight attendants announces that it is time for them to board. Marcos, Major, and Ben retrieve their carry-on bags from off of the floor and head for the front of the line.

"You've got to love first class," Major says to his friends as they walk down the runway.

Major, Marcos, and Ben enter the airplane and walk down the aisle until they reach a set of stairs. At the stairs, they climb up to the first class section. The three friends take their seats in the same configuration as the first leg of their trip: Major in the aisle, Ben by the window, and Marcos across the aisle from Major, alone.

As the airplane taxis down the runway, Ben makes himself comfortable in order to return to the slumber from which he was in during the last flight. Major pulls out his Disc Man and selects his favorite DJ Green Lantern CD to listen to. Marcos does the same as Major, except that he decides to listen to Tupac's newly released album.

Before Major presses play on his disk man, he speaks with the flight attendant who is walking to the rear of the first-class section, "Excuse me, ma'am."

"Yes, sir?" the lovely, tall red haired flight attendant responds.

"I was curious, when will you show the movies?"

"Not until we've reached our maximum altitude."

"Oh. Okay. Thanks."

"Is there anything else I can help you with, sir?"

"Naw, I'm good. Thanks for asking, though."

"Well, you have a good flight then, sir," the flight attendant says as she softly pats Major on the shoulder. She then goes to her seat in preparation for take off.

Major presses play on his Disk Man and immediately commences to bobbing his head with musical pleasure.

1730 HRS EST: SOMEWHERE OVER THE MEDITERRANEAN SEA

THE FLIGHT TO BEIRUT GOES RATHER smooth, just as the first one to Frankfurt had. The three friends relax in order to save their energy for a possible night out on the town. The flight attendant walks up and down the aisle, taking care of the needs of her passengers.

Gretchen, the flight attendant, as Major has already come to know her name and a few personal things about her, kneels down beside Major. Seeing that Gretchen is about to speak, Major lifts the headphone from over his left ear.

Now that Gretchen knows that Major can hear her, she asks him, "Do you need anything, darling?"

"Actually, yes," Major replies. "May I have another cup of tea, please?"

"With four sugars, again?"

"Yes, with four sugars."

"Just like my little brother," Gretchen laughs as she stands erect.

"Your little brother, huh?" Major jests. "I've got your little brother for you."

Gretchen returns to the back laughing. As she begins to prepare Major's tea, she is suddenly grabbed from behind and gagged. Gretchen kicks with all of her might and attempts to scream, but her voice is muffled from the rag that is shoved down her mouth. None of the passengers can hear Gretchen struggle for her life because they all either have headphones over their ears or are asleep.

A terrified Gretchen is suddenly spun around like a rag doll and, much to her fear, stares into the dark brown eyes of an Arab male. The man quickly duct tapes her rag filled mouth; thus, making the gag permanent. He then wraps the tape around Gretchen's wrists. He knocks her to the ground and tapes her ankles together. Secured, the man, forces Gretchen into the coat closet. In all, it only takes him fifteen seconds to subdue Gretchen.

Gretchen's acauster walks down stairs, then immediately returns to the first-class section, this time with two other men of Arab decent. Standing in the rear of first-class, one of the men presses the attendant's assistance button. A few seconds pass without a flight attendant showing, so he presses the button again. The second time pays off.

A short flight attendant whose hair is blonde and hangs at shoulder length, walks up the stairs saying, "Gretchen what's going on up there? One of your passengers is trying to page you."

The flight attendant reaches the top of the stairs and peers down the aisle. Not seeing Gretchen, she immediately turns around to look in the back. The sight of three Arab men shocks her to the point to where her knees waiver and she nearly stumbles to the ground.

Reacting to the flight attendent, one of the men whispers to her, "Speak and die."

The whimpering flight attendant is now shaking uncontrollably. She is able to muster enough strength to nod her head in acknowledgement.

Another of the men snatches the flight attendant forward and spins her around. He holds an airline issue steak knife to the flight attendant's throat and walks down the aisle, holding her close to his body to keep her from escaping. Flight attendant in tow, the man walks down the aisle, heading for the front of the first-class section. As he passes, those who are awake are shocked by the unexpected. Those who sit beside them immediately awake those who are asleep.

As the man and his captive flight attendant walk past Major, the sight causes Major to throw himself back into his seat.

'What the hell!' Major shouts in his head.

Major shakes Ben awake, quietly urging, "Ben, you've got to get up."

"We there yet?" Ben groggily asks.

"Dude, one of the flight attendant's is being held hostage."

"What?"

Major's news forces Ben to fully awaken. He throws the blanket from over his head and stares in disbelief as to what is occurring before him.

Standing in front of the first-class section and still holding the steak knife to the flight attendant's throat, the Arab male announces, "Everyone stay calm. We are not here to hurt anyone or crash the plane. If you attempt to interfere, I will be forced to kill her, and then you. We do not wish to harm anyone, but we will if it is the only way we can fulfill Allah's will."

As everyone in first-class processes in their minds what is occurring on their flight, the other two men walk confidently down the aisle behind their accomplice and his hostage, stopping at Marcos' seat. Much to Marcos' surprise and before he is able to react, one of the men knocks Marcos on the head with a blunt object.

In response to Marcos' sudden attack, Major nearly jumps out of his seat in retaliation. Fortunately for Major, Ben restrains him: keeping Major from doing anything foolish.

"Stay cool," Ben says to Major, calming his friend down.

Marcos does not pass out from the attack, but the blow to the head does cause him to become quite nauseas and unaware of his surroundings. One of the men grabs Marcos' limp body and drags him to the rear. The lone man joins his accomplice at the front of the plane, pulling a steak knife from out of his pocket.

The man holding the flight attendant walks her to the cockpit and orders, "Tell the captain to open the door."

Quivering, the flight attendant dutifully presses the intercom button, saying, "Captain, I have some Cokes for you."

"Heidi is that you? Where's Gretchen?"

The man presses the knife firmly against Heidi's throat. She begins to whimper, but attempts to hold in her tears.

"She had to go to the bathroom, sir."

"Oh. Well, we're good in here, Heidi," the captain answers.

Heidi presses the intercom button again and says, "I really think you guys need a drink, captain."

"We really don't Heidi, but you can leave them in here if it will make you feel better."

The captain presses the button to unlock the cockpit door.

Hearing the door unlock, the man holding Heidi throws her behind him. The man who only holds a steak knife grabs Heidi and forces her to the rear of the plane. He gags and binds Heidi, then throws her in the coat closet with Gretchen.

The man who was holding Heidi opens the door and storms into the cockpit. He snatches the navigator by the back of his collar and jerks his head up. The sudden commotion causes the captain and his co-pilot to jump in shock and turn their bodies around in order to see what the disturbance is.

Pressing the knife to the navigator's throat, the man states, "You are going to change your flight pattern. We are now going to Damascus."

The captain and co-pilot turn back around, facing their instruments.

The captain thinks to himself, 'Does this bastard really think that...'

"I know what you are thinking," the man holding the navigator informs.

"You want to continue flying to Beirut, while I think that we are heading to Damascus. I assure you that I know how the instrumentation of an airplane works. You will take us to these coordinates."

The man who had taken Heidi to the rear of the plane now stands beside the man who holds the knife to the navigator's throat. He hands the captain a small sheet of papers that contain the coordinates to the Damascus International Airport.

"You will input these coordinates," the man continues. "Deviate from them and people will die. I will stay here to keep you motivated."

Major leans over to Ben and whispers to him saying, "We've got to do something. We can't let them take Marcos."

"Are you serious?" Ben questions. "This isn't West Point, man. You didn't do all that by yourself, remember? You had real help that day. There are too many unknown variables for us to be doing anything right now."

"I hear you, but we have to do something."

"Yes we do, but we're not going to fight these guys. That's the dumbest thing we could do. We don't even know how many of them there are. I didn't get on this plane to die, and neither did you."

"Okay, you're right. So, what do we do?"

"You have Big Mac's number on you?"

"Yeah, I've got it on my phone."

"Good. You actually listened to Terry and got that international plan, right?"

"Didn't have much of a choice."

"Well, we need to find a way to call Big Mac, but we sure can't do it here."

After a brief moment of deep thought, Major says, "I've got an idea."

Major covertly rummages through his briefcase until his hand finds what it seeks, carefully pulling his cell phone out of his briefcase. Looking to ensure that none of the three men are watching him, Major quickly, yet smoothly, slips his cell phone into his pocket.

Major leans towards Ben and asks, "You seen *The Great Santini?*"

"Yeah," Ben replies.

"Remember the opening scene?"

"Of course: funniest part of the movie."

Major simply nods his head. Ben understands.

Major crams as much food that is on his tray into his mouth and chews it up. He then takes Ben's orange juice and fills his mouth up with it, but in such a manner that his cheaks are not puffing out. Major makes it a point not to swallow any of the contents, and rightfully so. The combination would turn his stomach and make him truly sick. Ready, Major nods his head slightly. Ben returns the gesture in compliance.

Out of nowhere, Major begins to gag. He rocks himself heavily back and forth and moans ever so slightly.

Ben jumps to his feet and tends to his friend, shouting in distress, "What's wrong, man? Are you all right?"

Major uses the seat to his front to slowly pull himself up. He continues to gag, while Ben makes every effort to help his friend. Ben holds Major up as he gradually steps out into the aisle. As soon as Major's foot steps in the aisle, he collapses to the ground. Seeing the commotion, the man who grabbed Marcos runs over to investigate, where he finds Major hunched over on the ground and Ben leaning over him.

"What go on here?" the man angrily asks in broken English.

"My friend is sick!" Ben answers, shaking slightly from the adrenaline rush. "I need to take him to the bathroom."

"No!" the man barks.

As soon as the man spouts the word 'no,' Major turns in the man's direction and throws up on his legs and feet. The man jumps back and shouts in disgust.

Upset, the man frustratingly gives in, "Okay! That way! No funny stuff!"

The man points to the rear of the plane where he wants Ben to take his seemingly sick friend. Ben carefully places Major's arm around his neck, then lifts him to his feet. With what little strength Major has, he assists Ben in walking down the aisle. The contents of the throw up dribble down Major's mouth as Ben carries him to the rear bathroom.

Beside the bathroom, Ben leans Major up against the wall as he opens the door. Ben then grabs his friend and escorts him into the bathroom and places him on the toilet. Inside, Ben locks the door: Then, and only then, does Major end the charade. Ben switches rolls with Major, making loud heaving sounds to give everyone in the first-class section the impression that Major is throwing up.

Quickly, Major retrieves his cell phone from out of his pocket. He turns his cell phone on and impatiently waits the five seconds that it takes for the screen to appear. The cell phone now on, Major goes immediately to his phone book and scrolls down until he finds the number he is looking for.

THE HAMPTONS, NEW YORK

ONLY THE TRULY RICH AND ELITE in society own a home in the area of New York known as the Hamptons. The level of wealth varies, but every resident, whether they live there regularly or seasonally, is valued in the excess of hundreds of millions. The summer is when most people frequent the Hampton's, using it as a quick getaway when one does not feel like doing any real traveling, yet still wishes to escape the hustle and bustle of New York City.

One house in particular is always bustling with people. Young men and women are always coming and going from the elaborate home. At least once a month there is a party at the house: Sometimes for a particular reason, for instance a birthday, others just, for the sake of partying and having a great time.

Last year after his big blockbuster film debut, X bought a house in the Hamptons. To X, his Hampton home symbolizes his success. The house is a status symbol. X bought the house in cash for four million dollars. For this reason, he gets as much use out of it as he possibly can, which is why he throws house parties so frequently.

One of the extremities that X added to the grounds was an indoor swimming pool. When X was a child, the only time he ever went swimming was the two times his mother sent him to summer camp in upstate New York. As a child, swimming always gave X a feeling of freedom. Unfortunately, he did not have too many of those free moments.

Today, X is hosting a pool party for Def Jam Records. The pool area is crowded with numerous people ranging in all ages. As it is with all of X's parties, it is going to go all night and creep into the early morning. During the day, as it is now, there are several children present, enjoying the giant pool and good barbecue. Because there are children around, X does not allow any heavy drinking until after they leave, which is around eight o'clock at night or so.

If and when someone is caught breaking X's alcohol policy, they are immediately kicked off of the grounds. The rule is not broken because that would cause the offender to have a very bad altercation with Mac, which is something no one wants to do. Mac takes X's alcohol policy very seriously. Rules and the enforcement of them are very important to him. More importantly, Mac loves the kids.

As it is with the majority of X's parties, Mac is present. Working for X is a little weird for Mac because as X's head of security, he has to ensure that people remain safe and abide by the rules. The problem is that X seems to always forget this whenever they are in a social environment. X always expects Mac to have a good time with him whenever they are out. Fortunately for Mac, the no heavy drinking policy is still in effect, so X is rather calm, which means that he is not looking for Mac to get into any trouble with him just yet.

Mac stands with a group of bikini clad young women, sharing with them the little knowledge he has about art and his favorite artist, Ernie Barnes. The girls are in their early to mid-twenties and have all been in a Def Jam video at one time or another. Mac easily impresses the young ladies. They are amazed that such a large and powerful looking man is so cultured and, of all things, is an artist. It is not too difficult for Mac to amaze the girls, being that they are not as aware of the world around them as they should.

"What style do you paint?" one young lady asks.

"I don't have a style, dear. I get a vision in my head, and I have to put it on canvas," Mac answers.

"That is so incredible!" another young lady exclaims.

"No it's not. What I do isn't anything special," Mac humbly comments. "You ladies can easily do it."

"You're so modest," a pink thong wearing young lady responds.

Mac simply smiles, thinking to himself, 'This is just too easy!'

He then says, "I would love to show you ladies my paintings sometime, if you're ever free."

"Oh, we'd love to," several of the beautiful young women gleefully reply.

As Mac happily converses with the young ladies, his cell phone rings.

"That's odd," Mac quietly comments as he reaches for his cell phone.

He pulls out his cell phone and looks at the screen.

Shocked, Mac says to himself, 'This can't be good.'

Mac returns his attention to the young ladies and says, "Excuse me ladies. I have to take this."

Mac steps away from the beautiful young ladies and simultaneously presses the answer button on his cell phone, while bringing it to his ear.

Major cups his mouth over his cell phone. He anxiously waits for the phone on the other end to pick up.

After three rings and much to Major's relief, he hears a familiar voice ask, "What's up, Major?"

"My plane is being hijacked," Major whispers into the phone, behind the sound of Ben's heaving noises.

"Holy shit! What happened?"

"They knocked out my friend Marcos and took him to the back of the plane."

"Okay. Marcos was the target. Don't do anything. These guys aren't looking to kill anyone or they wouldn't have snatched your friend. Where are you flying to?"

"Beirut."

"What the hell are you doing flying to Beirut? Nevermind, we'll deal with that later. Call me as soon as you land. Stay cool."

"We will."

"Damn," Mac quietly says aloud as he hangs up his cell phone.

Mac scrolls through his phone book and stops at Killer's number. Mac presses the call button and waits for a response.

"What's up, Mac?" Killer asks answering the phone.

"We've got serious trouble, man," Mac states.

Killer, who is sitting on his couch reading a book, slowly sits up.

Placing the book to his side, Killer asks, "What's going on?"

"Major's flight to Beirut's been hijacked."

"Beirut! What the hell's he doing going to Beirut?"

"Not sure. Something about a friend of his named Marcos who was kidnapped in the process. I have a bad feeling about this one."

"I hear you."

"I'm going to go and see what I can do. Can you come?"

"You know I can't do that. The wife would kill me."

"Understood."

"I will call some people, though: see what they can scrounge up and if they're willing to tag along with you on this rescue mission."

"A few people out there still owe us."

"True, but there's bad blood with some of them, now that we're out of the business."

"I know, but there's got to be a couple."

"There are. I'll give you a call when I get something. Keep your phone close."

"Thanks, Killer. I'll be standing by."

Mac hangs his phone up and returns it to his pocket. He then walks through the bathing suit clad crowd, making his way to X, who is surrounded by an uncountable number of women.

Sitting on the edge of the pool, X feels a heavy hand tap him on the shoulder.

"What's up Big Mac?" X boisterously asks his good friend.

"I've got to go, man. I'm not sure how long I'll be gone, but I'll give you a call when I return."

"I swear to GOD, man! I'm going to find out what it is you do one of these days."

"Not if you value your life," Mac jokes as he steps away from the pool, leaving the party.

Major turns his cell phone off, not saying a word. He nods to Ben, signaling that he is ready to return to their seats. Major rinces his mouth out, then hunches over. Ben gets underneath Major's right side to assist him out of the bathroom.

The two friends exit the bathroom to discover a large black bag lying on the floor. One of the men stands over the bag. He pushes Ben and Major out of the way and down the aisle out of concern of their suspicion.

Ben and Major linger down the aisle, heading for their seats. When they approach Major's make-shift vomit pool lying on the floor, Ben steps to the side to keep from getting their shoes dirty. At their seats, Ben assists Major down, then takes his seat, as well.

Situated, Ben carefully takes a pen from his pocket and jots on a napkin, 'Marcos = bag?'

Ben cautiously slides the napkin to Major. Reading the note, Major nods his head, answering yes.

The two men walk up and down the aisle to ensure that everyone stays calm and that things do not get out of hand. Another hour passes when the fasten seatbelt sign flashes.

'It's funny,' Major thinks to himself with a small smile on his face, 'even through all of this, the captain remembers to turn on the seatbelt light. That's funny.'

The airplane makes its decent down to the airport. For the current situation on the flight, the landing is actually pretty smooth, which is a testament to the captain's flying ability and expertise, especially under the current circumstances.

As the plane taxi's down the runway, the man in the cockpit holding the steak knife to the navigator's throat says, "You can stop right here."

The captain, not acknowledging the man verbally, does so by slowing the airplane down and bringing it softly to a halt in the middle of the tarmac.

Feeling that the airplane has stopped moving, the two men in the back of first class grab the black bag that lies on the floor and throw it onto their shoulders. The man in the cockpit jerks the navigator up onto his feet and forces him to the back of the first class section with him. Standing beside the coat closet, he shoves the navigator forward and to the ground. As the navigator tumbles, the man snatches Heidi from out of the coat closet and throws her on his shoulder.

The man carrying Heidi then states, "If you follow us, I will kill her. Stay where you are until the authorities arrive."

He and his two black bag carrying accomplices scurry down the stairs. Much to the shock of those below, they do not know how to react when they see the men rush down the aisle with their hostage and enormous package. The astonishment causes a few people to scream, but shock of what their eyes behold forces them into silence.

At the main cabin door, the man carrying Heidi tells the confused flight attendants, "Open the door, now!"

One of the flight attendants who is not frozen from fear complies. She leaps to her feet, spazzing just a bit, and opens the door for the men.

As soon as the men rush down the stairs, Ben and Major jump to the window to see if anything is occurring outside. On the tarmac, bordering the runway, is an immense marshland. The terrain is scattered with tall reeds and grass. Parked alongside the runway near a grouping of reeds is a rusted blue van. Standing beside the van are two men carrying a ladder that appears to be at least ten feet high, give or take a few feet. Ben and Major watch the two men rush to the captain's front side of the plane where the main cabin door is located.

A few seconds pass, and Ben and Major witness two of the men carrying the black bag to the van and the remainder of the men running with them.

Ben quietly counts, "One, two, three four, five. That's all of them."

"Where the hell's the other stewardess?" Major asks Ben.

With all of the men inside the van, it goes peeling off and exits the runway area, driving off into the distance.

With the van gone and the threat of danger seemingly over, Major and Ben immediately jump out of their seats. Major rushes towards the back to check on Gretchen. Ben makes his way to the cockpit to check on the flight crew.

When Major reaches the coat closet, he immediately swings the door open to find Gretchen tied and gagged. She is still conscious, but Major can tell that she is extremely traumatized from her experience. At first,

Major attempts to slowly remove the duct tape from around Gretchen's mouth.

Realizing that being gentle is not working, Major says, "Gretchen, this is going to hurt," then quickly rips the tape off of Gretchen's mouth and removes the rag.

"Thank, GOD!" Gretchen cries out. "I thought I was going to die."

"Not on my watch, dear," Major smilinly replies as he removes the tape from around Gretchen's wrists. Major then squats down and says to Gretchen, "I know this is hard, but I need you to be calm. The passengers need you to be strong. None of them know that you were tied up."

Gretchen wipes her eyes and straightens her uniform out, saying, "Okay. I can do that."

"That's my girl, Major replies as he assists Gretchen to her feet.

Ben pounds on the cockpit door. He would ring the bell, but he neither knows where it is nor does not have the time to check for it.

"Captain!" Ben shouts. "The terrorists are gone! They're not here anymore!"

Still, the door does not open. The navigator, who had been sitting on the floor all of this time, picks himself up and makes his way to the cockpit door.

"Here, let me try," the navigator states.

The navigator presses the intercom button and says to the captain in a calm voice, "Sir, it's all clear out here. It's safe to open the door."

The cockpit door slowly creaks open. The navigator waits for the door to open fully before entering the cockpit. Seeing that everything is all right, from the pilots' perspective, Ben runs down the aisle and meets Major in the rear of the first-class section.

"We've got to find that other stewardess," Ben states.

"Yeah," Major complies.

Major follows Ben down the stairs to the main section of the airplane. The two friends race to the main cabin door where, much to their relief, they find several flight attendants tending to the aid of their fellow flight attendant who was earlier bound and gagged.

Rushing to the scene, Ben asks the small group, "Is she all right?" He then kneels down beside the traumatized flight attendant to check on her condition.

"She's a bit shaken up," one of the assisting flight attendants answers, "but she'll be okay."

Major walks to the open cabin door. Hanging onto the edge, he leans forward to take a look outside. Much to Major's relief, he can spot in the distance, the airport's rescue personnel rushing to their location.

Major pulls himself back in and says to a kneeling Ben, "The airport's rescue team's on its way."

"Good," Ben replies. "I don't think anyone's going to need them, though."

"Thank GOD them dude's didn't hurt anyone."

Ben looks up at Major, who is now leaning beside the door, and asks, "What did Mac say?"

"He wants me to call him back."

"What do you think he's going to do?"

"Couldn't tell you, but I think he's going to find Marcos." Major pauses for a brief moment, then says, "How's this crap keep happening to us?"

Ben shakes his head and says with a smirk on his face, "Beats me, brother, but I'm telling you, I'm not getting shot and missing out on all of the action this time."

Red Bank, New Jersey

EVER SINCE THE WEST POINT JOB, Amos Man Killer Stewart has been out of the mercenary business and living the straight life—that of total peace and quiet, except during the summer when the New Yorkers go to the Jersey shore for vacation. As far as Killer is concerned, he is retired. The payout from the West Point job allows him to never have to work another day in his life.

Killer could go out and get a job, but he is more than content playing Mr. Mom. His two sons are in school, so he only has to watch his youngest child, Angie. She is a handful, on the curiosity side, but other than that, she is very well mannered, which makes her father's task of watching her quite simple.

Killer's days of killing people for money are long since over. He has made such a one hundred eighty degree turn that he is even active on the PTA at his sons' schools. Killer chaperones field trips and is on a schedule with the housewives in the neighborhood shuttling their children to and from their various activities and sporting events.

Killer has always loved working in his yard, but due to the several missions he had to regularly undertake, he was never able to put the time into his yard that he would have liked. Now that he is free of his employment commitments, Killer's yard now resembles a small Japanese garden. His yard has won the neighborhood yard of the month award so often that it is no longer judged. Killer's yard is the standard by which all of his neighbors aspire to achieve. Killer desperately wants his yard to appear in *Home and Garden* magazine and *Architecture Digest*. His wife laughs at him about his dream and tells him that he is silly.

Though Killer has no real regrets for his past life, to make amends for his actions at West Point two years ago, Killer took on the role of an assistant lacrosse coach at West Point's Prep school in March of 2001. He would have coached at the Prep School sooner, but Mac had informed him that Major was going to be there from July 2000 until January 2001. Killer did not want the awkwardness of seeing Major everyday. As far as Killer was concerned, the less Major knew of his and Mac's personal lives, the better.

After getting off the phone with Mac, Killer gets off of the couch and leaves the den. Killer walks outside towards the garage. He opens the garage door, goes inside, and immediately shuts the door behind him. On the left side of the wall hangs a flashlight, which Killer removes and instantly turns on. With the light as his guide, Killer walks to the shelf in the back where he keeps his tools and gardening supplies.

On the top of the shelf sits a green metal ammo can that Killer uses as a toolbox. Killer reaches for his make-shift toolbox and removes it from its position. Placing the toolbox on the ground, Killer presses down on the top with his left hand and firmly holds the bottom portion. With a quick jerk, Killer lifts the can up, thus leaving the one inch piece that he was holding, still on the ground. Killer then places the main portion of the toolbox down on the floor beside him. Inside the one inch piece lays a small brown book, which Killer retrieves.

Killer takes out an index card and a pen from his pocket and places them on the floor, as well. He then sifts through the countless pages of names and corresponding phone numbers. Finding the names that he wants, Killer jots them down on the index card. After a minute of number jotting, Killer returns the index card and pen to his pocket and places the book back in its original location. He fits the main portion of the toolbox back onto the smaller piece, then returns it to the top of the shelf.

Killer leaves the garage and returns to the house, heading straight for his wife's office. Before he sits behind her desk, Killer takes out his cell phone and index card from his pockets. Killer sits down in his wife's oversized brown leather swivel chair and places the index card on the desk.

When Mac and Killer left the mercenary business, J allowed them to keep their cell phones, identification numbers, and passwords: Partially out of respect and friendship, but mostly because he was hoping to one day bring Mac and Killer back into the fold.

Mac and Killer do not use their old cell phones anymore, yet out of force of habit, they always keep them on their person. As is the case today, it is a good thing Killer had his cell phone with him, as well as Mac, for that matter.

Killer dials the first number. After a couple of seconds, someone answers.

"Mother fucker! The Man Killer! I never thought I'd hear from you ever again!" the voice on the other end of the phone shouts.

"Sam, I need you to return a favor," Killer states.

"I do owe you. What do you need?"

"A plane was hijacked on the way to Beirut. I don't have any details on it yet, but you'll be forced to react fast."

"I can't do fast. I'm in the middle of a job right now."

Killer shakes his head, then says, "All right, man. I understand. Thanks anyway."

"I'm sorry," Sam apologizes. "Maybe next time."

The two men hang up simultaneously. Killer immediately dials the next number. The phone rings several times. After the tenth ring, Killer stops the call. Killer tries the next number. A few rings later, someone answers.

"You know, I shouldn't even be talking to you. You know some people want your head."

"So I've heard. I'll let you know when I'm scared."

"Well, whatever you want, I can't do it for you."

"You owe me, Diego."

"As far as I'm concerned, any debts I had with you and Mac were washed away the day you guys quit."

"That's bullshit, and you know it."

"Maybe so, but in your present status there's nothing you can do about it."

"You know, you're mouth's going to get you killed one of these days."

"You've been saying that for years, but here's one for you- your complacancy will be yours."

"I'll pretend I didn't hear that. Have good day, Diego." Killer ends the call, highly pissed off.

Killer then tries one more number. On the first ring, someone answers.

"Amos, I never thought I would ever hear your voice again."

"I didn't think I'd ever need a reason to call, but I need a favor."

"For you, anything."

"Well, it's not quite for me, but for a friend of a friend of a friend."

"Well, any friend of a friend of a friend of yours is a friend of mine. What's the situation?"

"A plane on its way to Beirutwas hijacked just a little while ago. I'm not sure exactly when or where yet, but I'll get the details from Mac when I call him back."

"Douglas?" There's a slight pause, then the voice continues saying, "I can't do it, Amos. You know how I feel about him."

"Rebekah, I understand what you're saying. Mac hurt you, but this isn't for him, it's for a kid we know."

"I don't know about this. Can't you call someone else?" Rebekah asks.

"I did. They all either said no or didn't answer," Killer explains.

"I don't know, Amos. I don't know how I'll feel around him."

"I understand, but this kid really needs you. He's a great kid. He helped us out last year on our last job."

"The infamous West Point job that forced you guys out of the business?"

"The very one."

"This kid isn't in the business too, is he?"

"No. He was a cadet at the time. He's now a second lieutenant in the Army. You'd really like him."

"I bet."

There is a brief moment of silence, which Rebekah breaks by saying, "Okay. I'll help you, but make sure you let Douglas know I'm not doing this for him."

"You got it," Killer says with a huge grin on his face. He then asks, "You still have the same e-mail address?"

"I do."

"Good. I'll send you the information that way as soon as I get it. I'll call you first, though"

"Okay. I'll be standing by."

"Thanks, Becca."

"It's always a pleasure, Amos," Rebakah states before hanging up her phone.

A blue van speeds down the highway. The five occupants sit in silence as they drive further and further away from Damascus International Airport. The men breathe heavily. They have just done the impossible; they hijacked an airplane during the post-9/11 era. No one in their right mind would have attempted such a foolish and brazen feat, but they all have Allah on their side, as these men believe.

The hijackers were smart enough not to begin their activities in the United States. That would have been a suicide mission. Since most of Europe did not change its airline policies and procedures after 9/11, the hijackers were able to accomplish their task with very little resistance. The worst thing that happened to one of them during their hijack is that one of the passengers threw up on their legs.

On the van floor lies a large black body bag. The bag has lied motionless on the floor for nearly an hour. As the men quietly sit, the bag begins to squirm.

A voice from inside begins to mumble, saying, "Hey! Where am I? Let me out of here!"

One of the men who sits across from the bag kicks it extremely hard. The person inside the bag grunts from the blow and moans in pain.

The man who kicked the bag then shouts, "You better shut your mouth if you want to see your family again!"

The person inside the bag does not say another word. The men can hear light whimpering coming from inside the bag, which causes them to laugh hysterically. Other than the driver, they all take turns poking at the bag.

Two hours into the drive and the five men finally approach a small town. They slow their speed down, adhering to all of the local traffic laws. The last thing the successful hijackers want to do is ruin their good fortune by attracting unneeded attention. The driver guides the blue van carefully through the town and does not stop until they reach a small mosque.

When the blue van pulls in front of the mosque, two men rush from the inner courtyard and swing the front gates open. The blue van comes to a complete stop. The side door opens and the van's occupants rush out carrying the black body bag and expediently enter the mosque courtyard. The gate is closed shut and the blue van takes off down the road.

The men carrying the black body bag are led to the mosque. Several men wielding AK-47s greet the men as they move through the courtyard.

"Salam muhlaykum! Allah ahkbar!" the AK-47 wielding men shout.

"Muhlaykum salam! Uh humdih Allah!" the four men from the blue van joyfully reply.

Inside the mosque, the men enter the prayer room, which is situated in the center of the mosque. They drop the body bag without any reservation.

"Ah!" the person in the bag grunts as he hits the ground.

The men laugh at the person in the bag's pain and discomfort.

One of the men laughingly says, "I hope he doesn't think he's in pain yet, 'cause he's about to discover what it really is."

The men flip the body bag over so that the zipper is showing on top. One of the men reaches down and unzips the body bag. As soon as the body bag is open, three of the men reach inside and snag its occupant.

Dangling in their arms is a battered and weary Marcos Bakoos. His hair is caked in blood, which was caused by the initial blow he took to the head on the airplane. There is a small bruise on his neck, which resulted from one of the beatings he took in the van ride from the airport.

The men drop Marcos to the ground with no care.

When Marcos hits the ground, one of the men barks at him saying, "Don't move or we will kill you!"

Marcos lies in place. He does not move in fear that the men will follow through on their threat. Marcos wants to cry, but the fear is so intense that he is unable to do anything. He can barely think. It is probably best that he is mentally and physically incapacitated. Death is all that is on Marcos' mind. Survival is not a possibility that he can fathom.

"Get the chains and cinder blocks!" one of the men shouts.

Two men run out of the prayer room as ordered. A couple of minutes later, they return carrying two long, heavy chains and two cinder blocks. The man carrying the chains kneels down beside Marcos and ties them around his wrists. Two other men then hoist Marcos into the air, while another stands on a chair and works the free end of the chain through a loop in the ceiling. The man steps off of the chair and assists the two men who were holding Marcos pull the chain. The force of the pulling throws Marcos' arms straight over his head, causing him to dangle in the air. Next, another man grabs the cinder blocks and places them beneath Marcos' feet. One man holds Marcos' legs to keep them from swinging in the air, while another wraps the other chain around his ankles, then through the cinder block holes. The cinder blocks, in their position, keeps Marcos from freeing freely in the air.

With Marcos properly secured, the man who was barking all of the orders walks to the far side of the prayer room. Alone, the man pulls his cell phone out of his pocket and dials a series of numbers. After a few rings someone from the other end answers.

"Hello?"

"Uncle, we have him."

"Good. I will inform the others. Have you made the video yet?"

"Not yet, uncle, but we are doing that next. I just wanted to inform you of our progress."

"Very well. Continue on as you are. Call me again when you have completed all of your tasks."

"Yes, sayed."

The man on the other end of the telephone ends the call. The man who made the call returns his cell phone to his pocket and walks back to the group.

"Get the video equipment!" the man orders the others.

One of the men hastily exits the prayer room and, within a moment's time, returns carrying a small video camera. The man who is seemingly in charge of the group pulls a sheet of paper from out of his back pocket and unfolds it. He carefully reads the contents of the paper to himself to ensure that it has all of the elements that his uncle had instructed him to have Marcos say.

After reading the paper, the man nods his head in favor, then says, "All right. Let's do the video so we can finish this."

The man holding the video camera steps in front of Marcos. Turning the camera on, the man focuses the lens on Marcos' face.

"I am ready whenever you are," the cameraman announces.

The man holding the paper stands beside Marcos and holds the paper in front of him at chest level.

"Start filming," the man orders.

The cameraman presses record. The red light instantly shines, signaling that the camera is recording.

"Read," the man softly, yet with much anger, whispers in Marcos' ear.

Marcos looks down at the paper and reads what is presented before him:

My name is Marcos Paulos Bakoos. I am the son of Paulos Bakoos Sargon, the President of Lebanon. The men who hold me do not belong to an organization. They do Allah's work and are willing to die for him. I cannot say why these men of Allah have taken me, but if you want me to return with my life, you must give them twenty-five million American dollars within five days of receiving this tape. The size of the bills does not matter. Place the money in black plastic trash bags at ten in the morning at the Beirut city dump.

Finished reading the statement, the cameraman stops filming Marcos. He rewinds the tape, then shows it to the others to ensure they filmed what they want President Paulos to see. Satisfied with the product, the cameraman re winds the tape again and takes it out of the video camera. He places the videotape in a small box and hands it off to someone, who then leaves the prayer room, never to return.

With all of their technical work complete, the man who was holding the paper for Marcos shouts, "Go out there and make sure they're securing the courtyard and the hallway! Things are going too well for us to mess up now!"

The men all rush out of the room, leaving the one man who was barking the orders, alone with Marcos. He slowly walks around Marcos' hanging body, staring at it up and down. The man stops in front of Marcos and throws his face directly in front of his.

The man spits in Marcos' face, saying, "You are nothing: nobody. I hope your infidel father doesn't get the money so I can have more fun with you. I've never killed a Christian before, but I read that the Romans had fun doing it. I don' have lions, but my knife will do just fine."

The man steps away from Marcos' face and moves behind him. He grabs Marcos' collar and tears off every layer of clothing covering his upper body until nothing remains but his bare skin. The man tosses Marcos clothes away from him, then takes off his brown leather belt and wraps the leather end around his hand twice. The man takes a step back, then unleashes a wild swing.

When the buckle impacts with Marcos' unprotected flesh, he lets out a loud scream. Marcos has never been struck in such a manner and has not felt such intense pain since he broke his arm playing soccer when he was eleven.

Again, the man strikes Marcos. This time the belt wraps slightly around his waist. Marcos lets out another yelp. Again and again, the man whips Marcos. The excruciating pain causes Marcos to cry uncontrollably. He does not want to cry, but what can he do in such a predicament.

In all, the man whips Marcos eleven times. The pain from the beating knocks Marcos out. His back is now nothing more than one large red, swollen, welt. The man laughs at Marcos' condition, pushing his body with his free hand.

Done amusing himself, the man wipes his bloody hand and belt clean on Marcos' pants, then loops the belt back around his waist. The man pulls his cell phone from out of his pocket and hits the re-dial button.

After two rings someone answers the phone saying, "Hello?"

"Uncle, we're finished," the man declares.

"Very good nephew. You sent the message?"

"Yes, sir. The tape is on its way as we speak."

"Very good. I am very proud of you and your friends. You are doing a great work for Allah and our people"

"Thank you, uncle. You always told me I would one day have a chance to serve Allah."

"And now you are. Go in peace, nephew."

"And you, uncle."

1930 HRS: DAMASCUS, SYRIA

MAJOR REMOVES HIMSELF FROM AGAINST THE wall. Tapping his front pocket, Major says to Ben, "I'm going to the bathroom."

"Got you," Ben replies, understanding what Major is up to.

Major enters the nearest restroom. Locking the door behind him, he pulls out his cell phone and calls Mac back.

After a few rings, Mac answers saying, "I'm glad you called me back. Is everything all right?"

"Yeah," Major replies. "No one was hurt."

Mac interjects, stating, "Tell me everything from start to finish."

"Okay. This Arab dude held one of the stewardesses hostage with a steak knife to her throat and walked her down the aisle. He told us that if we did anything stupid, he'd kill her. After that, these other two Arab dudes knocked my boy Marcos up side the head, then dragged him to the back. While they were taking Marcos to the back, the dude holding the stewardess stood by the cockpit door waiting for one of his partners to return. When one of them did show up, they forced the stewardess to coax the captain into opening the door. From there, them fools took over the friggin' plane. The two guys stayed in the cockpit for a while, then one of them left and went back to the back. I couldn't see what was going on in the back or in the cockpit. That's when I decided to call you. Anyway, after talking to you and going back to my seat, we stayed cool and waited to land. When we hit the ground, the dude that stayed in the cockpit walked out holding a knife to one of the pilots' throats. He forced him to the back, then threw him to the ground. They took off after that. I really couldn't see what happened after that. We didn't want to turn around in fear of getting someone killed. Anyway, me and Ben looked out the window to see if anything was going on outside. We saw a blue rusted out van, like a Chevy van, and two other Arab looking dudes holding a ladder. When the plane stopped, them dudes ran up to the plane with the ladder. After a few seconds, all five of them dudes ran to the van. Two of them were carrying a big black bag and two others were carrying the ladder. Anyway, as soon as the van left and we were sure that the three dudes from the flight were gone, too, me and Ben went to see what was up. When we got to the back, we didn't see Marcos and being that he hasn't popped up now, I'm assuming that they took him. Right now, the rescue people are on their way."

"Where'd you guys fly out of?"

"BWI."

"Any connections?"

"Yeah. We had one in Frankfurt."

"What was the model of your plane?"

"Beats me. It's the one with the two aisles downstairs, the business class in the far front, and the first class and cockpit upstairs."

"You guys fly coach or first class?"

"First class."

"Okay, so they had you guys isolated."

"Yeah."

"Not bad. Pretty smart, actually. Your friend, Marcos, is he anyone important?" Mac asks.

"No, but his dad is?"

"Who's his dad?"

"He's the President of Lebanon."

"You guys were heading to Beirut, right?"

"Yeah."

"Lot of nice women in Beirut."

"So people keep telling me."

"Other than the women, why were you going there?"

"Marcos' dad invited us for New Years."

"New Year's in Beirut. That's different. My knowledge on world affairs sucks at the moment, which definitely doesn't help you guys out any. I can tell you this much, though. If those Arabs made it a point to capture Marcos, they more than likely are not going to kill him any time soon. That's to our advantage. If I were a betting man, I'd say they're going to ransom him. Whether a money exchange will return your friend home safely is beyond my knowledge, at this time. I don't want to have to rely on the bad guys' generosity for your friend's safe return. You know what I'm saying?"

"I hear you. So you and Killer are going to work this?"

"The Killer's not in on this one, little brother."

"Oh. You can handle this on your own?"

"I don't know. Killer is working on getting me someone, though. Someone I can trust."

"Cool. Is there anything you need us to do?"

"You want to tag along on this one?"

"Hell yes!"

"All right then. Meet me in Athens tomorrow morning."

"We'll be there."

"I don't think I need to tell you this but, nonetheless, when you speak to the authorities, play dumb."

"We will."

"All right then. You guys take care of yourselves. I'll see you tomorrow."

2000 HRS: NEW YORK CITY, NEW YORK

A BLACK HUMMER RACES DOWN THE Henry Hudson Parkway. In and out of traffic, the Hummer races, passing vehicles as though they are moving at a crawl. The Hummer's driver is aware of his high rate of speed, but two variables are of a concern: one, his friend is in need of immediate help and two; he knows that the police rarely monitor the parkway for speeding.

As the Hummer speeds along its course, the cell phone inside rings. The driver presses a button to answer the incoming call.

"Mac, I got someone to tag along with you," Killer informs Mac.

"Who you got?" Mac asks as he rolls the windows of his Hummer up in order to better hear his friend.

"You're not going to like this."

"Who?"

"Rebekah."

"Hell no! That woman hates me."

"It's the best I can do, brother. No one else'll help us out."

"You've got to be kidding me."

"For both of your sakes, I wish I were. She isn't too thrilled about working with you either."

"Well, she shouldn't be."

Killer laughs at his friend's tirade, then asks, "You got anything for me?"

"Yeah. Three Arab dudes hijacked a plane heading from Frankfurt to Beirut."

"Tell me again why in the hell Major's in Beirut?"

"That's part of it. His friend, Marcos was kidnapped. What's interesting about Marcos is that he is the son of the President of Lebanon."

"Really? That's interesting because about a year or so ago, there was an assassination attempt on the Lebanese President."

"You think it's connected with this?"

"Knowing how that part of the world operates, I'd say yes."

"Tomorrow, I think they're going to announce that they want a ransom for Marcos."

"I agree. Let me do some digging, and I'll get back with you. Take your laptop so I can instant message you, just in case you're already in the air. Oh! Where are you staging?"

"Athens. Have Rebekah meet me at our regular spot at twelve."

"All right. I'll start making preparations. I'll call you back in a few."

DAMASCUS, SYRIA: DAMASCUS INTERNATIONAL AIRPORT

BEN AND MAJOR SIT INSIDE THE Damascus International Airport security office. With them is the US attaché to Jordan who, ironically enough, just happens to have been Major's first semester Arabic instructor from West Point: LTC Paul Jackman. LTC Jackman flew in as soon as the word spread that the Lebanese President's son was kidnapped.

"LT Johnson," LTC Jackman opens, "it's good to see you again, despite the circumstances."

"Same here, sir," Major replies. He then asks, "So, what happens now, sir?"

"We're going to fly you and LT Irons home," LTC Jackman answers.

"What about Marcos, sir?" Ben asks.

"Don't worry guys," LTC Jackman comforts the two lieutenants. "The State Department is working the situation. Because of who you guys are, though, I'll let you know that "other" agencies are working this, as well."

"So you think Marcos will get out of this all right?" Major questions.

LTC Jackman lowers his head and replies, "I can't guarantee anything. All I can do is assure you that our government, along with the Arab League, is doing everything in its power to ensure that your friend is returned home safely."

LTC Jackman's words of assurance cause Major and Ben to simply look at one another. Their confidence in the United States government and the Arab League in rescuing Marcos unharmed is not very high.

Breaking the silence, Ben asks LTC Jackman, "What time are you flying us out of here, sir? We may as well get back home as soon as we can."

"I agree, LT Irons," LTC Jackman answers. "There's a flight that leaves out of here at 2130 hrs. It'll fly into Munich, Germany and then to Dulles International Airport. We've already contacted your families, so they'll be standing by at Dulles upon your arrival."

"Great," Major cynically replies under his breath.

"What was that?" LTC Jackman asks, turning and facing Major.

"Oh, nothing, sir," Major quickly responds. "I was just saying that it's great that we'll be able to return home so soon."

"Sir, should we expect anymore questioning when we arrive stateside?" Ben asks.

"No, we've got everything we need, though if we do capture the guys who got your friend, we'll have to contact you to ID them. Other than that, we shouldn't need you."

"Good deal," Major simply responds.

"Are we free to go now, sir?" Ben asks.

"Certainly." LTC Jackman reaches into his inside suit jacket pocket and pulls out two airline tickets. "Here you go," LTC Jackman says as he hands Major and Ben their new airplane tickets. He then says, "The receptionist has your bags. You guys need any help getting to the terminal?"

"No, sir," Major replies. "We'll be fine. We've got over an hour to kill anyway."

"All right then," LTC Jackman responds.

As Ben and Major prepare to leave the room, LTC Jackman states, "Don't forget, guys, you did all you could. There's nothing more you could have done, under the circumstances."

"Thanks, sir," Ben replies as he and Major step out of the room.

The two friends walk to the receptionist's desk and retrieve their luggage. Their bags in hand, Major and Ben leave the security office and enter the main airport terminal and head for their new gate.

Away from prying eyes and ears, Ben says, "We're not going home are we?"

"Hell no!" Major blurts.

"Good. I was hoping you'd say that. So, how do you want to handle this?"

"Mac wants us to meet him in Athens tomorrow, but we can't go there from here. The Army and the State Department are looking for us to get on that plane home."

"Right, but we can switch planes in Germany."

"You think so?"

"Yeah. They're expecting us to go home. They're thinking that if we were going to do anything stupid, we'd do it here where we're close to where everything happened."

"I think you're right! They're probably not going to be looking for us to switch planes in Germany 'cause as far as they're concerned, we're already in the mindset of getting home. Throw in the fact that our parents are expecting us, too. These guys don't know who they're dealing with!"

Ben laughs, then continues, saying, "When we get to Germany, we'll simply go to the desk and get our destination switched from Dulles to Athens."

"Seems simple enough."

"It should be."

"Man! Mom's not going to like this," Major laughingly comments.

"You're telling me. First West Point, now this! How many times can lightning strike in one place?"

"Looking at us, I'd say at least twice. How about we just call my dad and let him tell my mom and your parents?"

"Yeah, that works for me. It's a shame we can't just say we're going to hang out in Germany for New Years instead."

"Why don't we do that?"

"You're crazy. We can't tell our parents that."

"I'm all about telling the truth, but do you really think your mom can handle hearing my dad tell her that her son is going to the Middle East to rescue a friend? I doubt she's going to be down with that plan."

"Good point, but what if we die?"

"We won't have to worry about it. We'll be dead."

"You're cold, Major."

"Got to be. I say we call my dad and tell him that we're going to do the New Years thing. If he buys it, then you call your parents and tell them the same thing. If my dad doesn't buy our story, then we'll tell him the truth and make him deal with it. He's a smart guy. I think that even if he doesn't believe me, he'll say that he does because he knows we're going to do what we're going to do. You know what I mean?"

"I hear you."

Major reaches into his pocket, where he had placed his ticket and looks at it with an upset look on his face, saying, "Cheap friggin' Army!"

"What's up, man?" Ben asks.

"They knew we flew first-class, yet they have us in mother friggin' coach! You've got to be kidding me. Some way to say thank you."

"We haven't done anything yet."

"Okay, but we will."

"Right, but we haven't yet."

"Yeah: yeah: yeah: Mother friggin' semantics. All I'm saying is we flew first-class down here. They should've put us back on first-class."

"Major, you need to calm down. We're flying three hours to Germany on coach. What's the big deal?"

"You're right, cousin. My bad."

Ben and Major continue on their way through the airport terminal. Walking unhindered is not much of a problem due to the time of the evening. There are not very many people remaining in the airport, and the majority who are just flew in on arriving flights. The two friends do not stop walking until they reach their departure gate.

Killer makes one final phone call to one of his most reliable Middle East informants. After a couple of rings a man answers.

"Killer, I was not expecting to ever hear from you again," the man says.

"I wish I were calling you to say hello, Majed," Killer replies.

"How can I help?"

"Mac needs some information, and he needs it like yesterday."

"What do you need?"

"You heard about the Lebanese President's son being kidnapped today on a hijacked plane?"

"I saw it on CNN just a few minutes ago."

"What do you know?"

"That's a good question. Technically, nothing, but I know who I can speak to to figure out what's going on."

"How confident are you that you can get the info by tomorrow night?"

"If the situation is what I think it is, I shouldn't have a problem."

"That's what I'm talking about. You always come through. Now, where and how do you want Mac to link up with you?"

"Have him fly to Beirut and drive to the town of Masnaa. It's on the Syrian border. I have a safe house there. When he gets to Masnaa, I'll be wearing an NWO t-shirt and a silver and blue ring with a blue stone in the center on my right hand. Mac can find me near a park. From there, I'll take him to the house."

"Sounds like a plan. I'll trust you to have the information and weapons ready for them upon their arrival."

"Them?"

"I'm sorry. Mac's going to have three other people with him: two guys and a woman. The guys are friends of the target and friends of ours."

"Okay: Understood. It shouldn't be a problem, and yes, everything will be ready for them."

28 December 2001, 0300 hrs: Beirut, Lebanon

MAJED TURNS HIS CELL PHONE OFF and returns it to his pocket.

'Going to see some action,' Majed says to himself as he grabs his jacket before heading out the door. As Majed walks down the empty downtown street, he continues to think to himself. 'Now, if everything is occurring as I know it is, I'm going to have to see Ibrahim about this. He always knows what's going on, and the fact that I have a feeling that the Grand Ayatollah Ali may be mixed up in this gives me more of a reason to speak with Ibrahim first.'

After walking for about ten minutes or so, Majed finally reaches the Al-Omari mosque and strides in.

In the front lobby, a man approaches Majed and asks, "How may I help you?"

"I need to speak with Sayed Ibrahim," Majed replies.

"Do you realize what time it is?"

"Yes, I do, but that is of no concern of mine. Tell Sayed Ibrahim that it's his old friend, Majed."

The man looks at Majed suspiciously, but nonetheless, he walks off to inform his leader of his visitor. Because it is so early in the morning, the man must exit the mosque and walk to Sayed Ibrahim's modest home, which is located in the rear of the courtyard. Majed only waits about twenty minutes before the man returns.

"Sayed Ibrahim will see you in his office," the man informs Majed. "I will take you to him."

"No thank you," Majed retorts. "I know the way."

Majed brushes by the man and walks down the long corridor, heading for Sayed Ibrahim's office. Majed knows exactly where he is going. He has made several visits in the past to pick Sayed Ibrahim's brain. Majed does not revere Sayed Ibrahim as others do, other than the fact that he respects him because he is an old man, who happens to also be wise.

Majed is a Muslim by birth, but that is as far as he gets with his religion. He and his family, as far as Majed can remember, were never practicing Muslims. In fact, Majed's father was a very active Communist during the 1950s and '60s. When Majed was a child, his grandfather used to attend mosque regularly on Fridays, but he was by no means overzealous in how he practiced his faith.

Sayed Ibrahim is one of the few men who has his finger on the pulse on the entirety of the Muslim world. Islamic leaders from all sects from every continent on the globe come to him for guidance, mentorship, and advice. Whenever Majed needs to know what is occurring in the Muslim world, all he has to do is visit Sayed Ibrahim and, without hesitation, he tells him everything he needs to know.

Majed is able to speak with Sayed Ibrahim freely because he saved his life once, many years ago. Through the course of that encounter, Sayed Ibrahim came to learn that Majed, though he was paid to kill and destroy, never did so against the good or the innocent. For these two reasons, Sayed Ibrahim has never had an issue divulging information to Majed.

Majed approaches Sayed Ibrahim's door and knocks lightly three times.

"Enter," Sayed Ibrahim says from the other side of the door.

Majed opens the door and enters Sayed Ibrahim's office.

At the first sight of Majed entering his office, Sayed Ibrahim says, "I hope this is important, Majed. You couldn't wait for the sun to rise before seeing me?"

"I apologize, Ibrahim, but to answer your question, no, this could not wait," Majed states as he walks over to the sitting area.

"So, what is so important?" Sayed Ibrahim asks as he gets comfortable in his cushioned armchair.

Because Sayed Ibrahim was awaken so unexpectedly in the early morning, he is not wearing his normal garb. Instead of the regular white dish dash, black cloak, and black headdress, Sayed Ibrahim is wearing a dark green bathrobe and a pair of slippers.

Side stepping Sayed Ibrahim's question, Majed asks, "You got a new guy guarding the front, huh?"

"You are so observant," Sayed Ibrahim replies.

"Where's the regular guy? I kind of liked him," Majed states.

"He went away for a while. He should be back in a few days."

"Where'd he go?" Majed asks as he takes a seat on the brown leather couch, across from Sayed Ibrahim

Sayed Ibrahim attempts to change the topic of discussion by asking, "Would you like some tea?"

"Why are you changing the subject, sayed? You know I rarely drink tea with you, and so you know, I will answer your question, once you answer mine."

"It's always best to be polite, but I swear: an Arab man who does not like tea: How unusual."

Majed smiles and nods his head, in response to Sayed Ibrahim's words.

Majed then says, "So, where is your regular night guy?"

"As I said, he is away for a while, but he will return in a few days or so."

"Sayed, I do not have time to play word games with you. Usually, I don't mind because you keep me on my toes and keep me thinking, but today, time is of the essence."

"How so, Majed?"

"Some people I know want to find President Paulos' son."

"May I ask why?"

"I'm not really sure why. I'm told that some friends of his want him back: Can't say that I blame them."

"It is a tragedy, is it not? First they attempt to take his life. Now, they kidnap his son."

"You said they."

"Yes, I did."

"Are you saying that the same individuals committed both acts?"

"I may? Or I could be saying that the same individuals are responsible for both acts. It's all semantics, my son."

"That's true, but right now, I'm not concerned with word games. I just want the information."

"What do you know?"

"I know that who ever did this isn't keeping the boy in Lebanon, or I'd already know where he is. That leaves Syria and Jordan. I don't think it's Jordan, though because of the politics behind the act. Syria's more ideal for activity like this. The obvious reason they're in Syria, though is because they landed in Damascus. They'd be stupid to attempt a border crossing carrying a hostage."

Sayed Ibrahim softly claps his hands in acknowledgment of Majed's words.

"You are such a bright young man," Sayed Ibrahim commends. "You've almost figured this out all on your own."

"And since you said that, Sayed," Majed replies, "it's safe for me to assume that you know the rest."

"That I do. There is some information that I just can't indulge."

"There's a life on the line!"

"That is true, but the real question is who's life?"

"What's that supposed to mean?"

Sayed Ibrahim rises from his seat, saying, "I want you to take a look at something."

Sayed Ibrahim gingerly walks to his desk and steps behind it. He bends down very slowly. His old body is not as agile as it once was. At the bottom desk drawer, Sayed Ibrahim unlocks and opens it. He sifts through the papers and items that fill the drawer, until he finds a manila envelope. Sayed Ibrahim retrieves the envelope and slowly returns to his seat.

As he sits down, Sayed Ibrahim tosses the manila envelope to Majed, saying, "I want you to look at this."

Majed opens the envelope, discovering a large photograph. He removes the photograph and stares at it for a moment.

"This isn't what I think it is, is it?" Majed asks Sayed Ibrahim.

"Yes, it is," Sayed Ibrahim answers.

"But." Majed pauses for a while, then says, "I know these guys are real, but how the hell are they involved?"

"You do not have to worry about them. On the other hand, those you seek do."

"This isn't good, sayed."

"For those you seek, no it is not."

"So tell me sayed, what is going on?"

"The boy was taken for blood money."

"How so?"

"The man bearing that tattoo was killed before he could complete his job."

"Yes, I know about that."

"But you do not understand the consequence behind his pre-mature death."

"Help me understand."

"Because he died without completing his contract, someone must pay for the loss."

"So those somebodies are the ones who kidnapped the president's son."

"Exactly."

"And the ransom is like another way of completing the contract?"

"In a way. It is better if you say that if the one you seek receives the money, then he will regain his life."

"What happens if I get the boy before the one I'm looking for gets his money?"

"All we can do my son, is pray for his soul because his life will be taken from him most earnestly."

"Where can I find the boy, sayed?"

"Why should I help you further, Majed?"

"Because me rescuing this boy is the right thing to do. That's why."

"If I help you, Majed, I will lose an old friend."

"Sayed, you lose old friends everyday. That's what happens to old people."

"Don't get cynical with me, boy. You know what I mean."

"No I don't. If I knew who your friend was, then maybe I would. I can only imagine all of the other people that this supposed friend of yours has hurt in the past. I don't know who the man is, but I already know that he tried to kill our president and now he holds his son hostage. This man is not a good person. Good people don't do these kinds of things. He's hiding behind the name of Allah, sayed. That's all he is doing."

"If I help you, my friend will surely die."

"Not by my hands, he won't, and not by my colleagues' either, if he doesn't get in our way."

"I know, but they will kill him."

"Maybe so, but that's the risk he was willing to take. A life for a life: Isn't that how they do it?"

"If the stories are true, yes."

"They're not stories, sayed. They're real, and it seems to me as though your friend got himself caught up in something that he cannot control. He was doomed to lose from the start."

Sayed Ibrahim holds his head down. He knows Majed's words are true. He was afraid that his old friend would get caught up in a vicious circle, unable to find his way out.

"I will not tell you who my friend is. If we are both correct, Allah will sort this all out in the end. I will tell you this, though. Go to the town of Ad Dimas in Syria. There is only one Shi'a'a mosque in the town. You will find the boy there."

"That's where your old guard is, huh?"

"Yes."

"Sheep." Majed then rises to his feet and says, "Thank you, sayed. I hope you understand that I'm doing the right thing."

"I know you are, son," Sayed Ibrahim replies as he too, rises to his feet. He continues, saying, "It's just that all of this death and violence. You would think that old people would no longer have a taste for it. I killed many men in my youth in the name of Allah, but there are days when I regret some of those killings, but that is neither here nor there. Go. Do what you must, Majed. May Allah watch over you and protect you."

"Thank you, sayed," Majed replies.

The two men shake hands, then kiss one another three times on the cheek.

SOMEWHERE OVER NORTHERN EUROPE

MAC SITS COMFORTABLY IN HIS SEAT. His flight from Newark International Airport departed at three in the afternoon. To bide his time while he waits for Killer to instant message him, Mac listens to a little Frank Sinatra: something to keep his spirits up and his mind off of the action to come. Mac does not fly nearly as much as he used to, but when he does, it is first-class all the way. On this flight, he is pleased that his adjoining seat is not occupied. On mission flights, Mac does not like people bothering him while he mentally prepares. Recreational trips are another story. Today is not recreation.

In the empty seat beside him, Mac has his laptop lying open with the internet connection on. Looking at the screen, Mac notices that Killer has finally contacted him.

"bought time,' Mac types.

'stop your crying. I did all the work,' Killer replies.

Mac laughs, then types, 'true true. what you got for me?'
'bekah will meet you at the café tomorrow.'
'fine.'
'i got you 4 plane tickets leaving tomorrow night for Beirut.'
'the kids don't fly in until tomorrow night.'
'don't worry. did some checking. they land tomorrow morning.'
'what time?'
'11 from munich.'
'ok. Have bekah meet me at 12.'
'that's cutting it kind of close.'
'she's a big girl. she'll be ok. what else you got?'
'got you a safe house in a border town called Masnaa. when you get to the town, find a guy wearing an nwo t-shirt and a silver and blue ring w/a blue stone in it on his right hand. he'll be near a park. he'll take you to the house.'
'how quaint. anything else?'
'no. he'll have more info for you. here's what i could gather.'
Killer forwards Mac a file attachment.
'I'll read it when I land. weapons?'
'in the house.'
'thanks brother.'
'always. call me when you get home. The kids miss you.'
'most def. Body slam 'em for me! HA!'
The two friends log off of the internet. Mac shuts his computer down and returns the laptop to its case. He then leans back in his seat and takes a much needed rest.

0420 HRS: AD DIMAS, SYRIA

AD DIMAS IS A VERY TRANQUIL town. With its small size of only ten thousand people, the population is still rather diverse. There is a strong Sunni community, comprising of roughly seventy-five percent of the population. The Shia'a population is only fifteen percent. The Christian population, which comprises of Chaldean Assyrians, makes up the other ten percent of the population.

Sunni mosques litter the entirety of Ad Dimas. There are two Catholic churches because the Assyrians live in the north and central sections of the town. The Shia'a, on the other hand, have only one mosque because the bulk of their people live in eastern Ad Dimas.

Majed drives through Ad Dimas in order to become situated with the town. He has been to Ad Dimas before, but only in passing. Until now, Majed has never had a reason to spend any time in Ad Dimas. During his reconnaissance, Majed parks his vehicle several times and walks throughout the neighborhoods to gain his bearings and get a better feel for the streets.

As Majed recons the town, his investigation brings him to the realization that he needs to head for the east side of Ad Dimas. Going to the Shia'a community makes since. The Sunni and Assyrians would not dare harbor the men who are holding Marcos Bakoos hostage. If his captors have half a brain, the community around them is ignorant of their activities.

Majed passes by the mosque in question. From the outside, all appears normal. The wall around the mosque is too high for Majed to see into the courtyard. The gate is not locked, which at first does not make sense, but in retrospect, it does. If the gate were locked, then the populace would be aware that something is going on in their mosque. By keeping the front gate unlocked, the people assume that it is business as usual at the mosque.

Majed drives past the mosque and turns right at the next street. Pulling up a few feet, Majed parks the minivan alongside the curb. Before getting out of the minivan, Majed takes his digital camera out with him. He walks down the street in the direction from which he was driving. At the next corner, Majed turns right, then takes another right at the end of the block. Continuing on his path, Majed reaches another corner. Now, he is able to see the mosque again, which is situated to his front right. Directly across the street from the mosque is a two-story primary school.

Majed looks down at his watch and says to himself, 'Fifteen minutes to morning prayers.'

To pass the time, Majed indiscriminately takes a few pictures of the surrounding neighborhood and the mosque. Having taken enough photographs, Majed turns his attention to the school. He looks at the mosque, focusing on the tower.

'There could be someone up there,' Majed says to himself. 'I need to get a closer look.'

Majed steps off of the corner and heads for the back of the school. Out of the sight of any possible prying eyes, Majed covertly climbs over the wall that surrounds the school. Within the perimeter of the school, Majed runs to the nearest set of stairs and sprints up. When he reaches the second floor, he runs to the side that faces the mosque.

Unfortunately, Majed has no means of seeing the mosque from where he stands, so he is forced to break into a classroom. The lock on the door is not very sophisticated, which makes breaking into the classroom quite simple.

Now in the classroom, Majed tactfuly moves to the window, ensuring that no one from the outside can see him. Majed takes his digital camera and takes a quick photograph of the mosque's prayer tower. The picture taken, Majed looks at the display screen, and zooms in on the picture as much as it is able.

'Just what I thought,' Majed thinks as he looks at the picture.

The screen displays a man in the prayer tower wielding an AK-47.

'We're going to have to take him out first before we do anything,' Majed says to himself as he runs out of the classroom.

Majed darts down the stairs and immediately scales over the same portion of the wall that he initially came over. Landing on his feet, Majed looks to his left and right, then heads for the same corner that he was standing on earlier.

When he arrives at the corner, Majed looks at his watch again and realizes that the regularly scheduled morning prayers are going to occur in a few seconds. Without stopping, Majed immediately walks across the street, directly for the mosque. On the other side of the road, Majed heads for the front gate. When he reaches the gate, he raises his hand to undo the latch.

As soon as Majed touches the gate handle, a man suddenly appears, ordering, "Do not open the gate!"

"But I have come for morning prayers," Majed replies.

"The mosque is closed for renovations. Didn't you get the word?"

"I just returned home from out of town. I didn't know the mosque was being renovated today."

"Well, it is!"

"Where should I go to pray? I always pray at the mosque."

During the middle of the conversation, the loudspeakers that are on the prayer tower begin to blare the morning prayer.

Talking over the prayer, the guard says, "Pray at your home. Allah hears you wherever you are."

"That is very true. All praises to Allah. Well, it's good to know that the money I give to the mosque every week is being put to good use."

"Yes it is."

"Well you have a good day," Majed says as he steps away from the mosque.

The man does not return Majed's kind gesture.

As Majed returns to his minivan, in the same direction from whence he came, he thinks to himself, 'Old Ibrahim came through, like always. There were at least thirty armed men in there. Marcos has to be in there. I'm not sure where, though, but that's not that big a deal. That mosque is small. It wouldn't take too long to do a thorough search. Being that Mac is as good as his reputation, he won't have any problems finding the kid. With four people and myself, we should be in and out in less than half an hour: assuming that all goes well, as it should.'

Majed reaches the minivan and casually gets in. Instead of continuing in a straight direction, Majed turns the minivan around and turns left at the corner. When Majed passes the mosque again, he raises his digital camera up just enough so that the lens is looking through the window, yet no one from the outside can see it. Majed fervently presses the button, snapping as many pictures as the camera will allow. After passing the mosque, Majed returns the camera to the passenger's seat.

Complete with his recon, Majed drives out of the Shia'a neighborhood and leaves Ad Dimas. He heads directly for Masnaa, without stopping. A short while later, Majed crosses the Lebanese-Syrian border with ease.

Majed quickly arrives in Masnaa and heads directly for a house. He parks the minivan in front of the house and immediately steps out. With the digital camera and a small black satchel in hand, Majed enters the house and heads for a small room in the back where there is a computer and high resolution color laser printer. Majed connects the digital camera to the computer and downloads the pictures. From the pictures that Majed downloads, he selects the best quality and information containing photographs, and then prints them in color.

Majed stacks the photographs and sits them on the desk. He then pulls out a notepad and a pen and commences to taking notes about each of the photographs. Majed retrieves a magnifying glass and peers close at some of the photographs. Attention to detail is a priority. He must be meticulous in his analysis. The more accurate information he can gather and piece together increases the success rate of Marcos' rescuers.

It takes a couple of hours for Majed to completely analyze the photographs. Finished, he matches each photograph with their respective set of notes, then neatly stacks the documents, places them into a folder, and then places the folder in his black satchel, along with the manila envelope.

Majed steps out of the room and enters another. He walks to the rear of the room where there is a large wooden cabinet. The cabinet door is locked. Majed reaches in his pocket and pulls out a set of keys. Finding the key he needs, Majed unlocks the cabinet and opens the door. Inside is an assortment of weapons: AK-47s, sniper rifles, forty-five millimeter pistols, daggers, etc. Majed conducts a functions check for each weapon to ensure that they all work properly. Satisfied, Majed returns the weapons to their original resting positions in the cabinet, then shuts and locks the door.

"This should do it," Majed says as he walks out of the room. "Now, all they need to do is get here."

MUNICH, GERMANY

MAJOR AND BEN ARRIVE IN MUNICH in the early morning with no problems. Flying coach was not as much of a hassle as Major thought it would be because the flight was nearly empty. Other than Ben and Major, there were maybe only fifty other people on the flight. Major and Ben were able to occupy an entire section to themselves, using the much appreciated space to get some much needed rest. Their long and interesting day had finally caught up with them.

When they exit the plane and enter the terminal, Ben says, "Call your dad. I'll see about switching our flights."

"Cool," Major replies handing Ben his ticket.

Ben and Major make their way through the airport until they find the airline ticket counters. Ben approaches the only open booth. It is not their airline, but experience has taught Ben that all of the airlines service one another, if and when they need to. While Ben handles the ticket issue, Major stands in the back to call his father.

Major retrieves his cell phone from his brief case, then scrolls through his phone book, stopping at his parent's home number.

After a few rings, COL Johnson answers the phone asking, "You guys all right?"

"Yeah, we're fine," Major replies.

"What happened? All they told me was that your plane was hijacked and that they were going to fly you guys home."

Major makes a conscience decision, and then asks to his father, "Do you want the truth or do you want me to tell you what you want to hear?"

"Give it to me straight."

"Marcos was kidnapped. Me and Ben're going to go get him."

"How're you going to do that?"

"The same way I got my medal."

"I don't like this."

"I didn't expect you to. I was going to tell you that we were going to stay in Germany and do New Year's with Ed, but I figured I'd tell you the truth instead."

"Well, for telling me the truth, I appreciate that, but other than that, I think it's best that you and Ben return home."

"We can't do that, dad."

"What makes you think that you and Ben can get Marcos better than the government?"

"We know people."

"You mean, Big Mac?"

"Yeah."

"I'm not going to even touch that one, but once wasn't enough for you, huh?"

"What do you mean?"

"How many times do you have to save the world, Milton?"

"I don't know about the world, dad. All I know is that my friend needs help and if roles were reversed, I pray that he would do the same for me. Nonetheless, this is something that we have to do."

"You're mother's not going to like this."

"When does she ever like anything I do?"

"That's true, but I think you need to think this one through a little better. There's a strong likelihood that you could lose your life on this rescue mission."

"We know that. It's a risk we're willing to take. There's nothing you can say that'll change our minds. We're doing this either way."

"You're right. I'll tell you're mom the New Year's story. She won't be able to handle the truth."

"Can you tell Ben's parent's too?"

"I could, but I'm not going to do that. Ben's going to have to do that one on his own. Personally, I think he should tell them the truth, as well. I can deal with your mom hating me for a while if you don't make it back, but I don't need his parents harping on me and blaming me for not stopping you two."

"I hear you."

"By the way, how are you calling me? You're cell phone number's showing on the caller ID."

"Terry had me get the international plan while I was on this trip."

"Good thinking on her part."

"Yeah. If you only knew."

While Major speaks to his father, Ben walks to the ticket counter and asks the attendant, "Do you speak English?"

"Yes, I do," the attendant replies.

"Thank, GOD. I was wondering, can you switch these flights for me and my friend?"

Ben points to Major who stands in the back talking on his cell phone. He then hands the attendant he and Major's airline tickets.

The attendant looks at the tickets and says, "Where would you like to change your destination to?"

"Athens," Ben simply replies.

"That should not be a problem, sir."

The attendant places the tickets in front of him and commences typing on the computer, in search of a flight to Athens, Greece.

After searching the computer database for a moment, the attendant looks up and says, "Sir, I have good news and bad news. The good news is that there is a flight leaving for Athens. The bad news is that the earliest flight does not depart until eight in the morning."

"That's not a problem. How much for the switch?"

The attendant punches away on the keyboard again. Finding the answers, he replies, "No charge, sir. Actually, if you like I can put you and your friend in first-class."

"Please do. My friend whined about us having to fly coach out here."

The attendant laughs, then says, "Very good, sir. I need to see some identification."

Ben pulls his passport out of his back pocket and hands it to the attendant.

"I need your friend's, as well," the attendant states.

"Hold on a second." Ben turns around and says loudly to Major, "You need you show your passport."

Major, who has finished speaking with his father, waives Ben over and says, "I need to holler at you real quick."

"Excuse me," Ben says to the attendant as he leaves the counter and walks to the position of his waiting friend. "What's up?" Ben asks as he approaches Major.

"I spoke to my dad," Major begins to explain. "I told him the real deal."

"What'd he say?"

"He doesn't like it, but he understands."

"Great."

"There's one thing, though. He says you should call your parents. He's not going to do it for you."

"Should I tell them?"

"I don't know, man. I mean, if they buy off on the whole New Year's thing and we make it back, then great, but if we don't, then what? I say you just give it to them straight and explain to them that it's something we have to do. Plus, your parents know you. When's the last time you backed away from a challenge? It's not their choice. They don't have to live with it. We do. You know what I'm saying?"

"I hear you."

Major hands Ben his phone and shows him how to call home.

Before Ben dials his dad's home telephone number, he says to Major, "Oh! I almost forgot. You need to show the guy your passport so we can get our tickets."

"Thanks," Major replies.

As Major heads for the ticket counter, Ben says to him, "By the way, we're flying first-class."

In mid-stride, Major pivots on his left foot, faces Ben, and says, "That's what I'm talking 'bout! Way to hook it up, cousin"

0700 HRS: BEIRUT, LEBANON

A HIGHLY DISTRAUGHT PRESIDENT PAULOS SITS behind his desk. In his office with him are the Lebanese Prime Minister, Rasul Haneen, the Defense Minister, Ziad Al Salah, the Minister of Justice, Hyder Abeer, and the chief investigative director, Arkan Mohamed. The four influential men convene with President Paulos to discuss the matter involving the recent hijacking and the situation around Marcos' abduction.

"Paulos," Prime Minister Rasul opens, "we all grieve for your loss. I promise you that we are going to use every resource at our disposall to find Marcos and his abductors."

"What do we know, so far?" President Paulos asks, attempting to distance himself form his obvious pain.

"Well," Director Arkan begins, "you've already read the report, so I'm not going to go into that. I have to be honest with you Mr. President; it doesn't look good for your son."

"What about Marcos' friends, LTs Irons and Johnson? Where are they now?"

"We sent a dispatch to the Jordanian attaché. He coordinated flights for them last night. They're not home yet, they will be soon," Minister Ziad explains.

"Very good," President Paulos says as he lets out a sigh. "Their parents must be relieved." He then asks, "Do you think that the same men who tried to kill me are the same ones who took my son?"

"That is highly probably and one that my men are currently following. I suspect that within the next couple of days or so, we will come across some solid leads," Director Arkan states.

"We don't have a couple of days," President Paulos protests. "They could kill my son at any moment!"

Full of frustration, President Paulos leaps to his feet and pounds his fists hard on his desk. At that moment, a knock is heard on his office door.

"Enter," Present Paulos barks.

The door opens and a small man enters the office carrying in his hands a small, rectangular, package.

"President Paulos, sir," the small man states, "this was just dropped off in the front lobby with explicit instructions for you to personally look at it. I think it is a video cassette."

"Do you know who brought it?" President Paulos asks.

"No, sir," the small man replies. "One of the janitors happened to come across it as he was sweeping this morning."

"Let me see that," Director Arkan states.

The small man hands the package to Director Arkan, then promptly steps out of President Paulos' office. With the small man out of the office, Director Arkan opens the package. When he removes the wrapper, Director Arkan discovers that the small man was correct; the package is a videocassette, after all. Director Arkan rise to his feet and walks to the television and VCR and turns them both on.

Before Director Arkan inserts the videocassette, he says to everyone, "I think we need to take a look at this."

The men all nod their heads in agreement.

Director Arkan inserts the videocassette and presses play. The five men watch the tape in shock. Before their eyes on the television screen is a bloodied Marcos Bakoos. Though it is not evident by watching the video, one can tell that Marcos is reading a pre-written message, which was obviously written by his captors. The Lebanese leaders boil with rage as the video progresses. Watching Marcos forcefully read the message makes their stomachs turn. Much to everyone's relief, after only a few seconds, the tape finally ends.

President Paulos rises from his seat and steps away from his desk, asking, "What is the likelihood of us getting twenty-five million dollars?"

"Not very good at all, I'm afraid," Prime Minister Rasul replies.

"I was afraid of that," President Paulos responds.

"We just don't have the money in the budget to risk losing that much money," Prime Minister Rasul tries to explain.

President Paulos walks towards the large window behind his desk and stares outside.

"I know. I know," President Paulos answers as he leans his right arm on the window.

While President Paulos and Prime Minister Rasul converse, Minister Arkan ejects the videocassette from the VCR.

Minister Arkan then states, "I'm going to take this tape and have my men analyze it as many times as it takes. We will not stop our efforts until we discover who these despicable men are who took your son, President Paulos."

"That is much appreciated," President Paulos replies.

It is now obvious to everyone present that gloom is beginning to set in President Paulos' demeanor. He does not sound at all confident with the current situation.

"I pray to GOD, gentlemen, that we are all able to find my son before a worse fate befalls him," President Paulos solemnly states. "I can only imagine what they will do to my Marcos if we do not deliver the money."

1130 HRS: ATHENS, GREECE

MAJOR AND BEN STEP OFF OF their plane and walk down the terminal, heading for the baggage claim. The two young men do not run, but they definitely move with a purpose as they make their way through the crowded airport. When they reach the baggage claim section, Ben and Major stand directly beside the baggage shoot so they can retrieve their luggage as soon as it appears on the carousel.

"Give Mac a call. I'll watch for our bags," Ben says to Major as they wait for their luggage.

"Yeah," Major says, taking a knee to retrieve his cell phone from his brief case.

Major rises, simultaneously scrolling through his phone book in search of Mac's number. At the same time, Ben and Major's luggage rolls out of the baggage claim shoot. Ben grabs his and Major's luggage and places it on the floor.

Ben gives Major a look, as though he were asking, "What's up?"

Major pulls the cell phone away from his ear and says, "I'm not sure what's up. I'm not getting anything."

"It's not like we can call him over the P.A.," Ben comments. "Do we even know his last name?"

"I think it's Pollard, but don't quote me on that."

"Well, let's go outside. If he drives up, then he'll see us."

"That'll work."

Ben and Major grab their luggage and walk out of the baggage claim section. The two friends step back out into the crowd, making their way for the nearest exit.

As they approach the door, on the verge of walking out of the airport, they hear a deep voice say, "You fellas ready to roll?"

Startled, Ben and Major jump slightly and look to their right rear. Leaning up against a pillar is Big Mac.

Seeing Mac, Ben and Major stride to where he stands. Mac takes himself off of the pillar and meets them near the exit.

"Mac! What's up, man?" Major cooly states as he walks forward. "I just tried calling you."

"I know," Mac smilingly replies. "This was more fun, though. How's it going, Ben?"

"I'm all right," Ben states, shaking Mac's hand.

Releasing Ben's grip, Mac says, "Let's get out of here. We have to go link up with one other person."

"Cool," Major blurts.

Mac leads Ben and Major out of the airport and onto the arrival pick-up section. Idling alongside the curb is a waiting cab. When Mac steps foot outside, He throws his right index finger in the air, signaling to the cab driver that he is ready to depart. The cab driver notices the two other young men with his original passenger, so he rushes to the back and pops the trunk so they can place their luggage inside. Major and Ben walk to the rear of the cab and place their luggage in the trunk. They then join Mac in the back seat.

"The Coliseum Café," Mac says to the cabbie.

The cab driver pulls away from the curb and heads for his next destination.

A little over fifteen minutes of driving through traffic, the cab driver says to Mac, "Here we are, sir."

The cab stops just short of the café.

Before Mac steps out, he says to the cab driver, "Take these guys back to the Hilton, then come back here for me."

"Certainly," the cab driver replies.

Mac says to Ben and Major, "You guys chill out at the hotel for a while: get some rest. Order some room service or whatever. I'm in room 2702."

"How long do you think you'll be?" Ben asks.

"No longer than an hour. We fly out tonight, though, so I won't be too long. Keep your phone close," Mac replies.

"Roger," Major answers.

Mac shuts the door and steps onto the sidewalk. The cab pulls out onto the street. As they pass the café, Major and Ben notice a very attractive woman sitting alone just outside of the café. She sits leaning back in her chair, legs crossed. The woman is rather tall, about five ten or so, with very long legs that gleam in the sun. Her long black hair is tied in the back. The ponytail lies across her right shoulder and ends at the bottom of her chest.

"That's nice right there, son," Major says to Ben, pointing to the sitting woman.

Ben nods his head in agreement of Major's assessment of the woman as the cab turns right at the next corner, heading for the Hilton.

Mac stands on the side of the road and watches as Major and Ben drive off down the street, before he heads for the café.

"This is going to suck," Mac quietly says to himself.

Mac walks slowly down the street alongside the café, stopping behind a black haired woman who sits alone sipping on a cup of coffee.

"You're late, Douglas," the woman says before Mac can let out a word.

"I just came from the airport," Mac simply replies.

"Well, are you going to sit down, or are you going to continue hovering over me? You're blocking the sun."

Mac steps from behind the woman and takes a seat across from her. As soon as Mac sits down, a waiter approaches. Mac immediately waves the waiter off. He does not plan on being at the café long enough to enjoy anything on its menu.

Situated, Mac takes a second to study the woman who now sits across from him.

'Man!' Mac thinks to himself. 'She's just as beautiful as the last time I saw her, if not more so.'

"I really appreciate this, Bekha," Mac thanks the woman sitting across from him.

"Don't thank me. Thank Amos," Rebekah states as she pushes her black sunglasses up on her nose.

"I already did."

"Well, I guess we got the pleasantries out of the way."

"Where are your things?"

"In your hotel room"

Mac shakes his head and chuckles some. He then asks, "You told them you were my wife, huh?"

Rebekah nods her head, complying with Mac's assumption.

"So you knew I was at the airport then?" Mac asks.

"I knew you had to pick-up the kid eventually."

"Two kids."

"Two? What the hell? Are you running a kindergarten or what?"

"Hey! If you don't want to help me and the guys, then go. Getting you was the Killer's idea, not mine. The boys may not be pros, but they're tough as hell and have already proven themselves to me and the Killer once before."

"Fine! If you feel so highly of them. Amos told me of the one. He didn't mention there were two."

"That's 'cause I didn't know that there were two of them on the plane until after Major called me back the second time."

"What kind of name is Major?"

"I don't know? That's the boy's name, as far as I know. That's what his dad called him when I met him the first time."

"You know this guy personally? You're really getting sloppy."

"Listen woman! I met Major when he was like twelve or something: back when I was still in the Corps. You know good and well not to disrespect me about how I operate. There's no one better at what we do. You know this better than most."

"I apologize. Who's the other guy?"

"Major's friend, Ben. They went to West Point together. Ben's a white guy: blonde hair, blue eyes. He's about six two or so: decent size for his height. He was the defensive captain and starting middle linebacker his senior year and was pretty damn good from what I hear."

"And Major?"

"Black kid: a bit shorter than Ben. Good size for his height, but not overly muscular, from what I can see: more of an athletic build. He was skinny as hell when I saw him when he was a kid. Major's got a lot of balls. He really proved himself that day at West Point."

"Does he know the truth about all of that and how you and Amos were involved?"

"No he doesn't, and he never will. It's better that he remains ignorant of the truth."

"That would be best. So, when do I get to meet these young heroes of yours?"

"Right now. They're waiting for me at the hotel."

"I guess we better get going."

Mac and Rebekah rise from the table. Rebekah stands in her high heels, placing her at the bridge of Mac's nose.

"You look good," Mac compliments.

"I always do," Rebekah replies as she places the money for her coffee on the table. She then walks out alongside the street to hail a cab.

Mac steps next to Rebekah and says, "You're too independent for your own good. I've got a cab waiting for us."

"That's why I hate you," Rebekah says to Mac and she turns from the street and follows him down the sidewalk.

"Why, 'cause I'm right?"

"No. Because you don't know when to keep your comments to yourself."

"It's funny how you're the only person who seems to think that."

"I'm not laughing."

Mac approaches the idling cab. It is the same cab that has taken him everywhere he has gone in Athens since his arrival early this morning. Mac opens the backdoor for Rebekah and lets her in. She slides all of the way over to the far side of the cab. Mac gets in after her and sits close to the side of the open door.

"Back to the Hilton," Mac instructs the cabbie.

After a couple minutes of driving and endless silence, Rebekah says, "Why Douglas?"

"Why what?" Mac asks.

Rebekah snaps her head at Mac and barks, "This is why I cannot deal with you!"

"What are you talking about? You know how I am. Be specific with your questions. Don't come at me with this open ended bull crap and expect the answer to whatever the hell it is you're asking."

Rebekah turns her head away from Mac and stares out the window. A tear drops from her right eye.

"We really need to talk, don't we?" Mac asks realizing Rebekah's emotional state.

Rebekah simply nods her head in agreement.

"We'll take care of business first, then we'll go somewhere and hash all of this personal stuff out. All right?"

"Okay," Rebekah answers.

The cab pulls into the main entrance of the Athens downtown Hilton hotel. Mac and Rebekah step out of the cab.

Before the cab takes off, Mac says to the driver, "Be back here at seven."

"Yes, sir," the cab driver complies. He then takes off into the streets to continue with his job.

Mac and Rebekah enter the hotel and head for the elevator. Inside the elevator, Mac presses the button labeled, '27.' The ride to the twenty-seventh floor is very quiet. Neither person says a word to the other. Mac and Rebekah barely look at one another.

After a slow and seemingly long ride, the elevator stops and the door opens. Mac and Rebekah step out of the elevator. Being that Mac reserved a suite, there are only two rooms on the floor: his and another. Mac turns to the right and only has to take a few steps before approaching his door. With Rebekah standing behind him, Mac swipes the door with his key and enters the suite.

Mac enters his suite, blocking the entire entranceway with his enormous body. The only light that escapes from the doorway enters through the gaps that his trapezius muscles form with the cracks in the top of the doorway.

Major lies on the couch and does his best to watch a little television, but all of the channels are in Greek. Hearing the door open, Major realizes that Mac has arrived.

"Mac!" Major excitingly states as he still lies on the couch. "Bro! It's a good thing me and Ben have some self-control, and what not, 'cause there are some serious females down in the restaurant and the bar. If we didn't have this mission to do, and what not: Man!"

"Trust me, I know," Mac replies with a small smile on his face.

"Did you see that woman at the café earlier?" Major asks as he sits up and stands to his feet. With his back to Mac, Major then goes to turn the television off, saying, "She was nice, son! She had some legs on her. She looked tall, too. I love tall women!"

"Just nice, huh?" Rebekah replies as she steps from behind Mac.

"Fudge!" Major silently exclaims at the sound of a woman's voice. "Man do I feel dumb."

"I've been referred to as a lot of things," Rebekah responds, "but nice is not one of them." Rebekah walks beside Major and, lightly patting him on the cheek, says, "How cute."

"You have to understand," Major embarrassingly attempts to explain, "nice for me is one of the best compliments I can give. Trust me when I say this."

"I guess I don't have much of a choice. Now do I?" Rebekah replies as she walks over to the couch to take a seat.

Major just shrugs his head, stating, "Not really."

"I like you," a smiling Rebekah says pointing to Major.

Rebekah's words cause Major to silently thank GOD that he is Black because, at this moment, he would be blushing in embarrassment

Mac takes a seat in an armchair and asks, "Ben sleeping?"

"Yeah," Major replies. "He was tired as hell. I couldn't sleep, though."

"You having problems sleeping?"

"Naw. I've never been one to fall asleep easily. It always takes me a couple hours at least. I'm just a little anxious, I guess."

"You know we can do this without you, right?" Rebekah informs Major.

"Yeah, I know, but they got our friend. Ben and I have to go. What would you do if you were us?" Major defends.

Rebekah smiles and says to Mac, "I like him."

"I told you you would," Mac replies.

Major, who is still standing says to Mac and Rebekah, "I'm going to go get Ben."

"Aight," Mac responds as Major leaves the room.

"He looks young, but not as young as I had thought," Rebekah says of Major once he is out of hearing range.

"I wouldn't bring him or Ben along if I thought they were a liability," Mac explains.

"I know you wouldn't."

The room grows silent again, this time, though, Mac and Rebekah gaze at one another as though they are looking into one another's souls.

Mac's mind takes him back three years to Hong Kong. He and Killer had just finished a job taking down an Indonesian pirating ring. Rebekah had called Mac earlier and asked him to meet her in Hong Kong. Killer flew to Paris to complete the paperwork with J, while Mac flew north to see Rebekah. Mac and Rebekah meet in a tranquil park outside of urban Hong Kong. Mac and Rebekah stand out like a polar bear in the forest, being that Mac is a big Black man and Rebekah is a tall Israeli woman.

Rebekah's family originates Thawra, which is located in the northeastern district of Baghdad, Iraq. Once Saddam usurped power, he renamed Thawra after himself, calling it Saddam City. When the Shia'a uprising occurred during the end of the Persian Gulf War, the Shia'a unofficially renamed it Sadr City after the martyred Shia'a cleric who led their seperatist movement.

When the Ba'ath party began gaining control of Iraq during the mid-sixties, Rebekah's grandparents relocated to Israel. Being native to the region, Rebekah's complexion is much darker than that of the average Israeli, the majority of whom migrated to Israel from Europe.

For the past three years, Mac does not go a week without him running the memory through his head. This was the second to last time he and Rebekah saw one another: the last time they had a civil conversation.

At the time, Mac and Rebekah were lovers. Dating would not be a good word to use because they did not see one another as often as

Rebekah would like and the simple fact that their line of work does not allow for much of what most people would consider a normal life.

Holding hands and walking, Mac opens the conversation by saying, "It's good to see you."

"You, too," Rebekah replies.

"Other than us seeing each other, which is important to me, 'cause I love you and what not, what do you want to talk to me about?"

"I know it's hard on the both of us because of the business, but I want to give us a chance."

"I don't know how we can have a real relationship living the way we do."

"I know it'll be hard, but I think we can do it."

Mac shakes his head in confusion. As much as he loves Rebekah, he also loves his life away from the business. Mac enjoys the fact that he can easily separate business from pleasure.

Gathering his thoughts, Mac finally says, "As much as I love you, you know how I appreciate my private life. I like the fact that I have this, but then I have my other world, as well."

"What about Killer?"

"What's this got to do with the Killer?"

"You two hang out like you're best friends."

"That's 'cause we are."

"You know what I mean."

"I owe the Killer my life. We didn't ask to be friends, it just happened."

"Well, I didn't ask to fall in love with you, but that kind of just happened, too."

"Rebekah, I'm honestly not ready for a serious relationship."

"But we love each other."

"I understand all that, but I have my own life, and I like keeping that to myself. Not even the Killer is a part of that."

"So you don't want me in your life. Is that it?"

"That's not what I'm saying."

"Then what are you saying?"

"I don't know what I'm saying."

"You need to know, because having you in my life is important to me, and if you loved me as much as you claim you do, it would be important to you too."

"It is."

"It obviously isn't if you're not even willing to give us a chance."

"It's not that. It's that I feel as though I'd have to give up a part of myself and my personal life."

"I'm not asking you to give up anything. I'm asking you to include me in it."

"I don't think you're ready for my life."

"I kill for a living, like you. Not much is going to shake me up."

"Okay. Fly home with me and I will give you a crash course in my life. If you can handle it, I'll give us, as you say, a chance."

"Thank you for that. I know how hard it is for you to let people in."

Major breaks Mac's personal thoughts on he and Rebekah's past by saying, "Ben's on his way."

"Good," Mac states, rising from his seat. Mac walks over to the dining room table where his laptop lies and turns it on. He then states, "Gather around. This won't take long."

Rebekah rises from her seat and stands beside Mac. Major and Ben, who is now out of the bedroom, walk over to where Mac and Rebekah stand.

"Here's the situation as we know it," Mac begins his brief. "Yesterday afternoon, your flight was hijacked for the sole purpose of kidnapping your friend, Marcos Bakoos, who happens to be the youngest child of the Lebanese President. On 10 January 2001, someone attempted to assassinate Marcos' dad. The assailant hit his target, yet was unsuccessful; the president did not die, as you guys know. The president's personal security was able to kill the assailant before he got away."

"What's interesting is that when the authorities ran prints on the assailant, they came up empty handed. His fingerprints didn't match in anyone's database, and being that this was an international incident: everyone's involved in trying to get to the bottom of this: Interpol, the FBI, CIA, etc. Everyone is clueless, or at least they're playing dumb. In my experience, nine times out of ten, if they say they don't know, then they really don't. There are those rare cases, though. Anyway, the assailant had a tattoo on his left forearm of a saber with the star and crescent in the curved part. I'm unsure as to what the tattoo means, if anything, but being that we're dealing in the world of Islamic fundamentalism, the tattoo could mean anything."

"Tonight, we fly out of here at eight for Beirut. Once in Beirut, we're going to rent a car and head for the Syrian border to a small town called Masnaa. In Masnaa, we have to find some guy in a park wearing an NWO t-shirt and a silver ring with a blue stone in the center on his right hand. This guy's going to lead us to our safe house and give us the remaining information that we need."

"What about weapons?" Ben asks.

"They'll be at the safe house," Mac answers. To strengthen Ben and Major's confidence, he continues, saying, "I've been doing this for years, guys. When one of my contacts gives me info, it's solid, and so you guys feel better, the Killer gave me all this data, so I know it's good."

Mac and Ben look at one another assuredly, and nod.

"Are we taking all of our stuff with us?" Major asks.

"Yes, we are," Mac answers. "We're taking all of our belongings to the safe house. From there, we're traveling as light as possible. Being that we're going in and coming out, there will be no need to take anything except our weapons and essential combat gear: i.e. rope, smoke canisters, grenades, etc. Take something to snack on though, like a Snickers or something: something that'll fit easily in your pocket."

"When do we look to execute," Rebekah asks.

"Hopefully early tomorrow morning," Mac replies. "I'm not looking to drag this out any longer than we have to. Kidnapping's can be tricky sometimes. It's better to go in quick, than wait. Also, someone as high profile as Marcos is not kidnapped for just any old reason. These guys want something."

"We've got something for 'em," Major comments giving Ben a pound.

Rebekah smiles at Major's bold statement.

"Major, Ben," Mac instructs, "I want you guys to go down to the restaurant and eat up. GOD only knows when we'll be able to eat again. After you eat, find yourself a pair of boots: Nothing fancy. Something you can move freely in. Don't get lost. When you return, take a shower and get some rest. We have a long twenty-four hours ahead of us. Hopefully, this time tomorrow, you'll be chillin' at the presidential palace." Mac digs in his pocket and hands Ben his American Express card saying, "I don't leave home without it."

"Thanks, Mac," Ben laughingly says as he receives Mac's American Express card and places it in his front pocket.

Major and Ben leave the suite and head downstairs to get a bight to eat.

As Major and Ben walk through the lobby, headed for the restaurant, Major's cell phone begins to ring.

Major and Ben share a funny look, with Major asking, "Who the hell's calling me?"

As Major reaches into his pocket to retrieve his cell phone, Ben replies, "It might be Killer. It did look like Rebekah and Mac had some serious talking to do."

"Maybe you're right," Major responds, but then, looking at his phone, he says, "or maybe it's Terry."

"I'll let you handle this. I'll go get us a table."

Ben steps away from Major to give him some privacy, while Major walks to a large marble pillar and leans his back against it. Major takes a deep breath before answering his phone.

"Hey, babe. What's up?"

"What's up? You were supposed to call me yesterday. Remember? Thank GOD your still alive! I saw the news last night about the hijacking. You weren't on that flight were you?"

Major shakes his head. He wants to laugh, but doing so would clue Terry in on to his current status. Honesty is the best policy, or so they say. Major understands though, that the truth is not going to make Terry feel any better. Lying to her, Major feels, is what is best, given the present state of affairs. Then again, lying, no matter how much good it does for the present, just does not feel right.

"Yeah, we were," Major replies, "but we're all right. We flew into Munich last night."

"When do you get home?"

Major takes a deep breath and lets it out, saying, "Terry, you're not going to like what I'm about to say..."

Terry cuts Major off stating, "You're doing something crazy that I don't want to hear, aren't you?"

"Yeah. Ben and I are in Athens right now."

"Athens? That's not so bad. I thought you were doing something crazy."

"Well, we're getting ready to."

"What do you mean you're getting ready to?"

"Our friend Marcos was kidnapped during the hijacking."

"Oh my GOD!"

"Ben and I linked up with a friend who's going to help us get him back."

"You're going to do what?"

"We're going to go rescue Marcos."

"Are you trying to die? How many times do you have to be hero?"

"As many times as the challenges present themselves. Listen, I know this is hard for you to digest, but please I understand that I am doing what I know is right. You wouldn't love if this were not a part of me."

"I just don't know what to do with you, Major. Do your parents know?"

"My dad does."

"Well, I know there's nothing I can say to change your mind. Just promise me that you'll come back to me alive and in one piece."

"I will. Oh, and by the way, thank you."

"What're you thanking me for?"

"If you wouldn't have made me get that international plan for my cell, I wouldn't have been able to contact my friend to help us."

"I'm glad I could help."

"You always do. I've got to get going. Ben and I hae to eat before we go."

"Should I ask where?"

"It's probably best that you don't"

"I'll call you when everything's over. I promise."

"Please, Major. Take care of yourself. Tell Ben to watch your back."

"I will."

"I love you.

"I love you, too."

Major hangs up his cell phone and returns it to his pocket thinking, 'Terry's the best thing that ever happened to me.'

Alone in the suite, Rebekah says to Mac, "You ready to have that talk?"

"I guess so," Mac replies. He pulls a chair out from under the dining table and takes a seat.

Rebekah remains on her feet, pacing across the room, as she begins her monologue. "You broke my heart Mac: more than I thought you ever could. You told me you loved me and yet you acted as though it meant nothing. What? Did you think I was running around spreading my legs for every good looking guy I could get my hands on when I wasn't with you? 'cause GOD knows you sure as hell were messing around with every bitch you could get your hands on! I could not believe that you were doing all of that, while at the same time telling me that you loved me. What the hell does love mean to you anyway? It can't mean too much if you can act any which way. Love must be just another word to you."

As Rebekah carries on with her tirade against Mac, he begins to ponder on the events that stir her anger.

Rebekah sits on Mac's brown leather sofa, relaxing in his orange Mr. T t-shirt. On Mac, the t-shirt goes just below his waist. On Rebekah, it is six inches below her waist. The couple had just arrived in the states around six in the morning. It is now four in the afternoon. Mac and Rebekah did not get much rest though. Instead of sleeping, they were busy doing other things.

"What're we doing tonight?" Rebekah asks Mac as he stands in the kitchen preparing him and Rebekah a cup of tea. Of course, a cup of tea for Mac is more like a Gulf cup of tea.

"Well," Mac answers, "you wanted to see how I live away from the business, so I'm going to throw you in the mix of things. Every Saturday, I meet up with X at one of his spots. If I don't see him the Friday prior, he calls me that night to tell me where to link up."

"So where're we going? I haven't been dancing in so long."

"I'm not sure. Probably Club NV, but it changes every once and a while. I have to check my messages."

Mac goes to his answering machine and runs through his several messages that accumulated while he was away on business:

"Hi, baby. It's Candice..." Beep. Mac quickly erases the message.

"Mac, honey. It's Janine. I missed you last…" Beep. Mac erases that message as well.

Rebekah sits up and gives the answering machine and Mac a funny look. Mac does not notice Rebekah's discontent as he continues going through his messages.

"Dark chocolate, me and Maria…" Beep. Mac presses the erase button yet again.

"Yo, dawg!" a voice barks through the answering machine speaker.

"Here we go," Mac simultaneously states as the message plays.

The message continues, saying, "NV at ten, son! Like we always do! Honestly, I don't know why I have to keep sending you these damn messages. We always start out Saturday's at NV, nigga! Anyway, I'll see you, player. Holler!"

Mac deletes the remainder of the messages on his answering machine, then turns and faces Rebekah, who is still sitting on the couch.

Noticing that Rebekah is pouting, Mac asks, "What's wrong?"

Rebekah leans back on the couch and says nothing. She simply crosses her legs and sits there.

Mac shrugs his shoulders and says, "Whatever. You want to go out to dinner first, or do you want to eat in? You know I'm the best cook in the world."

"I don't care what we do," Rebekah stubbornly replies.

"You're mad, aren't you?"

"No. I'm very elated," Rebekah cynically comments

"What's wrong?"

"What's wrong? How about all those women on your answering machine?"

"What women? You mean them?" Mac asks while pointing at his answering machine. "They're nobody."

"What's that supposed to mean?"

"I hardly know those women. They're a part of X's crew. You know how women get around big muscular men. They lose themselves."

"Then how'd they get your number?"

"Probably from X. I don't know."

"They seemed to know you pretty well."

"They know me well enough, I guess. I talk to them when I go out."

"You only talk to them?"

"That's all I do."

"All right, then," Rebekah says. She rises from the couch and walks over to Mac who is still standing next to the answering machine. She leans forward and lightly hugs him, saying, "My fault. I should trust you more."

Mac returns the hug and thinks to himself, 'Man, am I in trouble tonight.'

Mac and Rebekah arrive at Club NV a little after ten o'clock in the evening. The doorman, recognizing Mac, allows him and Rebekah inside, unhindered. As Mac walks past the cute young girl behind the register, he waves and winks at her. She smilingly returns the wave and blushes as Mac and Rebekah pass her. Mac never has to pay at any of the clubs he patrons: NV included.

The couple enters the main level of Club NV. Mac takes Rebekah's hand and leads her towards X's regular VIP section. NV is not overtly crowded yet, but it is congested enough to where Rebekah is forced to walk behind Mac. Every step that Mac takes, a beautiful woman approaches him and says or does something provocative.

Some of the women say simple, sexual salutations to Mac. Others walk directly up to him and rub his chest and his abs. Some squeeze his arm or reach for his free hand and give it a light squeeze.

Rebekah witnesses all of this and is not too pleased. Some of the women, after passing Mac, give her cold and dirty looks.

One woman, a mid-height Puerto Rican wearing three inch stilettos, which accentuate her legs very nicely, walks up to Mac and puts her hand on his chest and says, "You get my message, baby?"

"I get several messages while I'm away," Mac replies with very little emotion.

Mac gives the woman a look, in an attempt to inform her that right now is not a good time to speak to him. The woman, recognizing the look, takes a peak to see who is standing behind Mac.

Seeing Rebekah, the woman blows her off replying, "I'm not worried about her."

"You should be," Mac replies as he continues his forward progress.

"I'm from Spanish Harlem. I can't handle myself," the woman defends.

"She'll take you out in two seconds. Trust me," Mac says as he leads Rebekah past the woman.

When Rebekah passes the woman, she places her hand on the woman's shoulder. With a quick, heavy press down, Rebekah places so much force on the woman that she causes the woman's legs to buckle and break her heels. Rebekah smiles a devilish grin as the woman stands in her bear feet looking dumbfounded.

Highly upset, Rebekah gruffly withdraws her hand from Mac's. Not expecting this to occur, Mac turns around.

Facing Mac, Rebekah coolly says, "I can't do this, Douglas."

"What's wrong?" Mac asks, knowing what Rebekah is already going to say.

"What's wrong is the fact that you obviously enjoy your freedom much more than I was aware."

"We can make this work, if you want to."

"But do you want to make it work, Douglas? That's the issue we're dealing with."

"I don't see the big deal. I can easily drop these females right now."

"Sure you can, but how can I trust you when I'm not around?"

"You're just going to have to."

"I don't think I can. You're running around like a dog. I don't see you ending your way of life anytime soon."

"We can make this work. I love you."

"Maybe you do, but you don't love me enough."

As Mac and Rebekah speak, two women come from behind and tap Mac on his backside.

Seeing the overt public display of affection, Rebekah says, "That's it. I can't deal with this. You obviously aren't ready for a serious relationship. I don't have the time, and I don't have the patience to baby sit you. I shouldn't have to worry about you being faithful, but damn it, you're going to screw around like the wild dog that you are, and there's nothing I can do to stop you."

"Are you sure this is what you want to do? I mean, I can give all this up for you."

"No you can't. You've known X for forever. GOD! He's the reason why you moved into that hell hole of a neighborhood in the first place. Whenever you come home, you're going to party and screw every woman you can get your big paws on like you've been doing all these years. No. I think I'm making the best decision for me. I'm going to leave now."

Rebekah turns away from Mac and heads for the exit. Mac follows close behind her.

Feeling Mac's presence and still striding forward, Rebekah turns her head and asks, "What do you think you're doing?"

"I'm taking you home," Mac answers, unsure as to why Rebekah is asking him the question.

"No you're not. I'm going to a hotel and flying out in the morning."

"What about your stuff?"

"Give it to one of your whores."

"That's not right."

Rebekah now stands just outside of Club NV, on the sidewalk. Mac's ominous body stands blocking the entranceway. The doormen do not bother Mac. They stand to the side and allow Mac to take care of his personal business.

Rebekah stops in her tracks and quickly snaps her body around.

"Right? What's not right is the fact that you wasted my time out here. You brought me to this shit hole, knowing that all these hoes that you've been screwing were going to be here. What's not right is that you didn't take me seriously."

"I didn't think..." Mac begins.

Rebekah cuts Mac off in mid-sentence. Poking Mac in the chest profusely in the chest, Rebekah shouts, "That's your problem, Douglas! You don't think! You're selfish and you only think of yourself! You're not a Big Mac! You're a chicken mcnugget! "

"I..." Mac attempts to let out a few words.

Rebekah cuts him off again shouting, "I! I! I! Shut up! I don't want to hear from you or see you ever again! This is it! Lose my number!"

Rebekah shoves Mac in the chest. The force does not push him back, but the pain and humiliation does. Rebekah steps out in the street and hails a cab. Mac watches as Rebekah, the only woman he has ever loved drives off forever.

Mac shakes his head, ending his daydream of he and Rebekah's past. He looks up at Rebekah, who is still lecturing him on the meaning of trust and true love. While Mac was reminiscing, he was half listening to what

Rebekah was saying, not for the context or subject of her monologue, but so he would know when and how to react.

Looking at Rebekah, Mac breaks his long silence by cutting her off in mid-sentence, saying, "You're right."

Rebekah, who was not expecting Mac to say much of anything during their "talk" stops pacing and looks intently at Mac.

"What did you say?" Rebekah asks.

Mac stands to his feet and walks over to Rebekah, saying, "You're right. I was not ready for a serious monogamous relationship with you. At the time, I was not ready to settle down and I should not have put you in the position I did."

Rebekah takes a step away from Mac and says, "No, you shouldn't have."

"I know this now. The Beast is getting tired. He wants to settle down. He needs to rest."

"I've never known you to put a leash on the Beast."

"It's time for me to settle down. I'm getting too old to be partying like I do."

"You are getting old."

"Yeah I am, and I want you with me when I get old."

"What are you trying to say?"

"You're a smart woman. You know what I'm saying."

"I don't know, Douglas. Why don't you say it?"

"Listen. I don't want you to make a decision now. Take your time with this. Get back with me whenever you feel ready."

Mac places his hands behind Rebekah's upper back and pulls her inward. Rebekah rises on her toes as Mac smoothly pulls her in. Suddenly, the front door swings open.

Major boisterously states, "You guys have got to check out that restaurant! They've got some serious food up in that bad boy!" Seeing Mac and Rebekah and the position that they are in causes Major to stop his mode of speech and say, "Oh! My bad."

Ben punches Major on the back of his right shoulder and says, "Real smart, Major! Way to open your mouth."

"How was I supposed to know?" Major inquires.

"Come on. Let's go to the back so they can be alone."

Embarrassed, Mac and Rebekah release their hold on one another and take a step back.

"Maybe we should go eat," Rebekah suggests.

"Yeah. I am kind of hungry," Mac agrees.

Before Rebekah and Mac leave, Ben comes jogging from the back of the suite saying, "Sorry, Mac. I forgot to give you your Amex back."

"No problem, brother. Thanks," Mac replies as Ben returns his American Express card back to him.

Ben quickly retreats to the back in order to give Rebekah and Mac some much needed privacy.

"I like them," Rebekah says as she heads for the front door.

"Me too," Mac replies.

The couple heads out the door, heading for the restaurant for a much needed meal.

1500 HRS

WAKING UP FROM A TWO HOUR nap, Major slowly rolls out of bed and drags himself to the bathroom to take a bubble bath. At the same time, Ben gets out of bed and goes to the other bathroom to take a shower. Mac and Rebekah have just returned to the suite from their meal and a very extended conversation.

"You guys getting ready?" Mac shouts as he enters the suite.

"Yeah!" Major and Ben shout from their respective bathrooms.

"All right!" Mac returns the response. "We'll be out here getting packed."

"We won't be long," Ben replies as he lathers his hair with shampoo.

While Ben and Major continue bathing, Mac and Rebekah spend the time organizing and gathering their belongings. Packed, they then place the bags and luggage near the front door for easy access when they are ready to depart.

Ben steps out of the shower and with a towel wrapped around his waste, leaves the bathroom saying, "I'm done in here if anyone needs to take a shower."

"I sure need one," Rebekah replies.

Rebekah retrieves her shower kit from out of her luggage and walks out of the main room. She heads straight for the bathroom that Ben was utilizing to take a much needed, relaxing shower.

Major steps out of the other bathroom with a pair of shorts on, stating, "You can have this bad boy, Mac."

"No, thanks," Mac replies, "I'm good, you pre-madonna."

"Man!" Major responds. "Everyone's got jokes. Oh well," Major continues as he heads for his room to change, "real men take bubble baths. Yeah! That's right."

Mac laughs as his young friend marches down the hall complaining about people not understanding his love of taking hot bubble baths.

A few minutes pass and a luggage carrying Ben enters the main room where Mac sits. Major walks out behind Ben a bit later, followed by Rebekah.

Looking at his watch and noticing that it is fifteen minutes until seven o'clock, Mac informs, "All right, guys. It's time to get going."

"Bet," Major replies as he heads for the door.

"Make sure you guys have everything, 'cause we're not coming back," Mac instructs Ben and Major.

"We've got all our stuff," Ben replies as he heads for the door.

Ben and Major step out into the hall and press the button to raise the elevator. Mac and Rebekah step out of the suite, the door shutting behind them. They walk to the elevator where Ben and Major wait.

"You boys ready for this?" Rebekah asks Ben and Major.

"Yes, ma'am," Major replies with a huge grin on his face.

"Please," Rebekah replies, "I am nobody's mother."

"That's my bad," Major explains. "Force of habit."

"It's okay," Rebekah states, patting Major on the head.

Ben and Mac laugh at Rebekah coddling Major.

Ben leans over to Mac and says, "He likes the attention."

"Yeah, he does," Mac responds.

The elevator door opens and all four persons walk inside. A quick unhindered trip down and the elevator reaches the main floor. Mac, Rebekah, Major, and Ben step out of the elevator and head for the main lobby.

"I'm going to check out. Rebekah, get my cab. You guys go with her," Mac instructs.

Mac walks to the front counter to check out of his suite, while Rebekah, along with Major and Ben, head outside to locate the taxi cab that Mac has used during the entirety of his time in Athens. As was expected, the cab driver is waiting outside when Rebekah steps outside.

"The cab's here guys," Rebekah informs Ben and Major as they follow from behind. "Throw your stuff in the trunk and get in. We want to be ready to go when Douglas gets out here."

"Douglas?" Major asks as he and Ben walk to the rear of the cab.

"You didn't know that that was his first name?" Rebekah asks, some what stunned.

"Naw," Major responds.

"We didn't really think much of it," Ben replies.

Ben takes Rebekah's luggage from her, in order to place them in the trunk, along with his and Major's belongings, as well.

"Thank you, Ben," Rebekah graciously states as she hands her luggage off to Ben.

"It's no problem," Ben replies.

Ben places Rebekah's one carry on bag into the trunk. Mac walks out of the hotel and over to the cab where is companions wait. He throws his bags into the trunk and slams it shut. While Mac puts his luggage in, everyone piles into the cab.

Mac enters the front passenger's seat and says to the cab driver, "Take us to the airport."

The cab driver puts the car in drive, then pulls out onto the street, taking his passenger's to the airport. It is exactly seven o'clock, so the cabbie does not drive with any real haste.

Arriving at the airport, Mac graciously pays the cab driver and says, "Thanks for the help these past couple days, man. You did well. You have a card or something?"

"No I don't, but I can give you my number," the cab driver replies.

The cabbie writes his cell phone number on a small piece of paper and hands it to Mac.

"Thanks, man," Mac replies as he looks at the number that was handed to him. "If I am ever in Athens again, I'm going to hire you as my driver. I like punctuality."

Mac steps out of the cab and nods at the cabbie as he drives off. Major hands Mac one of his bags as Mac picks the other up from off of the ground.

"Let's get going," Mac states, leading the group into the airport.

2300 HRS: BEIRUT, LEBANON

THE FLIGHT FROM ATHENS TO BEIRUT was rather smooth, as most airline flights are. Ben and Major are relieved in the fact that they have landed in Beirut without any incident, as they originally were supposed to. Their current track record on unsuspecting incidents is not very good.

Once in the Beirut International Airport, Rebekah, Ben, and Major head for the baggage claim to retrieve their luggage, while Mac goes to the Avis booth to sign for their rental car. Everyone having completed their tasks, they all meet up and exit the airport area together.

With Mac driving, he turns onto the highway and heads due east for the Syrian border. Driving just short of an hour, the group finally makes its way to the town of Masnaa. Mac drives slowly through the town, looking for the park. Mac finds the main market area and slowly drives through it. Being that it is just after twelve in the morning, the market is empty, so the drive is not difficult, by any means.

In the Middle East, the winter is the rainy season. From December to February it rains sporadically everyday. The temperatures go down, to their lowest, in the high fifties on the Fahrenheit scale. To those from the region, the temperature is cold, but to those from the United States, it is very comfortable.

Because the weather is cold to those from the region, they do not sit outside and socialize during the evenings, as they would during the late spring to mid-autumn. For said reason, the streets are totally empty, minus the occasional pedestrian here and there.

"Well, we shouldn't have too much trouble finding this guy," Mac states as he takes a right turn down another street.

After a few more minutes of driving, Mac spots the park to his front right. Approaching the park, Mac slows the car down to a crawl.

"Bekah, I want you to get out and comb the park," Mac orders Rebekah.

Mac brings the car to a stop. Immediately, Rebekah jumps out and cautiously strides into the park.

With Rebekah gone, Mac continues saying to Ben and Major, "All right guys. Let's see if we can find this guy."

Ben and Major sit quietly in the back as Mac pulls away from the curb and continues driving around the perimeter of the park. A couple of seconds later, Mac's cell phone rings. Mac quickly answers his cell phone after only the first ring.

"I think I see him," Rebekah informs Mac.

"How far are you from him?" Mac asks.

"Approximately a hundred meters."

"Which direction is he headed?"

"To the north."

"All right. We're heading that way."

Mac, who is on the southeast side of the park, continues driving the car around the park, heading for the north side.

"Where's he now?" Mac asks.

"Still heading north: No clear destination yet," Rebekah informs.

"We're almost on the north side. Is he near the perimeter?"

"He's about fifty meters from the perimeter. It looks like he's heading for a bench of some kind. There's a water fountain and a weird looking monument or statue, some sort of funky, new age art work, near the bench.

"Okay. I see the art. I'm going to get out and meet you at that bench. Stay on him. Major when I get out, I want you to continue driving around the park. I'll call you when I need you."

Major nods his head in compliance. Mac slowly stops the car in such a manner that the breaks do not squeal; thus not giving away their location. He then steps out of the car. Major, instead of getting out of the car, rolls over the front seats and into the driver's seat.

"That was real smooth," Ben sarcastically says to Major

"Yeah: Yeah: Yeah," Major replies as he puts the car in drive and continues moving forward. "Take this," Major then says to Ben as he tosses him his cell phone.

29 December 2001, 0030 hrs

L EAVING MAJOR AND BEN ON THEIR own, Mac scrambles into the park and covertly moves towards the giant piece of artwork that is near the concrete bench and water fountain. Mac stands up against a tree and surveys the area. He spots the man sitting on the bench, smoking a cigarette. Rebekah is approximately fifty meters away from the man's position and out of his line of sight.

Mac puts his cell phone to his ear and says to Rebekah, "I'm going to swing around. I want you to do the same. Let's see if we can't trap this guy where he is."

"Got you," Rebekah acknowledges.

The two mercenaries make their way toward the sitting man, ensuring that he does not detect their movement. Closer and closer Rebekah and Mac approach the man: Rebekah from his front and Mac from his right rear.

Finally, Mac gets close enough to the man where he is able to speak to him and disallow him from running away, if he plans on doing so.

"You the one?" Mac asks the man, standing ominously over him, as though he could easily swallow him up.

A bit startled, the man turns his upper body around. Noticing Mac, the man says, "You are the Killer's friend?"

"Yes, I am," Mac replies.

The man stands to his feet.

Looking up at Mac's enormous form, the man says, astonished, "Yes you are. Please, come with me."

Half ignoring the man, Mac says to Rebekah, "This is him." Mac then turns his attention to the man and says, "I have a ride."

"We will take your vehicle then," the man agrees with Mac.

Rebekah comes walking out of the tree line, heading for the man and Mac's position. There, three personnel begin to walk out of the park.

Mac calls Major and asks, "What's your fix?"

"I think we're on the northwest side of the park," Ben answers.

"All right, Ben. Where are you in relation to the funky art?"

"It's behind us, about fifty meters or so."

"Okay. We're not far from there. I don't want you to turn around, though. Tell Major to slow down some. We've got our contact. We'll meet you on the southwest side."

"Okay."

Mac leads Rebekah and the man through the park, staying as covert as is possible. They skirt the inner perimeter of the park, keeping the west side of the park to their right. Mac and Rebekah are able to see Major and Ben's location to their front right.

"We should pick up the pace some," Rebekah suggests.

"Good idea," Mac agrees.

Mac and Rebekah begin to run through the park. Mac drags the man along to ensure that he keeps up with Rebekah and him. Major is driving at such a slow rate of speed that they are able to pass the vehicle within no time. Running dead even with the vehicle, Rebekah and Mac run out of the park. Seeing them, Major slows down even more and comes to a smooth stop. Major puts the vehicle in park and immediately jumps out. He keeps the door open, giving Mac easier access to enter the vehicle. Major opens the back door, allowing Mac to quickly lead the man into the vehicle. Simultaneously, Rebekah enters the front passenger's side.

With everyone situated within a moment's time, Mac drives off: this time driving at the regular speed limit of fifty kilometers per hour.

"Take a left at the next corner," the man instructs.

Mac turns left.

"Keep going straight for a while. After the school, turn right."

As Mac approaches the school, he slows down, then takes a right turn.

"Okay, slow down some," the man instructs. "You see that row of houses? Turn right down that alley."

Mac follows the instructions to a tee.

"That's the house there on the right. You can pull alongside the front," the man informs Mac.

Mac slows down and parallel parks the vehicle along the side of the house.

"Let's get inside and get to work," Mac orders the group.

They all jump out of the vehicle with haste and grab their luggage. The man leads them to the house. They walk through a black metal gate, entering a small courtyard. Walking, the man pulls a set of keys out of his pocket. When he approaches the front door, he sticks the key into the lock, twists, turns, and opens the door. The man holds the door open for Mac, Rebekah, Major, and Ben to enter.

When Mac enters the house, he spots out the first large table in his sights and heads directly for it. The remainder of the group follows Mac's lead as they enter the house. Everyone tosses their bags against the wall, then congregate around the table. The man goes to a separate room for a brief moment and returns carrying a blue folder in his hand. He walks to the table and stands beside Mac, placing the folder down and sliding it to his right.

"This is what I've got," the man says to the group.

Mac opens the folder and pulls the forms and maps out of the pockets and spreads them out in front of him. The man grabs the top page and begins his brief.

"My name is Majed Salah Al Cattan. Mac, Rebekah, I know who you are. Your reputations are heralded. Your two young friends, though, are unfamiliar to me."

"Milton."

"Ben."

After Ben and Major introduce themselves, Mac says, "Since you seem to know me, then you know that I don't care who you are. All I care about is accomplishing the mission and getting home unscathed. Just so my guys here feel a little more comfortable, why don't you tell us who you are."

"As I stated, my name is Majed. You could say I'm the man who knows things in this part of the world: Jordan, Syria, Lebanon, Iraq, and Israel. Info from Iran, Egypt, and Turkey, I can get, but it takes me calling in favors, as your friend Killer did."

"How do you know the Killer?" Mac asks.

"You guys did a job in the Sudan a couple of years ago and had to link up in Egypt prior to execution. I was the guy who got him the intel he needed on that gold mine."

"That was good work," Mac congratulates Majed. "That's all I need to know. You have my confidence. Let's get this thing started so we can get Marcos the hell out of where ever he is. Before you start, though, is there a reason why the Killer had us stage in this town, other than the obvious."

"Yes, there is, and actually, that will be a good place to begin. We are only one hundred twenty kilometers from where your friend is being held captive."

Majed sifts through the pile of papers and pulls out a map. Finding the map, Majed unfolds it to continue his brief.

"I threw this map together this morning," Majed says with respect to his make shift map. "We are here," Majed points. "Here's where we're going: Ad Dimas. The drive there should be uneventful, due to our departure time. There is nothing on this road: no shops, gas stations, or towns." Majed grabs another map. Continuing, he says, "This is a rough sketch of Ad Dimas. It has one police station with about two hundred officers. We don't have to worry about them."

"Why's that?" Rebekah asks.

"Because we're going into a Shia'a mosque," Majed answers.

"We're busting up into a mosque?" Major asks.

"That's correct, Milton," Majed replies."

"Continue with your brief, Majed," Mac states.

"Your friend, Markos Bakoos, is being held it that mosque. It is located across the street from a school. I do not know where in the room he is, but he's in there somewhere."

"How big's the mosque?" Rebekah asks.

"It's quite small, actually. Due to the fact that the town is not very large and there are not many Shia'a. When I drove by the mosque this morning, I saw roughly twenty some armed men inside."

"Not too bad," Mac comments

Continuing, Majed says, "It shouldn't be. None of you look Syrian, except for Rebekah, so, if we're going to go in at daybreak, we're going to have to go in hard and fast."

"Just the way I like it," Mac again comments.

"Why'd they kidnap Marcos, in the first place?" Major asks.

"That's the interesting part," Majed replies. "As you guys are aware, Marcos' father is the President of Lebanon and there was a hit on him earlier last year. What's interesting is who pulled off the hit and who ordered it. Let's start with the latter. Around here, it's public knowledge that the Ayatollah Ali Hussein Ishmael hates President Paulos. After some reforms that he spoke of at his address to the National Assembly, the Ayatollah wanted him dead. Here's where it gets interesting." Majed finds another sheet of paper and shows it to the group, asking, "You know what this is?"

"The Killer told me about that," Mac blurts.

"That's good," Majed states. "Not too many people see one of these on someone and lives. I only know of it. I've never seen one in person."

"What is it?" Ben asks.

"This tattoo is a symbol of the Ishmaelites, or better known as the Assassins," Majed explains. "The star and crescent represent Islam and the sword symbolizes strength. The man wearing this tattoo is said to be a weapon of GOD. You never see one of these."

"So the Ayatollah hired the Assassins to kill the president," Mac states.

"In a matter of speaking, yes," Majed answers.

"What do you mean in a matter of speaking?" Rebekah asks

"You don't pay the Assassins with money," Majed replies.

"What do they take for a job?" Rebekah counters.

"No one really knows, but definitely not money," Majed states. "Receiving money for dong GOD's work is not seen as an honorable thing."

"Let me make this make sense," Mac begins. "The pissed off Ayatollah hires the Assassins to kill the president. The Assassin fails, and now the president's son has been kidnapped. What we need to understand is why Marcos was kidnapped. Here's what doesn't make sense."

"What's that?" Major asks.

"The Assassins didn't kidnap Marcos. The Ayatollah's guys did."

"How do you know that?" Ben asks.

"'Cause they have Marcos holed up in a Shia'a mosque. The Assassins is a Sunni based organization. I could be wrong, but even if they are Shia'a, they wouldn't be in a friggin' mosque. The Assassins are an ancient secret organization. You don't maintain centuries of credibility by doing bone head stunts like these idiots who got Marcos."

"You're right," Rebekah agrees. "My grandfather used to tell me stories about them when I was a child, yet in all my years of working this area, I've never ran into an Assassin. As far as I knew they were nothing but fictional characters. Our fight is with the Ayatollah's guys at that mosque. I doubt we'll receive any contact from the Assassins."

"I agree," Majed affirms.

"How much is the ransom?" Marcos asks.

"Twenty-five million US dollars," Majed answers.

"Is there anything significant in that?" Mac continues with his questioning.

"No," Majed replies. "As far as any of my contacts knows, twenty-five million is just some number that someone picked out of the sky."

"Obviously there's a connection between the failed hit on the president and Marcos' kidnapping," Major interjects.

"That's a great point, Milton," Rebekah comments. She then asks him, "Why would you say that?"

"Well," Major begins to explain, "if the Ayatollah wanted to get at the president, he's already done so by taking Marcos. If he wants the president dead, obviously he would want Marcos dead as well, except he's not trying to kill him. Instead, he's trying to extract money out of his dad, which doesn't make any sense."

"Yes it does," Ben adds. "Mac, didn't you say that the president's body guards killed the Assassin who tried to kill the president?"

"Yeah, they did," Mac answers.

"That's what I thought," Ben continues. "This doesn't make any sense to me, but for whatever reason, it looks like the Ayatollah is paying for the failed hit."

"You're right," Mac agrees. "I didn't think about it like that."

"That doesn't make any sense, but I think you're right," Rebekah comments, as well.

"If you guys are right," Mac states, "I feel sorry for the Ayatollah when we take Marcos away from him."

Everyone in the group laughs.

Mac follows the laughter with, "I think we're good on the intel portion. Let's get down to tactics. Majed, since you know the lay of the land, fill us in on what you think our best course of action is."

Majed sifts through his stack of papers and selects the ones that he needs for the tactical portion of the brief.

"Here's the mosque we're going to hit," Majed begins. "I'm not sure of its name, but that's not important, anyway. Take a look at this photograph," Majed says as he directs the groups' attention to one of the many pictures that he took during his reconnaissance. "There's an armed guard in this tower. If we enter the mosque before taking this guy out first, then we're liable to get hit. Now, there's an easy way to fix this." Majed takes another photograph from the stack and slides it in front of the group, saying, "Directly, across the street from the mosque is a school. It has a six foot brick wall around it. I checked the school out and there's a clear shot to the tower from one of the classrooms. I can go up there and take the tower guard out before you guys go in."

"How good a shot are you?" Mac asks.

"I don't miss," Majed boasts.

"Well, I guess we don't have much of a choice. Now do we?"

"Not really. I can't think of any other way to handle the situation."

"Okay," Mac states, "This is what we're going to do." Mac takes the photographs from in front of Majed and spreads them out across the table, giving everyone the ability to see them all at once. Mac then continues, saying, "When we get to the town, we're all going to go into the school. Majed, you'll take the shot, as you said. I assume you have a silencer?"

Majed nods acknowledging that he has a silencer for his sniper rifle.

"Good," Mac responds to Majed's answer. "As soon as you take the shot, we're going into the mosque. Once we leave the school, Majed, I want you to drive around the town, appearing as indiscriminate as you possibly can. Do not go any further than four blocks away from the mosque, though. We want to be able to move out of there as quickly as possible. As for us," Mac says to Ben, Rebekah, and Major, "when Majed takes the tower guard out, we will sprint across the street and bust. I don't think we're going to have to worry about being quiet with the number of guards that Majed says are in the mosque." Mac returns his attention to Majed, saying, "Since you're the expert on the ground, you'll drive us to Ad Dimas. Do you have a cell phone that'll work out there?"

"Yes I do," Majed answers.

"Good," Mac replies, "give me your number after we're done with all this. We'll both keep our phones on so you know what the hell is going on inside. As soon as you take your shot, tell me. That'll be our signal to head for the mosque. Be ready for me to speak to you at all times." Mac returns his attention to Rebekah, Major, and Ben, saying, "When we get inside, guys, we're splitting up. Major, you're with Rebekah. Ben, you're with me. Lucky for us, mosques are not designed with a lot of rooms, so there aren't too many places they can hide Marcos. The center of the mosque, which takes up most of the building, is nothing but a large prayer area. We'll all go in through the front. I'll go right. Rebekah, you go left. Kill every male you run into. It'll be approximately five in the morning when we go in. I doubt very seriously that anyone with good intentions would be in the mosque at that time of the day. Rebekah, if you guys get Marcos, let me know. You'll have your phone on, too. Majed, as soon as you hear that we've got Marcos, you get your ass to the front gate. If everything goes according to plan, you should get to the gate as we're fighting our way out of the mosque. Try to have all of the doors open, if you can. Once we're all positioned in the vehicle, we're going to get the hell out of there. We will not slow down unless I feel there is no oncoming threat. We'll drive back here and grab the remainder of our gear. At this point, you can go your own way, Majed, or you can roll on with us to drop Marcos off at his house."

"As much as I would like to, my remaining discrete is key to my work. Thank you, but I will have to decline the offer. I will not continue on with you once we return," Majed answers.

"That's cool," Mac states. "No big deal. That's about it then. Any questions?"

"Yeah," says Major. "Where're the weapons?"

Everyone looks at Majed for an answer.

"They're upstairs," Majed replies. "Once Mac has completed his brief, I will take you to the room."

"Good. Anyone else?" Mac asks.

Seeing that no one has any following questions, Mac states, "All right then let's check out the arsenal. Oh by the way: before I forget. Ben, don't get shot this time."

Mac's statement causes Major to laugh to a great degree.

With a smile on his face, Ben defends himself by saying, "I don't plan on it. You guys aren't having all the fun without me this time."

Mac, Rebekah, Ben, Major, and Majed are all huddled around a large table cleaning their weapons. Before firing a weapon, it is always imperative that it is clean and lubricated. If one has a misfire while firing, it is better to know that all was done to ensure that the weapon was prepared for battle.

Weapons cleaned, Mac announces, "Let's get going. I want to be in Ad Dimas just before daybreak. I want to leave in ten minutes."

Everyone proceeds to put their clean, lubed, weapons back together. Major and Ben open their luggage and pull out the boots that Mac had them buy when they were in Athens.

Laced up and ready to go, Ben and Major grab their weapons and ammunition from off of the table and follow Mac outside.

Sitting in the driver's seat of a white Khia minivan is Majed. Rebekah patiently stands outside, waiting for Major, Mac, and Ben to exit the house. After a rather short time, the three men come trotting out of the house, making their way for the minivan.

"It's about time," Rebekah states as they pile into the minivan.

Rebekah steps into the minivan behind Mac, who is the last of the three to enter. As soon as Rebekah shuts the door and everyone is situated, Majed pulls away from the curb and out into the street.

It does not take the group very long to drive out of Masnaa. Fifteen minutes into the drive and they are in Syria. Majed does not drive through the legal boarder crossing. He and his companions cannot take the chance of anyone discovering their activities. Instead, Majed uses a side road that is unfamiliar to most. The road cuts through a small mountain range that is not heavily patrolled by neither the Lebanese nor the Syrian governments.

Majed drives the group across the boarder with ease. Their journey across the long stretch of desert is very dark. Only the luminance from the moon and the uncountable number of stars light their path. The drive is somewhat bumpy due to the fact that the majority of the road is unpaved. Some sections of the road are paved, but most of it is simply hard pressed dirt and rocks.

Mac looks at his watch and says, "All right, guys. We've got about another twenty minutes or so before we get on site. Major, Ben, who're you with?"

"I'm with you," Ben answers.

"I'm with Rebekah," Major answers, as well.

"Good," Mac replies. I want you guys no less than ten feet behind us at all times. You are our shadows. Understood?"

Major and Ben nod their heads in compliance.

Not satisfied with the response, Mac states, "I need to hear you say it."

Major and Ben both reply with, "Yes."

"Good," says Mac. "You guys are disciplined and you know that me and Rebekah know what the hell we're doing, so I don't need to go into too much detail in terms of following orders. We will be exact with you to the point where you won't have to analyze anything we say."

Rebekah enters the conversation, saying, "Major, I'm going to use you to do most of the hands on stuff; i.e. carrying stuff, knocking down doors, things like that. I'll do most of the killing. You may be a man, but you and Ben are far too young to cause so much death. Please feel free to defend yourself, of course."

"Of course," Major jests.

Everyone softly laughs.

"Ben," Mac continues, "If we find Marcos first, I'll carry him out while you cover me with suppressive fire."

"All right," Ben responds.

Mac continues speaking, saying, "Majed, I'll say, 'We've got him.' That'll be your clear signal to return to the mosque. If enemy fire is light, roll up to the mosque as we had planned. If it's heavy, though, see what you can do about bashing your way in."

"This van cannot take the force of crashing into the mosque's gate," Majed informs Mac.

"Then you'll have to find something that will, while at the same time remaining on schedule. We must stay in synch with each other at all times," Mac stresses.

The night sky begins to lighten some, signaling the coming of the dawn.

As the group enters the outskirts of Ad Dimas, Mac says, "All right, guys. It's time to get serious."

Major and Ben both take in a deep breath. They have both seen action and have been in some rather volatile situations in their short lifetime, but this is the first time they have purposely put themselves in harms way. The danger is well worth the risk of losing their lives, if it means rescuing their friend Marcos from his captors.

"The mosque is just down the street some," Majed states. "Look relaxed. There are lookouts scattered throughout town. I'm going to drop you off at the corner to throw them off some, just in case they happen to actually be doing their jobs."

"Yeah right," Mac states. "They're probably sleeping and using their AKs to hold their heads up."

The group laughs lightly, doing their best not to make a sound.

Majed gets serious for a moment and states, "There's the mosque, to the left. I'm going to go around the block, swing around, and park behind the school."

Mac, Rebekah, Ben, and Major take a look at the mosque as they casually pass. The mosque is a lot smaller than Mac had pictured. He was expecting something a little more formidable.

Majed takes the immediate right, after having passed the mosque. He stays straight for one block. At the corner, Majed takes another right. At the end of the block, Majed, yet again, turns right. When Majed reaches the next corner, he comes to a complete stop.

"See the mosque?" Majed asks.

Everyone nods in acknowledgement. The mosque is situated across the street from them, to their front right. There is no one in front of the mosque. The street itself is rather empty, as well, due to the fact that it is just after five o'clock in the morning.

As Majed leads the group through Ad Dimas, he says, "All right guys, we're approaching the school now."

Majed drives down a residential street that is empty of any life, minus that of a lone dog that wonders aimlessly with no clear destination. Majed pulls up alongside the back of the school and parks the van beside the wall.

The group grabs their weapons and necessary equipment, then hurry out of the van and move to the wall. Expeditiously, they scale over the wall, making very little noise as they take their weapons with them.

Inside the inner perimeter of the school, Majed runs to the stairs and sprints up to the second floor, while Mac leads Ben, Rebekah, and Major to the school's front gate. Mac and Ben stand to the right of the gate and Rebekah and Major stand to the left.

While Mac, Ben, Rebekah, and Major wait in position, Majed picks the lock to the classroom and enters without any problems. Majed silently enters the classroom. With an elongated case in hand, Majed places it onto the teacher's desk that is located in the front of the classroom. Majed opens the case and retrieves the multiple pieces of his .50 caliber sniper rifle. Quickly, yet carefully, Majed puts his sniper rifle together.

Complete with his rifle assembly, Majed moves into position at the window. He removes a small magazine full of .50 caliber rounds and places it into the rifle's magazine well. Majed then silently locks and loads his weapon.

Majed takes three deep breaths and thinks to himself, 'I've got to make this shot count. One shot, one kill.'

The distance from Majed to the target is only two hundred meters away: a very simple shot, even for a basic marksman. Majed can make the shot with his eyes closed, if he had to. He has definitely had to take harder shots in his career.

Majed carefully sights in on his target, a young male wielding an AK-47. He exhales one more time, letting out all of the air in his lung. Depleted of oxygen, Majed squeezes the trigger. The rifle makes a soft popping sound as the round is fired through the muzzle. A brief moment later, the round strikes the target and instantly, the man buckles over and falls dead.

With his target extinguished, Majed takes his cell phone out of his pocket and says to Mac, "Target's taken out."

As Mac stands beside the gate, he spies the mosque that is located directly across the street from the school. Simultaneously, he latches his cell phone around his left bicep and places the ear piece in the corresponding ear.

While Mac waits for Majed to take out the guard in the mosque's prayer tower, he thinks to himself. 'This shouldn't be too bad.' The place doesn't look like it's guarded too well. If they're smart it's because they want to keep a low profile. Of course, if they were smart, they wouldn't have done this nonsense and forced my ass out here.'

After only waiting for a few minutes, Mac hears Majed's faint voice in his ear say, "Target's taken out."

"Let's do this," Mac states.

Instantly, Mac throws the front gate open and moves at a fast pace across the street. Ben follows close behind him, followed by Rebekah, and then Major. As soon as Major's feet touch the sidewalk, he quickly turns throws his arm back and shuts the gate closed so that no one will suspect that they had broken into the school.

As soon as Majed informs Mac that he has taken out the tower guard, he quickly disassembles his sniper rifle and returns the multiple pieces to the case. Majed grabs his rifle case and sprints out of the classroom. Before heading downstairs, though, Majed makes it a point to quietly shut the door behind him. In the chance that the local authorities happen to investigate what is about to occur at the mosque, Majed does not want anyone from the implicated with his and the group's activities.

Majed springs down the stairs and expeditiously climbs over the school wall and lands beside the Khia minivan. Without pausing, Majed moves to the driver's side, opens the unlocked door, and hops into the seat. He places the sniper rifle on the floor to his right and immediately starts the engine. Majed pulls away from the side of the wall and drives through the residential neighborhood, doing his best to look as inconspicuous as possible. Now, all Majed is waiting for is Mac's call saying that the group has rescued Marcos.

Mac leads the group across the street at a very intense pace. Mac is not one to move slow and take his time doing anything. Expediency is key to everything that he does.

Ben stays close to Mac, ensuring that he is not less than a step behind him, as he was instructed. Major does the same: staying directly behind Rebekah, pulling the rear. The group sprints across the street, as they quickly approach the front gate.

At the gate, Mac comes to a sudden stop. Carefully, without making very little noise, he unlocks the gate and quietly swings the doors open. The gate squeaks some, causing Major and Ben to become paranoid, to a minor extent. Much to their relief, though, the opening of the gate does not cause a raucous.

With Mac holding the front gate open, Rebekah sprints into the courtyard, Major following at her heels. Next, Ben enters the courtyard, then Mac, who then closes the front gate behind him. The last thing that Mac wants to do is tip their hand to the enemy or the general public, for that matter, of their current actions.

Much to Ben and Major's dismay, just as Majed had briefed, the courtyard is filled with men carrying AK-47s. Most of them are asleep on the ground, but a few are awake: some pacing around the mosque and the interior perimeter of the wall. Others sit on the ground conversing with one another.

Seeing the men walking along side the left wall, Rebekah turns her attention to them, shooting the unsuspecting enemy. Major follows Rebekah's lead. Instead, though, he fires to the right, shooting the men who are walking around the mosque.

Rebekah and Major's fires create a shield of bullets, which gives Mac and Ben the cover they need to enter the mosque. At a full sprint and a bit of sporadic fire at aimed targets, Mac and Ben quickly make their way to the mosque's main entrance. As he makes his way to the door, Mac shoots the handle three times, shattering it and the lock. A few feet away, Mac follows through with a swift size fifteen boot to the door. Instantly, the door falls with a hard thud.

Having penetrated the mosque, Mac reports, "We're inside. Take the right. Ben, back-to- back."

Immediately, Ben turns around to cover Mac's rear. Mac turns left and quickly moves down the hall. The first door Mac and Ben approach, they lean their left shoulder up against the wall. Mac quickly checks to see if the door is unlocked. Discovering that the door is locked, Mac skirts to the other side of the entranceway. In position, he jumps in front of the door and kicks it in. As soon as the door makes the slightest crack, Mac throws his body back up against the wall to keep from getting shot. He then swings his body inside and does a quick scan of the room. Ben follows close behind Mac into the room.

The room contains four combatants. Mac turns to his right, where the nearest man is and shoots him dead. Ben takes the left, killing another. Mac quickly takes out the other two as Ben's victim falls to the floor.

"You all right?" Mac asks Ben.

"I'm good," Ben replies.

"Let's keep going then."

Mac and Ben burst out of the room. As soon as they enter the hall way, Mac and Ben are forced to kill again. Now, the mosque is filled with armed men. Most of the men are clueless as to what is occurring. They linger around in disarray, confused as to what they should do. The armed stand in small groups running back and forth, trying to figure out what is occurring.

Seeing the men carrying their weapons, Mac and Ben take them out as they move forward. In their defense, some of the enemy do return fire, but they miss their targets every time. Their lack of precision and accuracy are a result of their lack of quality training and ability and the fact that they do not use the butt stock of the weapon.

Mac and Ben easily pick off their bewildered enemy.

Hearing Mac's instructions through her earpiece, Rebekah says to Major, "We're going inside: cover my rear."

Rebekah spins around and runs full speed into the mosque and firing upon those who get in her way, while Major runs backwards, laying down suppressive fires.

Inside the mosque Rebekah, slows down, waiting for Major to catch up. When Major enters he notices Ben and Mac enter a room. Major re-focuses and turns around, following Rebekah to the right, down the hallway.

"Cover my rear," Rebekah commands.

Again Major turns around to ensure that no one sneaks up from behind and surprises them. Due to Mac and Ben's early entry, the hallway is now swarming with armed men. Rebekah and Major pick the enemy off one at a time.

When Rebekah reaches the first door, instead of informing Major of her actions, Rebekah simply kicks the door in. Major looks out of the corner of his eye to see what Rebekah is up to. Before Major can react and properly cover her, as he was trained in Ranger school, Rebekah is already inside the room. She mercilessly kills the three men who stand bewildered in the room. Major, on the other hand, covers the doorway: protecting Rebekah from possible enemy fire.

Rebekah taps Major on the shoulder, signaling him that she is ready to exit the room and continue on down the hallway. Rebekah and Major skirt the wall, moving skillfully down the hall, killing the enemy with every step.

As Mac, Ben, Rebekah, and Major fight their way through the mosque, in search of Marcos, Majed continues driving through the neighborhood. As time progresses, the streets begin to fill with people. Most just stand at their gates, curious as to why there is shooting occurring at the local mosque. Others carefully walk towards the mosque, in a hope to discover what all of the commotion is.

"Things are getting a little busy out here," Majed informs, speaking into his cell phone.

"Are they on to you?" Mac asks.

"No. As far as the people are concerned, I'm just another person driving down the street."

"Good. Randomize your route so they don't catch on to your actions," Mac states as bullets blare in the background.

"What is happening!" a man shouts to his four colleagues.

"We're under attack!" another replies, running frantically in circles around the room.

"Check the hallway to see what's going on," one of the men suggests.

"Do it yourself! I don't want to die!"

"Fine! You coward!" the man who made the suggestion barks.

The man walks towards the black velvet curtain that separates the room from the hallway. Shaking somewhat, the man pulls the curtain back slightly: just enough for him to witness what is happening out in the hallway.

Lying on the floor in front of him are several dead bodies. The walls are spackled with small holes and gashes, which obviously originated from the constant gun fire. The air is filled with the immense sound of AK-47s firing in all directions. The only human voices that the man hears are the sporadic shrieks from his brothers who now lie on the ground in agony: Those who are fortunate to still be alive.

The man throws his head back into the room. What his eyes and ears had just witnessed causes the man to shake even more. His breathing becomes very deep and shallow. The man's face has turned a pasty color and sweat pours profusely down his face.

"What did you see?" one of the men asks him.

"Our deaths," the man simply replies.

"We must call for help," another man states.

The man runs to a table that is positioned against a wall and retrieves the portable phone that sits on it. While frantically pacing, he sporadically dials a series of numbers.

After a couple of rings, someone answers the phone saying, "You're not supposed to call unless it's an emergency."

"Uncle!" the man desperately shouts, "It is an emergency!"

"This better be important, Ali. You're disturbing my morning coffee," the voice on the other end of the telephone barks.

"Uncle! We are under attack! Everyone's dying! What do you want us to do?"

Ali's words stun Jabar in such a manner that his coffee cup unknowingly slips out of his hands. The coffee cup and saucer instantly hit the ground, shattering into an infinite number of pieces.

"Uncle Jabar! Uncle!"

Ali's desperate pleas for help bring Jabar back to reality.

"Ali, you better not fail me!"

"Uncle Jabar, we are here to assist you and serve Allah."

"Then Allah help you if you don't keep the infidels from taking the Christian's son."

"How do you know they want him, uncle?"

"Why else would they attack the mosque?"

"Yes, sir. Thank you for helping me understand."

"Don't give me your thanks. You just ensure that you do Allah's will or I swear by the prophet that if the infidels don't kill you, I will."

"We will not..."

Ali's words are cut off. Sporadic gunfire fills the room for a brief moment, followed by a deadly silence.

"Ali! Ali! Answer me!" Jabar shouts!

Frustrated and confused at the current events, Jabar hangs up his telephone. Sitting in an armchair, Jabar leans forward and puts his head in his hands.

'This is not good,' Jabar thinks to himself as he rocks back and forth in his chair. 'The Ayatollah will not be pleased.'

Mac and Ben have cleared all three rooms on their end of the hall, but there search for Marcos has them still empty handed. The two Mac and Rebekah led groups meet at the end of the mosque. The hallways that they cleared just so happen to wrap around the prayer room and meet in the rear: the hallway was just one long circle. After all of their searching, they still have yet to find Marcos.

"He isn't down there," Mac states.

"We came up empty, too," Rebekah informs.

"Check the rear court yard. We're going into the prayer room," Mac orders.

"Moving," Rebekah responds.

Rebekah and Major exit the hallway through a rear door that they all were standing beside. Mac and Ben sprint back down the hallway in order to search the prayer room.

At the entrance to the prayer room, Mac and Ben stand on opposite sides of the black velvet cloak that drapes down to the floor. Mac carefully moves the drape so he can take a quick peak inside. Much to Mac's relief, he spots Marcos inside, but his condition does not look too good.

Positioned in the middle of the prayer room, Marcos is tied up, hanging from the ceiling. His hands are tied and hang above his head: wrists wrapped tightly several times with a chain. Marcos' feet are tied in the same manner, but instead they are weighed down by two heavy cinder blocks. Marcos lightly swings back and forth from the ceiling in an unconscious state. His limp neck forces his head to lie forward to the right with his chin touching the top of his chest.

Marcos is shirtless and shoeless. The only clothing that remains on his body is the pair of pants that he wore on the flight two days ago. His body is littered with cuts and bruises. It is obvious that Marcos' captors had their fun with him: abusing and beating his body as they saw fit. Marcos' left eye is swollen shut and there is a small bruise on his left cheek. His back has welts and streaks on it, giving the appearance that someone had struck him severely with either a belt or some form of a leather strap.

Other than Marcos, there are five men wielding AK-47s in the prayer room. They move back and forth sporadically: waving their arms in the air and arguing with one another. It is obvious that the men are petrified as to what is occurring out in the hallway. The men are disorganized and confused. They do not know what they should do: whether they should stay and do their duty or attempt to escape with their lives. A couple of the guards push one another in frustration. One of the men stands near a wall, speaking to someone on a telephone. The conversation does not look too positive, which is expected, under the current conditions.

Seeing the display of disarray causes Mac to smile on the inside. The enemy's disorganization and inability to focus under stress makes his job that much easier. Mac's only wish is that the enemy does not do anything stupid; i.e. kill Marcos before he and Ben can get to him.

Mac grabs the edge of the curtain. While simultaneously swinging the curtain open, Mac springs into the prayer room, with Ben following close behind. Mac and Ben's entry startle the men. Panicking, two of them drop their weapons and run. Instinctively, Ben shoots them dead. Mac turns to his immediate left and kills the other three as they were in the process of firing their weapons.

With the enemy all dead in the prayer room, Mac says, "We got him."

"Copy," Majed states.

"We're heading around front to clear the way for you," Rebekah informs.

"Hold him up," Mac instructs Ben.

Ben dashes to where Marcos hangs limp from the ceiling and holds his sweaty, bloody, body.

"Shut your eyes," Mac commands.

Ben does as he is told. Mac stands about ten feet away from Marcos, aims carefully, and shoots the chains that are attached to the ceiling. Instantly, Marcos' body falls limp into Ben's arms.

Mac then instructs: "Stretch him out. We've got to get his feet as far away from the cinder blocks as we can."

Ben carefully drags Marcos' unconscious body across the floor, creating as much distance between Marcos' feet and the cinder blocks, in which they are attached to by the chains. With Marcos properly situated, Mac shoots at the point where the cinder blocks and chains meet. The flash from the metal on metal contact is followed by concrete and metal shattering, thus freeing Marcos from his bonds. Mac immediately lifts Marcos from off of the ground and throws him over his shoulder like a sack of potatoes.

"Ben, take the front," Mac orders. "We're coming out."

"We've got you covered out in the courtyard," Rebekah informs. "The hall's cleared for movement."

Without hesitating, Ben strides to the draped curtain. He immediately reaches his free hand up, grabs the top of the curtain, and tears it down.

The curtain now lying on the bloodied stone floor, Ben peers down both ends of the hallway to ensure that it is clear of any enemy personnel. With their safety assured, Ben leads a Marcos carrying Mac out of the prayer room and into the hallway. Three and a half strides later, Ben and Mac are outside in the courtyard. Rebekah and Major are in position, to the front and twenty meters from one another providing cove fire. There were a few enemy stragglers in the courtyard, but Rebekah and Major took care of them prior to Mac and Ben's return.

Seeing that Mac and Ben are safely outside with Marcos in tow, Rebekah and Major run to the gate to cover their forward movement. Rebekah swings the gate open. Major jumps through the gate opening and clears the sidewalk area of any possible enemy personnel.

The sidewalk is covered with innocent bystanders. Much to Major's relief, none of the people are carrying weapons of any sort, so he is not forced to shoot anyone. As was planned, Majed comes rolling forward as Mac steps out onto the sidewalk. Assessing that the situation is not highly volatile, Major opens the side minivan door, instead of waiting for Majed to do so.

While Major opens the door, Rebekah and Ben stand outside on the sidewalk, on both sides of the gate, covering Mac's movement to the minivan. The area fully secured, Mac, who still touts Marcos on his shoulder, runs out of the courtyard and leaps into the minivan. Ben jumps into the van behind Mac, followed by Major, and then Rebekah, who slides the door shut behind her.

Everyone inside, Majed peels off and drives down the road at immense speed. The only thing that occupies Majed's mind is getting out of Ad Dimas unnoticed. Though the crowd outside of the mosque had grown to a very large size, the group's actions only took a matter of fifteen minute or so: give or take a couple of minutes. They were fast enough that the police did not have adequate time to react to the commotion.

Spotting two police cars heading their way in the distance, Majed slows down some, in order to look as inconspicuous as possible. The police officers zoom by without paying the Khia minivan any mind. Before the group's departure from the mosque none of the citizenry was aware that the white Khia minivan that was driving around the neighborhood was an accessory to what was occurring at their local mosque.

With haste, the group drives out of Ad Dimas unnoticed and unscathed. Most importantly though, they are leaving with what they came for: Marcos.

"Nice work, guys," Ben congratulates.

Ben and Major give each other a pound and smile.

"That's how it's supposed to be done," Mac continues. "In and out: Just like that."

While Mac speaks to the group, he takes the chains from around Marcos' wrists and ankles. Free from his bonds, Mac takes an ammonia capsule and sticks it up both of Marcos' nostrils. A couple of breaths later and Marcos wildly shakes his head from side to side. Calm, Marcos opens his good eye.

Recognizing his two friends, Marcos says with a raspy voice, "Ben, Major, I didn't think I'd ever see you again."

"We weren't going to let you go out like that, Marcos" Major boasts.

Marcos laughs at Major's remark. The strain on his chest causes Marcos to cough as he laughs.

Ben lightly squeezes Marcos' shoulder and says, "It's good see you back alive, man."

"Thank you, friend," Marcos states, grasping Ben's hand.

Marcos takes a look around him and realizes that he does not recognize the other three passengers in the minivan.

Marcos asks Ben and Major, "Who are they?"

Before Major or Ben can say anything, Mac interjects saying, "We can't say. All you need to know is that we're friends of theirs. We're going to take you somewhere to get cleaned up, then take you home. Now, sit back and get some rest. You've had a long two days."

Marcos nods his head in compliance. He leans his head up against the window, closes his eyes, and, for the first time in nearly seventy-two hours, is able to sleep in peace.

0600 HRS

THE AYATOLLAH SITS IN HIS LIVING room, surrounded by his four closest confidants: Kareem, Jabar, Ahmed, and Assam. They all have received the news that the president's son was rescued from the mosque in Ad Dimas, Syria just a short time ago.

"What do we do from here?" the Ayatollah openly asks.

"What can we do, sayed?" Jabar opens.

"Your plan was full proof," Assam states.

"Who could have done this?" Kareem asks the group.

"It wasn't the Americans or the Zionists," Ahmed states. "From what I was told, less than ten people attacked the mosque."

"Less than ten?" the Ayatollah asks with a bewildered look on his face. "And we have no idea who could have done this?"

"None, sayed," Ahmed replies.

"Can we check the neighboring towns?" the Ayatollah asks his men. "Maybe we can re-take him before he makes it to the city?"

"That's not going to work, sayed," Assam disappointingly responds. "The Shia'a community is not strong enough for us to make that happen."

"I'm afraid we have no options, sayed," Kareem states.

"The plan was fool proof," Kareem states.

"If that is the case, sayed, how do we explain our current situation?" the Ayatollah asks his colleagues.

"With the way things are today, sayed, anyone could have informed someone of our activities," Assam suggests.

"I can't think who would have sinned against Allah and spoken of our plans," the Ayatollah states.

As the five men talk, a series of loud bangs from the door disrupts their conversation. The men stop speaking and look at one another in a confused manner. Instantly, a ghostly silence fills the room. A second later, an envelope slides from beneath the crack in the door. Ahmed steps forward towards the door and picks the envelope up from off of the floor. The envelope in hand, he then promptly hands it over to the Ayatollah, who stares at it with a bit of fright.

"You must open it, sayed," Assam softly says to the Ayatollah.

The Ayatollah nods his head. He rips the side of the envelope off and pulls its contents out. The Ayatollah unfolds the paper and silently reads it to himself. Unexpectedly, the Ayatollah releases the paper from his hands. The paper glides gently down to the ground. Landing, Kareem bends over and retrieves it from off of the ground. Kareem raises the paper to his eyes and reads it to his colleagues:

Ali Hussein Ishmael:

The Great Khan requests the immediate presence of you and your four associates at the mountain. Be there at eleven o'clock this evening. Do not be late.

Having read the note, Kareem places it on the table and looks at each of his friends. They all have the same look on their faces: that of uncertainty and eminent doom.

Assam breaks the silence, saying, "Is this it, sayed?"

"I fear so, old friend. There is no way we can run from this. We must face our fate with dignity and pride and allow Allah to sort everything out."

MASNAA, LEBANON

IT TAKES MARCOS' VICTORIOUS RESCUE PARTY about an hour to return to Masnaa. They could easily have kept on to Beirut, but Mac felt it best that they stop at the safe house so Marcos can clean up, eat, and get some much needed rest. Since Marcos is no longer in harms way, Mac feels no need to rush him home. This not being Mac's first rescue mission, he understands the importance of the rescuee "looking good" when he reunites with his loved ones. The scene is much easier to take in for both parties.

The group slowly pulls up in front of the house and quickly exits the van.

As Majed leads the way towards the house, he suddenly stops dead in his tracks and softly says, "Something doesn't feel right. It's too quiet."

Mac takes Majed's words as the sign for him to move to the front. He turns and intensely looks at everyone; thus signaling for them to be vigilant. Ben hands Marcos his .45 so that he is able to defend himself, if need be.

Mac places his left hand on the door knob, his right hand lightly gripping his AK, and slowly opens the door. There is no explosion or gunshots. Good.

Mac enters the house, followed closely by Majed, Rebekah, Major, Ben, and then Marcos. The group begins to sweep the room from the right of the door when, unexpectedly, the door slams shut behind them.

Mac spins around and aims his AK at the door, yet finding no target. Suddenly, the entire house turns pitch black, as though thick curtains were draped over the windows. The darkness is so extreme that they all may as well be blind.

Reacting to the surprise attack, Mac loudly orders, "Everyone, circle in, facing out! Marcos, get in the center!"

The group forms a circle in the order in which they entered the house: all facing outward: and surround Marcos. For all they know, Marcos' life is still in danger. Before they can react any further to the sudden mysterious happenings, several gushes of wind, like fast moving cars, race past and around them.

As they feel the mighty forces passing around them, their weapons are suddenly snatched out of their hands. Those with secondary weapons quickly draw them, but with no targets and the inability to see, smartly, no one fires their weapon. Doing so would cause possible fratricide. Either way, as soon as the weapons are drawn, the mighty gusts of wind make another series of passes and snatch them, as well.

Frustrated beyond belief, Mac shouts, "What the hell is going on?"

"I knew something didn't feel right," Majed states with a bit of cynicism in his tone.

Before anyone else has a chance to respond to Mac and Majed's words, an unkown voice from amongst the dark states, "Do not be alarmed. We are all friends here."

"You took our weapons. I don't take that as a friendly action," Mac retorts.

"Under normal circumstances, I would agree, Mr Pollard, but today is not a normal day, now is it?"

"How the hell you know my name?" Mac asks.

"And your other question is, "How am I here?" but there is no need for me to explain that. As for your voiced question, I find it my responsibility to be aware of all activities of those like yourselves and your two colleagues. As for the young lieutenants with you, they seem to have attained a great deal of skill and ability from their experience at West Point and their Ranger school training."

"Okay, so you know who we all are, but who the hell are you?" Mac calmly asks. He would love to get upset, but being in the position that they are in, Mac knows that it is best that he act with a cool head.

"Who I am is not important. Why I am here, is. I wish to thank you for cleaning up a mess that should never have occurred. Marcos, my deepest apologizes for the pain that was inflicted upon you. You were not meant to get dragged into of all of this. Allah has granted you the gift of life."

"Dragged into what?" Mac asks. "Obviously, there's more to all of this than a simple hijack and rescue mission."

"Much more than you will ever know, but know this: I am forever indebted to you. I must now tend to more pressing matters. May Allah bless and guide you, my friends."

Suddenly, the room again stirs with immense gusts of wind whipping in all directions. And, as though nothing mysterious and out of the ordinary had even occurred, the lights turn back on, leaving the group standing there in the house looking at one another with little understanding as to what had just happened.

As they all attempt to piece everything together of what had just occurred, Major looks over at the table where they had prepped for Marcos' rescue mission and just happens to notice that something seems out of place. Major makes his way to the table and finds a small ceder box lying on top of the strewn out papers.

"Mac, check this out," says Major, not wanting to touch the box.

Mac turns in Major's direction to see what he wants. He then walks over to Major and says, "What's up?"

Major points to the ceder box. Mac takes the box into his hands and opens it. Much to his surprise, Mac finds five gold chains, each of which have an emblem of a crescent, star, and dagger hanging as the centerpiece. At the bottom of the box, Mac spots a note. He takes the note out from under the gold chains and reads it to everyone.

Dear Friends,

I present these gifts as a token of my extreme gratitude. Wear them knowing that Allah's arms will always embrace you with his glorious protection. Continue along your honorable paths and our bond of friendship shall never break.

With all Praise and Honor to Allah,
The Great Khan

"I knew it!" Majed proclaims. "The Assassins did have a hand in all of this!"

"The Assassins?" Rebekah states. "They haven't existed for centuries."

"I would agree," Majed responds, "Except for the fact that the man who attempted to assassinate President Paulos bore the Assassin's mark and used a dagger as his sole weapon. Other than the mark on his arm, which is identical to the emblem on these chains, the assailant had no identifiable markings: not even fingerprints."

"Who the hell is the Great Khan? Is he related to Ghengis?" Mac asks as he attempts to piece all of the recent events together.

"Yes, but no. It would take too long to explain," Majed begins, "but then again, anything that's public record is nothing more than myth and legend. Our interaction with the Great Khan alone is more knowledge than anyone has of him or the Assassins. I think that it is best that we keep this to ourselves."

"I have to agree with Majed, Douglas," Rebekah agrees. "If we go around telling people we encountered the Great Khan or any of his Assassins, at best we'll be ridiculed and labeled as fools. At worst, we'll be killed by people looking to make a name for themselves, or by the Assassins for our not being able to keep our mouths shut."

"You guys are right," Mac replies. "We'll mention this to no one. Agreed?"

Everyone nods their heads in agreement.

Mac holds the gold chains in his hand and says, "You guys can do whatever you want with these, but I'm sure as hell taking mine. If this Great Khan is who you says he is, I'm not pissing him the hell off."

They all laugh, knowing that there is some underlying truth to Mac's words.

Mac hands Majed, Rebekah, Major, and Ben each a chain. Marcos does not receive one because, as the Great Khan had stated earlier, Marcos' life was his gift. They all take their chain from Mac and place them around their necks and tuck them under their shirts. Mac simply slips his chain into his pocket.

Changing the subject, Mac, "Go get cleaned up, Marcos. We should get you home to your family before word breaks out about our op."

Marcos nods his head in agreement.

"Come with me," Majed says to Marcos, escorting him to the bathroom.

While Marcos takes his shower, everyone else finally takes advantage of the dead time and gets some much needed rest and a chance to unwind.

0800 HRS

NOW THAT EVERYONE IS RESTED AND their nerves have calmed from all of the activity, it is now time to return Marcos to his family.

Mac walks up to Majed and, firmly shaking his hand, says, "Well, Majed, it was a pleasure working with you. You're a true professional."

"The honor was all mine, Mac. I always heard how you operated, but it was much more amazing being able to work alongside you and watch you in action," Majed replies.

Mac turns his attention to Major, Ben, and Marcos and asks, "You guys ready to go?"

"Yes, sir!" Marcos answers with a great deal of enthusiasim in his voice.

Major and Ben grab their and Rebekah's luggage, and take it to the car that Mac had rented from the airport, and quickly return to the house.

Ben stands in the doorway and announces, "We're loaded up, Mac. Ready when you are."

"Well, let's get going then," Mac states.

Before exiting the house, Marcos approaches Majed and says, "Thank you sir, in helping rescue me. I am forever in your debt."

"I'm just doing what I do and helping friends," Majed simply replies.

The two men shake hands and embrace.

Rebekah is the first one out the door, with Mac following close behind. Major and Ben walk out the house with Marcos. The three friends jump into the back seat, while Mac gets in the driver's side and Rebekah the front passenger's side. With everyone situated, Mac pulls out onto the road and drives out of Masnaa, heading straight for Beirut.

The drive to Beirut is rather smooth and quite free of traffic. As Mac drives, he notices a white Mercedes Benz speed past them in the opposite direction. Mac does not pay much attention to the car, but what he does see causes him to laugh slightly.

"What's so funny?" Rebekah asks, curious as to why Mac is laughing for seemingly no reason.

"Did you see that Mercedes we just passed?" Mac asks, smiling.

"No. I wasn't paying attention," Rebekah answers.

"I haven't seen that many old dudes packed in a car before in my life and they were all turbaned up," Mac explains.

"What's so funny about that?" Rebekah asks, not understanding the jest.

"Oh, never mind," Mac replies, frustrated at the fact that Rebekah does not see the humor in what he saw.

1030 HRS

AS THEY ENTER THE OUTSKIRTS OF Beirut, Mac says, "Hey, Marcos. Where do I go from here?"

"Oh. I am sorry," Marcos apologizes. "Let me direct you to my home."

Marcos gives directions to Mac as he drives, guiding the group through the immense and culturally diverse Lebanese capital.

After driving for nearly half an hour through Beirut, Marcos announces, "There's my house, up ahead to the right."

Upon Marcos' words, Mac slows the car down to a complete stop.

Putting the car in park, Mac says to Marcos, Ben, and Major, "It's best that Rebekah and I drop you guys off here. Ben, Major, you guys know where I coming from on that."

"We understand," Ben replies. He then asks, "How do we explain our rescuing Marcos."

"You're smart kids. You handled the West Point thing without a hitch. You'll know what to say when pressed," Mac answers. He then turns to Marcos and says, "That means you can't even mention our names: me, Rebekah, or Majed."

"Let's get you boys home," Rebekah states as she opens the door and steps outside.

All of the men follow suit and get out of the car. Mac tosses Ben the keys so that he can get his and Major's luggage out of the trunk.

While Ben gets the luggage out of the trunk, Major says, "Hey, Mac. Thanks a lot, man! You really came through for us in a way I never thought you would."

"It's like I told you, Major," Mac replies as he lightly punches Major in the chest. "Call me when you need me. I always look out for my people."

Mac and Major give each other a pound.

Rebekah then says to Major, "You take care of yourself, sweetie." She then touches Major's cheek with her soft hand and kisses him lightly on the other.

"Ben," Mac says as he shakes his hand, "I'm glad you were able to hang around for this one."

"You and me both," Ben replies with a slight chuckle

Rebekah then says, "Way to have my back today, Ben. You're definitely going to do your army proud." She then gives Ben a hug.

Mac stands before Ben and Major and places a hand on both of their outer shoulders, saying, "I'm extremely proud of you guys. You stepped up in a way that most people could never fathom. That thing at West Point was one of the worst days of my life, but encountering you two that day was one of the best. You guys are like little brothers to me, and I will always be there for you. Know that."

The three men embrace for a second.

Once they release, Rebekah says, "Okay, it's time for us to get going. You three take care. Make sure to have some fun. GOD knows you've earned it!"

Rebekah and Mac get back into the car and slowly drive off into the distance.

"I can't believe this is over," Major comments as he picks his luggage up from off of the ground.

"Tell me about," Ben concurs. He then asks, "How you feeling, Marcos?"

"Ready to see my family," Marcos replies with a huge grin on his face.

"Well, let's do it," Major states. "Lead the way!"

Marcos leads his two friends a few yards down the street, then takes a right into a long driveway. The three young men immediately halt their forward progress because a large black gate impedes their path.

A large man, not as big as Mac, but still a formidable presence nonetheless, slowly walks down the driveway and sternly shouts, "What is your business?"

"George! It's me! It's Marcos! Let us in! These are my friends!"

Hearing Marcos' proclamation, George jumps back in shock, shouting, "Sir! How? When?"

Realizing that Marcos needs to enter the compound, George sprints to the gate with all of his might, and without pausing, opens it.

"George these are my friends who just rescued me," Marcos informs.

"Allah be prasied!" George shouts, giving Marcos a big bear hug.

George grabs his radio from his inside blazer pocket and excitedly shouts, "Marcos is home! Marcos is home!" George then snatches Marcos' hand and says, "Come, sir. Your parents are dying to see you!" George speedily strides with Marcos in tow. Remembering the other two young men, George turns around and says, "Forgive me. I forgot all about you. Please, follow me inside."

George presses an eight digit code on the control panel, which is positioned ten feet from the gate. A slight pause later and the steel black gate opens, allowing Major and Ben into the Presidential compound.

As George leads Marcos towards the Presidential mansion, several people on the compound, within eye sight, cease their activities and stare in disbelief. After hearing of Marcos' kidnapping and the $25 million ransom video, none of them expected to see Marcos ever again. Marcos waives to the onlookers with a huge grin on his face.

Dragging their luggage, Major and Ben do their best to keep up with Marcos and George, of whom they walk stoically behind, as Marcos celebrates his triumphant return home. The pace that the group moves is somewhere between jogging and fast walking

President Paulos sits in his study reading a book. He attempts to keep his mind off of his son as best he can. The past couple of days have been extremely hard on the president. He does not sleep very well and is unable to eat. Whatever President Paulos tries to do to forget about his loss does not work and seems to cause the pain to grow even more.

Frustrated with reading, President Paulos closes the book and tosses it on the floor.

"Why me, Allah?" President Paulos pleads to higher as he throws his head back against the couch.

Unexpectedly, President Paulos' personal secretary bursts into her boss' study.

"Sir!" the secretary shouts. "Marcos! He's home!"

The unexpected news does not hit President Paulos immediately. Slowly, he raises his head and sits up on the couch. Seeing that the president has not yet processed her joyous news, the secretary runs up to him and drops to one knee.

The secretary takes President Paulos' hand into her own and softly says, "Sir, did you not hear me? Marcos is home."

President Paulos' eyes open wide as the information begins to slowly process in his head. He stares down at his secretary who is still on one knee. Finally, after a few moments of digesting the informtion, President Paulos grips his secretary's shoulders with immense pressure. Instantaneously, he leaps to his feet while tossing his secretary up into the air with him.

"Marcos is home?" President Paulos joyously asks.

"Yes, sir!" his secretary happily answers, while she balances herself.

Without warning, President Paulos grasps his secretary's head with both hands, pulls her in, and kisses her four times on her cheeks.

"Thank Allah!" President Paulos shouts as he releases his secretary's head.

President Paulos' secretary joyously laughs at her employer's happiness.

"Come, Fedah!" President Paulos says to his secretary. "You must take me to him!"

Fedah takes President Paulos by the hand and says, "This way, sir."

Fedah, running as fast as her little legs will move, drags President Paulos out of the study and into the immense foyer. She heads directly for the front door, reaching for the doorknob as soon as she is able. With the doorknob firmly gripped, Fedah turns it and swings the door wide open. She stops in her tracks and forces President Paulos to stand in front of her in the doorway.

Much to President Paulos' greatest prayers, he witnesses the one thing that he thought he would never in his life see again: his youngest child, Marcos, alive.

"Get Vienna," President Paulos softly says to Fedah of his wife.

"Yes, sir," Fedah replies with a huge grin on her face.

Fedah takes off, leaving the President's side. She runs upstairs to find Mrs. Paulos to inform her of the glorious news.

"Marcos!" President Paulos joyously shouts.

Hearing his father's voice, Marcos halts in place and looks up at the doorway.

"Father!" Marcos replies with a loud shout.

Ecstatic over seeing his father in the distance, Marcos runs full speed towards the doorway. Likewise, President Paulos darts out of the doorway and runs as fast as his tired body will allow. Reuniting in the middle of the driveway, the father and son embrace. President Paulos hugs his son with more love and strength than he has ever had. He fervently kisses Marcos several times on both cheeks.

"Thank Allah he brought you back to me," President Paulos happily states, while crying tears of joy. He then asks, "How did you escape?"

Marcos signals behind him and says, "Major and Ben."

President Paulos, with yet another shocked look on his face, looks up and sees his son's two friends standing a few meters back.

President Paulos and Marcos release their hold on one another and quickly walk over to where Ben and major stand.

"I am forever in your debt," President Paulos says to Ben and Major. "Allah definitely blessed this family when he brought you into my son's life!"

"Thank you, sir," Ben and Major humbly reply.

Full of joy, President Paulos embraces both Ben and Major.

"I thought I had lost him," President Paulos somberly remarks. He then takes a small step back and says, "Well, Major and Ben, I guess you gentlemen got an interesting introduction to our part of the world, huh?"

They all laugh at President Paulos' sarcastic comment.

Collecting himself, President Paulos then says to Major and Ben, "I was going to cancel the New Year's festivities, but now, I am making it my duty that you gentlemen have the time of your lives!"

"Man, yeah!" Major happily responds.

"George!" President Paulos shouts.

George who was standing a few yards off to the side to give the joyous group space and privacy, runs to where President Paulos stands, saying, "Yes, sir."

"Tell Fedah to get on the phones and tell everyone that the New Year's party is still on as scheduled!" President Paulos happily commands.

"Yes, sir," George replies with an enormous smile on his face.

Following his president's instructions, George immediately runs into the house in search of Fedah.

President Paulos returns his attention to Major and Ben and says, "We should all go into the house now for some refreshment. By the way, not taking anything away from your efforts in returning my son home, but how did you do it?"

"Let's just say, sir," Ben begins to explain, "that we have friends with special skill sets."

President Paulos looks at Ben inquisitively and says, "I think I understand, but won't the authorities want to know you were able to rescue Marcos all on your own?"

"Trust me, sir," Major begins to explain, "We're experienced in dealing with the authorities."

President Paulos now gives Major a funny look, then turns and curiously looks at Ben, thinking, 'What have these boys been up to in the past?'

Reacting to President Paulos' gaze, Ben and Major do not know how to respond, so they simply shrug their shoulders and crack a smile. President Paulos returns the smile in kind as they all enter a once again joyous home.

2000 HRS: SOMEWHERE IN THE SYRIAN DESERT

THE AYATOLLAH AND HIS FOUR ASSOCIATES stand at the base of the mountain. Assam, Kareem, Jabar, and Ahmed wait behind the Ayatollah as he attempts to find the secret lever to allow them passage into the mountain.

"It has to be here somewhere," the Ayatollah frustratingly states as he fervently feels every piece of rock with hands, in the hopes of finding the lever.

"Sayed, did you not tell us that the Khan would move the lever elsewhere?" Kareem reminds the Ayatollah.

"Yes, he did," the Ayatollah replies, "that is why I'm checking in other places, as well. Come! Help me."

Upon the Ayatollah's desperate plea, Kareem, Jabar, Assam, and Ahmed rush to their leader's side and help him search for the secret lever that will allow them passage into the mysterious mountain.

The five desperate men have been at it for nearly half an hour and have made no progress. Being that they are at the base of the mountain, there is no way for them, with only a half an hour, to properly search the entire side of a mountain for something that is supposed to be a secret. The five men do not think in that manner because at the present, their lives are on the line: Desperate people do desperate things during desperate situations.

The Ayatollah and his four associates scamper all over the side of the mountain. Some are on their knees; others have actually climbed a few feet up, in the hopes of discovering that which they seek. Their clothes are dusty and dirty. Rips and stains cover their once clean and pristine garments. Instead of looking like the revered men of society, their desperate search has now caused them to appear as the lowest of peasants.

From out of no where, a loud voice startles the five men, saying, "You look like peasant dogs: Scratching at the mountainside in such a manner. I guess it is fitting, considering your present state."

The voice seems to come from all directions, yet from no where, at the same time. The Ayatollah and his men jump back from the mountain and prostrate themselves on the ground: nothing but intense fear consumes their minds. Their bodies begin to shake unnervingly from extreme dread.

Losing all control and allowing fear to take over their actions, Ahmed and Assam pick themselves up from off of the ground and run with all of their strength out into the empty desert, screaming pleas to Allah. Assam and Ahmed do not run very far or very fast, due to their current physical condition and their old age.

"Why do you run?" the voice asks. "Your effort to escape is frivolous. There is nowhere for you to go."

Suddenly, two cracks cut through the night sky. A moment later, Assam and Ahmed fall to the ground hard: lying face first in the desert sand. Kareem runs to their sprawled, still bodies to check on his two friends' condition. Assam and Ahmed have two clean shots to the head. The entrance wounds are located where the head and the neck meet. Because the bullets traveled at such a high rate of speed, very little blood is splattered on the corpses.

"Sayed, they're dead!" Kareem shouts.

The Ayatollah rises from off of the ground and turns towards the mountain, shouting! "Why do you torture us so?"

The voice responds, "Why do you ask me questions in which you already know the answer."

All of a sudden, the ground shakes and rocks and dirt cascade from the side of the mountain. Jabar, who is still kneeling on the ground, scampers to his feet and runs back a few yards. A moment later, a large piece of the mountain slides inward and to the side, creating a passage.

"Enter," the voice commands.

The Ayatollah, Jabar, and Kareem dutifully enter the mountain opening. They are cautious with every slow step that they take. Their feet shuffle in the rocky dirt as they move forward. As much as they want to run away, they have already seen the penalty for attempted escape.

The opening that the Ayatollah, Kareem, and Jabar enter is very dark and dry. It is extremely dark to the point where they are barely able to see their feet. The darkness disallows them from knowing exactly how large the room is that they now occupy. Fear of the unknown forces the three old men to huddle close to one another.

Inside and scared, the mountain begins to rumble, once again. Behind the old men, the mountain slowly closes in on them, leaving them in extreme darkness. The Ayatollah, Kareem, and Jabar do not move a muscle. They remain where they stand, frightingly waiting to see what happens next. Fear courses through their bodies in such an intense manner that their minds are completely empty. All they know is that death is apparent.

Without notice, the room fills an extremely intense light. The light is so bright that the Ayatollah, Kareem, and Jabar cover their eyes to keep from going blind. They have been in the dark for such an extended period of time that the sudden increase in illumination is too much for the old men's eyes to handle.

"You can keep your eyes covered," the voice says after an extended period of silence. "There is nothing for you to see. The light is for my purpose only."

"What do you want with us?" the Ayatollah pleads.

"Your questions amuse me, Ali," the voice replies. "You know what I want."

"But I tried!" the Ayatollah cries.

"Yes you did, and your trying illustrates your failure."

"I did not anticipate the infidel's guards killing your Assassin!"

"That is the risk we take. He is now in heaven basking in Allah's glory. Where will you be in the next few minutes, I ask you?"

"Great Khan! I implore you! Give me more time to get the money!"

"I don't think you seem to understand, Ali. I never meant for you to get the money. So you are aware, since I'm going to kill you anyway, I never meant for you to succeed at any of your schemes."

The Great Khan's words stab the Ayatollah in the heart. He cannot believe the words that have just touched his ear. The Ayatollah stops breathing for a brief moment. The Great Khan's ill news knocks the breath right out of his lungs like as sledge hammer to a wall.

"You're surprised, Ali?" the Great Khan cynically asks. "Ask yourself this. Why did you seek me out in the first place?"

"The infidel wanted to ruin our way of life! He was sinning against Allah!"

"That is not what I am getting at, Ali. Maybe I should explain, since you have blinders over your eyes. I told you before that I did not care about your holy crusade. Your personal grievances with Paulos are none of my concern. My having you attempt to produce $25 million was nothing more than a test of your character. Blood can only replace blood. You cannot replace it with money. If I knew you had the capabilities and resources to raise $25 million, then I would have set the bar higher. Do you understand me now, Ali? Only your blood can replace that of my fallen Assassin. The fact that you kidnapped and abused Paulos' son is despicable and shows just how evil and self-righteous you really are."

In tears, the Ayatollah interrupts the Great Khan, shouting, "But Great Khan! We did not beat the boy! I swear on my father's grave!"

"Do not interrupt me again, Ali, or I will painfully cut your life off even sooner than I plan!" The Great Khan then laughs at what the Ayatollah has informed him. Gathering himself together, the Great Khan says, "Now, you must either think I am stupid or you have no real control of your people. Looking at the situation you are currently in, I will take the benefit of the doubt and say that it is the latter. So you know, if for some unknown reason you would have come up with the money, then you would not be in your current condition. See: I am fair."

During the seemingly one way conversation between the Great Khan and Grand Ayatollah Ali, Kareem intently listens, in the hopes that the Great Khan will have pity on them and release them. As the conversation stretches out, Kareem realizes that there is only one fate for he, Jabar, and the Ayatollah: death. It is apparent that the Great Khan is not going to show them an ounce of mercy.

With the realization that he is dead anyway, Kareem, from somewhere deep within, straightens his back and takes a step forward.

The Great Khan looks at Kareem puzzlingly, thinking to himself, 'What is this crazy old man doing?'

From deep within his heart, Kareem raises his arms high over his head and shouts, "We have lived great lives! Everything we have said and done has always been for the glory of Allah! We have lived our lives by the direct instructions given in the Holy Quran! If we must die, then so be it! Let is always be said that we lived for the glory of Allah and the teaching of his blessed prophet, Mohamed; blessings be upon him! Great Khan, if you are going to kill us, then do so! We are prepared to meet Allah and his martyrs in Heaven!"

The Great Khan leans forward. All this time, he has been sitting in a high back wooden chair with gold trim. Again he laughs, this time, though, not in amusement. The Great Khan laughs because Kareem's outburst has caused his perspective of the situation to slightly change.

"You, Kareem! You're a brave one. You always have been," the Great Khan declares.

"My bravery means nothing-only Allah's will and plan!" Kareem replies.

"Oh. And wisdom, too."

"Great Khan, do not chastise me as though I am a child! Let us die with our honor. You owe us that much!"

"I owe you nothing, but this is what I'm going to do with you."

The Great Khan effortlessly waves his hand. Instantaneously, Kareem is snatched up from off of the ground and is separated from the Ayatollah and Jabar.

Dropping to his knees, the Ayatollah asks, "Where are you taking him?"

"Kareem was always the brave one of the group," the Great Khan states as though he does not hear the Ayatollah's question. "I like his bravado: His bravery in the face of certain death is much like that of the first generation of saints. Yes, very brave." The Great Khan, through with his outspoken thoughts, returns his attention to the Ayatollah, saying, "Now Ali, do you want to know how you are going to die, or do you want me to surprise you?"

The Ayatollah lowers his head in defeat, not saying a word.

Seeing that the Ayatollah is not going to answer his question, the Great Khan replies, "Very well then. I hope you have asked Allah to forgive you of your transgressions. Maybe I will see you in the next life: maybe not."

The lights that fill the room instantly shut off with the end of the Great Khan's words. The Ayatollah and Jabar are all who remain. Nothing but silence fills the air.

A few moments later, a small rumbling is heard from above. Slowly, dust begins to fall and fill the room.

"Sayed, what is happening?" Jababr desperately asks.

"I do not know," the Ayatollah replies, unsure as to what is occurring.

The Ayatollah and Jabar stand in place, covering their faces from the thick dust that fills the cavernous room. Small rocks drop from high above. First in small numbers, but as time quickly passes, the rocks increase their rate of decent. Dirt and sand now accompany the rocks on their decent. As the debris falls, it slowly begins to pile up: gradually rising on the ground.

The Ayatollah and Jabar frantically raise their feet, as though they are dancing. Their efforts work for a short while, but as the dirt, the rocks, and the debris continue to fall, it rises over their ankles, up to their shins.

Faster and faster the small cavern begins to fill. The Ayatollah and Jabar cover their heads for protection. Their attempts are to no avail, though, being that the dirt and rocks are rising at such a high rate that their wastes are now buried. The Ayatollah and Jabar attempt to move around, but the force and pressure around them is too great to allow them to move effectively.

"Allah! Have mercy on us!" the Ayatollah shouts as the debris continues to rise.

"I don't want to die! I don't want to die!" Jabar loudly pleads.

No one answers the two old men's pleas. The dirt continues to rise and rise and rise. As it reaches their necks, the Ayatollah and Jabar scamper for their lives. They throw their arms into the air, while they attempt to pull themselves up. Their efforts are nothing more than a waste of energy. For every inch they are able to climb, debris simply fills in the space that they create.

The debris fills all around them. The Ayatollah and Jabar are at the point where they are unable to move their bodies. They swing their necks in all directions. Though they know that death is imminent, it is simply man's natural instinct to fight for one's life to the end.

"No! Noooo! It wasn't supposed to end this way!" the Ayatollah cries as the sand rises over his chin, touching his lower lip.

Suddenly, the debris stops falling around the Ayatollah and Jabar. The two old men, with great effort, strain their necks to look at one another. Neither man knows what is occurring now. The fear still continues to swell. The silence and lack of activity, though causes their fear to shift over to hope. Though they were not prepared to die, the Ayatollah and Jabar did not expect the Great Khan to spare their lives.

"What is happening, sayed?" Jabar asks the Ayatollah.

"Allah has shown his divine mercy," the Ayatollah replies.

"All praises be to Allah," Jabar shouts.

As the two trapped old men give glorious praises to Allah, the mountain begins to rumble again.

"Sayed, no! We were spared! Allah spared our lives!" Jabar shouts as he begins to sob like a small child.

The Ayatollah does not say a word. He simply raises his head and waits for his fate to befall him. The debris continues to fall again, this time, though, instead of small rocks and sand, large boulders fall from above. The boulders fall fast and hard, easily crushing the heads of the Ayatollah and Jabar. With their deaths, the small cavernous room quickly fills with boulders until there is barely any room for air.

Kareem has been taken from one cavernous room to another and thrown on the ground like a sack of rocks. Kareem hits the ground hard. The force of the impact causes a small dust cloud to rise. The room in which Kareem now lies is just as dark as his previous location.

"Lie where you stay! Move from this spot and die!" a loud voice commands.

From his current experience, Kareem realizes that the loud voice is not that of the Great Khan's, or at least he does not believe so, being that tonight was the only time he has ever heard the Great Khan's voice. Kareem's only reference comes from that of his old friend, Grand Ayatollah Ali Hussein.

Kareem does as he is commanded and does not move a muscle. Even if he wanted, Kareem could not move very far. The fall has bruised his right knee. Old age made him slow. The injury now makes him immobile.

The pain is excruciating, but Kareem does not let out a sound, concerned that someone may punish him for his actions.

Suddenly, from afar off, Kareem feels the mountain rumble, followed by a weird sound, as though sand were falling down the side of the rocky mountain. The strange noises coming from within the mountain is accompanied by horrific screams and pleas to Allah for mercy. For those who scream, Allah, unfortunately, does not answer their prayers. At present, Allah is answering the prayers of another.

The rumbling ceases, but the sound of falling sand and the pleas for mercy continue for what seems an eternity. As with all things, though, the falling sand ceases, as well. The screaming stops, and a short period of time passes with nothing but silence. All Kareem can hear is his breathing: the air pushing and forcing his lungs up and down and the breeze lightly blowing through the mountain cracks. The silence, though does not last long, as the rumbling returns and the sound of falling rocks emits from inside the mountain. This time, though, there are no screams. It is as though those who were screaming have accepted their fate and made their peace with Allah.

The sound of the falling rocks comes to an end. The realization that the Ayatollah and Jabar are now dead hits Kareem hard. Kareem lowers his forehead to the ground and silently weeps for his two friends, praying for their souls and safe passage into Heaven.

Without notice, the cavernous room fills with light. The light, though, is not as bright as when Kareem was in the other room. The room, full of light, forces Kareem to shut his eyes. Because he has been in the dark for such an extended period of time, it takes a while for his eyes to adjust.

Kareem squints, attempting to see what is around him. As his eye sight improves, Kareem notices four men standing around him. The men are dressed in all black and stand in a powerful stance around Kareem with their arms folded over their chests.

"I am going to spare your life, Kareem!" the Great Khan informs.

Kareem scurries on the floor, turning his head in all direction, attempting to find the Great Khan, but to no avail. The Great Khan is not in the small cavernous room. Kareem is forced to communicate with the air.

"Your search is futile, Kareem." The Great Khan says in response to Kareem's investigation. He then continues, saying, "As you are more than aware, your illustrious Ayatollah and your coward of a friend, Jabar, are both dead. Now, you're probably wondering why you are not dead, as well. Am I correct in my assumption?"

Agreeing with the Great Khan, Kareem nods his head.

"Let me tell you why I have spared you Kareem," the Great Khan begins to explain. "You showed courage in the face of imminent death. I do not know if it was bravery or a touch of insanity. Nonetheless, it was inspiring. Not too many people speak to me in such a manner before I take their lives. They usually either stand in silence or cry for mercy. I prefer silence. You, on the other hand, Kareem, stood up to the Great Khan. You tossed your fears to the side and challenged me: Quite awe inspiring."

"What will you do with me?" Kareem interrupts.

The Great Khan lets out a slight chuckle, saying, "Your fate, Kareem, is to remember this day and the days that led up to this day for the remainder of your old years. The catch is that you will no longer be allowed to see this place. I warn you though, if you attempt to return, I will deal with you accordingly."

Kareem looks up into the air, confused. He is unsure of what the Great Khan means. Allah knows that Kareem never wants anything to do with the mountain, the Great Khan, or his Assassins ever again.

Abruptly, three of the men in the room grab onto Kareem. Two of the men hold each of Kareem's arms, while the other firmly grips his head. Kareem does not squirm under the pressure, until his fate stares him dead in his face.

The fourth man stands before Kareem holding a hot poker in his hands. The iron rod glows white from the immense heat. Now, Kareem begins to squirm.

"What is this?" Kareem shouts.

No one answers Kareem's question.

The men holding Kareem, with great strength and ease, pin his back to the ground. The man holding his head positions his knees around it and squeezes: immobilizing Kareem and disallowing him from moving his head. Without hesitation, the man with the hot poker skewers both of Kareem's eye sockets.

Kareem lets out a mighty scream as the hot iron melts his eyes and the skin around them. Never in his life has Kareem felt such intense pain. Kareem's body shakes and he slides his feet on the dusty ground, in a feeble attempt to find some comfort and relief.

Having completed his task, the man carrying the hot poker steps away from Kareem and quickly returns with two ice packs. He places them over Kareem's eyes. The men who have Kareem pinned to the ground raise him slightly, enough to where the man can wrap a bandage around his head to keep the ice packs in place.

"This is your fate, Kareem," the Great Khan states. "I was going to cut your tongue out, as well, but Allah has mercy on the righteous. Living with no sight and speech is worst than death. I could not have you suffer a worst fate than Ali. At the same time, if I really wanted to silence you, I would have had to cut your hands off, as well. Could you imagine having no eyes, tongue, or hands? Definitely worst than death. Taking your sight, on the other hand, is a fitting punishment. You will adjust. Now, go with Allah, Kareem."

The lights suddenly shut off, leaving Kareem in the darkness with the four men. He can still feel their presence around him. Instantaneously, Kareem is hoisted up from off of the ground and thrown over someone's shoulder. Kareem bounces up and down as he is carried through the mountain.

Moments later, Kareem feels the cool evening air hit his face, causing him to realize that he is now outside. The one carrying Kareem continues on his destination. They stop, and Kareem hears familiar noises like those of moving mechanical parts, but he is unable to distinguish the sounds from each other. Kareem is suddenly thrown from off of the man's shoulder and lands on a soft surface. He cannot make out what he is lying on. It is not a mattress, yet at the same time, it is not a pad, either.

An engine starts and with Kareem inside what he now realizes is a vehicle of some sort, he and his secret escort begin to move at a high rate of speed.

'I must be in a van,' Kareem thinks to himself as he lies still.

Kareem makes his deduction based on the fact that if he could feel the wind on his face, then he would be in the bed of a truck. If he did not have room to stretch out, he would either be in some sort of a car or a minivan. Kareem carefully feels the space around him, but is unable to touch anything.

The drive continues for what seems an eternity. The van maintains a high rate of speed for the entirety of the trip. Some time later, though, the van slows down. As the van moves at a much slower rate of speed, Kareem's body rolls slightly in several directions, which signals to him that they are making several turns through a town or a city.

A few minutes later, the van comes to a slow halt. Kareem hears men step out of the van. Next, he hears what he realizes is the side door open. The men retrieve Kareem from where he lies and carry him out of the van.

Again, Kareem bounces on someone's shoulder, towards an unknown destination. This portion of the trip is not long, though, for he abruptly stops. Kareem is lowered from off of the shoulder and placed on his feet. He then hears several loud knocks on what seems to be a metal door. The noise sounds like a banging steel gate, but Kareem is not quite sure.

Kareem hears the men scamper away from where he stands, followed by the sound of the van driving off down the street. He now realizes that he stands alone.

Before Kareem can say or think anything, he hears a very familiar, yet confused, voice say, "Father, is that you out there?"

Kareem stretches his arms out in front of him in an attempt to feel where he is, and says, "Hannah, my daughter, is that you?"

Hannah runs from out of her doorway to the front gate. Seeing her father's condition brings Hannah to near shock.

"Father, what happened to you?" Hannah asks as she rushes to her father.

"I am unable to say."

"What do you mean you're unable to say?"

"Hannah, do you trust me?"

"Of course I do, father."

"Then trust me when I say that I cannot tell you what has happened to me."

As Hannah opens the front gate for her father, she asks him, "Can you at least tell me who did this to you?"

"I cannot reveal that, either. Darling, it's wise that you never ask me anything concerning my blindness." Kareem, realizing that Hannah saw him outside rather expediently, asks her, "How did you know I was out here?"

"Someone just called and said you were standing outside at the front gate. I assumed it was a prank call, but when I looked through the window and saw you, I was rather shocked. I was not expecting you to be outside at this time of the night. I thought someone from your mosque had dropped you off, but obviously I am wrong."

"Why would you say that?"

"Because you're alone, father. I can't recall the last time I saw you without an escort. Here, let me help you."

Hannah reaches out and takes her father's arm into her own. She leads him into the small courtyard, heading for the house.

"Don't worry, father. You're going to be fine. I'll take care of you," Hannah says as she softly kisses Kareem on the cheek.

31 DECEMBER 2001, 2000 HRS: BEIRUT, LEBANON

THE PRESIDENTIAL BALLROOM IS FILLED TO its safety capacity to celebrate the coming New Year with President Paulos Bakoos and his family. Leaders and celebrities the world over are in attendance. The current Vice President of the United States and his wife are two such influential world figures present for the evening's festivities.

President Paulos' New Year's Ball is always the hit of the Middle East and Arab world, but this year's ball is special. Tonight's celebration required Fedah to issue more invitations for the ball. Those who generally would have answered another's invitation are in attendance. Tonight's New Year's Ball is very special for two reasons.

Generally, people do not begin arriving for the New Year's Ball until around nine o'clock in the evening. Due to the special occasion, though, the attendees arrived early: just before eight o'clock at night. Other than dancing, which will take up the majority of the evening, President Paulos is going to use the beginning of the celebration as a casual awards ceremony.

President Paulos stands at the top of the stairwell, ten feet over the immense crowd. To his right stands Marcos and to his left stand Ben and then Major. In President Paulos' left hand are two small flat green boxes.

The smile that shines across President Paulos' face lights up the room. All of those who look at him can tell that he is extremely happy. President Paulos probably has never been so happy before in his life. Tonight is special for him and his family.

President Paulos takes a small step forward. He is now ready to address the joyous crowd and make his presentation.

"First, thank you all for coming this fine evening to toast the New Year with my family and me. Tonight, as most of you know, is a very special occasion for us." President Paulos wraps his arm around his son's shoulder and says, "Just a few days ago, our son, Marcos, was brutally taken away from us. I thought we would never see him again. Well, tonight, along with this glorious New Year, we celebrate Marcos' safe return home. I thank Allah for his town friends, lieutenants Milton Johnson and Benjamin Irons. If it were not for the bravery and selflessness of these two upstanding young gentlemen, I dare not think where Marcos would be right now. By Allah's grace, we are all able to celebrate the New Year together." President Paulos releases his hold on Marcos and turns, facing Major and Ben. Without pausing, he says, "Gentlemen, I thank Allah for you. He truly blessed my son and our family when you became friends. You are like sons to me now." President Paulos gives both Ben and Major a bear hug. He releases the two friends and says, "This is a small token of our appreciation. On behalf of the great and proud people of Lebanon, I present you with this medal of honor and distinction." President Paulos places the medal around Ben's neck, then Major's. He then quietly says to Major and Ben, "This medal is the highest award our government presents for heroic military actions and government service. Would you like to say something to everyone?"

President Paulos places his hand in the small of Ben's back, politely forcing him to take a step forward. Ben moves forward from the light force.

Ben holds the medal in his hand, looks at it, and says, "This award I accept with great pride, not because of the accolades that come along with it, but because of the actions it took for me to receive it. My honor was tested the day Marcos was violently taken from the airplane that fateful day. Major and I could have easily have returned home and no one would have thought less of us. We couldn't do that though. There's an old Ranger saying: Never leave a man behind. In our good conscience, we could not return home without the assurance that Marcos was home safe, as well. Friendship means more to me than anything. Without your friends, you're nothing. To me, this medal represents the friendship that we have with Marcos. It symbolizes that there is nothing stronger than the bond of true friendship. Thank you."

The ballroom erupts with the roar of applause. Ben blushes from all of the direct attention he is receiving. He has spoken before many crowds during his young life, but not one that acted with such adulation.

An overjoyed President Paulos looks at Major and rhetorically asks, "Would you care to share a few words, Major?"

Major steps forward with a broad smile streaking across his face. He is a bit nervous, but like Ben, Major has done his fair share of public speaking. Unlike Ben, though, Major has spoken before politicians and dignitaries.

Major begins his speech, saying, "When I called my dad in Frankfurt to tell him that Ben and I were going to return to Syria and rescue Marcos, he asked me, "How many times do you have to save the world?" Well, to make a long story short, saving the world never came to mind. Saving our friend did. Watching Marcos being taken from us was one of the most horrific things I have ever seen. All that raced through my mind was what could we do to get him back? From that moment, nothing was more important to me and Ben than finding Marcos alive. President Paulos, I am humbly grateful for the award. I appreciate the commendation. You know better than most, sir, that Marcos' safe return home is reward enough for me."

Finished speaking to the immense crowd, Major raises his hand slightly and takes a step back. Again, the regal audience roars with applause and cheer. To further move the jovial crowd, President Paulos takes both Major and Ben's hands and raise them high over their heads. After a moment of celebration and cheer, they drop their hands. Full of joy, President Paulos then turns and embraces Ben, and then gives Major the same attention. Marcos follows his father's lead and hugs his two life-saving friends.

President Paulos takes a step forward and faces the joyous crowd, stating, "And now that the formalities are out of the way, let the festivities begin!"

President Paulos leads the three young men down the massive staircase to ground level, amongst the vast crowd. The Vice President of the United States and his wife are the first to approach Ben and Major.

"LT Johnson, LT Irons," the Vice President opens as he extends his hand out. "I don't know how you young men do it."

Laughing slightly, Ben and Major shake the Vice President and the Second Lady's hands. President Paulos and Marcos, seeing that Major and Ben are comfortable, move along and intermingle amongst the crowd.

With a huge smile on his face, the Vice President continues speaking to Ben and Major, saying, "You know, you two have caused quite a stir amongst the upper brass and DoD. When it was reported that you guys didn't arrive at Dulles as scheduled, people were running frantic to locate you. Who would have guessed that you young men had returned to Syria to rescue your friend?"

"We did what we had to do, sir," Ben speaks first.

"Roger, sir. We were just doing our duty," Major follows.

"That's right, sir. There's no way we could have gone home knowing that Marcos was in danger."

"Well, I don't think your superiors are too upset with you anymore. You accomplished the mission and everyone returned home safe. At the end of the day, that's all that matters. I do have one question, though?"

"What's that, sir?" Major asks.

"How were you able to rescue Marcos? The reports state that you had some assistance, but the details were rather vague as to who helped you and how you did it."

Major and Ben give one another a glance, as though they are telepathically speaking to one another. The two friends know exactly to what the Vice President is referring.

When the two young men reported to the United States embassy the day after they had rescued Marcos, they had to scue their story some to protect Mac and Rebekah's identities. Instead of the truth, Major and Ben reported that when they arrived in Frankfurt, they ran into a man and a woman. The man just happened to be the same one who had assissted them during the West Point incident. You have to love coincidences.

From there, the remainder of Ben and Major's report was totally factual, except for the fact that they do not know the proper names of the three individuals who assissted them. Of course, they smartly did not mention the Great Khan or any plausible interaction with the Assassins.

When the US ambassador to Lebanon asked Major and Ben how they could not have known the names of their accomplices, they simply stated that things were moving so fast that there just was not any time for formal introductions. Because of the continuous, fast paced action, Ben and Major barely had time to shake hands and say good bye to those who had assissted them in rescueing Marcos.

Major looks at the Vice President and answers, "The report is what it is, sir."

"Very well then," the Vice President replies. "I guess I'll have to take the report as gospel."

The Second Lady of the United States leans forward and says to Ben and Major, "You young men are such heroes. It is gentlemen like you who make our country so great."

"Thank you, ma'am," Major and Ben reply as they both shake the Second Lady's hand.

"Well, gentlemen," the Vice President states, "since all of these important people are here to meet our two heroes, I guess I should introduce you to everyone. This should be fun," he concludes as he smiles and raises his eyebrows.

Grinning, Major and Ben nod their heads in acknowledgement. The two second lieutenants follow the Vice President and the Second Lady to begin the long and tedious task of formally meeting and greeting all of the foreign politicians and VIPs present at President Paulos' New Year's celebration.

Once again, the year has ended on a positive not for Milton Johnson and Benjamin Irons. As in the past, things began with a crisis, but ended in jovial triumph. Ben and Major are beginning to become quite accustomed to being in the right place at the right time. Their youth keeps their thoughts from dwelling on the negative aspects of their activities. There is nothing more exciting than living the life of an action adventure hero. Major and Ben are living that life and have loved every moment of it.

EPILOGUE

Physical Training for the Second Armored Cavalry Regiment begins every weekday, except Thursdays, at six thirty in the morning. Each of the TCBs (Troops, Companies, and Batteries) holds formation in front of their respective S&As in order to take accountability of the unit, prior to conducting PT.

There are not too many positives that result from being stationed at Fort Polk. One of those positives though, is the fact that it rarely gets extremely cold. Of course, weather is all relative. What is bearable to one is unbearable to another.

The Cobra Battery stands in formation preparing for its regular Friday motivation run. The uniform that everyone in the formation wears is that of their basic issue PT shorts and black Cobra Battery t-shirt. They do not wear any winter gear: no hat, no gloves, no cold weather pants, no cold weather top. Though it is forty-two degrees outside, the temperature does not factor into the uniform decision. The Cobra Battery rarely ever wears their cold weather gear during the winter. It is one of the many things that the Cobras do that separates them from the rest of the Regiment.

Each platoon is formed up and prepared to stretch and perform calisthenics, prior to the run. From the rear and starting at the right, is first platoon, second platoon, and headquarters platoon. First and Second platoons are the firing platoons, while headquarters consists of the service and service support elements.

First Sergeant Martin Gonzalez stands at the front of his formation and barks, "Battery! Right face!"

Upon the command, the three platoons execute a right face.

"Forward, march!" 1SG Gonzalez shouts as soon as his battery executes the right face. Once the battery takes two steps, he then shouts, "Counter column, march!"

The Cobra Battery executes a counter column, which has them now marching in the opposite direction. If they would have stayed on their current path, first platoon would have marched into the HHT

(Headquarters, Headquarters Troop) formation. 1SG Gonzalez marches Cobra across the street and down a small hill, to a parking lot.

Centered in the parking lot, 1SG Gonzalez shouts, "Mark time, march!"

Cobra stops moving forward and marches in place.

1SG Gonzalez then gives the command of, "Battery halt!"

The battery comes to a halt.

Next, 1SG Gonzalez shouts, "Sergeant Cochran, post!"

The fire direction NCO, Staff Sergeant Joseph Cochran dutifully, responds with, "Moving First Sergeant!"

SSG Cochran takes a step back and runs out of the formation from the most expedient point and jogs to the front of formation. At the front of formation, SSG Cochran faces 1SG Gonzalez and renders a salute.

1SG Gonzalez returns the salute and says so only SSG Cochran can hear, "Stretch the battery out, then take us to LA 10."

"Roger, First Sergeant," SSG Cochran replies.

SSG Cochran drops his salute and 1SG Gonzalez faces right and trots to the rear of the formation with the remainder of the battery leadership: the two platoon leaders, platoon sergeants, gunnery sergeants, fire direction officers, the executive officer, and the commander.

"Open ranks, march!" SSG Cochran commands.

Instantaneously, a loud roar fills the air as the Cobra Battery, one hundred twelve strong, run to the side to get to double arm interval.

The battery stretched out an additional thirty feet, standing at double arm interval, all of the soldiers and the NCOs in the formation come to a halt and cease their shouting.

SSG Cochran then commands, "Right face!"

The battery executes a right face.

"Open ranks, march!" SSG Cochran again commands.

The battery opens ranks once more, shouting as they move. This time, though, the Cobra battery does not move too far because there are only four ranks in the formation.

The battery comes to a halt.

SSG Cochran shouts, "Left face!"

With the battery now facing him, SSG Cochran commands, "From front to the rear, count off!"

Upon the command, the soldiers and the NCOs in the formation snap their heads to the left. Instantly, the front rank shouts, "One!" the second rank shouts, "Two!" the third rank shouts, "Three!" and the fourth rank shouts, "Four!" As each rank counts off, they snap their heads back to the front and waits for the count off to end.

Finally, SSG Cochran commands, "Even numbers to the left, uncover!"

Following SSG Cochran's command, the second and fourth ranks take one step to the left and say, "Woosh!" as they move.

Now that the Cobra Battery is properly formed for stretching and calisthenics, SSG Cochran is ready to lead them in their exercises. He starts the battery off with a series of push-ups and flutter kicks. Flutter kicks are when one lies on his back and raises his feet six inches off of the ground. To perform the exercise, one kicks his legs up and down, while not allowing the feet to touch the ground. SSG Cochran completes the exercise session by leading the battery in side straddle hops (jumping jacks): the unofficial exercise of the United States Army.

Finished with the exercises, SSG Cochran shouts, "Close ranks, march!"

The Cobra battery soldiers scream their heads off as they run and push themselves back to their original formation positions.

"Right, face!" SSG Cochran commands.

The battery immediately executes a right face. The guidon bearer jumps out of the formation and grabs the guidon, which he had planted in the grass to the battery's front. With the guidon in his hands, the soldier races to the front of the formation.

The battery now ready to run to LA 10, CPT Amsterdam struts to the front of the formation. The guidon bearer positions himself one step and to the right of the commander. The lieutenants go to the rear of the formation and gaggle with the senior NCOs. Generally, the lieutenants are supposed to form the first ranks of a running formation, but CPT Amsterdam does not allow that to occur. Major does not know why CPT Amsertdam breaks from this Army tradition, and when he did happen to ask first platoon's platoon leader, 1LT Luke Arnold, Major did not receive a response that seemed to make much sense to him.

With everyone in their proper positions, SSG Cochran then gives the command of, "Forward, march!"

The Cobra battery marches forward and works its way to the left.

When the battery reaches the reach the road, SSG Cochran shouts, "Column left, march!"

The battery executes a column left and walks up a small hill. At the top of the hill, the Cobra Battery approaches a one way, two lane road, which runs in the southern direction.

When the battery reaches the top of the hill, SSG Cochran again gives the command of, "Column left, march!"

Once again, the Cobra Battery executes a column left, which now has them marching south along the one way.

With the entire battery now on the road, SSG Cochran shouts, "Double time!"

Instantaneously, all of the Cobra soldiers shout at the top of their longs, "Double time!"

"March!" SSG Cochran commands.

Upon the command, the Cobra Battery begins its Friday morning battery run. Down the one way they run, calling and sounding off with cadence. The Army is known for its cadences, but the Cobra Battery has a few special ones of their own.

As Cobra passes units that are still stretching and giving the appearance of laziness, they sound off with, "Hey you! On my left! Your mama should've told you! You ain't shit, boy! I thought I told you! You ain't shit, boy!"

When the listening units hear the cadence, they annoyingly wave their hands at Cobra, upset at the fact that they are the brunt of Cobra Battery's fun.

Cobra runs down the road passing other units as they move, full of motivation and pride. Some of the untis are running in formation, just as they are. Others run as though they are stragglers. They give the appearance that they have fallen out of their unit's formation somewhere.

Continuing on with the run, the Cobra Battery finally makes it down to Louisiana state highway ten, or better known as the sign says, LA 10, which is roughly a two mile trip, making the two run distance just over four miles.

The run back towards the battery area is just as the run out. This time, though, the Cobra Battery spreads trails. The first and fourth ranks spread out and run alongside the edge of the road and the second and third ranks split the lanes. Spreading trails truly motivates the Cobra Battery because it is a show of strength. There is nothing they love more tan showing and telling everyone that there is no unit better than the mighty Cobra Battery.

As the battery approaches a small formation, instead of running around it, they run as they are, without flinching. The other formation ends up in the middle of the Cobra Battery formation and is forced to suffer through a series of taunts and sneers. The show of dominance does not last long, as Cobra continues moving on, faster than the formation they had just enveloped.

After a nice relaxing run, or at least relaxing to some, anyway, the Cobra Battery finally finishes. They turn left into the parking area and stop in front of the S&A to stretch out before dismissal.

Finished stretching, 1SG Gonzalez dismisses the battery. The soldiers and NCOs fall out of the formation. The single soldiers and junior NCOs make their way to the barracks and the dining facility. The married personnel race to their cars in an attempt to beat the seven thirty horn, which announces to the entire post that PT has ended and that cars are now permitted on the one ways.

Before Major can get to his 4Runner, CPT Amsterdam pulls him to the side saying, "Let me holler at you, LT."

Major changes his direction, and dutifully jogs over to where his battery commander stands. As he approaches CPT Amsterdam, Major sees that his commander is standing with three senior NCOs from the squadron. Though Major recognizes the NCOs, because he has not been in War Eagle for very long, he does not know the men by their names yet.

The three senior non-commissioned officers pop to the position of attention, salute, and say to Major, "Morning, sir,"

"Major returns the salutes and says, "How're you guys doing?"

Standing amongst the group, Major does not say much. He just stands and smiles as CPT Amsterdam carries on a relaxed conversation with the NCOs.

Turning the conversation to Major, CPT Amsterdam asks him, "How was that run there, LT Johnson?"

With a slight smile on his face, Major simply shrugs his shoulders and replies, "It was fun, sir."

The senior NCOs all laugh at Major's answer, noticing that there is neither a drop of sweat on his PT shirt nor is he breathing heavily. CPT Amsterdam, on the other hand, lets a big smile show on his face.

Softly laughing, CPT Amsterdam says to the group of senior NCOs, "This is my stud right here."

ABOUT THE AUTHOR

TERRON SIMS II GRADUATED FROM WEST Point in 2000. An Iraq veteran, he helped establish Baghdad's local governments and was the Wasit Province military liaison officer. He sits on the board of principals for the Truman National Security Project and is active in Virginia and national Democratic politics. He currently lives in Virginia.